ALSO

NIGHTHAWKS SERIES

Find Me in the Rain

Find Me on the Ice

Find Me Under the Stars

Not My Coach (Novella)

Find Me in the Fire

MRS. CLAUS STANDALONE DUET

Stealing Mrs. Claus

Becoming Mrs. Claus

HEAU HOCKEY LEGENDS SERIES

Saving the Beast

Redeeming the Villain

SAINT ELDRITCH SERIES

Shut Up and Bite Me

THE WICKED TRILOGY

The Wicked Truth

The Wicked Love

The Wicked Ending

ISBN-13:

redeeming THE VILLAIN

PRU SCHUYLER

redeeming
THE VILLAIN

Thank you!

Brook and Melissa,

Thank you so much for sharing your POTS experiences with me. I could not have brought such care and authenticity to this story without your help.

You are both angels, and I'm so grateful this book has brought us closer together. Thank you so much for being exactly who you are.

This book is for you. <3

Xoxo
    Pru Schuyler

Hockey Terms

Apple

An assist

Barn

The home rink of a team

Breakaway

When there are no opponents between the offensive player and the goalie, this is usually very fast-paced as the offensive player wants an attempt to score before the defense catches up.

Check

A number of defensive moves aimed to disrupt the player with the puck, doing so by crashing into the opponent with their body

Chippy

Often used to describe a game or moment where the aggression in the game heightens, typically resulting in more shoving, checking, chirping, and fighting.

Chirping

a term for 'trash talk' often used in hockey. Chirping can get under the opponents skin and distract them.

Dangle

Completely embarrassing the opponent with impressive stick handling offensively. Practically "dangling" the puck in front of them but they can't get to it.

Defender

A hockey position that is responsible for preventing the other team from scoring, as well as other tasks.

Deke

'faking' an opponent out using a deceptive movement in order to get them out of the way of a pass, or to bypass them altogether

Fivehole

The gap between a goalie's legs, typically referring to scoring.

Hat Trick

When a player scores three goals in one game, often celebrated by the fans throwing their hats onto the ice

Michigan

A Michigan is a lacrosse style goal where the player picks the puck up on their stick, skates around the back of the net, and throws it into the net to score.

Penalty

A punishment imposed by a referee for breaking a rule.

Power play

When a team has more players than their opponent on the ice as an outcome of the other team committing a penalty.

Screening

When a player on the opposing team attempts to block the goalie's view

Sin bin

Also known as the penalty box. An area where players are sent, off of the ice, to serve the allotted time from the committed penalty

Playlist

Nobody Sees This Part, Taylor Ocano

Burning Down (Alex's Version), Alex Warren

after you, jordn day

Glow, Livingston

Are You With Me, Nilu

Tell Me You Love Me, Shaya Zamora

Chasing Shadows, Alex Warren

Gravedigger, Livingston

my tears ricochet, Taylor Swift

Last Man Standing, Livingston

Castles Crumbling (Taylor's Version), Taylor Swift [feat. Hayley Williams]

Soul Tied, Ashley Singh

River, Myles Smith

Better Days, Will Swinton

masquerade, Abe Parker

Traitor, Livingston

Somebody to Someone (I Just Wanna Fall in Love),
Natalie Jane

Soulmate, Chanin

Gilded Lily, Cults

War of Hearts (Acoustic Version), Ruelle

Haunt Me, Blindlove

Hear You Me, Jimmy Eat World

SCAN ME TO PLAY

H E A
University

Dear Reader,

It is with great pleasure that we announce your acceptance into Happily Ever After University. As the most elite school in the country, we are proud to have selected you out of hundreds of thousands of applicants.

As a HEAU student, be prepared to immerse yourself in the lux campus culture. You will have the opportunity to study in our breathtaking castles alongside the brightest students and highest-regarded faculty. You will also spend time in beautiful blossoming flower gardens, hedge-lined student quads, vine-covered gazebos, and state-of-the-art facilities.

Along with your course load, there are endless extracurriculars to indulge in, including cheering on our Legend's hockey team at the astounding Kensington arena. Based on your application, it is clear that you are driven and dedicated. We have no doubt that you will be an excellent fit for our student body, and we look forward to having you join our campus in the near future. Welcome to Happily Ever After University.

Sincerely,

Dean of Admissions.

TRIGGER WARNINGS

This book is recommended for readers 18+.

This book contains depictions of bullying, death of a sibling, explicit sexual content, sexual harassment/assault, degradation.

For the readers who first fell in love with fairy tales from the Little Golden Books.

For readers who crave both degradation and praise from a tattooed villain with a tragic past.

author's note

This isn't a story about a girl who pricks her finger on a spindle and falls into an eternal sleep, only to be awoken by Prince Charming's true love's kiss.

This is the story about a reserved girl named Alora Briarwood, who is cursed by her father's choices and destined to be tormented by Malik Ravenwell, a hockey player who wants nothing more than to bring her kingdom to ruin.

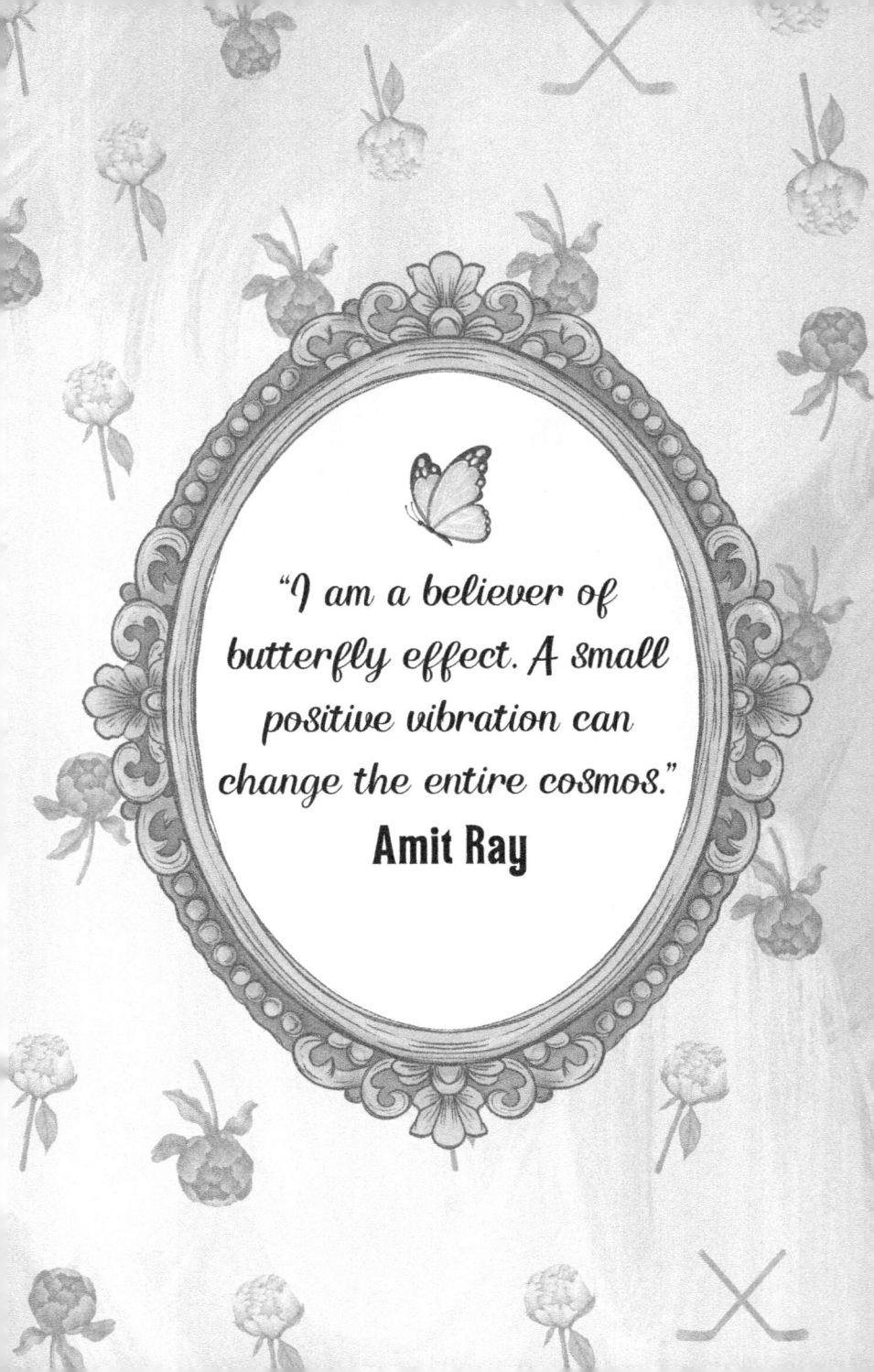

"I am a believer of butterfly effect. A small positive vibration can change the entire cosmos."

Amit Ray

prologue
malik
two years ago

My gaze locks on to her the second she steps inside the school doors, following her as she hesitantly walks through the foyer and down the hallway.

Cautiously, she takes in her surroundings, scanning the hall full of students, studying each of their faces. The same thing she does every day.

I doubt anyone else even can see her tiny movements and glances. But I do. I've noticed everything she's done since her first day here. Even before I found out what her last name was this past weekend.

Unfortunately, it doesn't matter how cute she might be, not since I discovered who she really was. As far as I'm concerned now, she is just as much my enemy as her dad is.

Her strides close the distance to where I'm leaning

back against my locker—waiting and watching. She could not have picked a worse school to transfer to. She doesn't know it yet, but she will come to hate me. I'll make sure of it.

Following her down the hallway, I hook my arm over her shoulders and lean into her blonde hair, breathing her in and telling myself that I hate how sweet she smells … like strawberries and vanilla.

My voice drips with venom as I say, "You are as small and insignificant as a bug, Alora. Have I told you that yet?"

She slams to a halt, peels herself out from my arm, and looks straight up at me with a quivering lip and wide, naive blue eyes. "Y-you've never talked to me. Do I know you?"

I slide my finger down the length of her nose before bopping the tip of it. "Not yet. But I know *you*."

Those doe eyes fall to my lips for a second, and I wonder how pretty her mouth would be while moaning my name and begging me for more. But I force those thoughts away—the same ones I have late at night in bed with the image of her in my mind.

Her brows pinch in confusion, and she tightens her hold on the books in her arms. "If I did something to offend you, I apologize.

So polite. So rehearsed. So fake. Her political-esque response earns a guttural laugh from deep in my chest.

My face falls flat, and I stare down at her, hatred boiling in my blood as I force myself to feel disgust

2

rather than lust. "Your existence offends me. Is that something you can change? Huh, *Bug?*"

She glances around for help before looking back up at me. But there isn't anyone who is going to come to her aid, not here.

This is my school, my domain, and no one will dare to interfere.

Pursing her full pink lips, she sucks her cheek between her teeth, considering what to say. But unfortunately for her, nothing she says will change the inevitable future. It was written in the stars before she ever stepped foot in this town.

Her gaze meets mine again, wetter than before. "N-no, I don't think I can change that."

Twisting a loose lock of her honey-blonde hair around my finger, I sigh, my saddened expression twisting into a devious smirk.

"Tsk-tsk. What a shame." I chuckle, glancing away as a shiver sweeps across my shoulders.

Grabbing her jaw, I hold her stare intensely so I can watch my words imprint themselves in her mind like a curse.

"Every day for as long as you live, I will ensure your life is as unbearable and empty as you've made mine, *Briarwood*."

I take a shuddering, chilling breath, her last name a curse on my tongue. Her eyes widen slightly with shock that I know her name at all.

But that's not all I know about her. I've studied her

since I learned she was one of *them*, one of the rich monsters who had flipped my world on its head. I know her likes, dislikes, dreams, fears, and I'm going to use each one of them against her.

There is only one thing I am certain of in this world: never trust a *Briarwood*. Not the pretty blonde one who just transferred to my school and, more importantly, not her father—the monster who stole all happiness from my life as if it meant nothing.

She deserves everything I have planned for her because no one from the kind of endless money and greed she was born into can possibly be good. She's just like her father, flaunting her luxury brands and car, as if the cost of them weren't more than what I could make in the next twenty years.

I tried to be nice—I really did.

Well, that's a lie.

But it's not my fault. I can't look at her without seeing what her father, Congressman Daniel Briarwood, did. I might not be able to get to him, but *she's* right in front of me. Besides, the best way to hurt someone is to hurt the one they love most.

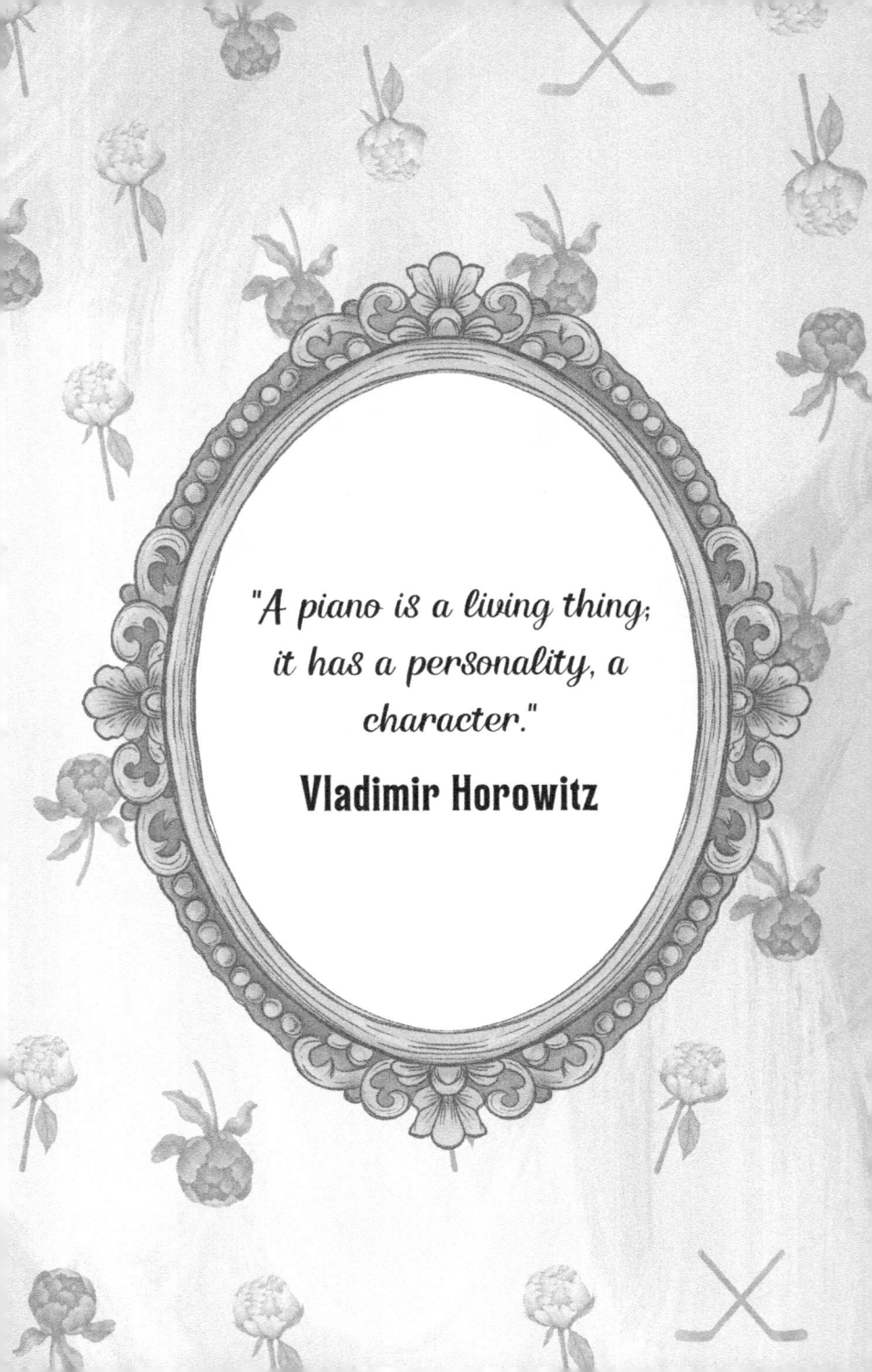

"A piano is a living thing; it has a personality, a character."

Vladimir Horowitz

chapter one
alora
present

My entire life, I have navigated the balance between being forced into the spotlight by my father and hiding in the shadows cast behind him.

Don't draw unnecessary attention. Don't make a scene.

I was taught to be the perfectly behaved daughter who never spoke out of turn or had a hair out of place. But I suppose that's what's expected of a congressman's only child and the future heiress of the Briarwood fortune.

That's all he ever refers to me as in his interviews—his sole heir, his legacy. But perhaps that's because that's all he truly knows of me. I've barely seen or spoken to him since he handed me over to his three sisters just before my senior year of high school because I had become *too much to handle* alongside his work.

When I turned eighteen on my birthday, to be exact —I was diagnosed with POTS, postural orthostatic tachycardia syndrome.

For years, my dad and doctor had diagnosed my symptoms as anxiety. But they were wrong, and deep down, I knew it all along. Do I have anxiety? Yes, frequently. But that was certainly not the entirety of what I was going through.

It didn't matter how doctors many I went to; they all gave me the same diagnosis. When my primary doctor retired and was replaced with a new one, I'd finally felt listened to for the first time ever.

My dad was deep in his congressional campaign amid my diagnosis, and I think it was all a bit much for him to handle. At least that's what it felt like. Because two days after my appointment, his assistant had my bags packed, and my dad informed me that I would be going to live with my aunts for the rest of high school.

With a hug and tears streaming down my face, I was gone. He might not have been the most doting dad, but he was all I had, especially after my mom passed when I was seven.

He has always been emotionally unavailable, but it got so much worse after we lost my mom thirteen years ago. She was the sunshine to his shadows, and since she's been gone, he's been consumed by the darkness. He became ice cold, never showing any emotion, and the man I remember from my childhood is long gone.

As for my aunts—Flora Merryweather, Fauna

Merryweather, and Freya Merryweather—they are the epitome of love and affection.

They all chose to bear their mother's maiden name rather than their cruel father's—a similar choice I have considered many times over the last couple of years.

Thankfully, they are nothing like my dad. Although they were raised under the same roof by the same parents, somehow, the three of them turned out to be compassionate, selfless, and kind.

The media would have you believe the same about Congressman Daniel Briarwood. A mourning widower who will never remarry out of the love for his wife. A father who misses his daughter every single day, but knew she deserved a life out of the spotlight, so he selflessly sent her away.

Although if that were true, he would have called or at least texted. The only correspondence I've gotten over the last couple of years are bank notifications from him sending money on my birthday and a few cards that were clearly sent from his assistants.

As a teenager, "*I love you*" was only spewed when I had been acting up and needed to be reeled back in. He knew before I did that I thrived on praise and acceptance, and he knew exactly how to use it to mold me. He also learned over the last couple of years, that the love tactic doesn't work on me anymore.

Most of our hugs were in front of a camera or crowd. Aside from the one on the day I left, when his assistant had to drag me from him as I cried, begging him not to send me away.

I can picture that moment so clearly. It still haunts me. The coldness in his gaze, the heartlessness in his touch. I didn't know him anymore, not in the same way I used to.

He throws money at my aunts and me during every holiday, not bothering to attend himself—unless, of course, a news outlet is doing an exposé and he needs to once again paint the perfect family image.

Now, I am merely my dad's asset more than his daughter, and only recently have I come to terms with that fact...for the most part at least.

Since then, I've been more comfortable tapping into my bank accounts and trust fund that became mine when I turned eighteen. My trust fund was set up by my mom, and no matter what, he can't hold that over my head because he has no access to it. It's solely mine, no guilt attached.

For the longest time, I could never treat myself or splurge because I knew the money came from him trying to buy my love. But that is just one of the many things that I've been working on over the last year or so.

After graduating high school, I took a year off before coming to Happily Ever After University. My acceptance had already been signed, sealed, and delivered before I was even born. I was a politician's daughter and an HEAU legacy, so my application was more of a formality.

But I needed time first before going to school. I needed to spread my wings and try to find myself because I had no clue who I was and what I wanted out of life. To be honest, that's still a work in progress.

But getting out of Avandale and away from the horrors of my senior year, something changed in me. I used to be shy and a pushover, taking anything the world threw at me with a smile on my face. The way my dad had taught me.

But not anymore.

If I have discovered anything this past year abroad, it's that I'm done taking shit from anyone.

My blood boils as *his* face flashes in my mind—my tormenter, the dark and twisted villain of my story. The one who made every single day of my senior year a living, breathing nightmare from the moment I transferred to Avandale High School.

Malik Ravenwell. A name I will never forget, no matter how hard I try.

If my dad taught me the lovelessness in the world, then Malik taught me the cruelness. *Over and over.*

He is the reason I graduated high school two months early, the reason that I spent countless nights crying, and the reason I fled the country the second I could. I didn't even want to be on the same continent as him. I still don't.

But I'm done hiding from the villains in my life. I'm not a princess locked in a tower, waiting to be saved by some honorable prince. I'll wield the sword and slay the dragon myself.

Besides, I know I won't have to see him anytime soon—or *ever* if I can help it. The last I heard, he graduated from Avandale and had no plans on college. I don't care what he's doing as long as he's far from me.

Tearing my mind from the running thoughts, Sunny, my golden retriever, stands up and stretches her cute legs as a big yawn overtakes her sweet face.

"Big stretch, baby girl," I swoon, reaching over and running my fingers across that ultra-soft spot on her snout.

I've had Sunny since I graduated from high school —a gift from my aunts. While a lot of individuals with POTS don't have service dogs, I'm lucky to have her. She's able to detect an episode coming on before I can. But more than her gifts, she's my best friend and my anchor. I don't usually go many places without her, and I can't imagine that changing much now that we're here.

We are a package deal, and when I enrolled at HEAU, they were more than happy to accommodate, giving me a large corner room with a private, grassy, fenced-in area they'd installed, with direct sliding-glass-door access right inside my unit.

I'm a quiet person who enjoys keeping to myself. Well, Sunny doesn't count; she's a part of my soul. People always talk about finding your soulmate in love, but there is something special about meeting your soul-pet. The one who finds you when you need them most, who loves you unconditionally.

Sunny is mine.

Besides, she's an active girl with loads of energy, and she needs more room to play around inside. Along with walks and enrichment activities.

I cried the first time she jumped into my lap. I'd never known I had a hole in my heart for her to fill until it was bursting at the seams with love. She's not only my best friend, but my protector too.

She's trained to detect if my heart rate and blood pressure are starting to get too high. She will nudge my hand with her head and even bark and signal me by sitting on my feet if I don't notice her first attempt.

I also have my watch that I wear if I don't have Sunny with me, but aside from a handful of situations, she's typically with me so I don't need to use it.

When she signals, I know I'm at risk of a flare-up. Once she lets me know, I get my water and find a good place to sit down, preferably a place where I can put my legs up to avoid blood pooling in my feet.

Sometimes, my body will regulate itself after a few minutes. And sometimes, my body makes it feel like it's fighting against itself. It can be frustratingly unpredictable. Both in its longevity and its symptoms.

POTS patients' experiences can have similarities, but each still unique.

Everyone has a different journey with POTS. Some have various triggers or stressors that I don't, and I have struggles that others don't. I think that's what can be most frustrating with the invisible illness—there's no simple solution for any of us. We just have to listen to our body and let it be our guide, whether we want to or not.

I mean, of course, some of our symptoms are the same—muscle fatigue, brain fog, body temperature regulation, a risk of fainting, and more.

One of the most frustrating parts of getting diagnosed is learning how it affects you because there isn't a handbook built just for your symptoms and body. You have to teach yourself how to navigate it, listening intently to your body.

Luckily, a few pills help me regulate my symptoms for the most part, but that doesn't mean I don't still have bad days. Days that require me to lie in bed with my feet elevated, resting until the episode passes. Sometimes, it's just a few hours, sometimes an entire day, and occasionally, it's multiple days. But thankfully, I haven't had a flare-up that bad in quite a while.

But the biggest misconception of POTS is that a lot of people assume that we just pass out when we stand up or get lightheaded. Although that may occasionally be true, that is the tip of the iceberg. I've only lost consciousness a handful of times over the last year.

It was worse when I was first diagnosed, until I learned how to manage my symptoms. And until I got on medication to help regulate my heart rate.

It's the little things that affect me the most. Watching what I eat so my sugar isn't too high, making sure I always stay hydrated, listening to my body, even when I don't want to. The headaches, the muscle fatigue, the lightheadedness—I could go on and on.

I know I'm one of the luckier ones when it comes to POTS, and I'll never take that for granted, even when it feels impossible.

I don't think it's very common for individuals with POTS to have service dogs, but I'm grateful for Sunny nonetheless.

My aunts planned on getting me a puppy when I

graduated, and when they found out that there were POTS service dogs, they knew they had to follow that path. But I can say that since I've had her, the episodes are so much smoother.

She can detect it in me far faster than I can. She's made all the difference during our time together, especially easing my transition of moving here.

Stress can be a big trigger for my symptoms, and having her to keep me company has been the biggest blessing. And when I go on adventures without her, I wear my watch that keeps my heart rate.

We moved into our room three days ago, and I'm finally unpacked. Instead of keeping the small twin bed they usually provide, I had a queen bed brought in since I have so much extra space.

Besides, Sunny needs her spot next to me. We've never spent a night apart. And fitting us both in a twin bed would have been *snug*.

The rooms here may be excessively large, but I'm not complaining. And it's part of what HEAU is known for—the opulence and extravagance threaded into every inch of the campus.

But I suppose when your student body is composed of some of the wealthiest families in the world, money isn't hard to come by.

Besides, I also needed room for my piano so I can play every chance I get. It would have been much more of a hassle to walk to the music hall every day for practice.

Music has always been tied to my being, feeling like an extension of my heart and soul. It's been the one consistent part of my life.

I brought all of Sunny's things along, including a few new additions—a lofted pink princess dog bed with a custom-embroidered rug with her name positioned beneath it. I spoil her—I can't help it.

Sunny happily pads across the comforter, licking my cheek, and I giggle.

"Did you have a good nap?"

I talk to my dog incessantly even though she can't talk back. We talk about everything and anything. Like I said, she's my best friend.

Her fluffy golden self jumps off of the bed and onto the fluffy pink rug, and I follow suit, stepping into my slippers. She needs to go potty—her usual habit after waking up.

Wrapping my cream-colored throw blanket around me, I walk over to the sliding glass door and unlock it, letting her run outside, across the patio, and onto the lush green grass beneath the starry sky.

It's chilly out tonight, but I suppose it's the end of August, and we're moving into fall, so I should be prepared for the drops in temperature. Especially being in Evermore, Washington, located in the very northern part of the state.

"Go potty," I tell her, watching her bound around the big yard, enclosed by a seven-foot privacy fence.

No one can see inside, which is my favorite part. I

don't have to worry about anyone trying to stick their hand in to pet her or feed her something she shouldn't have.

Zoomies hit her almost instantly, and she starts doing figure eights, pure happiness in every leap and bound of her stride. A cool breeze blows over me, and I shiver, goose bumps breaking over my arms.

"Hurry up, baby," I tell her before stepping back inside and closing the door behind me. I'll watch her from here, where it's nice and toasty.

As she continues to race around the grass, my mind drifts to thoughts of classes starting in two days. I am *so* ready.

I'm double majoring in business and music, which is definitely a heavy load, but I'm confident I can handle it. If I set my mind to something, nothing can hold me back.

Business is boring, and I don't really care for the course load, but I know the knowledge will be useful to have. Especially when it comes to investments and managing the Briarwood fortune when the time comes.

Our money goes back generations, and it takes a lofty staff to help manage all of the assets. From hotels and properties to stocks and airlines, we have our hands in a lot of cookie jars, and I don't want to be blind to the responsibility of it all when I take over.

But my true passion, the one I've always had, is music. Playing my piano is what fills me with purpose and joy. But even more than that, it's my gift. I've been musically inclined since I was very young.

My aunt Flora always says that I got that blessing from her. But from the times I've heard her sing or play, I can't help but disagree with her.

The one thing I can thank my dad for is providing me piano lessons since I was four years old. I was a prodigy, the keys a mere extension of my fingers. Even though he might have financially supported my musical endeavor, he insisted that my passion for playing remain out of the spotlight, no matter how much I pushed and begged.

He's always kept my talents from the public. He said that people would use it to extort us. To turn my love and passion into hatred. That keeping my gift private was for my well-being. For the longest time, I believed him. I mean, he was my dad, so what else was I supposed to think?

But the older I got, the more I began to question a lot of what he said and did, wondering who he really made his "thoughtful" decisions for—us, me, or just him?

Sunny bolts toward the door, yanking me from my thoughts, and I slide it open as she slows down and bounds inside. I lock it behind her and close the curtains.

Wiping her paws clean with one of her wipes, I let her go, and she jumps right back up onto our bed, nestling and relaxing on my heated blanket.

"I'll be right back. I'm going to run to the bathroom," I tell her, tossing my blanket onto the bed next to her, leaving me in my super-soft, short-sleeved pink button-up with matching shorts set. I can tell she wants to come along when her body stiffens up. "Just wait here."

Grabbing my key fob and phone, I step into the hallway and secure the door behind me, hearing the automated lock slide into place.

The marble floor glistens under the soft, warm light from the sconces on the walls and small chandeliers, which hang from the tall ceiling every ten feet.

I could have gotten my own place off campus, but to be honest, I wanted this experience. I've been dreaming of college for years. It doesn't matter that this fate was constructed by my dad since I was little; I'm here for me, not anyone else.

This is the best school in the country. Getting handed an HEAU diploma is a fast pass to success in life. Which is why the application process is so grueling and invasive and only the smallest portion of applicants are selected.

I know my last name got me into this school, but I worked hard to make sure that I earned it with my own merit as well. That I was a perfect applicant regardless of my dad and his more than charitable donations over the years.

The room and setup they provided is perfect, and I couldn't extend enough gratitude when I moved in.

Although I'm not sure if their generosity is because of Sunny and their excitement for my attendance or because of my dad's position.

After using the bathroom and washing my hands, I smile politely at a few girls who walk past me before heading back to my room.

Turning the corner, I bump into a tall, hot guy with wandering eyes, dark hair, and a cute smirk.

"Shit, sorry about that," he grumbles, his voice low.

"No problem." I smile politely.

He spins, walking backward as he strolls away from me, biting down on his bottom lip. "See you around, pretty girl."

My heart flips in my chest, and I giggle lightly, feeling my cheeks warm. I know it's ridiculous how good his compliment made me feel.

But most of the ones I've gotten were in proximity with my dad, and it was hard to tell if they were genuine or just coming from people trying to gain his favor. Which has happened more times than I'd like to admit.

Besides, I'm not on the hunt for a guy. I'm focused on my music and Sunny. There's no time for unnecessary distractions.

Without a word, I continue to my door, unlocking it with the fob and stepping inside, inhaling the sweet cinnamon-and-apple air freshener. The door starts to swing shut behind me, and I yawn as I kick my slippers off, ready to crawl into bed with my girl and watch a movie.

Footsteps race down the hallway toward my door, and I instinctually spin around, just in time to see it fly open with force as someone deeply calls out, "Coming in!"

Voices echo down the hallway behind him, laughter and anger intertwining into a slew of curse words and shouts.

He quickly ducks behind my door and slams it shut with his back to me as he tries to catch his breath and look out of the peephole for whoever is chasing after him.

A cold, spine-chilling snake slithers up my back and wraps around my throat, constricting tightly as that familiar, unsettling voice registers in my brain.

My gaze travels from his black hair to his bare strong arms, every other inch of the taut skin scattered with black-and-white tattoos. His fitted T-shirt outlines his strength and impressive physique, and my breath gets caught in my throat from fear.

Sunny brushes against my leg, standing guard at my feet, more so out of curiosity than anything. She isn't trained to be protective, but maybe she can sense the enemy in the room.

His shoulders rise and fall rapidly as images of our past start to flash in my mind. I'm frozen in place, unable to move a finger as shock rocks through me to my core.

"You fucker! Where'd you go?" someone yells in the hallway.

It's not him. There's no way it could be him. Right?

The six-foot-three monster, with ruffled black hair and haunting purple eyes, turns around, his gaze locking with mine. And as much as I try to fight it, I can't ignore the truth any longer. Standing in my room is the cruel and menacing man I hoped to never see again ... *Malik Ravenwell.*

hat trick

When a player scores three goals in one game, often celebrated by the fans throwing their hats onto the ice

chapter two
malik

My eyes travel from the familiar, stark blue eyes to the parted rosy lips, and all air expels from my lungs as my words fill the silence between us. "No *fucking* way."

My body warms, and my palms sweat as I realize that I'm not hallucinating, that this is real and she's actually standing right in front of me.

Alora Briarwood.

I never thought she would step foot in the same town as me again. Not after she ran to the other side of the fucking world to escape me. But it doesn't matter how far she runs; my claws will always be sunk into her.

She stays silent as we study each other, both of us in a frozen stupor at the fact that we're mere feet away from one another again. My gaze wanders over her flowing blonde hair and down her body before meeting her confused and angry gaze.

Out of the corner of my eye, I notice a dog by her legs, and I'm not surprised. Of course, the prissy princess would have her dog here with her. I'm sure her daddy even paid extra to make sure it was allowed. I see the greed of the Briarwood family hasn't lessened in our time apart.

The innocence in her eyes is the same as I remember, but as she blinks away her daze, I notice something new in her stare. A confidence that certainly wasn't there before. Including how she carries herself. She isn't cowering down in my presence like I'm used to. She's standing tall and facing me head-on.

She must have forgotten who I was during our time apart. But that's okay; I won't hesitate to remind her and refresh her memory on exactly how unimportant she is.

Her mouth shakily closes before parting once more. "Get the *fuck* out of my room." Her voice isn't meek or shy; instead, it's proud and demanding.

I think it's the first time I've ever heard her swear, and I can't help but chuckle at the sound of her innocent mouth cursing.

Her lips curl as she crosses her arms, disgust exuding from every cell in her body.

A haunting laugh vibrates from deep within me, waves of anger vibrating through the air.

Taking a step toward her, I bite down on my bottom lip and smile. "Well, that's a rude way to greet an old friend."

Scoffing, she widens her eyes and strides forward, jabbing her finger into my chest as an aroma of delicious vanilla and strawberries engulfs me. I breathe in deeply without thought, my mouth watering at how good she smells.

Her words whistle through her teeth, quiet but powerful. "Y-you are not my friend. Now get the *hell* out of my room."

I laugh in her face as she struggles to meet my eye, her neck craning straight back. God, I forgot how short she was in comparison to me.

It would take such little effort to pick her up and move her away from me. I contemplate it, but I don't want her to think I'm trying to make a move on her.

Besides, I want her to think she has the upper hand; it will be so much more entertaining when I rip the power away from her.

Her dog approaches, sniffing me cautiously, and I reach my hand out, letting her get a good whiff.

"Cute dog. I guess when you can afford to buy the school, they let you get away with anything."

"Malik," she growls.

I lean closer to her, her body stiffening from my nearness. Her breathing picks up like crazy, and her cheeks burn bright red.

"Yes, *darling*?" I tease her, my voice melodic and smooth.

She falls for the sweetness, her eyes and posture softening at my tone. The fact that she thinks I could ever forget what her family had done to mine is laughable. I will never forgive her, and as long as she's near me, I won't let her forget it either.

Reaching my hand out, I grab her chin firmly with my fingers and jerk it up higher, showing her how easily I could bend her to my will if I wanted her. But I'll never fuck a monster as seemingly sweet as her.

My voice starts out kind but by the time I finish, my tone twists into something cold and venomous. "Yell in my face again, and I'll remind you just how malicious I can be."

She gulps hard, but doesn't move, and my chest blooms with satisfaction because I know she's taking me seriously. Because I mean every. Single. Word.

Her eyes shift, anger igniting in her stare. "Get your hand off of me."

The coolness and sharpness of her tone slithers down my spine, and I can't hide my surprise at the boldness.

"Remember your place, *Bug*."

Bug. Insignificant, little creature. A nickname to remind her how easily I can stomp her existence out with my shoe.

The use of her old nickname—the one I called her

in high school—catches her off guard, and her fierceness wavers.

Dropping her chin from my grip, I hold my hands up in defeat. But we both know it was my choice to surrender. Her sassy tone did nothing to convince me.

"Get out." Her voice cracks, and her eyes well up with tears, triggering images of her from years ago to flash through my mind.

But I have no sympathy for the girl who lives on a bed of money, luxury, and the bones of my dead brother.

It's late. I want to be in my own room, not standing in hers, looking into the saddened eyes of the girl I hate the most in this world.

Leaning forward, I lower my face to hers. "Good night, Bug."

She doesn't say a word as I spin on my heel.

As I reach for the door handle, something shiny hanging on the back side of the door catches my eye, and I snatch it sneakily, stowing it in my pocket before leaving her room. This could most definitely come in handy later.

She deserves everything that I've done to her. And everything I will do now that she's in my kingdom.

That new attitude of hers only provokes me more, but I'd be lying if I said it wasn't hot, seeing her standing up to me after all this time.

Her getting in my face to prove that she's no longer the tiny bug on the bottom of my shoe—it's cute. But she's only just made it more dangerous for herself because I never back down from a challenge. This just got a whole hell of a lot more interesting.

She will cower and kneel before me once again—I'm sure of it.

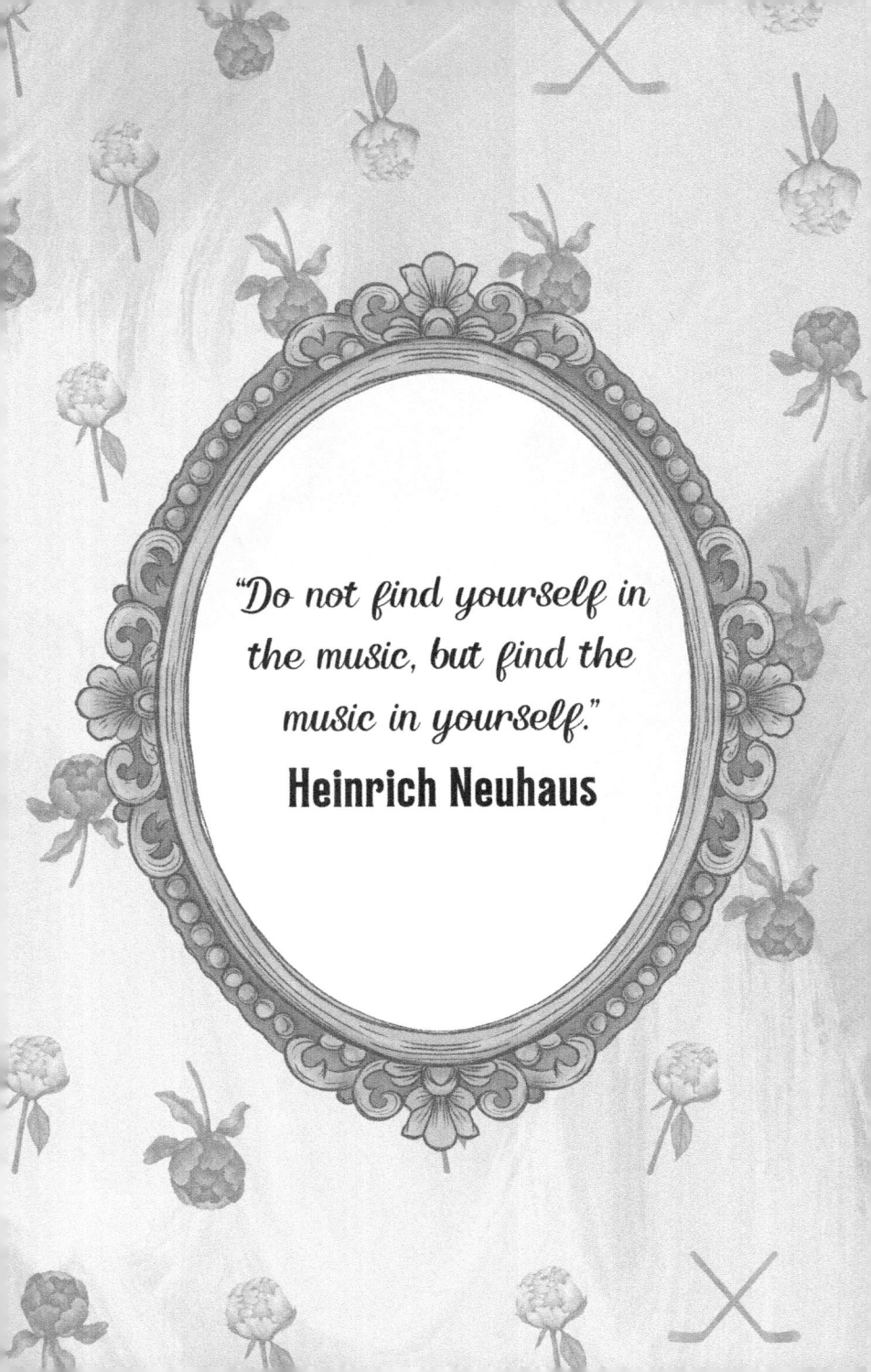

"Do not find yourself in the music, but find the music in yourself."

Heinrich Neuhaus

chapter three
alora

My eyes fly open, air heaving in and out of my lungs as reality starts to sink back in.

It was just a nightmare. It was just a nightmare.

I fling my blanket off of my legs as I quickly become aware of how much sweat is dripping down my body.

Deep breaths. Calm down.

Sitting up on my elbows, I start taking slow, deep breaths and reach for my water bottle on my nightstand. Hydration is one of the most important things when it comes to POTS. Taking a few sips, I continue to relax my breathing, feeling my heart rate begin to slow.

My nightmare flashes as I remember that it wasn't a

torturous image conjured up by my imagination; it was very real. A memory from my time at Avandale High.

As the purple eyes appear in my mind, a chilling shiver races down my spine, goose bumps erupting across the tops of my arms.

Last night ... Malik really was here, in my room. I still can't believe it. A horrifying scene that even my mind couldn't create.

He shouldn't be here at all, especially in my room. But to be fair, I never double-checked from the rumors I had heard during our senior year.

That's an oversight on my part, but there won't be another. I need to be on my A game from now on. I won't let him make a mockery of me, not anymore.

Never again.

Once my breathing returns to normal, I start sitting up slowly, focusing on my body for anything out of the ordinary.

My head isn't hurting, which, so far, is a good sign that I might have avoided triggering an episode. But it's still early; they can come out of nowhere sometimes.

Thankfully, my body is being kind to me this morning.

Glancing at the nightstand, I grab my phone and check the time. Seven forty a.m. A whole twenty minutes before my alarm is supposed to start going off.

Sliding off of my tall bed, I step into my slippers. No harm in getting an early start to the day.

Sunny is starting to stir, slowly rolling over onto her

stomach from her favorite sleeping position—upside down on her back with her head cocked to the side.

"Good morning, sweetie," I greet her, reaching my arm back and brushing her golden bedhead.

She stretches back into a downward dog pose and yawns.

Walking to the sliding glass door, I pull back the curtains and unlock the door before sliding it open. Hopping off of the bed, she lazily saunters out, getting more energy back into her with each step she takes. And before I know it, she's leaping and bounding in figure eights across the dewy grass.

Leaning against the open doorframe, I take a deep breath, inhaling the crisp fall Washington air. I've only been to Evermore a few times in my life—with my dad for publicity of his donations to the university. But even then, I saw how special this place was.

It's like the town and school were conjured from a fairy tale. The shops downtown are crafted from brick with flowers overflowing every windowsill—fake or real, they look incredible. Not a penny left in the budget when it came to the aesthetics. The town square has a gigantic marble fountain that puts on a water and light show every four hours.

I can't wait to get out and explore on my own with Sunny, without the crowd of photographers and journalists looking for a good story, like all the other times before.

After a quick potty break, Sunny prances back over

to me. I quickly clean her wet paws before letting her pass me.

My phone pings, and I pick it up off the bed where I left it, finding a text from Flora in my family group chat—consisting of my three aunts and myself.

> Flora: Good morning. Sending all of the love your way today. Call us later! We love you!
>
> Freya: Or call now. Whenever. Anytime. We miss you so much!
>
> Fauna: Don't forget to take your meds and drink lots of water!
>
> Flora: And avoid too many sweets!
>
> Freya: Give Sunny extra pets for me!
>
> Fauna: Keep your purse stocked with everything you need. Don't hesitate to call if you need anything, honey!

They're ridiculous. I love them so much. They may be my aunts, but they feel more like three mothers than anything.

They raised me far more than my dad ever did—at least in the ways that matter most. Even if I spent seventeen years with him and only two with them.

Although my dad did teach me lessons that I'll

never forget either—like how little someone's word can weigh.

> I miss you all too! I'm about to take
> Sunny for a walk. I'll FaceTime you guys
> later tonight. I love you all so much!

Setting my phone down on the bed, I walk across the room to my dresser and grab a pair of leggings and a hoodie before quickly changing and slipping on a pair of socks.

After washing my face, brushing my teeth, and putting light makeup on, I brush through my blonde hair and throw it in a high ponytail, calling it good enough for the day. Taking Sunny on a walk this morning is the only thing I plan on doing outside of my room today, so a ponytail will do just fine.

Besides, I don't have the mental energy to sit and curl my hair like I usually do.

Maybe I'll feel up for it when classes start in two days.

Sunny jumps back up in bed and curls up with a blanket, watching me as I settle down onto my piano bench and lift the lid of my piano, revealing fifty-two pearly white keys and thirty-six black ones.

"Ahh," I sigh, feeling peace settle in the depths of my shoulders as my fingers brush against the keys and my feet against the pedals.

From memory, I begin playing *La Valse* by Ravel, the upbeat tone filling the room around me, creating a shield from the rest of the world. My sanctuary, my true happy place, is when my music surrounds me and wraps me up in a warm hug.

I get lost in the notes, my body rocking back and forth as my hands dance the familiar pattern.

I love this piece; it's one of my favorites. It's beautiful with bursts of clarity during the melody. But there's an undertone in it, building as the song continues.

The first time I heard it, the resolve took my breath away, leaving me on the edge of my seat.

When I'm anxious or overwhelmed, this is the song I listen to, the one that slowly brings me back from the edge of panic. Or I play it if there's a piano nearby, but when I was on press tours with my dad, that wasn't always an option.

Especially when he wouldn't allow me to publicly play throughout my entire childhood.

Sunny huffs behind me, and I turn to face her, my fingers continuing to play. She is alert with a new burst of energy. I know what she wants, and after this song, I'll give it to her.

Closing my eyes and finish, taking a deep breath when the final note sounds through the room. I hate that I have to use an electric piano in the dorms. But I understand that a full grand piano would be very loud in comparison. I chuckle to myself at the thought. This one will do just fine.

Closing the lid, I get up and walk over to my shoe rack, grabbing my sneakers and tying them snug on my feet. Sunny is watching me very cautiously, waiting for the slightest movement toward her leash.

Lifting my crossbody strap over my shoulder, I secure my purse at my side and tuck a water bottle inside.

Turning to face my girl, I can't help the smile that starts to lift my lips. She has kept me sane the last couple of years and helped more than I'll ever be able to repay her. But I'll start with this.

"How about it, Sunny? Do you wannaaa"—I drag the *A* out, and her ears perk up in anticipation of what's coming next—"go for a … *walk?*"

Her entire face lights up with excitement, and she looks at her leash hanging by the door. Then she jumps from our bed and sprints over to me, her body vibrating with excitement.

"I'll take that as a yes." I grin and grab her leash and harness, I slip it on her.

Slipping my phone into my purse, I lead the way out of the room, Sunny snug at my side. The door automatically locks behind us and we head outside for an early morning tour of campus.

Sunny stays glued to my hip as we wander through the hall and down the steps outside of the dormitory.

Making the way to one of the dark cobblestone pathways that connect all of campus, I stay to the right side, out of the way of the bustling students. Some flutter past in a rush while some lackadaisically pass by —both groups stealing glances at Sunny. I knew she would draw some attention from my fellow students, but I'm honestly surprised no one has approached us yet. She is wearing her pink service dog vest, but that hasn't stopped people before.

The wide walkways are lined by four-foot vibrant green hedges, perfectly trimmed into sharp rectangles with no gaps between them. The chilly morning's only reprieve is the sunlight warming my back. Birds tweet in the trees scattered around us while squirrels race up and down the branches.

This campus really is breathtaking in every way possible. It's like stepping into a fairy tale. The buildings are all structured like old castles, and there are flower gardens spread throughout the grounds, tall grassy hedges lining the walkways, white marble fountains, and even a hedge maze.

I take a right at Hubert Hall, where I have Economics class. I might have created the path based on where my classes will be so I feel more comfortable with getting to them when the time comes.

I'm a master planner with everything I do. I like having control as much as I possibly can. I like habits, patterns, and routines. It helps with my POTS and my mental health.

Malik was not part of my vision. He is a very unwelcome addition, catching me completely off guard. I wish I had punched him in the face yesterday just to make myself feel better, although I'm sure my hand wouldn't feel the same way after colliding with that annoyingly sharp jaw.

Turning the corner toward the Student Union, I slam to a stop with Sunny when I spot the devil himself twenty feet away from me with a group of other tall and obnoxiously well-built guys, and a brunette girl. He laughs at something one of them said, his head tipping back and eyes squeezing shut before slapping one of the guys on the back of his head.

I've never seen him look so ... *happy*. It's unnerving.

As if he can sense my stare, his head turns my way, that piercing gaze locking with mine. I suck in a sharp breath at the intensity.

Even from here, I can feel his stare like a physical touch, pinning me in place.

His jaw clenches, and every joyous feature he just had hardens to stone. His black-and-white-inked arms cross against his muscular chest, as if he's standing his ground.

Stomping my right heel lightly on the cobblestone, I do the same, quickly covering the shock and fear on my face with confidence and annoyance.

He turns his whole body to face me, ignoring the group of people he's with, and a shiver twists down my spine, goose bumps erupting. He's intimidating and good at using it as a weapon.

But I'm not backing down. I take a step forward, Sunny following suit—completely unaware of the game she is tied up in. His eyes narrowing as he takes a step toward me. As childish as this feels, I won't let him win. I take another step.

With thirty feet still between us, this will take quite a while.

But we're already out of time.

One of the guys next to him pats his chest, eyebrows furrowed and head cocked to the side.

The dark-haired guy follows Malik's stare—right to me—and his confusion only deepens.

Like dominoes falling, one by one, everyone else in the group does the same until they're all staring at me.

But they aren't looking at me with disdain, like Malik; they just seem utterly perplexed. I don't blame them.

It's probably odd to see your friend in a stare-off with a girl across the courtyard.

One of the other guys mutters something to Malik, and a second later, he hesitantly retreats from his post, turning his back to me. Only now, I can see just how fast he's breathing, his shoulders rising and falling rapidly as he storms off in the opposite direction. Two of the guys follow after him, but the rest of the group hesitates, studying me for a moment more.

The brunette girl with a bow in her hair tugs at the biggest guy's hand, and he lets her lead him away. The rest of the group follows behind them.

A smile tips my lips up, and a sense of pride blooms in my chest.

I interpret that interaction as a success. He didn't

charge over here and dump his drink on me. Or have everyone around us start laughing at some obscene rumor.

He just left.

And I just won. For once, *I won*.

But as fast as the giddiness appeared, a gloomy eerie storm settles into my bones. He won't let it end like that. He'll find a way to get back at me.

Malik's a sore loser, and he'll make sure he comes out on top, no matter the cost.

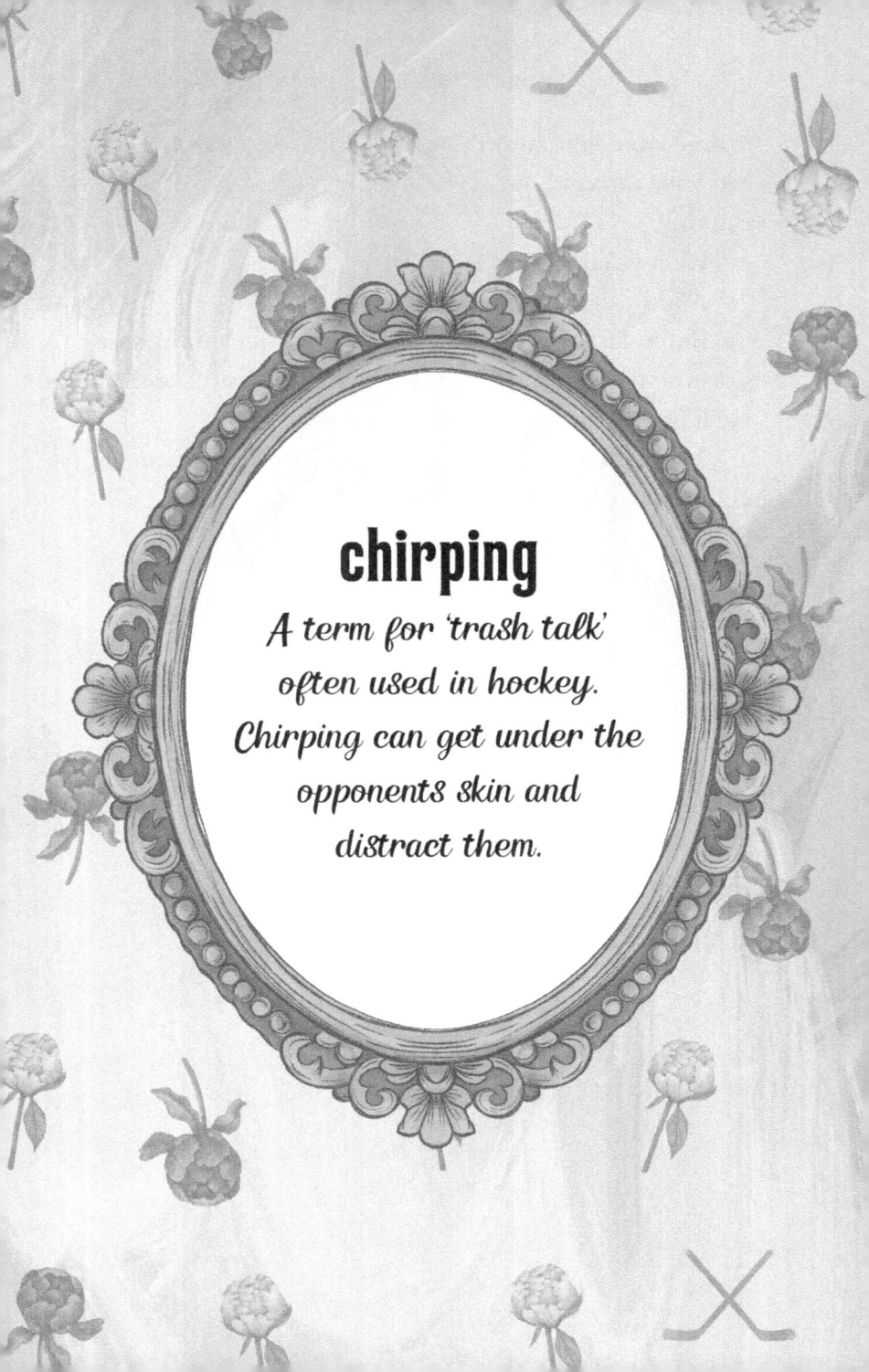

chirping

A term for 'trash talk'
often used in hockey.
Chirping can get under the
opponents skin and
distract them.

chapter four
malik

"Malik, for the love of God, don't do anything stupid." Griffin Hawthorne—a HEAU Hockey Legends defenseman and my best friend—sighs, dragging his hand down his face.

"You do realize who you're talking to, right?" Asher Kensington scoffs, laughing as he starts taking his sweaty clothes off from our workout.

Asher's brother, Dean Kensington, chimes in, "Malik, stupid? *Never.*"

While the brothers have a lot of similarities, their differences lie on the ice, Asher being a forward and Dean being a defenseman.

"Why is everyone trying to get their ass kicked today?" I exhale through my words. "All I said was that I need to get some energy out."

Griffin scoffs jokingly. "Yeah, and I've seen firsthand how destructive *your* energy can be."

Twisting my face, I groan. "That's not fair. I just happen to have a lot of it that regularly needs to be expelled. Sue me."

Fisting my T-shirt behind my neck, I pull the sweat-soaked black Legends shirt off and toss it onto the bench beside me.

"Did you get *more* tattoos?" Asher chuckles, looking at my exposed inked chest and arms.

"No, smart-ass, no more than I had the last time you saw me." Although I can't quite blame him for asking because even I have lost count.

"What's got you all riled up?" Griffin asks, changing into his sweats and hoodie. "You've been on edge the last couple of days, more so than usual."

Those annoyingly pretty blue eyes and blonde hair flash in my mind, but I force the unwelcome imagery away.

"Nothing."

"Are your teeth okay?" Asher asks, concern etched into his pinched brows. "I've never seen someone clench their jaw that tight before."

"Ha-ha," I deadpan.

"Seriously though, you know we're here if you need to vent about shit," Dean chimes in. "Better out."

"Than what? In?" Asher slaps the back of his head, scoffing. "Did you just fail to quote … *Shrek*?"

Dean shrugs with his arms in the air. "What? It's a great movie."

"Shut up." Asher winces, shaking his head in brotherly disappointment.

A beat of silence passes between all of us, and my heart starts to race because I know they are anticipating a response. But I'm not going to talk about her ... not to them.

"Yeah, seriously, guys, I'm good. Thanks though." Throwing my black Legends hoodie and joggers on quickly, I haul my backpack onto my shoulder and stride toward the exit. "I'll see you at the house, Griff."

When I lift my fist to his, he bumps it, and I repeat it again with Asher and Dean as I pass them.

Griffin looks at me like he knows there's more I'm hiding. "Sounds good, man. I should be right behind you."

Heading out of the locker room, I'm more annoyed than I was when I walked in, which is impressive, given I spent the last hour and a half weight lifting and pushing myself past the point of exhaustion.

But the built-up rage isn't what's suffocating me. It's *her*. Her presence here.

She's going to destroy the peace I've built for myself.

She's the resurrection of my past, blending with my present, and it's mind-fucking me. I hate it—*all* of it.

This school and team are my future. I buried the version of myself she knew, along with the pain, so deep inside of me that I'm scared of what will happen if it breaks free.

I spent the last year forcing Avandale and everyone in it out of my mind. Everyone but the three people I'll never be able to forget.

My high school hockey coach, Darius, and his wife, Alicia—who took me in when I needed help most. They're the only sense of family I have left in this world, aside from my team.

And my brother, Micah, who's still trapped in that town, in the same urn that my blackened heart and soul lie in. The only person in this world I've ever let in beyond my thorny walls.

When he died, so did I. My mind and body are just stuck here to live in a hell without him. My uncle hid Micah's remains from me, threatening to dispose of them if I ever opened my mouth about the truth of what had happened the night Micah died.

For now, I can live with that distance between us if it means he stays safe, even if it's away from me. One day, I'll get Micah back, if it's the last thing I do.

I'd break into my uncle's house if I knew Micah's ashes were there, but he already told me that it would be a waste of my time. That the urn is being kept somewhere I'd never find on my own.

And I believe him.

I've been keeping my head down, focusing on my classes and hockey. I've been distracted, surrounded by new people and a new school that have helped me hide from the ghosts of my past.

Everything was going to plan until Alora showed up here. Now, it's like every thought and memory I've spent running from are all rushing back to me. My head feels like it's going to explode.

If it's not visions of my uncle's fist or belt, my little brother forever still, or the countless freezing nights spent sleeping under the stars, it's of Alora. All haunting nonetheless.

Strolling out of the arena, I spot her walking away from me across the quad, with her dog on her heel.

Without thought, I do what I probably shouldn't and take a step toward her and then another, until I'm following her into the music hall.

Music, really?

I wouldn't have guessed Miss Nepo Baby would care enough about anything that took genuine skill and effort. If it didn't make her money, I thought she wouldn't pursue it.

Maybe she's just cutting through the building to go somewhere else; it's just part of her path.

Twisting my fingers tightly around my backpack strap, I stay behind her, keeping a significant distance so she doesn't get spooked.

Why am I following her? I have no plan or smart-ass comment locked and loaded if she catches me. Although I'm not concerned that she wouldn't quiver before me if I stood tall and sneered.

Even with doubt and Stop signs flashing in my mind, I push onward after her.

She approaches the steps and very slowly ascends one at a time, her golden retriever doing the same beside her. I have to come to a stop at the hedges around the corner so I don't catch up with her.

Once she slips inside the double doors, I climb the steps behind her and hesitate for a second as my hand hovers over the handle, once more debating whether to turn around or go inside.

I pull the door open.

Whoa, this place is insane.

The lobby is gigantic, stretching upward by at least thirty feet. Giant skylights fill the open space with natural light, reflecting off the huge chandelier hanging from the highest point. The second and third floors are open to the foyer, separated by a tall railing.

A swoosh of blonde hair in the corner of my eye reminds me why I'm even here in the first place, drawing me from my stupor.

She disappears around a corner, and I dig my heel into the ground, my long strides carrying me down the trail of her strawberry and vanilla perfume. I breathe it in without thought.

Drifting behind her, I can't help but wonder if I've completely lost my mind. Chasing after her and watching her, just like I did in high school. But I never once caught her in the music room. Although I was never near it myself.

This feels all too normal. But I didn't care about anything back then. I had nothing to lose. But now? Now I can't be as reckless as I once was.

I have a scholarship to the most prestigious school in the country and am on a path to go pro afterward. I can't lose that because of her.

She steps through a door to her left and closes it behind her and her dog. A sign hanging on the wall above the doorframe reads *Practice Room*.

Slowing my pace, I cautiously approach the door, spotting a narrow window above the doorknob. What is she possibly practicing?

Students turn and shuffle down the hallway, heading this way.

I quickly dig my phone out of my pocket and casually scroll through the home screen, pretending like I'm not trying to peep through the window next to me.

They pass by me, all three girls glancing my way with variations of a flirty smile. When I nod at them, they blush and scurry away.

Breathing deeply, I take a step closer to the window. *What is she doing in there?*

But she answers my question without a word.

As if a switch was flicked, the room bursts with life as Alora begins to play the piano. She isn't pecking the notes like a chicken, but like she has a thousand fingers, dancing through all of the perfect strokes.

Why has she been keeping this part of her a secret?

I've seen her social media accounts, stalked them

intensely for years, and not once has she posted anything about this.

I didn't know she was even musically inclined, let alone play like *that*. Inching closer toward the window, I hesitantly peek inside, leaning my cheek against the frame of the window.

My mouth dries, and my lips part at the sight before me. I don't know what I was expecting, but being mesmerized wasn't even close.

The piano sits perpendicular to the door, tucked against the right wall. Alora's side is to me, giving me a perfect outline of her profile, just a few feet away.

She continues to play with vigor, her eyes sealed shut and lips slightly parted. She is a stark difference from the dark, haunting song flowing from her fingers. She's completely transported into her music, swaying with the movements of her hands as they travel the keys by pure memory alone.

Through the small window, I watch her head tilt backward. Her wavy blonde hair falls from her face, further exposing the pained expression etched in her every feature.

So delicate, so fragile, yet ... she looks so *powerful*.

Maybe this is her *hockey*, the one part of life where she feels most comfortable, where her true purpose lies.

The brief moment of empathy seizes my body, my muscles going rigid. A thrum of self-hatred blooms in my chest as I remind myself that she doesn't deserve empathy.

This is something I could take away from her or turn against her if I wanted. I could make her hate the piano. Ridicule her to the extent that anytime she touched one again, she couldn't help but think of me.

I should throw this door open and show her that no matter where she goes on campus, she isn't safe from my reach.

But I don't move. I'm frozen, my body weakened by the sight of her. Feeling helpless and under her control.

Add that to the list of reasons for my hatred. She was never supposed to have this power over me, to manipulate my wrath. It's infuriating on a whole new level.

I've gone years hating her; that isn't about to change now. But I have a feeling that my fascination with her won't either.

Alora was always the object of my obsession, sitting at the center of everything I did back then. Even before I learned her last name.

She caught my eye the first day she walked into Avandale High. Drawing me in with that blue stare and pillowy lips. With her aura of warmth and gentleness. I wanted to feel the fragility crumble beneath my desire as she came apart around me.

Then everything changed when I heard the teacher mention who she really was. It was like a bomb went off in the room, destroying the reality I'd thought I was living. My lust transformed to an all-consuming hatred.

But as much as I've tried, that desire has never

faded. It still tortures me with thoughts and feelings of the one girl I can never have, of the one girl I will never *want* to want.

Her fingers and movements slow, and I shift out of view of the window, flattening my back against the wall.

Suddenly, everything feels wrong.

My blood rushes through my veins, racing as my heart thumps faster and faster. My palms begin to sweat, and my clothes feel heavier and tighter than before.

What the fuck is happening to me?

I run my hand down my throat as my body warms a thousand degrees.

I need to get out of here.

Pushing away from the wall, I stride toward the door I came through, each step harder than the last, like gravity is weighing down more than before.

I can't breathe. I can't breathe.

Am I ...

Am I having ... a panic attack?

Shit. I haven't had one of these in years.

She's not just bringing memories back; she's unleashing the literal pain I've managed to keep beneath the surface.

Crashing through to the doors and into the crisp fall air, I inhale deeply and race down the steps, heading toward the first thing I see to keep me upright.

Bracing my hands on the rough bark of the great oak, I squeeze my eyes shut as my mind works through the muscle memory of what to do. The same muscle memory my mind created from having countless attacks before.

Inhale for five. Exhale for ten.

Over and over.

I repeat it until my breathing begins to slow and I can feel myself finally gaining control again.

My phone rings in my pocket, granting me a much-needed distraction from the shadows in my mind.

Coach Darius Sherwood.

"Hello?" I answer, my voice cracking and shaky as I settle the phone against my ear.

"Are you all right?" His question is twisted with worry.

He may have only been my hockey coach, but he became much more than that when he found out I was sleeping in my car outside of the arena at night during my senior year. He and his wife opened their home to me without a thought. The only parental figures I've ever been able to look up to. I owe them everything.

"Yeah, I'll be fine. Just a … moment." I brush it off. "What's up?"

"Just checking in. You've been quiet the last week, and I wanted to see how you were doing. From what I can tell from our talk so far, I can tell you're not great." He chuckles softly, concern still evident in his tone.

Lifting my head up, I turn around and rest my back against the tree. "No, no. I am fine. Really."

"Malik," he sighs. "You know you don't always have

to keep the world shut out. What's going on? Classes okay? Hockey? Need more money?"

"No," I snap, instantly regretting the sharpness of my response. I just hate taking their money. Not after everything they've done for me. "That's all going fine," I continue.

The door of the music building swinging open draws my attention. Someone walks through, but it's not her.

"So, what's *not* fine?" he pushes.

"You remember …" I trail off, debating whether or not to keep going.

"Malik, what's got you all up in a twist, huh? Just talk to me." Darius's comforting voice hums into my ear, a stark difference to his coaching voice that I used to know.

Darius is the reason I even graduated high school. The reason I had a roof over my head the second half of my senior year. The reason I have a scholarship to this school. He submitted the application on my behalf and surprised me with the acceptance letter.

I didn't think I would get anywhere in life. And I don't think I would have without him and Alicia.

So, the least I can do is give him a real answer.

"Alora Briarwood." I mutter her name, and as if by magic, she appears through the doors of the music hall, pausing on the top of the stairs as she focuses on her phone.

"Oh." He exhales heavily, instantly remembering. "Got it."

"Yeah …" I trail off, uncertain of what to say next.

As if she can feel my gaze, she lifts her head, her eyes locking on to mine immediately, causing shivers to wrap around my spine.

"Well, just stay focus—"

I cut him off, "I've got to go. I'll call you later. Bye." I grind my teeth and start walking, away from the music hall.

"Soon!" he calls out as I end the call.

I jam my phone into my pocket, making a beeline to the parking lot my car's in.

I need to get home, get on the ice, get anywhere but here. Racing down the cobblestone walkways toward my car, I wonder if this is what the next few years will look like with her here.

My anxiety and sorrow begin to blossom into anger, the kind that only exists for her and her family.

My phone buzzes in my pocket, and I'm sure it's Darius, just sending a follow-up text, like he usually does after our call, telling me that he and Alicia miss me and to call again soon.

I don't mean to be blunt with him. I owe them so much. But sometimes, my mouth gets in the way of my intentions, like the words lash out before I can choose the ones I mean to say.

Approaching my Corvette, I dig my keys out from my pocket and unlock it with the fob.

God, I have such a love-hate relationship with this car.

Once upon a time, it was my dream to have a Corvette—a black one, just like this. But how I got it will always tarnish its beauty.

Every time I slide into the driver's seat of it, all I can think about is how my uncle took a bribe to cover up the murder of Micah.

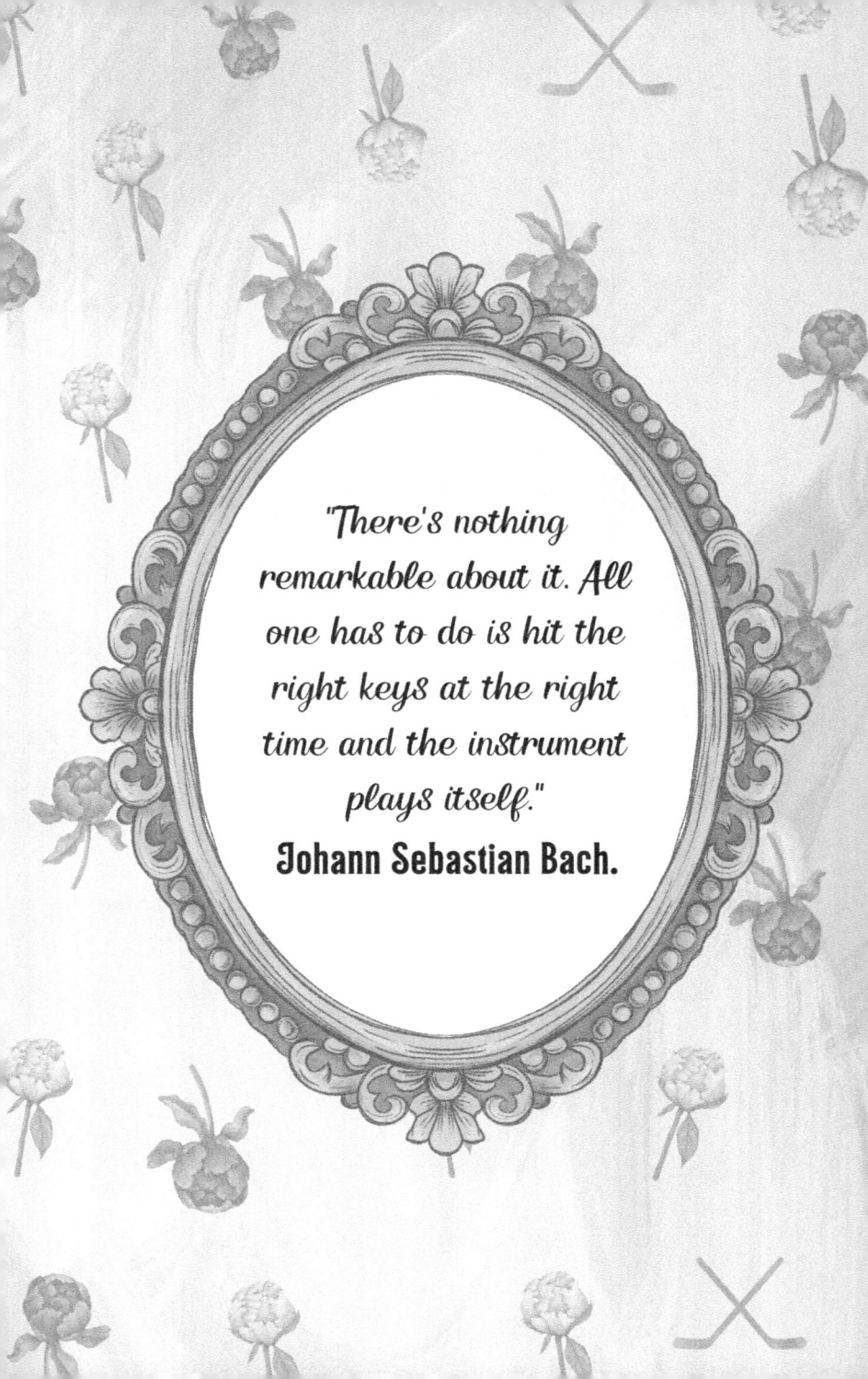

"There's nothing remarkable about it. All one has to do is hit the right keys at the right time and the instrument plays itself."

Johann Sebastian Bach.

chapter five
alora

When I walk into Hubert Hall with Sunny for my first class, my nerves are at an all-time high, more erratic than I was expecting.

Maybe it has to do with the fact that this is my first day and everything is a bit uncertain.

Will the professor be kind? Witty? Strict? Dry? Will I have any POTS flare-ups? Will a thousand people try to pet Sunny?

But I know where my anxiety lies. The constant chance of running into Malik. This may be my first year here, but I'm not a freshman as far as credits go. I have a plethora of credits from classes I completed in high school. Academically, I'm a sophomore. Which raises the stakes of sharing a class with *him*.

Thankfully, I haven't seen him since the night he barged into my room.

A shiver runs down my back, reminding me of the coldness of that night. Not only from the cool air outside, but also the wintery chill of his tone and touch. The bite of his words and threats.

A reminder that he doesn't have a soul to warm his bones. He's empty and hollow, and he always will be.

Mumbling to Sunny, I nervously blabber, "Come on, baby. Let's go to our first class."

She wags her tail and looks up at me with big, round eyes beaming with purity. I swear dogs are angels sent to show us the true meaning of unconditional love.

"I'll take you to do something fun after this, I promise."

She looks ahead and continues striding beside me with ease. We may have to make it a shorter walk today though because this morning was a bit shaky for me.

Mornings are usually a good indicator of how the rest of my day will go. And with the headache and tiredness I woke up with this morning, I need to take it a bit easier than normal.

Every morning, before I ever get out of bed, I drink a few big gulps of water from my water bottle and give myself a minute to adjust while I slowly stretch my limbs out. Gradually, I sit up, taking my time and listening to my body as I go.

I'm a bit more cautious than usual with how this morning went, but I'm taking it minute by minute. I feel okay right now—not great, but good enough to go on with the day as planned.

I wonder if there will ever come a day when I'm used to the level of decorum at this school. Or the opulence in every nook and cranny. I know that I grew up wealthier than most, but this place is something else entirely.

I mean, how many chandeliers is *too* many? The electric bill for this place must be insane. But when your student body consists of politicians' children, royals, gold medalist athletes, and every other elite qualifier, money isn't a problem.

Everyone wants the best for their kids—or at least to make the biggest show of it all. It's a bragging right both for the student and their family.

Whether it's donating a few million to have the family name slapped on a building or sponsoring the school with your family's billion-dollar sports drink company, like the Hawthornes, everyone fights to for the favor of this school. And everyone wants the shiny golden ticket we'll receive at graduation.

I'm sure my dad thinks I'm doing this to impress him, but I stopped trying to do that a long time ago. I'm doing this for me and me alone.

Turning into the classroom, I find it completely empty—exactly as I was hoping. I eye my seat immediately and cross the distance with Sunny to the first seat on the bottom row of the tiered seating. Easy in, easy out. And if I need to slip away, I can without having to cross the entire class, drawing unwanted attention.

I think I might have spent so much time hiding in the shadows that I'm scared to step into the light. I like to stay hidden from the rest of the world. It's comforting, safe.

But with Malik back in the picture, I'm scared that my presence will be glaring. Especially to him.

Sitting down in my seat, I unload my laptop, book, notepad, and pen from my backpack as I hear footsteps turn into the room and approach me.

But they aren't the heavy stride of a big guy; they're softer.

Glancing up, I find a brunette girl with a kind smile walking toward the seats to my left.

She looks vaguely familiar, but I can't place her.

"Wow, I'm surprised someone is here before me. I'm usually always first." She chuckles softly. "Impressive."

"I don't know that *impressive* is the word I'd use. More like anxious." My lips tip into a grin as she slides into a seat to my left, leaving the one between us empty.

"I've been there. Trust me. Is this your first year here?" She opens her shoulders to me, giving me her full attention.

I nod. "Yeah. I took a year off after high school to … I don't know … figure some stuff out, I guess."

A few students walk into the room, filling the silence with their muffled chatter.

"So, did you figure it out?" She lifts her hands up.

"I'm sorry. I feel like I should apologize for coming in here and interrogating you. I'm not usually this ... extroverty?" She chuckles at the made-up word.

Laughing with her, I brush her apology away. "Don't worry about it. And, yeah ... I mean, it's complicated."

"*Complicated* I can understand. I'm Blair, by the way." She officially introduces herself.

"I'm Alora." I smile softly.

"It's nice to meet you." She smiles back.

Her eyes fall to Sunny, who's now lying down on the ground between our feet.

"This is Sunny." I pause as her ears perk up at the sound of her name. "She's my service dog."

"May I ask what for? I totally understand if that's too personal though." Her eyes widen from fear of overstepping.

"No, it's okay. I have POTS—postural orthostatic tach—"

She cuts me off by finishing my sentence. "Tachy-cardia syndrome. Yeah, in high school, a friend of mine had it."

"Oh, really?" I sit up taller.

"Yeah. We weren't super close, but I helped her a time or two with it when she needed someone. Whether to vent or hold her through an episode. But I'm sorry I cut you off."

"Don't apologize," I assure her. "It's actually rather

refreshing to talk to someone about it here. It's just been Sunny and me, so it's nice."

Sunny looks up at me, and I think that she somehow understood that conversation and is offended that my talking solely to her isn't fulfilling enough.

"Oh, stop that. You know I love you." I pet the top of her head, brushing her ears down.

Blair fidgets in her chair, and I can tell she wants to pet Sunny, but doesn't want to be rude.

Turning my attention to Blair, I ask, "Do you want to pet her? She loves attention."

"Are you sure?" she asks, already moving her way toward Sunny.

"Yes." I chuckle. "Of course."

"Thank you." She reaches down, and Sunny encourages her hand even more by sitting up and leaning into her touch. "I'm always here if you need someone to help you. I mean, I'm sure that your girl here is great at her job. But if you ever need a vent session, I'm here."

I know I just met this girl, but I can tell she's genuine. Maybe it's from being surrounded by lying politicians most of my life that gifted me with the ability to spot a liar a mile away.

"That means a lot." My eyes burn, and I instantly shut the sensation down.

What the hell? Why am I tearing up at her simple offer? It's ridiculous. Get it together, Alora. She is just trying to be polite.

But I can't help it. I've felt the sinking claws of loneliness my entire life, but there's a special kind of ache reserved for the absence of friendship. Something I've gone a long time without.

Apart from an old family friend I spent some time with after high school—Phillip Stephens, my oldest friend. We were brought together from our fathers' dealings in politics, forced into friendship, but a natural one blossomed over the years.

I appreciate him greatly, but it's not the same as having a real best friend. The one person you can trust with your life, the one person you tell absolutely everything to. No barriers. No lies. No walls.

I've experienced it countless times—always jealous of the connection everyone else in the world but me seems to have. I know there are worse things I could be a victim of. But that doesn't change the ache in my chest, a hole that's never been filled.

It would be nice to have a friend here, even someone just to get coffee with on occasion.

"Can I get your number for when I'm in need?" I smile at her.

Blair's movement yanks me from my spiraling thoughts. She digs her phone from her purse. "Of course. Here." She sets her phone on my desk with a new text screen pulled up.

I type my number into the designated spot, put a smiley emoji in the body of the text, and hit Send. My phone vibrates on the small attached desktop in front of me.

"Perfect." She beams.

I didn't even notice, but the classroom is nearly filled up, almost every seat taken.

An older woman enters the room, beelining it straight for the desk.

Professor Samson.

With a hand tucked into her white dress pants, she drops her bag on her desk and leans back against the front of it. "Good morning, everyone. Today will be a short one. We will cover the syllabus. Then you will be sent on your way. No point in making your first week of classes hell. I'm sure there are plenty of other professors who will do that for me."

"Fuck yeah!" someone in the back of the room shouts, followed by some sporadic clapping.

"Please pull it up on your laptop or phone. We'll be starting on page five," she announces. She's clearly done this enough times that she has it memorized.

She continues, "Attendance. It is your job to care about your classes. I can't make you show up. But I can be sure that if you don't, you won't pass my class."

Page by page, she breaks down her rules, expectations, workload, and pretty much every single little thing we could want to know. It's impressively thorough.

By the time she's finished, we still have thirty minutes left on the clock, but like she said earlier, she's releasing us early.

"Thank you all for showing up today. You're dismissed." She walks around her desk and sits down in her chair, opening her laptop and typing rapidly.

Students file out of the room, happier as ever that it's over so quickly. To be fair, I don't think that anyone is too upset about getting out of an Economics class early.

"Best class so far." Blair chuckles as we both gather our things and stow them in our backpacks.

"Yeah, I'd say so." I smile, throwing my backpack on as I rise from my seat.

She glances down at Sunny. "She is the best girl ever."

"Be careful. She loves compliments. She might never leave you alone if you keep doing that."

Blair crouches down in front of her, giving her gentle pets. "Oh no," she mocks. "That would be *horrible*," she says sarcastically.

She stands up, and we walk out of the room together, falling into the flow of traffic down the hallway toward the exit.

"I'm so glad you're going to be in this class with me. I was worried I would be stuck with people I didn't get along with," I sigh.

"Me too!" She opens one of the big arch doors, and sunlight flickers through. "What other classes do you have?"

She pulls her phone out, and a huge smile takes over

her face. "I have to go, but send me a picture of your schedule! We should grab coffee sometime!"

"Yeah." I nod as she starts backpedaling. "I'd love to. Have a good day!"

"You too!" she calls back to me as her pace increases.

She turns away and takes off in the opposite direction as me, picking up speed. It takes me less than a second to see exactly what she's rushing toward—or rather ... who.

As she reaches the beast of a guy wearing a Legends hockey T-shirt, I finally place where I saw her before, and my stomach sinks.

A perfect storm from the universe.

I've finally found someone who I think may actually be a good friend, and of course she has to be dating one of Malik's teammates.

Why couldn't she have been in the Anti-Hockey Club? That would have made this so much easier. But, no, she has to be in the same circle as the one person I'm desperately avoiding.

Exhaling, I turn the opposite way to head back to my room. Sunny walks beside me as we follow the path I've committed to memory. Maybe I should take her on a scenic trail back to our place instead of the straight route. She would probably love it.

"A quick one. And then home," I tell her.

Guiding her down a new route, I let her sniff and explore as much as she likes, letting her set the pace.

Her collar jingles against her harness, reminding me that I need to order her a new service vest since she was a *very* naughty girl and chewed hers up a couple of days ago. Something she has *never* done. I have no clue why, all of a sudden, she decided it had to go, but there's not much I can do about it now.

I know she isn't marked as a service dog right now, which is technically against campus policy. But I have her card on me, so in the worst case, if someone stops me, I can show them that. But to be honest, I'm sure my last name is the only proof I need to halt any questioning.

Entering the walking roundabout with a vine-covered gazebo in the center, we drift right with the flow of foot traffic. As we pull right to turn on the first break of solid green hedges, I stop in my tracks, sighing at the sight.

You have got to be kidding me.

I think the universe is starting to have too much fun, messing with my life.

"Fucking hell," he mutters, his jaw locking and arms crossing over his chest as he stops in the middle of the walkway.

Malik Ravenwell is five feet from me, with four of his hockey players at his side. But I can't look away from Malik's unique purple glare.

Surprisingly, he doesn't snap at me or plow through me, as expected. His anger at me is ever present, as always, but his lips are sealed shut.

Interesting.

I wonder why. It's not like he's had a change of heart toward me.

Maybe he doesn't want his friends to know he was such a piece of shit in high school. Does that mean that I have the high ground for once?

His friends, noticing our obvious staredown, look from me to Malik, back and forth, waiting for one of us to make a move.

But instead, one of his friends does.

With dark brown hair and dark blue eyes, the two friends look vaguely similar, and I can't help but wonder if they're brothers. But to be honest, I don't care. I just want to get away from them. And even farther away from Malik.

"Excuse me," I mutter with annoyance in my voice, stepping to the side.

But one of the brown-haired boys politely stops me with his hand stretched out to mine. "Look, I don't know what Malik's done to make someone as beautiful as you so angry, but please don't run off just yet." His smile widens. "I'm Asher."

"I'm Dean." The other one introduces himself with a shining smile. "You know, we're having a party this weekend. You should come."

Like I'm going to fall for that setup.

Been there, done that with Malik. I'm not going to walk straight into his trap all over again.

"I appreciate that, and it's nice to meet you both.

But I'm going to …" I trail off, but Malik's sharp-edged words stop me.

"Alora doesn't like parties. It's not her place anyway. Besides, I'm sure she's too good to go to some college party." His words snap with anger, sending a shiver down my spine. Malik steps forward, closing the distance between us to a mere two feet. "Don't waste your breath with this one."

"I don't know." Asher sighs. "I think that's for me to decide, Mal."

"Trust me, you'll want to steer clear of her. She's a waste of effort."

I roll my eyes, and he inches closer to me.

Whoever I was five seconds ago is gone. I'm replaced by a pent-up ball of hatred that has spent years piling up. And I'm done with it.

Looking around him, I decide to fight fire with fire.

I bat my eyelashes and flash an award-winning smile. "Asher, I would love to tell you just how much of a waste I am over dinner." Grabbing my phone from my pocket, I hand it over to him to type in a new message.

He happily takes it with a big smile on his face. "Sounds great to me."

But Malik snatches it from his hand before he gets a chance. "No need to do that. Alora, you're not allowed to date anyone on the team."

"Excuse me?" I laugh viciously. "That's not your place to decide."

I rip my phone out of his hand.

He leans down and snarls, his warm breath caressing my lips, "You want to bet?"

"Malik, take a fucking breath, huh?" Asher scoffs. "If you're marking her off-limits, I got you. But if not … then I'm inviting her to dinner or our party at least."

He painfully tears his gaze from mine. "Asher, would you fuck off for two seconds, please?"

Asher holds his hands up in defeat with a shit-eating grin on his lips. Dean laughs at the awkward situation.

I hate that Malik has still found a way to have power at a new school. To make others obey his orders.

But it sounds like it's more of a respected rule among the team. Although if it's some off-limits rule that I have to worry about, then I'm not worried at all.

Malik would never claim me as his to anyone, but especially to his team.

"You're not going to that party. You're not going to dinner with Asher," he commands like I'm a dog.

My words leave my lips before I even realize it. "I don't take orders from you, Malik."

His lip twitches. "Yes, you do. You did back then, and you will now. Like the good little bug that you are."

Now it's me who steps toward him. Jabbing my finger into his ridiculously firm chest, I stand tall. "*You* have no idea who I am anymore. You don't call the shots. Not when it comes to me." I huff out a sharp breath. "You don't scare me anymore, Malik."

Wrapping his hand around mine, he yanks it down

and off of him. I stumble from the force, but his grip keeps me steady.

His eyebrows pinch, and his nostrils flare. "I should." His voice vibrates through every bone in my body.

He does. He scares the shit out of me.

Everything in me is telling me to run, to cower in the corner. But I don't back down.

Standing up higher on my toes, I grind my next words through my teeth, my mouth inches from his. "You are nothing more than a bully and a sore loser, desperately clinging to a power that you no longer have over me."

"Careful, Bug. You're about to start a game you won't be able to win." The words he utters are only loud enough for me to hear.

His pupil-blown stare flashes to something behind me before returning to mine.

Backing up from him, I flick my hair over my shoulder, hanging on to every shred of fake confidence I have.

Striding past him, I glance up and address Asher once more. "I'd love to come to the party. You can get my number from Blair. She's dating one of your teammates, right?"

He nods and smiles. "Can't wait."

Turning back around to Malik, I smile with nothing but poison in my words. "And, Malik? You're wrong. It's my game now."

Without another word, I spin on my heel, and Sunny and I stride away with ease, as if that was the calmest and most carefree conversation I'd ever had. But inside, I'm dying. Desperate to get home and relax.

I can feel my heart rate starting to race. And Sunny has been looking at me far more frequently, as if she's waiting for signs to tell me to slow down.

But I don't want to give Malik the satisfaction of slowing down a step. I don't want him to see a crack in my foundation.

Once we're out of view of the guys, we chill our roll. Taking full deep breaths, I lean back against one of the tall hedges, calming my heart.

Retrieving my water bottle from my bag, I take a few sips and continue to take steady breaths. Moments later, I feel better already, and Sunny and I head straight for our room.

It only takes us a couple of minutes to reach the dorm and tuck ourselves safely inside our sanctuary.

She immediately goes for a snack from her food bowl as I drop my backpack and settle into my comfortable bed to rest for a bit.

My headache from earlier is beginning to creep back in—thanks to the Malik run-in, I'm sure. My time at HEAU would be so much easier if he wasn't here at all.

Regret and worry start settling into my chest, pressing down with every breath I take.

Ugh … I never should have said anything to him. I should have turned around and walked away.

What the hell got into me?

He's right … I know he's right. This is a game I'm not going to win. Perhaps neither of us will. I think, in the end, we will be each other's ruin.

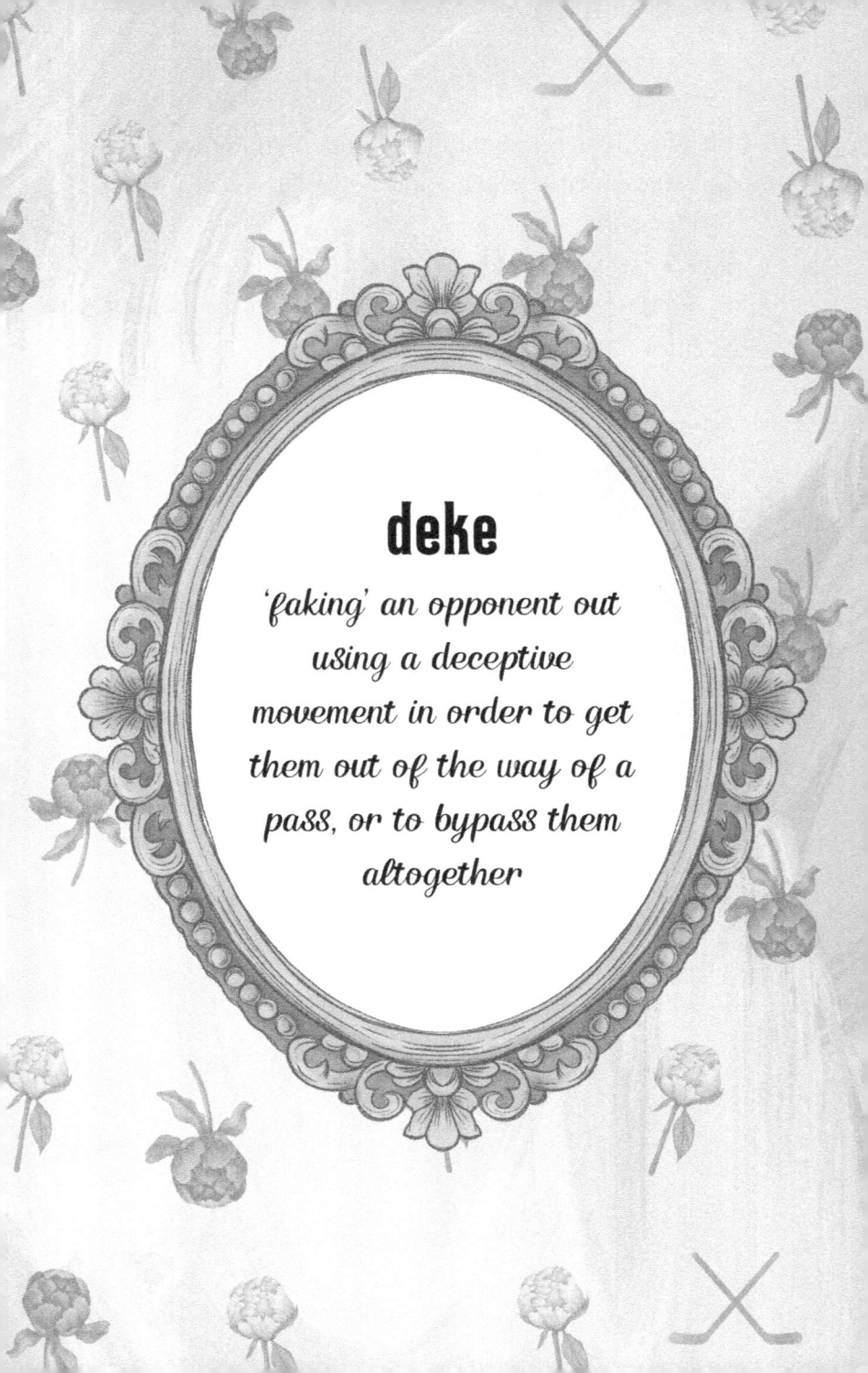

deke

'faking' an opponent out using a deceptive movement in order to get them out of the way of a pass, or to bypass them altogether

chapter six
malik

My body's aching as I roll out of bed this morning. The pain is doing little to kill the immediate thoughts of Alora, who has seemed to permeate more of my mind than I'd ever like to admit.

God, it would be so much better for the both of us if she stuck to her corner of the world and I to mine. This campus is big—big enough for us to not see each other as much as we have.

And now Asher is inviting her to a party at the Kensington mansion. Another part of my world that she's forcing herself into.

But I highly doubt she's going to show up. She never went to any of the hockey parties in high school, and I'm sure that hasn't changed. Even though *she* clearly has.

This new attitude of hers needs to be checked. She thinks she can call this *her game*. She's sorely mistaken.

I might have let her get away with that comment, but only because I haven't decided if I want my teammates to know our real history. Of how badly I tormented her.

My teammates mean a lot to me—more than I ever expected. They've become my family in a sense, and I don't want them to look at me poorly because of what I did to her.

But even I have a breaking point, and she does not want to shove me over the edge. At some point, I'm not going to give a fuck who knows what if she keeps pushing me.

There is a knot in my chest that appeared when I saw her again. One that won't leave, no matter how hard I will it away. It's fucking suffocating.

"Hurry up! We're going to be late!" Griffin pounds his fist on the door as he walks past my room.

Tapping the screen on my phone, I see just how right he is. Shit, we should have left, like, five minutes ago.

Rushing across the room, I grab one of my Legends hoodies and black joggers, quickly slipping on boxers and socks before putting on the rest.

After stepping into a pair of sneakers, I brush my teeth and run my fingers through my black hair. When I glance in the mirror for a brief second, my breath catches in my throat, slicing my heart with shards of glass.

The light-purple gaze glaring back at me has become one I don't often look at.

They say having purple eyes is a rarity, something saved for less than one percent. Yet, somehow, my brother and I have the same eyes. And every time I look in the mirror, all I see is him. A memory, a ghost of what he looked like. I can't see myself without seeing him, and I can't bear to look upon his image without feeling like the world around me is going to crash and burn.

Tearing my attention away from my reflection, I stride across my room, grabbing my backpack and tossing a black T-shirt inside for after weight lifting.

Heading out of the room, I throw my door open.

"I'm coming!" I shout loudly, hoping it manages to travel through this stupidly large house to him.

Traveling down the long, winding hallway of the lower level of the east wing, I climb the few steps that lead me into the grand foyer, finding Blair and Griffin waiting for me near the front door.

"About fucking time. Sleep through your alarms?" Griffin asks, spinning his keys in his hand.

Lifting my hands up as I approach the front door where they're standing, I plead my case. "Yes. But to be fair, if your house wasn't gigantic and it didn't take me ten minutes to get from my room to the front door, we wouldn't be in this mess."

He opens the door, and we step out into the sunny day, the warmth happily welcomed. "So, you're blaming your irresponsibility on the fact that my house—which you're staying in for free—is *too big*?"

Clicking my tongue, I wink at him. "Yeah. Of course. It could never be *my* fault."

He laughs. "It never is, is it?"

"Now you're catching on." I chuckle, sliding into the back seat of his pickup.

Blair hops in the front, and Griffin gets in the driver's seat.

I don't typically ride to campus with them, but since there's a party tonight, I didn't want to have to worry about my car and getting it home.

"Ready for our first day in World History?" Blair asks the both of us.

"Nope. But it's a good thing I have a really smart and hot girlfriend to be excited for me." Griffin lifts their intertwined hands and kisses her fingers.

"You know what? I'll just walk." I groan.

Griffin turns his head and blinks rapidly with a straight face, calling my bluff.

"Shut up and drive." I flip him off, and he turns back around chuckling.

This is really the first time that I've seen Blair since my Alora run-in, and I think of the words that Alora muttered to Asher.

"Hey, Blair. Question for you." I sit up further, positioning myself between the two front seats as Griffin starts driving out of his private driveway.

"Oh God," she murmurs, and Griffin laughs. "What's up?"

"First off, rude. Secondly, do you know a girl named Alora?" My palms begin to sweat, and my body feels oddly uncomfortable when I say her name aloud.

Like talking about her with my closest friends is causing my body to have some kind of allergic reaction.

Blair turns her head, squinting and studying me for a moment, clearly deciding how she wants to answer my question. "Y-yes. I have a class with her. Why?"

"Don't look so nervous. I was just curious." With my hands planted on both of their seats, I push myself back until I hit the backrest.

She spins fully around in her seat, her eyebrows pinched tightly together. "Nothing with you is ever so simple. Why are you curious?" She sighs. "Malik, she seems so sweet, and I don't want you to toy with her."

Holding my hands up in defense, I scoff. "I don't toy with people."

Griffin cackles. "Malik, don't lie to yourself. You are a grade-A menace."

Sitting up taller, I meet his stare in the rearview mirror. "Thank you."

Blair points her finger at me. "I'm serious."

Blair's automatic defense of a girl she just met signals everything in me to start locking down. It was this simple for her to take Alora's side that easily. Like I don't mean anything in comparison.

Stop, dude. Get out of your fucking head.

But the rage inside of me has already begun to swirl, slowly bubbling to the surface. "You had what, one class with her? You don't know her, Blair."

"And you do?" she challenges me with a feisty gleam in her eye.

"More than you'd think," I mutter under my breath.

Shit. I need to learn to just keep my mouth shut. I didn't mean to say that thought out loud.

She cocks her head to the side. "What?"

Her brown eyes holds mine as she waits for a response. But I don't want to spend any more of my morning talking about this girl. She is occupying far too much of my damn time.

"No, I don't." Fuck, I shouldn't have lied to her.

Griffin relieves me from the interrogation. "Baby, play that song you wanted me to hear earlier."

Blair lights up. "Oh my God, I almost forgot." She grabs her phone and connects to the Bluetooth of Griffin's pickup.

A moment later, some new pop song plays through the speakers. I tune it out almost immediately, getting lost in the never-ending spiraling thoughts in my mind.

This isn't going to end well. However this goes, Alora is going to crash my world to the ground with her pretty smile and kind words. She already stole Blair from my corner. Who's next? Asher? Griffin?

Clenching my fists in my lap, I force myself to take a breath, realizing that this is getting out of control. I need to expel some energy before I explode.

Thankfully, we are almost to campus, and I can wear my muscles down in the weight room until I have nothing left to give.

Maybe I should just skip the party tonight. It'd probably be a smart idea, especially if Alora plans on attending. God, she'd better not though. She's getting too confident. Like she's forgotten our dynamic and who makes the rules.

Let tonight be a test. I'll go. We'll see if she shows up. She'll choose her own fate. If she does, I'll give her a reminder of our past together. A taste of what she ran far away from.

"Malik, are you coming back home or what?" Griffin asks me as we walk out of the locker room after practice.

"Yeah. I've got to shower quickly and change beforehand. Is Blair coming with us tonight?" I ask out of curiosity.

Sometimes, she comes out with us, and sometimes, she'd rather stay home, curled up with one of her books in that giant library Griffin had built for her at the end of last year.

"Yeah, she is. My best friend, Lumi's coming too. He's going to meet us at the house and ride with us." Griffin dumps his backpack into the bed of his pickup and slides in the driver's seat.

Griffin starts the truck as I sit down in the passenger seat and says, "Blair is staying here a while longer for another class, and Lumi will bring her home. So, it's just us. Do you want to grab any food? I'm starving."

"Sure, yeah." My stomach grumbles, reminding me I haven't eaten anything, aside from a smoothie, after weight lifting earlier.

His phone dings.

"Hey, Mrs. Potts is going to make us some food. She and Chip are on their way home now. If that's good with you?"

Mrs. Potts and Chip live with Griffin. Mrs. Potts cooks and cleans for him. She's been with his family for years. They're practically Griffin's only family now.

"Yeah."

Griffin starts driving and I get lost in thought, looking out the window.

I owe him a lot. More than I'll ever be able to repay. It seems like there's more people like that than ever. The list keeps building, as does my guilt for accepting the help.

He took me under his wing this past year. Let me move into his place so I wouldn't have to worry about rent. He never lets me pay for groceries or anything when Mrs. Potts—his housekeeper and chef—goes shopping.

I have money, but it's a drop in the bucket in comparison to him. He comes from money—like the kind where you never have to check your bank account, you buy a brand-new car just because, you live in a multimillion-dollar mansion, and your family is worth billions.

I know what he spares for me might be nothing to him, but it's everything to me. And one day, when we're both playing pro, I'll pay him back.

Darius tries to offer me money any chance he gets, not wanting me to struggle. But I won't take another dime from him or Alicia. They have already done too much for me.

Besides, when it comes to family—which is what they have become—I don't have a great track record of family doing favors out of the kindness of their heart.

My uncle, who raised me, only ever did a favor so he could shove it back in my face later. When I couldn't repay it, he made me pay in other ways—being a punching and kicking bag for him to get his anger out.

That's all I knew for most of my childhood. I thought everyone's family was like mine. I didn't know any different. When I showed up at school one day with my arm in a cast and bruises on my neck, I learned just how wrong I was.

But the second anyone started questioning the

marks on my body, I was yanked from the school and plunged into another one. Eventually, my uncle got better at hiding his damage, ensuring the only marks he left were beneath my clothes.

I could've stopped it. Told the police. Told my teachers the truth. But that wasn't a part of the deal my uncle and I made. As long as I lay down and took the beatings, he wouldn't touch Micah.

I remember I tested that theory one time, and I'll always regret it. I was fourteen years old, and Micah was nine. I confided in our neighbor, a sweet couple. They were so concerned when I showed them the bruises on my ribs. They confronted my uncle, and to my absolute disbelief, they left us there with him and never stopped by again. I have no clue what he said to them and why on earth they believed him, but that's something I'll never get to learn.

That night was the worst it ever was. The pinnacle of all his rage. I seriously thought I was going to die. I met the devil that night in the basement, and he wore my uncle's face.

He punched me mercilessly, kicked me until I heard my ribs crack and break. I never knew how painful simply surviving could become. But my pain wasn't the most excruciating thing I felt that night. It was Micah's.

I tried to fight, to keep my uncle from him. But every time I gained enough strength to peel myself from the cold floor, he pushed me right back down to it, landing a few more blows as punishment for interfering.

Micah's screams and cries haunt my nightmares.

When my uncle started beating him like he did to me … that was the moment I wanted to die. Because it was my fault he was getting hit. It was my fault that he would never smile the same way again. It was my fault that my uncle fractured his jaw and killed his spirit.

But we survived that night together, and when we were finally left alone and locked downstairs, I dragged myself to him. He was conscious but in agonizing pain. I couldn't walk, let alone stand. I tried over and over, falling to my knees each time.

We slept curled up on a rug on the cold floor.

That was the last night I ever let Micah feel my uncle's wrath. After that, I obeyed whatever my uncle wanted.

I listened. I spoke when spoken to. I cleaned the house daily and learned to cook for all of us. I became his pet.

I learned to take beatings without making a sound or any expression.

My soul and heart caged themselves in with thorns and vines, protecting themselves from what I was going through and anything to come.

But the problem is, my heart and soul are still there, tucked away, and anytime I try to free them, everyone around me ends up getting hurt and I'm left bleeding out from the inside.

"Malik, you in there?" Griffin bumps my arm with

his fist, yanking me out of my thoughts and forcing me back to reality.

"Yeah. My bad. Did you say something?" I don't look his way, not wanting him to see anything in the depths of my gaze.

His voice is softer than usual, chock-full of concern. "What's going on?"

I sigh, dragging my hand down my face. "It's ... complicated."

He turns into his long driveway. "Trust me when I say that you can't keep everything buried deep inside. It will find its way out, even if it has to tear through you to do it. It's a hell of a lot easier if you free it on your own."

"When did you get so wise?" I chuckle, my throat burning and getting tighter.

"When Blair forced me out of my comfort zone and showed me a mirror of who I had become over the years." He rounds the oversize water fountain, parking near the grand staircase leading to the front door. "What's going on? I know something is wrong, so don't bother denying it. I was just trying to give you space, but clearly, it's not going away on its own."

My chest feels tight again, and I'm scared this conversation is going to send me spiraling. But I know what Griffin went through, growing up. He knows pain similar to my own.

At the same time, Griffin is one of the only people that I think would understand what's going on and not judge me. But deep down, I'm scared that my wounds will never heal, that I'm cursed to be raw forever.

"Mal," he hums, "come on, man. It's just me."

"I know." My voice breaks, and I wince at the crack showing in my foundation. "I just … I'm …"

A fucking pussy. A fucking coward. Worthless. Garbage. The thoughts, said in my uncle's voice, echo in my brain, vibrating against my skull.

A car comes into view behind us, pulling up behind Griffin's pickup. It's Mrs. Potts and Charlie, saving me from sharing anything I might regret, and I mentally thank them for their perfect timing.

"I'm good, Griff." I end the conversation, throwing my door open and rushing out, probably noticeably fast.

But I don't care. I need to be alone. This was too much. I can't handle it. I know that's pathetic, but vulnerability makes me want to peel my skin off.

After I take a quick shower, get ready, and eat, Blair, Griffin, Lumi, and I load up into Griffin's pickup to head to the Kensingtons'.

Griffin's wealthy because of the empire his parents built. But the Kensingtons are old-money rich, generational wealth on a whole other level. It's daunting, to say the least. But somehow, those cocky shits turned out to not be complete douchebags.

It's ironic that I grew up hating anyone and everyone who had this level of money, and now I'm surrounded by some of the most extravagant wealth I've ever seen or heard of.

But I think that has to do with the Kensington's parents. I've only met them once, but they seemed so down-to-earth and humble. It was shocking.

They even made the brothers move into the dorms for the first two years of college, just to be forced to be on their own and be self-sufficient. I respect the decision a lot.

Luckily for them, they only have this year left, and then they are free to get their own place or move back in with their parents.

As we pull into the Kensington estate, I can't imagine not choosing to stay here. It's ridiculous. I've only been here once or twice for team dinners, but I'm awestruck every time. I can't fathom being used to this.

A tall wrought iron gate seals the property off from the world. We stop at the gated entry and are greeted by the older man who works in the booth.

"Good evening." He smiles at Griffin.

"Hello, sir. Good to see you again." He shakes his hand.

"You as well." He presses a button, and the gate slowly opens, parting from the middle and revealing the breathtaking grounds inside.

It still blows my mind that people can live like this every single day and become accustomed to it. It's insane.

Griffin pulls through, and the gate swings close behind us. He takes a right at the first intersection, heading toward the main house.

Picture-perfect landscaping stretches across every inch of the property. Pristine flower beds, trimmed hedges, water fountains, and controlled vines that cover the old brick. Birds decorate the baths scattered about. Life blooms all around us, like the grass is greener in between the Kensington fences.

Shit, it just might be.

A motorcycle revs behind us, and I turn my head to see two bikes racing closer, weaving to our sides and passing us. They salute-wave as they zoom by, beating us to the front of the house … if you can call this place a house.

The brothers take their helmets off and rest them on their bikes, both smiling at their victory of beating us.

Griffin slams on the gas, gaining speed and heading straight for Asher and Dean, only stopping at the last minute. Their smiles falter as fear flashes in their eyes.

We burst out laughing as Griffin parks next to their bikes. When we exit the truck, Asher and Dean greet Griffin and me with our habitual handshake, and the other two with a quick hug.

People are setting up speakers and decorations as we start ascending the large staircase to the house. The Kensingtons usually only throw one or two parties a year, which are over the top and absolutely wild.

Everyone wants an invite. It always starts out pretty tight, with a list of attendees who are checked at the gate, but by the end of the night, the place is packed.

As we walk into the foyer, Asher grabs a bottle of whiskey from a worker strolling past with an arm full of bottles. "Anyone?"

My hand is outstretched before I realize it. "Fuck yes. Give me that."

Griffin's stare finds me instantly, and I don't miss the look of worry hidden in his gaze. But I need this, whether it's a good decision or not. Besides, I wouldn't be living up to my reputation if I went easy at a Kensington party.

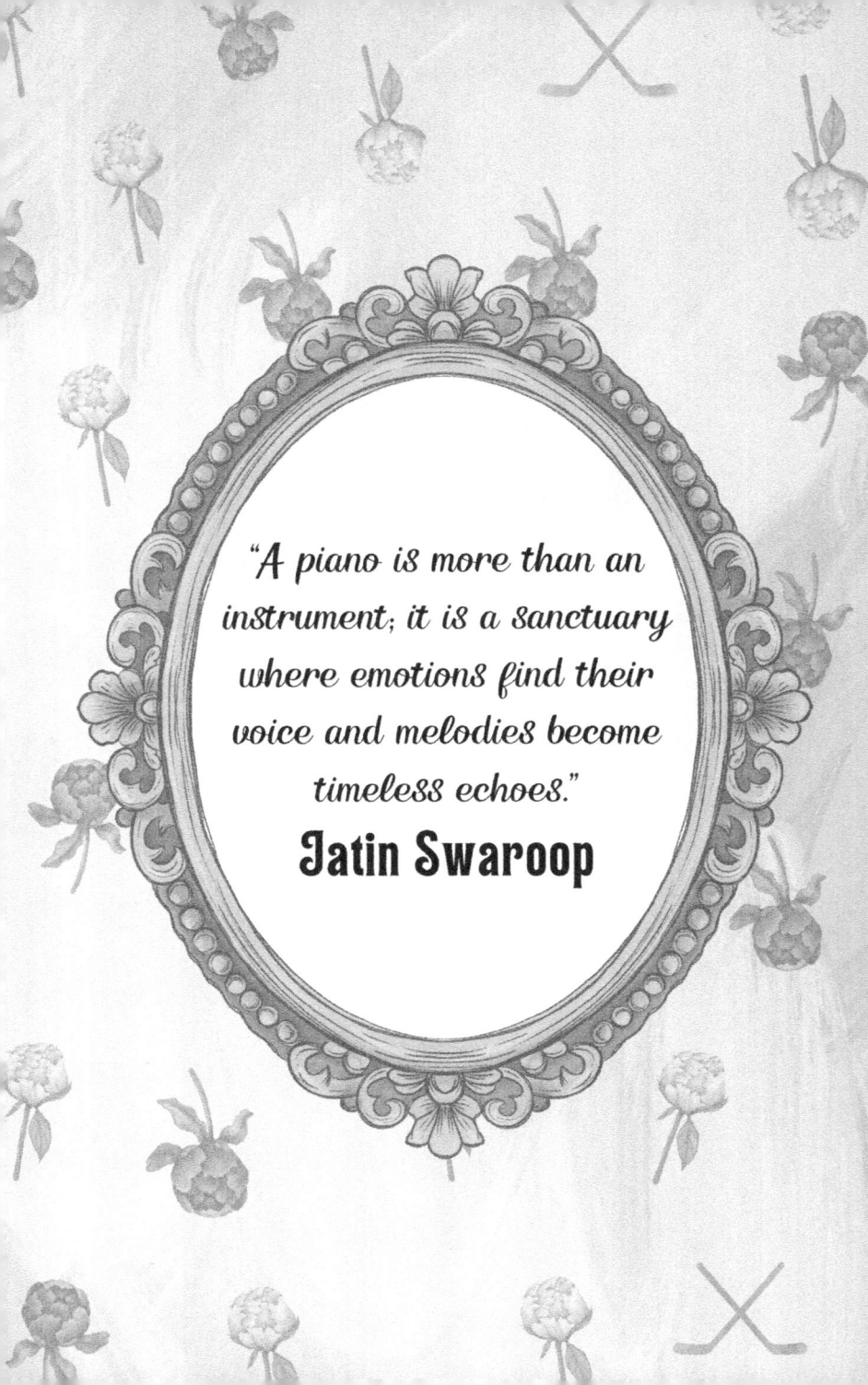

"A piano is more than an instrument; it is a sanctuary where emotions find their voice and melodies become timeless echoes."

Jatin Swaroop

chapter seven
alora

G oose bumps erupt along my skin as I step out of the Lyft and onto the paved entrance to the Kensington house. The air has a crispness to it, fluttering through my dress as the wind blows around me.

This estate's really nice. My eyes travel over the gated entrance. I've heard of the Kensingtons, even before coming to HEAU as a student. When my dad used to drag me to this school for donation ceremonies, I heard the Kensington name. The only higher contributors than us, which is saying something since I've seen the checks he cuts for HEAU.

There are already so many people inside the gate. I'm scared to see how crowded the house is. Sardines packed in a can?

I'm sure they have the space to manage it though. I

mean, for God's sake, there are multiple properties on the estate.

As I approach the booth at the gate, I wait in line as a few people list off their names. The man checks them on his computer and waves them ahead.

I will say that I'm impressed so far by the structure and staff for tonight. Security workers are everywhere, guarding who comes in and also strolling back and forth on the property. It's nice to know that they are taking precautions to keep people safe.

I'm up next, and as I step forward, my heart is in my throat.

This is a prank. I'm not really invited. I'm not on the list.

Malik is going to pop out at any second and laugh at me. Just like the old days.

"Hello. Your name?" the older man asks politely as I reach the open window.

I clear my throat softly. "Alora ... Alora Briarwood."

There is no gleam of recognition in his eyes, making me feel slightly better that this isn't all some elaborate scheme.

"Ahh, here you are." He types into his computer. "Welcome. Please grab a wristband and secure it around your wrist."

An assortment of colored bands decorates the table set against the booth. Which one should I choose? Do they have any meaning behind them, or are they just fun?

Oh God ... the choice begins to shut me down.

"Everything okay?" the polite man asks.

My gaze flicks to his, and I already feel way too overwhelmed by everything happening, and I haven't even stepped inside the actual party yet.

"Um … yeah. Thank you," I mumble, hesitantly reaching out and selecting a pink band.

It matches my dress at least. Glancing down at the ruched pink satin fabric, I slowly stride forward, fidgeting with the strap of my purse.

The sky is dark, the only light created from the lamp posts, and sconces on the building ahead. The gate is blocked open, and I follow the couple ahead of me inside, my short heels clicking on the pavement.

My gold bracelet reflects the light next to the party band. A gift from my dad. One of the many he threw my way in order to buy my love. Back when I was too naive to recognize it.

I might not be close with him anymore, but I'm not going to just throw away gold jewelry. I'm not an idiot. Besides, I also have a matching gold dangle choker that goes perfect with this ensemble.

But the luxury and pretty dress are doing little to settle the nerves and adrenaline coursing through my body.

Asher never sent me a text, and I wonder if that has anything to do with Malik. But Blair sent me the address and told me that I was more than welcome to hang out with her when I arrived.

I appreciate her warmth and welcoming spirit, but

part of me can't help but think she's playing along with some game Malik coordinated.

Which is why I got dressed up tonight. I'm not the same shy girl I was back then. Well, I mean, I am, but now I'm more confident in my skin and in doing things that scare me.

So, if Malik wants to pull a stunt tonight, I know that at least I feel good about myself—something he can't take from me.

Music begins pulsing from the house, thumping beneath my feet as I round the corner to the front entrance.

Squeezing between two big groups drinking on the twenty-foot-wide staircase, I use the railing to help me up the stairs to the first landing and then the second until I reach the front double doors, stopping every now and then to take a few deep breaths and breaks.

Blair wasn't kidding … the Kensingtons can throw one hell of a party.

My nerves overload me, and I stop myself, sinking to the side of the doors without going through.

Oh God. This was such a bad idea. What am I doing here?

This is so not my scene. Way too much alcohol. Way too many people. One too many Maliks.

What the hell am I getting myself into?

Closing my eyes and taking a deep breath, I contemplate if I've gone insane for doing this. For challenging Malik and showing up tonight. What if I just make everything worse?

"Alora?"

I recognize Blair's kind voice behind me instantly.

Shit.

Slowly spinning on my heel, I lift my head a little taller and relax my shoulders just enough to sell the part.

But my confidence fades when I see she's not alone. She has a wall of hockey players behind her, all staring right at me. Including Malik.

Stay calm.

Blair strides forward, pulling me into a light hug. "I'm so glad you came!"

Pulling away, I glance at the group, finding their eyes at different levels of my body, all but Malik's, whose gaze is locked so aggressively on mine that I'm scared I won't be able to move. He's pissed—royally so.

His nostrils flare, his jaw is clenched, and his fists are squeezed tightly against his sides. He crosses his arms, his sharp glare trying to gouge my eyes out.

All because I'm here. My chest flutters at the satisfaction of pissing him off. It's a nice change for once.

Asher whistles, walking toward me with a shiny white smile. "Alora, you look fucking hot."

Malik clears his throat, deep and rough, like a growl.

But Asher doesn't skip a beat. He hooks his arm over my shoulders and turns me toward the door, bringing me along with him without question.

I barely hear Malik say something behind me; the only words I catch are, "… fucking kidding me?"

Blair and a shorter guy with blond hair catch up to my other side.

Asher murmurs down into my ear, "How about a drink?"

"Oh, I'm okay. I don't drink." I refuse his offer as nicely as I can. "Thank you though."

He tilts his head back. "Come on, Aloraaaa. Live a little."

It's too much to explain that alcohol is hard on my body. As a diuretic, it can rapidly dehydrate me and exasperate my POTS symptoms. And if it's chock-full of sugar, it's even worse. But that answer feels drawn out, so I just say no.

"You can beg all you want, but my answer will still be no." I flirt with him playfully.

Asher clicks his tongue. "You like it when I beg, Alora? I can grovel as much as you want, babe. Even get on my knees for you."

The air on the back of my neck chills as someone steps behind me, so close that I can feel my dress shift from their nearness.

I can smell him—that cologne of his that is burned into my mind from the night he barged into my room.

Malik.

"*Asher.*" His voice is sharp, each letter a serrated notch on a blade.

Blair hooks her arm in mine, pulling me out of

Asher's grasp, who turns to face Malik. "Come on. I'll take you to get a nonalcoholic drink."

I let Blair pull me a step away from the boys, but I can't resist turning my head back just enough to see Malik staring at me with ferocity.

My lips part, and I suck in a sharp breath. There's not just hatred and anger in his gaze. His purple eyes are on fire, burning red hot as he stares at me with a hunger I've never seen before.

He looks back to Asher, his jaw locked tight. He hooks his arm over his shoulders in the same way Asher did to me before dragging him in the opposite direction.

Turning my attention back to Blair, I find her and the blond guy staring at me with anticipation.

But I stay quiet.

"I'm Lumi." The blond guy introduces himself as we walk into a huge white kitchen, the island transformed into a bar with a few bartenders mixing drinks. Who are most definitely not checking IDs.

But I'm not dumb. When you have wealth like this, rules and laws are guidelines, not requirements.

We stop in line behind a few girls swaying back and forth to the music.

"I'm Alora," I tell him, my gaze bouncing between Blair and him.

"Spill it—" Lumi chuckles, but Blair cuts him off with a light smack on the chest.

"You don't need to tell us anything," she assures me.

"About what?" I ask, half playing dumb, half wondering how much they already know.

"Next!" the bartender in front of us calls out, and we step forward to the roped-off divider. "What can I get you guys?"

"Just water for me, please," I order.

He quickly fills a cup with ice and water before handing it to me in mere seconds.

"Thank you," I respond, and he nods.

"I'll have a Sex on the Beach," Lumi orders, followed by Blair's, "Vodka cranberry, please."

"Of course." He steps away to get their drinks, grabbing bottles of liquor from the tiered tower behind him on the island.

Lifting my purse from where it dangles on my side, I dig a twenty-dollar bill from my wallet.

"You won't need that," Blair says, leaning toward me to talk over the music. "Drinks are free."

"That seems like a dangerous thing to do for a bunch of college kids," I retort, my mind running rampant with images of overly drunk guys and girls struggling to get home later tonight.

She shakes her head. "They have security, and the bartenders cut people off who get too intoxicated."

Wow, that's actually insanely ... nice. Asher and Dean don't have to go the extra miles that they have, but it speaks volumes for who they are as people. Protectors.

The bartender brings over their drinks and hands

them off. I still give the bartender my twenty, not taking no for an answer. I'm sure they still take tips.

Blair starts walking away slowly, and Lumi and I follow behind. She snakes through the crowds of people, leading us who knows where.

One glass of water, and then I'll go back home. I know Sunny is having a good time with her sitter, June, but I miss her and don't want to be out too late anyway.

Bringing her here would have been so chaotic, and I'll be just fine without her for a few hours, if I'm even here that long.

The crowds end, and a huge room opens before us. I spot Griffin as we pass through the arched walkway, sitting on a couch with two guys whose names I don't know. But I recognize them from being with Malik from when we had our stare-off.

A sofa sits across from the couch, and two oversize chairs close the square in with a coffee table in the center.

"There you are. I was about to come find you." Griffin beams, his entire face lighting up as he talks to Blair, lifting his arm for her to sit down and lean into.

"Oh, stop. It didn't even take that long." She giggles as Griffin leans down and peppers her with kisses on her cheek and hairline.

He whispers something to her, and her cheeks instantly redden. I feel myself staring, and I force myself to look away, feeling a twist in my chest.

I've always wanted something like that. A comfort

and warmth. Unconditional love from someone you choose and who chooses you. I want that, but I won't pressure someone into it. I'm patient and willing to wait for love to find me instead of trying to squeeze it into a mold that it's not meant for.

Lumi walks around me and sits down next to Blair, crossing his legs and whipping his phone out instantly.

The sudden urge to pee makes me remember that I definitely didn't do that before I left when I totally meant to. *Dammit.*

"Know where the restroom is?" I ask the group, setting my water down on the coffee table.

"I can show you. I'm going to head that way," says one of the guys that I don't recognize. "I'm Finn, by the way."

Noted.

He smiles at me, and I offer my name. "I'm Alora. Nice to meet you."

"I know who you are. But it's nice to *officially* meet you." He looks at me humorously.

My chest tightens. Oh God, why does he know me? Because of Blair? Or because of Malik? Because of my dad? All of the above?

"You know who I am?" I ask with a playful sass in my tone.

He nods and gestures with his hand to start walking. I join him, once again following someone through the intense crowds.

Finn leans down toward my ear to shout over the

music. "I know you are the only person I've ever seen get under Malik's skin. And that is something to be proud of." He chuckles. "You're my hero."

I chuckle. He's easy to talk with even though we just met.

"Be careful saying that too loud. Malik won't like it."

We turn down a hallway.

"What's up between you guys anyway? Did you used to date?" he asks, and I choke on my spit.

Coughing a few times, I swallow past the agitated pain. "God, no." I clear my throat. "We actually went to high school together."

He widens his eyes in shock, clearly hearing this information for the first time. "Oh shit. Really? He didn't mention that."

I huff, rolling my eyes. "I'm sure he didn't."

His questions continue. "So, what is it then? Out of curiosity, what happened in high school?"

I'm already pushing the envelope tonight, so maybe I should refrain from exposing all of the shit he did to me. Then again, he never stopped to question his actions back then.

"Finn!" Dean races over to us, his gaze falling to me and instantly widening. "What's, uh—" One side of his lips tips up, a gleam in his eyes. "What's going on here? Whatever. Doesn't matter. We need you."

"Umm—" Finn hesitates, but Dean's eyes widen, and stress tightens his features. "Yeah, uh, let's go."

Clearly some kind of silent conversation commenced. But I'm not privy to the details.

"Do you think you can find your way back?" Finn asks me, already stepping toward Dean.

"Yeah. Go. I'll be fine!" I assure him, mentally tracing my steps back to the group.

He flashes me a smile before taking off after Dean, who is nearly running between people down the hallway.

Weird.

Doing my best to divert my attention back to my overfilled bladder, I try the handle to the bathroom, happy to find it unlocked and empty. I quickly lock the door behind me before taking my seat on the porcelain throne.

Feeling immensely better after peeing, I wash my hands and take a look in the mirror.

God, it's eerie how similar I look to my mom when she was younger. The same eyes, nose, and lips. And the same long blonde hair.

My father used to tell me I was the spitting image of her. Which must be why he couldn't stand to be around me as I got older, looking more and more like the woman he had loved and lost. That's one of the excuses he gave me anyway.

Refreshing my lip gloss, I run my fingers through my loosely curled hair, detangling any errant strands. When I open the door to the bathroom, a girl rushes in past me, slamming the door behind her.

That would've been me had I waited any longer.

I giggle as I wander down the hall, taking a moment to appreciate the fine details in the design of the house. Crown molding; spotless, dark hardwood floor; intricately carved doorframes. Every room was custom built with character.

Turning the corner, I bump straight into someone. "Oh crap. I'm sorry!"

The tall guy with defined arms and shaggy brown hair smiles down at me. "Don't be. I'm happy you ran into me."

Something about him looks familiar, and a light bulb goes off in my head. It's the guy from my dorm that called me pretty in the hallway.

What are the odds of that?

"Let me get you a drink. Your hands are empty." His full lips outline his stark white smile, charisma oozing from him.

He's cute. But I also don't want to make Blair or anyone else wonder what happened or why I didn't come back.

"I have a drink. It's just back with my friends. I appreciate the offer though." I rock on the balls of my feet, nerves fluttering in my stomach.

"How about some fresh air?" he offers, and to be honest, it sounds amazing. "Come on. I'll behave, I promise. Although, *fuck*, you are the most stunning girl I've ever seen, and it's going to be hard not to touch you."

My cheeks warm from his compliment. There's no harm in just a moment. Right?

"For one minute, then I have to get back." I extend my hand, and his face lights up.

"I'll be happy for just a minute with you," he leans in and whispers in my ear as his fingers interlock with mine.

Is this stupid? Is it dumb to just go hang out with a guy I don't know? Probably. But I deserve a chance at meeting *someone*.

I can hear my father's tone in my ear, telling me this isn't responsible. But I push his irritating voice away.

Besides, this guy is sweet. I have no reason yet to question his intentions.

As we approach the front doors, a cool breeze skates across my shoulders, and I shudder.

"Are you cold? We don't have to go all the way out if you don't want to." His attentiveness doesn't go unnoticed.

He's in only a T-shirt and jeans, so I can't imagine he's much warmer than me. But my body temp is always fluctuating, so it's hard to tell if it's just me or the weather.

"Is here okay?" I ask, and he immediately nods.

"Yeah, of course." He steps in front of me and turns to face me.

His hands lift to brush up and down my arms. Which actually does wonders to warm me up.

"What's your name, beautiful?" he asks, inching

closer to me until my hands are together and my elbows are bent, resting against his chest.

I think I've introduced myself more tonight than I have in the last couple of years. Or at least it feels that way.

"My name is Alor—"

"Alora." Malik's deep and ragged voice slices through the air behind me, and I feel his breath flitter through my hair.

"Ravenwell?" The nice guy holding me looks up behind me with confusion. "What's up? You two know each othe—"

"Get your hands off of her." Malik lashes out, grabbing my shoulders and yanking me back.

I stumble into him, my back flattening against his chest. "Malik, what the hell?!"

Hints of bergamot, ocean waves, and spiced vanilla wrap around me and I try to remind myself that I hate him even if he smells so good.

His hands stay on my shoulders, his fingers firmly planted on my neck, so I have no room to wiggle away.

He ignores me, focusing solely on the cute guy whose name I still haven't even gotten.

"Is she with you?" He lifts his hands up in surrender. "My bad, bro. I didn't know."

Malik scoffs with disgust, and I can't ignore the sting that pinches my heart. "Fuck no. But you still can't touch her."

Cute Guy cocks his head to the side, clearly just as confused as I am. "Then what's the deal?"

I feel Malik stiffen behind me, and I notice how rigid his muscles are beneath his shirt and how seamlessly we line up together, even with our stark height difference.

"She's been with almost every guy on our team, so trust me when I say you should stay clear of her."

My ears begin to burn as my blood starts to boil.

"Excuse me?" I gasp, my head whipping around to glare at him, but he keeps me in place with his hands on my neck. "I have not!"

Lifting my arm up, I drop my elbow sharply into his ribs. He grunts, but doesn't move a muscle or loosen his grip.

Cute Guy steps forward, standing taller and puffing up his chest. "And if I keep talking to her … then what? Huh?"

Malik chuckles hauntingly, the sound sending shivers down my spine.

I don't have to see his face to know the daggers that are shooting the cute guy's way.

Malik steps forward, guiding me right along with him, and he closes the distance between them. "Well, you seem to know my name, yet I don't know yours. I imagine you've heard rumors about me too—violent ones. Want to find out if they're true?"

Cute Guy holds his stare, but remains silent. I wait

in nail-biting anticipation for him to say something snarky back to Malik.

But instead, he does the one thing I was hoping he wouldn't do—he lets Malik win.

His stare drops to me, softening instantly. "Alora, it was nice meeting you. Maybe I'll catch you around another time."

"You won't," Malik grunts like a warning.

I stare at the cute guy with my jaw on the floor, absolutely speechless. Because what the hell just happened?

Cute Guy turns and walks the other way, disappearing back into the crowd, leaving me alone with Malik.

Twirling in his grasp, I look up at him and shove his chest with both of my hands, putting some much-needed distance between us.

"Are you fucking kidding me?" I shove him again, and he backs up a step with my force. "Really, Malik? Grow the hell up!"

Something ignites behind his eyes, his lips tipping up into a smirk, and I don't know if I should keep fighting or turn and run.

He laughs, soullessly and cold. "Oh, I need to grow up? *Really*? Because it seems like you're the one imagining that you could ever be close with my friends. That you could have a place at our table. You're a *joke*."

My eyes burn, welling with tears, no matter how hard I try to fight them back.

A lump forms in the back of my throat, and everything inside of me wants to run and hide. But there's something else there—a rage that is desperate for release.

Malik continues to taunt me, leaning down so his face is mere inches from mine, his next words clear as day. "When are you going to learn, Alora? You're a *bug*, insignificant and weak. You will never be more than that—"

My hand lashes out, slapping his face with force I didn't know I was capable of.

His head whips to the side, as he was completely taken off guard.

My palm instantly stings, burning the same way as my eyes. Tears drop from my lashes, rolling down my cheeks and falling to the floor between us, slicing through the tension in the air.

He's frozen, leaning down and staring deep into my eyes with a rawness I wasn't ready to see. But he doesn't deserve my sympathy or mercy.

He deserves to feel the same pain I do.

I'm done playing it safe or calm and collected, as I was raised. I'm not a punching bag for anyone. Especially *him*.

This is what he's done—turned me into someone I don't even recognize.

"It's sad, Malik. Pathetic really. That you hate yourself so deeply that you have to take it out on everyone else around you just to cope with the world."

I stand up taller. My words leave my mouth, but they don't sound like my own—confident, cold, and calculated. "But what's even more disappointing is that you are a ball of wasted potential and effort. Your life has and always will amount to *nothing*. No matter how hard you try to prove to the world that you belong here, you don't. But *I do*, and you damn well know it."

His nostrils flare, and his mouth twists in disgust, but he says nothing in response, only stares at me with absolute rage.

Something clicks inside of me, something I'm not sure can ever be undone. But one thing's for sure: I won't fear Malik any longer. His power over me is gone for good. I'll stick to my side of the world as long as he does the same.

Turning around, I cut off his chance to say anything at all as I stride away with my head held high, walking out of the front doors of the Kensington mansion.

Sunny and I barely left the room after the party this weekend. The next morning, I felt hungover even though I hadn't had a single sip of alcohol. But I imagine it had more to do with the stress of dealing with Malik.

Stress can trigger my POTS symptoms occasionally, and it most definitely did on Friday night.

Saturday, when I woke up, I knew it was going to be a rough day. My head was already pounding, my feet and hands were cold, and I felt nauseous instantly. Sunny was extra attentive yesterday, not wandering more than a couple of feet from me the entire day. I was laid up in bed with my legs elevated, only getting up for bathroom breaks and to get food from the delivery drivers who brought me all of my meals.

One of the most annoying parts of an episode is the fact that I have to stay as hydrated as possible, but then I have to get up so much more than I want to because I have to pee constantly. Slowly sit up, ease into standing, and go slow, every time.

Thankfully, I felt a lot better yesterday and even more so this morning, so I can still attend my classes today. I wouldn't be as stressed to attend them, but it's the first day for my history one as it was scheduled to start a week late and I would hate to miss it.

My phone dings on my piano bench. I pick it up, finding a text from Blair.

Blair: Feeling better today?

When I left the party on Friday, I texted her as I got into a Lyft and let her know. I still felt horrible for just leaving. But I couldn't be there any longer. I wanted to be home and in bed. I told her I wasn't feeling well, which wasn't a complete lie, as my episode started shortly after I relieved Sunny's sitter.

> Much better. Thank you!

Blair: Grab lunch or coffee soon?

> I'd love to!

I know it's safer to avoid her if I don't want another Malik run-in. But she's my friend, the first one I've met here that I trust. I haven't known her long, but there's something really genuine about her.

Stowing my phone in my purse, I slip my backpack on and grab Sunny's leash, hooking it to her collar. Our first class of the day doesn't start for another hour. But it's a little bit of a walk, and I want to take it easy, especially since I felt so rough yesterday.

My phone chimes in my purse. I lead Sunny out of our room and hear it lock behind us before checking my phone, expecting a text from Blair.

But instead, it's from an old friend—one of my only friends.

Phillip: Hey, Alora. I'm transferring to HEAU. I'll be on campus tomorrow. Meet for coffee? I've missed you!

> Are you serious?!

Phillip: One hundred percent!

Excitement skyrockets in my body. I haven't seen him since I got back to the States. The year I took off after high school, I spent all of my time with him at his family's place in Italy.

I've known him since I was really young. His dad's also a politician, and our dads were good friends once, forcing us to spend a lot of time together as kids. But we were never in the same place at the same time. He was studying overseas, and I was shipped off to live with my aunts in Avandale.

I can't believe he's actually going to be here. I sigh, feeling a tiny bit of weight fall off of my shoulders. I didn't realize how lonely I had felt until now.

I like Blair a lot, and I think we'll be great friends, but she's in the same group as Malik. Being near her is being near him.

But Phillip is solely mine. He knows what Malik put me through and always threatened to beat his ass. Of course, I don't want any unnecessary drama. But it would be nice to have some support on my side and brute force if Malik needs a lesson.

My mind flashes to the party and the moment I slapped him. I still feel like I blacked out when I snapped. I had a moment of fearlessness, but the fear has indeed returned. At least a little bit.

To be honest, I just want to forget all about him and just focus on my music and classes. But now there's a new thing entirely I have to force from my mind—how good his hands felt on me, how his touch lit me on fire.

Whether it was anger or something else, he ignited me in a way I've never felt before.

I want to forget it all, pretend he doesn't even exist. Maybe Phillip can help me do just that.

screening

When a player on the opposing team attempts to block the goalie's view

chapter eight
malik

One day, I'm going to get out of this town. I'm going to take Micah with me, and we're never looking back. We're going to go far away from here and start anew together.

Opening the front door to the house, I enter first, keeping Micah positioned behind me in case my uncle swings the second we're inside.

"You're late," my uncle grunts, waiting for me the moment I walk in the house. Arms crossed and fuming.

I shoo Micah to the side, encouraging him to go up to his room. He doesn't need to see this. He sneaks away as I distract my uncle, stepping forward with my hands raised.

"I-I'm sorry. A road was closed, and we had to take a new path home."

"What do I say about excuses?" His nostrils flare.

"They're for weak people." I repeat his words back to him.

"And what are you? Are you weak?" His voice is cold and steady, the calm before the storm.

He walks toward me, and I brace for impact, but nothing comes. Striding past me, he pushes the door shut behind me, closing us off from any potential onlookers.

And then he makes his move.

Grabbing the back of my neck, he whips me around and pulls me down, bringing his knee up at the same time.

Oh fuck, I wasn't ready for head pain. He usually prefers my torso.

I take the blow, his kneecap colliding with my nose, hearing a crunch as excruciating pain erupts through my face.

Oh shit, I think he just broke my nose.

Blood gushes from my nostrils, spilling to the floor. I cup my nose with my hands as he shoves me down to the hardwood.

"Great. Look at the mess you made. Clean it up," he snaps, smacking me in the back of the head, making the pain throb even more. "And if anyone asks, you got hit during a game."

He walks around and crouches before me.

"And what should I tell my teammates?" I ask, immediately regretting opening my mouth. I know better. I've learned from previous mistakes.

He grabs my jaw, squeezing tightly. I struggle to keep my hands around my nose to contain the blood as he pulls my head forward.

His spit flies from his mouth with his next words. "Tell them whatever it takes to keep them from the truth. And if someone comes to me with concerns, then Micah will get a matching nose."

"No one will say anything." I avoid his gaze, looking anywhere but at him. *"I promise."*

He lightly slaps my cheek a few times. "Good."

He stands up and strolls off with ease, as if what just happened was absolutely normal. But I suppose when it comes to our house, it is.

When I turn eighteen, Micah and I are going to run far away from here. Only a few more years to go.

I fly up in bed, clutching my neck as ragged breaths tear through my throat, leaving it raw. "Fuck!"

These never get easier. The nightmares. I've had them for as long as I can remember, but they've been worse since Alora got here.

I thought I was doing better. I mean, I have been since last year, but I'm starting to think that I just got better at hiding my pain, even from myself.

Micah's face appears in my mind. I really thought we were going to get out of that house together and never imagined that I would be leaving alone.

A framed butterfly in the corner of my eye catches my attention, the sunshine reflecting off the glass from my open window.

One of the few things I kept from that house and one of the few things I have left of my brother.

Sitting up taller in bed, I grab the frame from my nightstand, gently cradling it in my hands as I bring it into my lap. The blue butterfly is so fragile and beautiful.

I can't help but feel immense guilt every time I look

at these, but they deserve to be seen—they were Micah's. His collection that he kept hidden from our uncle. The butterflies were his most prized possession, and I … I made fun of him for it.

Something I'll never forgive myself for.

I wish I could go back to that time and tell him how cool these were and how unique each one was, just like him.

I would give anything to change his frown to a smile.

My punishment for being cruel to Micah all those years ago is to be forced to live without him, knowing that I can never change the bad things I said to him.

My stomach turns at the thought of him. God, some days, I wish I could just forget this pain, live life with ease and without the weight of the world crushing down on my chest. Deep down, I think I deserve this agony.

Honestly, it's a miracle I've gotten this far without him. But I definitely couldn't have done it on my own. If it wasn't for Darius and Alicia taking me in, I would've joined him a long time ago.

But I won't let them down. For some godly reason, they believe in me more than anyone ever has. Selfishly proving that not everyone in the world has an agenda when it comes to love and trust.

So, as much as I don't want to get out of bed right now, as much as I want to stay here and get lost for hours, staring at the preserved butterflies, I throw the comforter off of my legs and set the butterfly back on my nightstand before heading to the bathroom to shower before practice.

We have a quick morning skate today in preparation for tonight's game against the Royals. My body is eager for the exertion.

It's always been my outlet, my one place to unleash the pit of anguish inside of me without catching a felony for beating someone to a pulp. When I do it on the ice, everyone cheers.

And I'm sure that someone tonight will be lucky enough to feel my wrath. We're playing against one of our rivals, and I know they'll be out for blood. We beat them our last five matchups, and they're desperate to break that streak.

I quickly shower, trying to scrub the memory of my nightmare from my mind and my uncle's touch from my skin.

But that bone-chilling fear that I once felt, staring into my uncle's eyes, still sits at the base of my spine. The feeling of fight or flight constantly courses through my veins.

After quickly changing into Legends sweats and a T-shirt, I grab my backpack and head upstairs.

The most delicious scent of chocolate chip muffins fills my nose, and my stomach grumbles in response.

I'm not typically a breakfast guy in the morning. If I do eat, it's usually a smoothie from the rink, but I'll be leaving the house this morning with one of those delicious muffins.

Turning the corner into the kitchen, I find Blair and Griffin sucking on each other's face.

I know this is more their place than mine. It is the Hawthorne Manor, but I can't resist making a scene.

"For God's sake, guys, you have a literal wing to yourself, and you can't resist making out in the kitchen?" I roll my eyes as I approach the cooling rack filled with chocolate chip muffins, grabbing one and wrapping it in a paper towel as they peel away from each other.

Griffin laughs—no shame in his actions. "Just because you're jealous that you don't have someone to make out with early in the morning, don't take it out on us."

"Oh, fuck off. You know damn well that if I wanted to, I could have a new girl in here every morning, but out of respect for you and Blair, I've never brought anyone into this house."

Griffin mockingly places a hand over his heart. "Oh, you're so kind, Malik. So thoughtful. Everyone should learn to be as selfless as you." He chuckles.

"God, you're such a dick." I laugh at his sarcasm. "I'm stealing one of these muffins, by the way."

I turn my back to them, heading out of the kitchen with my free hand lifted in the air, flashing Griffin the bird.

Walking out of the front door and down the ridiculous amount of stairs, I slip into the driver's seat of my Corvette, stowing the chocolate chip muffin in my cupholder as I rev the engine to life.

Rounding the fountain, I head down the driveway toward Grimm Street. The nice thing about living with Griffin is that he only lives about four minutes from campus.

My car purrs as I speed down the street, heading straight for the arena. This morning's skate will last about an hour, and then I have one class—a new one before I'm free for the rest of the afternoon leading up to tonight's game.

Pulling into the arena parking lot, I find a spot near the front and head inside.

I'm greeted by security, the staff kindly smiling, and I return the favor whether or not I feel that joy inside myself.

By muscle memory, I stroll to the locker room, my legs moving of their own accord, as they've done so many times before. But no matter how many times I've been in this building, every time, I'm struck by the facilities and money that went into this place.

State-of-the-art tech. The best of the best for the best of the best. And for some odd reason, I get to play here. I get to do the one thing I've always loved in a place I don't always feel I belong. But I try not to question it. I try to take it as a blessing from Micah and from Darius and Alicia. They are who I live for.

I can hear the other guys chattering as I enter the

locker room, immediately swatted in the back of the head from a towel.

Great. Everyone's on bullshit today.

"The next person who hits me with a towel isn't going to play in tonight's game," I threaten the room with a comical edge to my voice. But it's more of a taunt. I'm dead serious.

"Oh, yeah? Do you think you hold that power?" Asher teases.

Lightly patting his cheek, I chuckle. "I don't mean that I'll get the coach to keep you out. I mean that you physically won't be able to play."

Elias Lancaster, one of my best friends, a center and our captain for the Legends, giggles in the corner. "Careful, everyone. Malik's in a bad mood today."

These little shits. I swear they are professionals at getting under people's skin. Which is great when we're on the ice, playing another team. But it's awfully annoying when they're using those skills on me.

"I'm about to be in an even worse one if you keep that up." My stern facade breaks, my lips lifting into a slight smile as I start changing into my gear.

Griffin strolls into the room with a shit-eating grin on his face. It never ceases to amaze me how much of a difference Blair has made in Griffin's life. He's so much happier now. It's crazy that one person could come in and flip someone's life completely upside down for the better. It sounds like the fairy-tale bullshit that I've never believed in.

I'm happy for them—I am. But I'm also bitter. Although I think that's something that will always stay with me until I'm an old man.

"Let's go, boys. Big game tonight!" Griff hollers. "You guys done bickering?"

Laughter breaks out among us as I finish getting changed. "I suppose."

"Good. Because we have some ass to kick later. Not our own, preferably."

We finish getting ready and take the ice, preparing for the battle ahead of us tonight. No matter what small bickering moments happen between us, we're a team. A family. Tonight, we are going to destroy the Royals.

After running through a few different drills and lines, we're dismissed.

The chilly air feels nice when I walk out of the arena with the boys as we head to our classes. It seems to be colder earlier this year than normal. But I'm not mad at it. I've always preferred it over the heat.

Blair and Lumi seem to appear out of nowhere, joining our group.

I've been waiting for Blair to scold me for scaring Alora off the night of the Kensington party. But the more time that goes by, the more I think that she hasn't mentioned that incident to Blair. I don't know whether to be grateful to Alora or not.

The wave of rage and jealousy that came over me when I saw her with Garrett ... it surprised me, coming out of nowhere like a bolt of lightning to my body.

But what struck me even harder was how I felt when she was pressed up against me with her back to my chest. How *good* it felt. And how much I hated myself for feeling it.

But I'm a mess when it comes to her. Uncontrollable and raw. A tornado, wreaking havoc on everything around me. I don't know how to change it or fix it.

All I know is that every time I'm near her, I feel like I'm touching a live wire. But I don't know if it's because she makes me feel alive like no one has before or if it's because I feel like I'm being electrocuted to death.

Fuck, even thinking about her has my brain scrambled.

We head into Ivy Hall, Blair leading the way to the classroom—of course knowing the route by heart. It's nice that we all have this class together—Blair, Lumi, Griffin, Asher, Dean, Finn, and Elias. I might not have any interest in history but at least we can suffer together.

You've gotta be fucking kidding me.

I can't escape her if I try.

Sitting in the front row is none other than Alora with a golden retriever in the space next to her.

What's with her in this dog? If she wanted one to flaunt around like an accessory, she could've at least gotten something smaller to be respectful to the people around her.

But I'll save that taunt for another day.

Blair does the one thing that I was hoping she wouldn't—beelines it straight to the seat next to Alora. Lumi goes to her left.

Griffin walks to the second row, all of us guys following suit, sitting behind the girls. And of course, Alora's positioned directly in front of me.

If it wasn't for Blair, we wouldn't have been nearly as punctual, and maybe, if we had shown up later, these seats would have already been taken, and I wouldn't have been forced to be near her.

She doesn't acknowledge my presence or anyone else's, except for Blair and Lumi. But I should've known that wouldn't mean that the guys wouldn't acknowledge her.

Asher leans forward, resting on the pull-up half desk that he flipped up over his lap. "Alora, I didn't know we'd be blessed with your presence in this class." He doesn't skip a beat. "I'm sorry you weren't feeling well and had to leave the party early. I was hoping to see more of you."

"… *see more of you.*" I know exactly what parts he's hoping to see, and something about the thought of them together has me wanting to storm out of here.

Knowing that he's only doing this to push my buttons, I pinch the spot right above his knee and dig my fingers into his flesh. He sits back in his seat.

You know, I don't remember Asher being as much of a pain in the ass last year. I worry that maybe I rubbed off on him.

Alora turns to face us, her blonde hair cascading down her back in loose waves as she tilts her head back.

She flashes a big smile at Asher … actively not looking my way.

"It's okay. Malik was right about one thing: parties aren't really my thing."

I think those might be my favorite words I've ever heard her say. That I was right about something.

"Probably the only thing he's ever been right about."

The guys collectively gasp and burst out laughing at the second part of her comment. My jaw tics at her audacity.

What is she hoping to gain from this?

Is she just trying to provoke me?

Because it's working.

Leaning back in my chair, I lift my arm and rest it around Asher's seat as my stare drops down to her doe eyes—bright blue and wide with curiosity.

And absolutely stunning.

A flashback of them welling up with tears appears in my mind, and I can't help but think of how beautiful she looks when she cries.

She holds my stare without saying a word, and I feel everyone looking her way, waiting for one of us to make a move.

But I'm not ready to have this conversation with all my friends, so I avert my gaze, looking straight ahead to where the professor is unloading his bag.

Asher mumbles something inaudible, and I glare at him from the corner of my eye.

I can feel Alora's gaze still burning into me, but after another moment, she faces forward.

Griffin glances at me a few times, and I'm guessing he's wondering if I'll share any of this with him. But I remain silent, waiting for the class to begin.

And I remain silent for the next fifty minutes, until we're dismissed.

The moment our professor signals us, I grab my bag and book it out of the room, hopping over Asher's and Dean's outstretched legs.

My chest feels tight, and my lungs are struggling for air. Something I desperately don't need right before a game … another panic attack.

I need to get away from *her*.

A few of the guys call my name to get me to stop, but I ignore them and continue on until I'm out of the building and in the nice fresh air.

I stop only for a moment to catch my breath before I cross campus to my car and seal myself inside.

What is she doing to me?

She's ruining *everything*.

Eventually, my heart calms down, and I know I'm safe from spiraling.

I should probably go home and suit up for tonight's

game, but there are still a few hours before I need to change.

So, instead, I head in the opposite direction of Griffin's house, to a lookout with a walkway over the coast, where the waves lap against the rocks on the shore.

I haven't been there in a few months. I haven't really needed it. But I need it now more than ever because I feel like the seams that are holding me together are drastically deteriorating, and I'm scared what will happen when I fully fall apart.

My isolated safe space. The place where I go to clear my mind and think. Micah's always wanted to go to the ocean, so listening to the waves makes me feel closer to him. It makes me feel grounded.

Which is exactly what I need right now.

Walking into the arena in my suit and tie, I feel the shy and nervous pieces of myself shift into the background, the confident persona taking over. The broken version of myself doesn't win hockey games, so if only for tonight's game, I'll push everything back inside.

In the quiet moments when no one's watching, Malik, the boy—who was abandoned by his parents, then given to his ungrateful uncle, who saw him more as a punching bag than a loved one—gets easily overwhelmed and has panic attacks; it's a version of myself that no one will ever really know.

But here, at this arena, I am Malik Ravenwell, a legend. To any opponent who steps on the ice, I am the villain, their biggest threat.

I can't let my past get in the way of my future. I have to make it to the pro league. And if I have to pretend to be okay in order to get there, I will. Every step of the way.

But that doesn't mean that I won't exert some of that built-up anger. After all, it's expected of me. I'm a monster on the ice, doing anything and everything possible to win. Getting under other players' skin is my favorite pastime. To agitate them. Score. Dominate.

Standing up for my teammates when they're getting picked on is the easiest way to flip the switch inside of me. I become unglued, uncontrolled, and if anyone is going to bring that out of me, it's going to be our rivals.

The photographer takes photos of us players as we file into the building, one by one, all pretending the camera doesn't exist.

The second I breathe in the locker room air, my skin starts to tingle, excitement looming beneath the surface. The only time I truly feel comfortable in my own skin is on the ice, and I'm dying to get out there.

After gearing up, we head to the tunnel to hit the ice for warm-ups, and before we know it, the announcer is listing off the starters, and we're lining up on the blue line.

Our center, Elias Lancaster. Our forwards, me and Asher Kensington. Then we have our defensive pair, Dean and Griffin. Between the pipes is a legend of his own making, the best goalie in collegiate hockey, Finn Rutherford.

The air is electric as we set up for puck drop at center ice. Readying to face off against the Royals, I huff out a breath and lock eyes with number fourteen, my lips tipping into a cocky smirk.

A second later, the ref drops the puck, and the game's underway. Using my stick, I fling the puck back between my legs to Asher. Digging my skates in, I take off down the ice. Ash breaks into the zone, keeping the puck in front of him.

He dishes it over to Griffin and passes it back to me. Asher skates his way around the net, and I see the play in my mind before it even happens.

I pass the three defenders, and the puck finds Asher's stick in the blink of an eye. He wraps it around the goalpost and tucks it in the corner of the net, and the arena erupts. His arms and stick fly into the air as he cheers.

"Off the first face-off? Let's fucking go!" Griffin shouts as we race toward Ash, crowding around him in celebration.

The score may be one to zero, but we are just getting started. And if there's anything I know about the Royals, it's that they're going to give us one hell of a fight. We are nearly identical in terms of skill.

The first period continues to fly by, every shift on the ice more gruesome than the last. But so far, they have been playing clean, which is a nice surprise, as I haven't had to beat anyone's ass yet. But there's still time.

Adrenaline is flowing through my veins—my favorite feeling in the world.

When I glide over to the bench for the media time-out, long blonde hair catches my eye. My head whips that way, seemingly of its own accord, as if I'm desperate to see who it is.

Alora?

But it's not her, and I don't know why I expected it to be her. The last time she had come to one of my hockey games, I had her escorted out in front of the whole student body, claiming that she was stalking me, and the staff didn't bat an eye.

For a split second, my heart sinks, a sharp burn stinging deep in my chest.

Was I hoping it was her?

God, that thought is confusing as fucking hell. But I push it away. Now is not the time to start dissecting that reaction.

There's only a minute left in the first period, and the score hasn't changed since the first goal. We've gone back and forth this entire time, but both goalies are on fire, not letting anything by.

Since everyone's playing fair, there haven't been any penalties either. But this could change in the blink of an eye. It takes one turnover, one bad pass, one steal to completely change the course of the game.

Skating into our defensive zone, I use my stick to try to intercept a pass, but it manages to get through to the other teammates. Not a moment later, one of their players slap-shots the puck toward the net. Our goalie catches it in his glove.

We reset on a dot, and another face-off resumes. Asher wins it, and we take off down the ice. Asher to Griffin. Griffin to Elias. Elias back to Asher, who's flying through the slot. He catches the pass perfectly and cuts across the crease. With the flick of his wrist, the puck shoots over the goalie's shoulder, landing in the back of the net.

The arena explodes as he scores with three seconds left on the clock of the first period. He skates around the net, gaining speed before dropping to one knee and pulling an imaginary bow and arrow.

As the horn sounds around us, we pile on Asher, patting his head and shouting our praise over the blaring noise.

"Are you fucking kidding me, Ash? Another one! Hatty watch, baby!" I scream as I palm his helmet with my glove and shake him with glee.

We skate toward the bench, Asher leading, followed by Elias, who got the assist. We bump gloves with our teammates before setting back up for the last face-off of the first period. And three seconds after the puck is dropped, the horn sounds again, ending the first twenty minutes with the score two to zero.

The second period and the first half of the third seem to go by in a blink of an eye, the Royals managing to get one goal on the board during a power play.

With ten minutes left on the clock, all we have to do is keep them from scoring. But we'd be lying if we said we weren't trying to get Asher a hat trick tonight. Of course we are.

There's a high chance that in the final couple of minutes, which are starting to dwindle away, the other team will pull their goalie to gain an additional player on the ice, leaving their net wide open. Which would be an easy opportunity for Asher to complete the three goals for his hat trick. An empty netter isn't exactly the most exciting goal, but it's still points in the book.

We set back up in our offensive zone, Asher taking the face-off. He wins it, dishing it over to me.

I get shoved from behind, the stick digging into my neck and whipping my head forward. When I crash forward onto the ice, the refs' whistles go crazy as chaos ensues.

Bodies begin piling up above me, and fists are flying. Griffin begins to pummel the guy who checked me from behind. Getting to my feet, I decide to lend him a helping hand, but one of the other players steps in front of me first, clearly wanting to take the challenge for himself.

A gleam in his eyes answers the question in mine,

and in a matter of a second, we flick our gloves to the ice.

I sigh, knowing how good this is about to feel.

Maybe I shouldn't enjoy this part of hockey as much as I do. But I haven't questioned it my entire career, and I'm not about to start now.

We grab the collar of each other's jersey, our arms locked out between us. Cocking his arm back, he swings a right hook, but I dodge it, leaning my head out of the way.

I want to let him land a punch to trigger the ferocity inside of me. Which is the only reason his next hook lands.

Smiling through the pain in my jaw, I see the second absolute fear settles into his wide-set eyes. He knows I let him hit me, and this is the moment he realizes that he's going to lose this fight.

Taking control, I cock my arm back and crack him right in the side of the head. Again and again, alternating between uppercuts and hooks.

Blood flies from his nose, decorating my knuckles and staining the ice.

He crashes to the ice, and I land on top of him. I could stop here, and I should. But I give him one more for the hell of it.

It's kind of an unwritten rule to cease the fight when one of the fighters hits the ground. Well, if you want to avoid racking up extra penalties.

The refs pull me off of him, and I go willingly.

The crowd goes feral.

After the refs clean house, we're put in the penalty box—Griffin, me, and the two Royals players involved. Although a moment later, the one I was fighting skates to his team bench and disappears into the tunnel—probably to get some medical treatment.

We watch the teams reset for face-off. Griffin and I have a front-row view, sitting side by side in the sin bin.

We win the face-off and take off into our offensive zone, looking to widen the gap of our lead.

One of our freshman players—an absolute rock star —leads the puck into the zone with Asher and Elias hot on his tail. The freshman takes the puck deep into the zone behind the goalie's net. Elias dives through two defenders, catching the pass from the freshman, and dishes it to Asher.

He's got this. The slot is wide open, and the goalie is out of place, having expected Elias to shoot it.

Asher pulls back and fires, and the puck flies into the back of the net. The horn sounds, and the rink vibrates from the noise of our fans.

Hats begin to fly onto the ice, tossed from fans.

Griffin and I jump up, smacking the glass with our sticks, gloves, anything we can use in celebration.

It's Ashy baby's first hatty with the HEAU Legends. Something to commemorate and definitely something to remember.

Our guys skate along the bench, bumping gloves as the ice crew skates out and collects the hats into a big bin. The puck is tossed to one of our coaches, set aside for Asher to keep.

With Griffin and me receiving ten-minute misconducts, we won't see any more ice time this game.

But it doesn't matter. Because when the clock runs out, we'll have won three to one.

This is the high, the serotonin I'm always chasing that only this sport can give me.

"The piano keys are black and white but they sound like a million colors in your mind."

Maria Cristina Mena

chapter nine
alora

Rupert Von London, my idol and world-renowned pianist, is my new private lessons instructor. It still seems so surreal.

When I heard he was going to be doing lessons on campus this semester, I was the first to put my name on the list.

I still can't believe I get to work with him. It's a dream, and in the next five minutes, it will come true.

Early as usual, Sunny and I are waiting outside of the door to the reserved practice room.

But with no sign of him yet, my brain starts running rampant as we wait, muted sounds of instruments playing throughout the other rooms softly filling my ears.

At least I know that I won't be running into Malik in

any of my music classes. The one History class we have together is more than enough.

Although I'm beginning to wonder if I'm getting under his skin more than he is mine. But I know it's because he's letting me.

If he wanted, he could flip my world upside down, just like he did back then. But something's different now —our dynamic has shifted and changed into a new unknown.

That hatred and cruelty still stir in his gaze, but there's something else that I don't remember seeing before. I've been noticing it more and more lately—a gleam in his eyes that seems to shimmer only when he looks at me.

And I have absolutely no idea how to feel about it.

An older gentleman in a suit rounds the corner, and I recognize him instantly. Just the man I'm waiting for, the legend himself.

Professor Von London strides to me with confidence. His face lights up as I smile at him, lifting my hand up for him to shake.

"You must be Alora." His hands are full of books, but he shifts them in his arms to shake my hand.

"Yes, sir. It's an honor to meet you. I am such a fan of your music."

I open the door for him, and Sunny walks in before him and sits beside the bench—her usual place when I'm playing.

Professor Von London follows us inside, setting the

books down on the table. "We have an hour today, and for a good portion of that, I would like to just listen to you play. I want to see how you move with the music, feel the music, and bring it to life. There will be a structure moving forward, a plan and course of action after I get a good grasp on who you are as a pianist. How does that sound?"

My heart races with excitement as I take a seat on the bench and lift the lid of the piano. "That sounds— oh my God—incredible." I don't try to hide the absolute giddiness coursing through me. "Do you have a piece you would like me to start with?"

"Let's start with something moderate. Your choice."

I've never been more nervous to put my fingers on the keys in my life. But this feels like a *moment*. One of those moments that can change everything that happens after.

If he's impressed with me, he could alter my life. Whether it's with his connections, setting me up with a professional job, or helping me take my music to the next level.

My fingers brush against the keys, and adrenaline begins pumping through my system.

Something happens to me when I begin to play, taking over my body and soul as my being melts into the piano and music.

I become the chords I'm playing, whether by memory or by sheet music. I dance with the notes.

My old piano teacher used to hate that I swayed so

much when I played. But how can I not? The music demands to be felt.

I get lost in the upbeat tempo of the song, and before I know it, I'm striking the final note, listening to it pulse through the room as I'm left breathless.

With his pen and eyes still on his paper, he instructs me to play another, one with a much higher difficulty, one of his own songs, one I have memorized.

My fingers shake with nerves, and I set my hands free, executing his music with passion and precision. My hair swooshes back and forth over my shoulders as I play, only stopping when it finally comes to an end.

I turn on the bench and direct my attention toward Professor Von London, but I don't dare interrupt. I'll wait for him to speak first.

"You played that with ease, vigor, and tenacity." He pauses, studying me carefully. "I gave that to you as a challenge to see where your limit was, but you surpassed it …" He trails off, and my heart jumps into my throat. "Play another. Something to push you."

Forcing myself to take a breath, I set my iPad on the rest and debate between two pieces, both hard. One that I've recently played and perfected and one that I haven't played in a few years, but it's still considered one of the most challenging pieces.

Deciding on the latter, I click on Ravel's "Ondine," a haunting and dark composition, the first movement of *Gaspard de la Nuit*.

When I play just the first few notes, he huffs out a short breath, one that sounds happy … I hope.

I want to sit and question if I chose the right or wrong one to perform, but there's no time. I'm already too deep into the song to turn back, so I let myself once again get lost in the performance.

Six and a half minutes later, I remember exactly where I am and who is listening to me play. Pride bursts in my chest. That was the first time I'd played it in years, and it was nearly perfect.

Hesitantly, I turn to look at Professor Von London, finding him watching me in awe.

"That … was beautiful. I haven't heard it live in quite some time." He clicks his tongue. "You played a lot of that from memory. How long had you studied it?"

Shrugging, I tuck my hair behind my ear. "I hadn't played it in a couple of years. I think the first time I'd played it was when I was thirteen or fourteen."

His eyes widen, but he stays silent.

Thankfully, he doesn't make me wait too long. "You are a marvel, Miss Briarwood, unlike anything I've seen at this university in decades. Quite honestly, I haven't met many students your age at this level." He stares at me with a slight shake and tilt to his head. "Where have you been hiding?"

My cheeks warm at his incredible compliments. "I've always had a natural gift with music, but piano has always been my passion. I've been in lessons since I was four years old. There's nothing like it." My words only build the eagerness more.

"Have you performed anywhere?" He taps his fingers against his leg—fingers that have played at recitals I would've killed to attend.

I'm nervous to answer this question. I know how I must, but that doesn't mean I want to. I want to speak the truth. To tell him that my father always preferred that my gift be a secret. That it would only put me in more danger, more risk.

But I give the political answer, as I always have to anyone who overheard me play. "I've always been too shy to perform. But I think I'm getting over that. I want the chance."

"I think you're in the right place." His eyes twinkle with what almost looks like *pride*, but it's hard to believe that to be true, as I met him less than ten minutes ago.

I think perhaps I'll pretend just for a moment that maybe he is proud of me.

"How about we hear one more?" he asks with a glowing grin.

Maybe one day, I'd like to play some of my own music. Not to toot my own horn, but I know that my pieces are good.

For the remainder of the hour, I play pieces for him back to back. After each one, he asks for just one more song. Some fast, some slow, some upbeat, and some haunting. By the time I'm done, I feel a warmth in my chest, a satisfaction that I've never felt before.

After Professor Von London leaves when our session is over, I stay in the room, continuing to practice for about another hour before I realize that I'm going to be late.

Gathering my things and throwing them in my bag, I rush out of the room with Sunny. A cold shiver runs down my back, and I stop dead in my tracks in the empty hallway.

Hints of bergamot, ocean waves, and spiced vanilla invade my nose, as if he was standing in this very spot.

Malik.

Part of me wants to know if he was watching me play. But then again, would that be so he had something to use against me in the future? To twist the things I loved into weapons? I don't really want to find out.

Besides, I'm sure a lot of people on this campus wear that same cologne. I just can't help but associate it with him.

I get a text from Phillip, and I quickly check it as I walk out of the building.

Phillip: Can't wait to see you later!

He's finally in town, and I'm so excited to see him tonight after my study session with Blair.

Phillip and I are just gonna grab coffee or walk around somewhere and catch up. Nothing too formal.

I shoot him a quick text back.

So soon!

June meets me outside of the building to get Sunny from me, as she's going to watch her while I'm gone for the next couple of hours. I pass my baby girl off to her, knowing she's about to have the best night, going on a super-long walk that I can't really take her on without problems.

Blair wants to meet up to study for our Econ class. And to be honest, I could use a study buddy for it. Especially one as smart as her.

We're going to her house—or her and Griffin's house since they live together. Honestly, after seeing the Kensingtons' place, I'm excited to see theirs.

This town is known for its unique architecture. I mean, this town is known for a lot of things. Opulence. Wealth. Being one of the most expensive places to live and hardest to move into because no one ever wants to leave.

But there is something magical about it. It's unique, unlike anything I've seen from the traveling I've done. The air seems cleaner, the wildlife happier. It's … special.

I text Blair quickly to let her know that I'm on my way to Hubert Hall, where we agreed to meet up.

On my way. Should be there in just a few. Thank you so much again!

I know that it's just my anxiety talking, but there's

still a part of me that thinks this is just some elaborate plan of Malik's. But to be fair, he would do something like this. There's no length he won't go to win.

I wonder why he hates me. I've asked myself that for a long time. Was I just in the right place at the right time? Do I remind him of someone? Did I do something to him?

But I never seem to find an answer, and I certainly don't get any from him.

Was there something I could've changed? Apologized for? Something about me that I could've altered to save myself from the torment he put me through? Unfortunately, no matter how many times I go down this rabbit hole, it always ends the same...in disappointment.

I wanted to ask him so many times. The words have formed on my lips, but never come out. It's not like he and I have a lot of conversations to begin with. There's never really been a chance for an opening.

As I reach Hubert Hall, I find Blair waiting next to the steps outside. She hasn't looked up yet. She's typing into her phone. But as I approach her, she jams it into her pocket and greets me with a smile on her face.

"Are you ready?" She brushes her hands down her plaid skirt.

"Yes. Very. Unless, for some reason, I should be worried that you're a psychopath who is bringing me back to your house to murder me. Then, in that case, I think I'll change my mind."

I chuckle, and she laughs along with me.

"It's funny you used that line. Because the first time I ever went over to Griffin's house, I made the same joke to him." She smiles, her eyes seeming to drift as she reminisces.

"That makes me feel better—I think."

We head toward a parking lot that I'm sure her car is in.

"How did you and Griffin meet?"

"Well, it's kind of … funny and embarrassing." She giggles.

"I have to know now." I encourage her to continue.

"Well, we were both taking English. He was horrible at it. I had a perfect score, of course. His coach threatened to kick him off the team if his grades didn't go up. While I had no desire to help him at first, I needed money for my dad for his treatment, and Griffin had plenty of money to spare. We were a match made in heaven."

"So, sunshine and rainbows then?" I ask, genuinely curious about what her journey with love has been.

Having no experience myself, I can't resist being wrapped up in their love story, wondering what it would be like to have one of my own. It's not like there hasn't been opportunity. There's been plenty. Something just always went wrong.

In high school, I would go on first dates, but they never wanted a second. I used to think something was wrong with me until I got out of that town.

When I spent time with Phillip overseas, there were plenty of chances for me to have second and third dates.

I think my time at Avandale High was just cursed. And if I had to guess who put it there, it would be Malik.

But I've dreamed for years of having one person who's meant for me. A true love. I just haven't found it yet.

"Oh God, no. It was not sunshine and rainbows. It was snarkiness, treacherous, and one of the hardest paths I've ever walked. But I wouldn't trade it for a single thing."

"Is it bad if I say that makes me feel better about my own love life?"

She slides into the driver's seat of her car, and I get into the passenger seat.

She waits until the doors are closed before asking, "Is there someone in the picture?"

"No. Not in the slightest. But I always used to think that when it came to love, it should be easy."

"If it were easy, everyone would have it. Love can be messy, especially when it's with someone you care deeply about. Sometimes, the pieces don't fit perfectly right away; they need some shaping. But if you're willing to try, it's always worth it, if it's meant to be." She starts the car and lightly laughs off how deep our conversation has become in such a short amount of time. "Sorry, I feel like I overshared."

"Honestly, it's been incredible just to have someone to talk to from time to time. Usually, I'm a lot more isolated than this, sticking to the four walls of my bedroom. It's been really nice, talking with you, Blair." I suddenly feel very vulnerable. Like I'm setting myself up to be the butt of a joke.

But the only way I'm going to know if this is real or not is to follow the course and hope for the best.

"I have Lumi. And I love him to pieces. But I'm happy to be that person for you. Everybody needs somebody." She smiles softly at me and then pulls onto the street.

It takes us only a couple of minutes to get to her house, and once again, we're pulling into a gated entrance, but unlike the Kensingtons', the Hawthornes' doesn't have a booth with security.

But the wealth is on full display nonetheless.

In the driveway, there's a pickup and a minivan, which is surprising. Who else lives here? Does Griffin have siblings? A big family?

I keep my questions internal as we quickly go inside and set up at their giant dining room table.

The topic of love falls to the wayside as we dive deep into Economics. We go back and forth with questions to quiz each other until an hour and a half has passed by.

Phillip will be here soon to pick me up to get coffee.

"Can I ask you something?" she asks hesitantly.

A lump is already in my throat before I agree, nodding my head.

Her voice is low and soft, as if what she's about to ask is meant to stay between us. "I haven't known Malik for a very long time. But I know him enough to know that he feels a certain way about you." She glances away and purses her lips before continuing, "He may be an absolute fucking idiot—I'm not saying he's not. But I'm saying that I've caught him looking at you when you didn't notice. And I've never seen that look in his eyes before." She takes a breath. "Have you guys ever …"

My head is shaking before I can manage to get the words out. "No. God, no."

"Are you not interested?" she quickly asks, catching me off guard.

"He really hasn't told you guys how we know each other?" I don't know why it hurts me that he's kept our past hidden from his friends. But it does nonetheless.

"What do you mean?" she murmurs.

But before I can answer, I'm cut off as Malik, of all people, strolls into the room with arrogant confidence, as if this is *his* house. And from the lack of a shirt, I'm starting to wonder if it is.

I'm starting to wonder about a lot of other things that I should most definitely *not* be thinking about when it comes to my bully.

I'm not blind. I can see how attractive he is. How toned his body is. How the ink wraps around his skin, decorating his arms, chest, torso, v-line, abs, and thighs.

I want to know what they mean. I want to know what each one represents.

I hate that I want to know any of that at all. But I want even more. I want to know how the tattoos shudder when he's touched. I also wanna scrub my brain out of my skull for thinking that.

"Blair, you've got to be fucking kidding me," he snaps when he locks eyes with Blair.

Griffin slaps his back as he walks past him into the room, the skin-on-skin contact sounding like lightning striking. "Watch your tone when you're talking to her, Malik."

"You're right; I'm sorry. Let me direct that attitude where I mean it." His gaze shifts. "To *you*." He steps forward, leaning down and resting his hands against the back of a chair across the table from us. "What the hell are you doing here?"

"Isn't it obvious?" I snap, my tone sharper than expected.

Blair's head whips my way in shock.

Malik cocks his head to the side, his eyes running up and down my body.

"Blair invited me over to study. But don't worry; I'm leaving now." I hook my backpack over my shoulder.

Malik pushes away from the chair, rounding the table toward me and getting in my face. "I don't want you to come back to my house."

I cross my arms as my face twists into a scowl. "In my defense, I wouldn't have come if I had known you lived here. The last thing I want to do is be in the same house as you."

His head whips over to Blair, who is avoiding looking at us, Griffin's arm wrapped around her. He snarls, "Blair, seriously? Did you do this on purpose? Stay out of my damn business."

Griffin's voice is cold yet hesitant as he warns Malik, "Careful, buddy. You need to chill out before you take it too far, especially with my girl."

Malik chuckles manically, reminding me of the Malik that I know well. "Or what?"

"*Malik.*" Blair exhales his name in disappointment.

Griffin strides around the table toward him, shoving his shoulders. "Go for a walk, dude. You need to calm down. Love you, man, but you're being a fucking prick."

"Well, I'll see you guys later. Or hopefully, *not* all of you. Thanks for having me over, Blair." I wave kindly to her before turning back toward the exit of the dining room, which, of course, is behind the now-dueling boys.

Malik tears his angry stare from Griffin, aiming it straight down at me. "Where do you think you're going?"

I throw my hands up in the air as frustration weighs me down. "What?"

His eyebrows pinch together, and he steps toward me. "Where are you going? I didn't see a car out front when I got back from my run."

I run my hand down my face. "So, you don't want

me here? But you also don't want me to leave? And you want to know how I'm leaving? As if you deserve any of that."

When I stride past him, he catches my forearm in his grasp, surprisingly gentle but firm enough that I can't budge. "Answer me."

I roll my eyes at him and then look up into his darkened eyes. "Let me make sure you hear this plain as day." I clear my throat. "Fuck. You. Malik."

His eyes brighten, and ever so slightly, a smirk tips up the corner of his lips. Of course, he finds this amusing. "You wish."

"Believe me"—I stand up on my toes, closing the gap between our faces by a couple of inches—"I would rather cut my hands off and never play piano again than sleep with you."

His tongue flicks against his bottom lip before he bites down on it, his eyes falling to my lips.

And *there* it is.

That spark in his eyes that I'm getting weirdly accustomed to seeing when he looks at me. Burning bright and uncontrolled.

Maybe I could taunt him with the answer to his question, even if it's not true. "I have to go. I have a date."

Spinning on my heel, I stride through the arched entryway of the dining room and cross the grand foyer to the front door, quickly slipping on my shoes.

"Oh, yeah? With who?" he demands, charging after

me, his feet stomping on the marble before coming to a stop two feet behind me.

"Jesus!" I jump, not realizing how close he is.

"Who is it?" he asks again, his eyes boring deep into me.

My phone dings, and I'm sure it's Phillip, letting me know that he's here. "You don't know him. He just transferred in."

I walk toward the door and pull it open, but Malik stops it, slamming it closed.

Spinning around, I realize he's still touching the door, and I'm caged in beneath his arm. His body's close enough that I feel the heat coming off of him in pulsing waves.

"What's his name?" He leans down further, crouching low enough to meet my eyes, pinning his other hand against the door near my waist.

There's no way … right?

He's not … jealous?

Is he?

Oh, I *so* do not have time for this.

"I'm not telling you. Now get out of my way before my knee finds a new home in your balls." I smile up at him, knowing it doesn't reach anywhere near my eyes.

His eyelids twitch, probably out of annoyance. "Who's watching your dog?"

I scoff, crossing my arms. "That's none of your concern."

"Oh, so you're being a bad dog mom, hoping to get

laid?" he challenges me, making me feel like I'm going to explode from frustration.

He knows how to wind me up—it's a skill he's perfected over the years.

"Of course not. I have a sitter, you imbecile." I roll my eyes. "Now get out of my way."

He stays where he is, stubborn as always.

Pressing my hands against his bare, tattooed chest, I ignore how warm he is and shove him hard, but he doesn't falter a single step.

My heart rate is picking up, racing faster because of his nearness. It's putting me on edge in all of the good and bad ways.

I can smell his cologne, even now, without a shirt, like it's his natural scent. And it's delicious.

It also happens to be exactly what I smelled outside of my practice room earlier.

"Were you in the music hall today?" I ask him, changing the subject and gaining an odd boost of confidence.

His face hardens, his sharp features shifting back into stone. I didn't even notice the softness and the warmth in his face until now, when it's gone.

Leaning down, he hovers his mouth over my ear, and my heart starts to thump louder in my chest for his answer.

Was he watching me? Why the hell does that excite me as much as it does?

Anticipation rattles my bones, and a shiver runs down my back.

Then he opens his mouth and ruins any hope of a new version of him in my mind. "Get the *fuck* out of my house."

Flattening my hands on his chest—on the large letters of the word *villain*—I push him off of me, flipping him off. "With pleasure."

Throwing the front door open, I walk out into the chilly air—a stark difference from the heat burning in my cheeks. The door shuts behind me almost immediately, slamming closed with force.

Slowly walking down the stairs, I see Phillip's car. Of course he had it flown in—his precious Rolls-Royce.

The driver's door flings open, and he rushes out of his seat, looking up at me coming down the stairs with his arms held out.

"Alora!" he calls out happily.

He knows I have POTS and can't run down the stairs toward him, no matter how excited I am.

"Hi!" I call out, my voice giddy.

He starts climbing the steps, two at a time, and he meets me halfway on the first landing, wrapping his arms around me and gently picking me up.

The aroma of citrus and burning wood—nostalgic and familiar—floods my nose, replacing Malik's overbearing scent. I breathe him in as he slowly lowers me back to the ground.

"How are you feeling? Still up for a quick bite or coffee or something? I'm totally down for cruising a bit, too, like old times." He smiles, his blue eyes bright with joy.

After Malik's heated confrontation, I'm suddenly feeling a lot more tired than I was beforehand. "Honestly, cruising sounds great. But nothing too crazy. Straighter roads, please," I request with a shy grin.

Guilt at requesting anything because of my illness seeps into my chest, as it always has. I hate feeling like a burden, like I'm hindering someone else's day.

"Sounds great to me." He winks and offers me his arm to help me down the rest of the stairs.

"How were your flights? Good?" I grab my water bottle from my purse and take a sip through the spill-proof straw.

He nods, stepping ahead of me and getting the car door. "They were actually. But I slept during most of them."

"I would too." I chuckle, knowing all too well how I handle flights. With a sleepy drug and a fat nap.

"After you."

He holds the door open for me, and I slide inside, the custom starry roof glittering above me.

Politely shutting the door behind me, he walks around to his side of the car and gets in the driver's seat. "Away we go."

He pulls around the fountain and out of the drive-way, and we fall into conversation as if we saw each other yesterday.

Tate McRae plays through the speakers as he tells me how the last couple of months have been for him since I left.

He fills me in on his ex, who he recently broke up with. How transferring to HEAU was a business decision and not because he wanted to flee to the other side of the world to get away from her.

Apparently, his dad wants him to take on more responsibilities with his family—the opposite thing he wants. Which is why he's here. His father supported this, as any parent would—but especially those who care more about public opinion and image than they do their own children's happiness.

Our fathers are the reason we bonded right away, getting along on the disdain for them. But we stayed friends because we liked spending time together.

I remember the first time we went out in public together in Italy. Our photo at lunch ended up in the news. Headlines were everywhere, like *Political Alliance Forming? Daughter of Congressman Briarwood and Son of Senator Stephens—a Match Made in Heaven.*

But I've never thought of Phillip that way. He's my friend, and that's all I want him to be. Is he cute? Sure, yeah. He's hot. But there's no spark, no jolt when we touch. It's platonic.

I also fill him in on the last few months of chaos. Specifically going into detail on the last two weeks after running into Malik.

Phillip, of course, has his own opinion of him, and I know he's not wrong.

But there was a moment today, a brief second, when it was like I saw a glimpse behind the fortress. But as fast as it appeared, it was gone.

I keep today's outburst to myself, unsure if I want him to know where Malik lives in case he decides to try to play hero.

He may be my closest friend, but I worry that he might try to confront Malik about everything, which is the last thing I want.

Unfortunately, he'll only be here for a day or so before traveling to the Bahamas for a family vacation, but he'll be back soon.

We spend the next hour or so just driving around and chatting about anything and everything, and by the time we head back to my dorm, I'm exhausted.

He pulls up in front of the building, putting the car in park and turning my way. "I missed you, Lore."

"I missed you too." Pulling him into a hug over the middle console, I squeeze him tight.

My eyes burn slightly, and my body settles against his. It's been a while since someone other than my aunts hugged me so tightly. Sometimes, I forget how starved I am for physical touch.

"Call you tomorrow? Send me your classes." He unlocks the doors, and I push mine open.

"Yeah. I'll send you my schedule," I tell him, sliding

off the front seat and dropping a couple of inches to the ground.

He smiles at me and offers a wave as I close the door and head inside.

When I cross the sidewalk and approach the dorm building, I can't shake the feeling that I'm being watched. It's that sixth sense that makes the hairs on the back of my neck rise.

Nonchalantly scanning my surroundings, I don't notice anyone, and I quickly make my way inside of the secure building, using my key fob to unlock the door.

That feeling begins to disappear as I slip inside one of the elevators.

I'm still uneasy, but as I reach my room and relieve June from watching Sunny, I feel much better.

Changing into PJs, I take my evening medicine before curling up with Sunny in bed to watch *Legally Blonde*, one of my favorite comfort movies. But I barely make it to the scene at the dress shop before my eyelids drift shut.

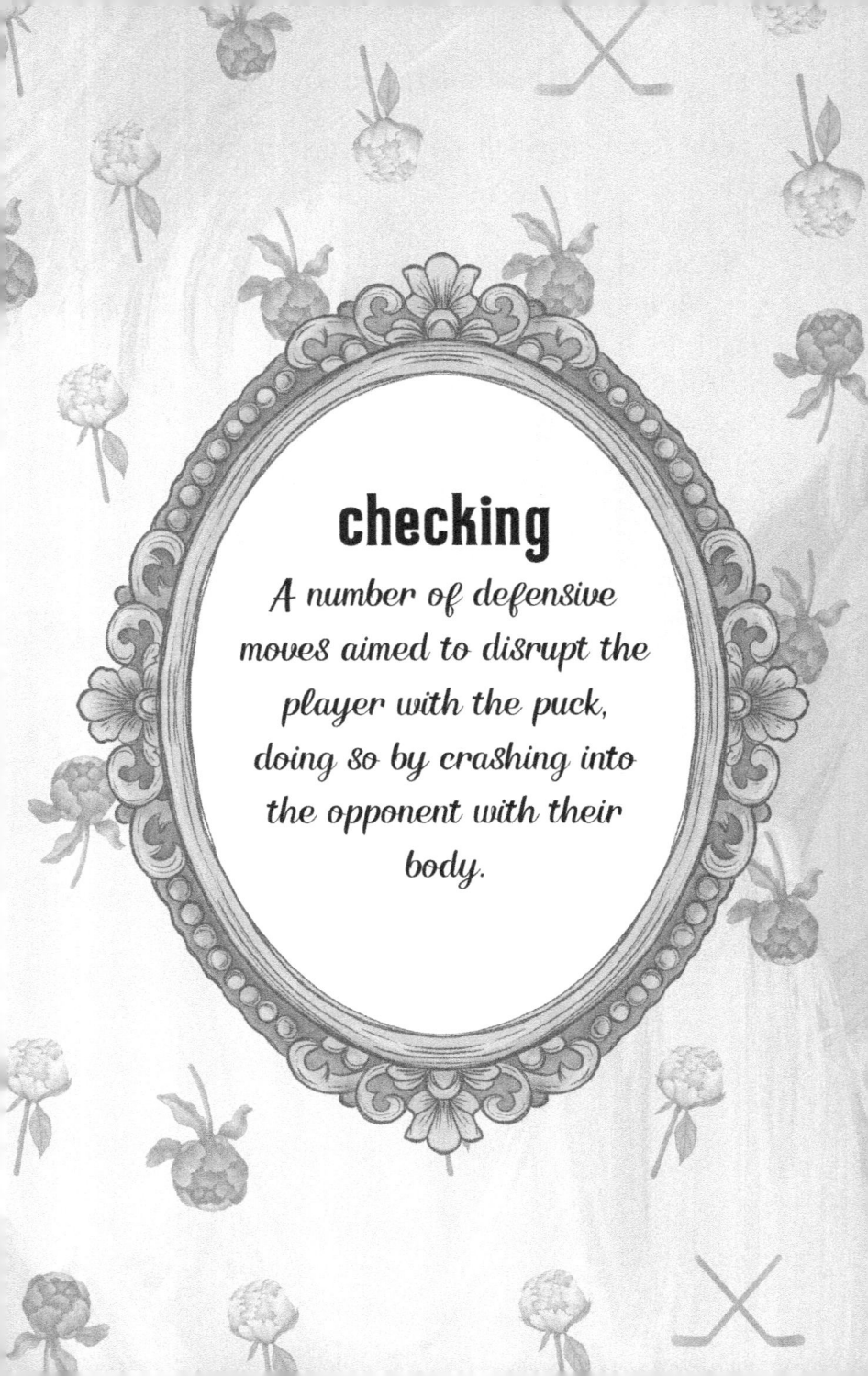

checking

A number of defensive moves aimed to disrupt the player with the puck, doing so by crashing into the opponent with their body.

chapter ten
malik

L ifting the red cup to my lips, I tip it up, but nothing pours into my mouth.

Shit.

It's already empty. I sigh.

"Already what?" Dean asks, and I realize that the thought wasn't just in my head. Either that or Dean can now read minds. Which would be pretty fucking cool.

"I'm out." I set the empty cup down on the desk and lean back in the gaming chair, closing my eyes as my body feels like it's spinning and floating in place while a comforting warmth spreads throughout my veins.

God, I had way too much to drink.

I should have stopped hours ago. But the more I drank, the more my brain went quiet. I'm just here, existing, thoughtless and numb.

My eyes flutter open, and when I sit up, Dean has magically disappeared. "What the fuck?"

The dorm room door swings open, and he walks in as if he didn't just teleport into the hallway.

"Why does your face look like that?" Dean looks up from the pile of clothes in his hand, his wet hair falling across his forehead as his brows furrow.

"Forget about me. How the fuck did you get on the other side of the door?" I ask the important question, ignoring his.

He bursts out laughing, Asher joining in, and he plops down on his own bed. "You're fucking wasted, Malik. *Jesus*. I left and took a shower. I've been gone for, like, fifteen minutes. You need to sober up, buddy."

That makes a lot more sense ...

"Yeah ..." I trail off in agreement.

My bladder feels like it's going to fucking explode soon if I don't piss.

Rising to my feet, I sway back and forth as I step toward the door to the hallway. "I need to piss."

"Thanks for letting me know." Asher laughs as I fumble for the doorknob, twisting it open. "Come straight back though. I already took your keys so your drunk ass can't even think about driving."

Annoying but thoughtful. "Thanks, man. I'll be right back."

Pulling his door open, I walk through the doorframe and take a right.

Ping-ponging against the walls, I make my way

down to the end of the hallway, stopping in front of a door that most definitely doesn't say *bathroom*.

I know whose room this is. That damn infuriating and intoxicating creature.

The one who's been wrapping herself around my brain, consuming all my thoughts. She's a virus, and I'm completely infected.

Fuck, I shouldn't be standing outside of her door right now. I need to actually find the bathroom and then pass the hell out in the Kensingtons' room.

I don't even know how I ended up here. One moment, I was taking shots with Asher and Dean in their room, and the next, I'm standing in front of Alora's room, questioning whether or not I should knock.

Is she sleeping?

Does she sleep naked, like me?

I can't imagine how perfect her bare body is. Those luscious curves. Fuck, I want to taste them, devour them. I want to know exactly what it's like to feel her thighs wrap around my neck. To hear what she sounds like, coming apart by my touch. I need it. I need her.

What the fuck is wrong with me right now?

I smack my forehead, hoping to hit the dirty images of her out of my head. But it doesn't work.

I need to go back to the room and lock myself inside because the thoughts running through my mind are going to get me in trouble. Like thoughts of how red her cheeks were earlier when I had her caged against the door. I wonder how red she'd get if I slid my hand around her throat and claimed her lips with mine.

Or how flushed she'd become if I tasted every inch of her soft skin until she melted into my grasp, writhing with pleasure.

My cock twitches in my joggers, making my boxers uncomfortably snug.

Fuck.

My body is floating in midair, every cell tingling as I stand on the precipice of crossing a line or not.

I drank too much. Way too much to be trying to make a decision like this.

Hearing the sound before I look up, I find my fist against her door.

Oh shit, I just knocked.

Malik, I'm going to need you to get it together right now, okay?

Pressing my ear against the door, I don't hear anything. It's quiet. She's probably sleeping. Which is a good thing. She shouldn't open this door. I'm way too out of control.

My hand knocks again with a mind of its own, and I start to wonder if this is all a dream because there's no way I would do this in real life.

"I-hear-something," I mumble, my words one continuous slur.

The lock clicks on the door, and it gently gives way, as does my weight.

I fall forward as the door swings inward.

"Ahh!" Alora shrieks as I crash into her. But I catch her, stabilizing her against the wall before I drop to the floor. "Malik? What the hell are you doing here?"

My eyes drift shut, only for a moment before I sit up and struggle to my feet. "What are *you* doing here?"

I chuckle to myself.

"You're *so* drunk," she sighs. "And I have no idea what you're doing here, but you need to get the hell out of my room."

She crosses her arms, and my vision finally clears enough to notice her fully.

My mouth waters at the sight of her before me. Her cami red silk top does little to contain the full, round weight of her tits, her nipples poking through the thin fabric, begging to be brushed by my thumbs.

The bottom of her top is bunched together, just above the waistband of her matching shorts, leaving a gap that exposes her bare skin. My eyes travel lower, down over the red silk to those plump, full thighs that I want to dive between.

My God, she's perfect. Every single inch of her.

My fingers twitch, desperate to reach out and stroke her smooth skin.

The words fall from my lips without my consent. "Fucking hell."

My gaze flicks back up to her face. Her lips are parted, and her cheeks flush a deep pink, almost matching those pajamas that are teasing me with the way they hug her body.

But her eyes … her eyes are otherworldly—bright, stark blue. Like the sky on the clearest day. Or the lightest part of the *Morpho didius* butterfly. Right now, they are wide, stretched with caution and a pulse of something resembling … desire.

As if she forgot herself for a moment, she shakes her head softly, just enough for a few stray strands to fall into her face. Her hair is all disheveled and messy from her sleep. But with her body flushed and plump lips parted, she looks like she just got ravaged by me, and, fuck, I wish it had been me that left her like that instead of her sheets.

Although, if we had been together, there would be visible marks on her—collarbone, throat, thighs. I would pepper her with my sin, burning it into her skin with pleasure. Maybe a bite mark here or there.

She steps toward the door behind me as she clears her throat. "You need to leave."

Right before she passes me, I throw my arm out, flattening my hand against the wall, stopping her from going any further. She slams to a halt, gasping with surprise as her hands latch on to my forearm as she braces herself.

She's so short. I tower over her, the top of her head barely hitting my collarbone.

"Malik." Her voice is breathless when she speaks, and I wonder if she feels the same way I do right now.

Leaning down toward her, I wet my lips. Watching

her eyes fall to half-mast and her lips part, I whisper, "Say it again, baby. It sounds so good on your lips."

Her eyes widen for a second, and she sucks in a breath. "Y-you should go."

Delicately, I lift my other hand up to her waist, brushing my thumb back and forth on her side. A shiver runs through her, and I bite down on my lip.

She follows my gentle push like a good girl, backing herself up against the wall, and I take this perfect opportunity to cage her in. Positioning my left hand against the wall higher, I rest it above her head and slide my left leg to the outside of her tightly pressed thighs.

My right fingers sink in her side of their own accord, desperate to feel how soft and pliable she is. I want to mold her body around mine. Memorize the way it feels.

She looks up at me, her lashes breaking up her bright blue gaze. "W-what are you doing?" she asks breathlessly.

Turning my palm up, I drag my fingers higher up her waist, around the side swell of her breast. She shudders and bites down on her bottom lip.

Inching higher, my fingers trail across her bare collarbone and up the side of her neck.

Gently, I wrap my fingers around her throat, and her eyes widen in response.

"Don't worry, Bug. I won't choke you until you ask me to."

Brushing my thumb back and forth, I can feel her pulse pick up at my words. She wants this too.

Dropping my head, I tilt hers up. "I hate you."

She wets her bottom lip and wiggles her neck in my grasp. My dick twitches in my joggers, hard as a fucking rock.

Our bodies drift together, our lips ghosting across one another as a shock runs through me.

Her warm breath skirts across my lips, her voice so soft that her words are almost inaudible. "Then why are you here?"

Shit.

I don't fucking know.

I stay quiet because I don't have an answer.

Staring down into her eyes, I take a shaky breath.

The small amount of mental effort it takes to process her question does just enough to clear my mind. Just enough to make me realize that I'm a second away from pinning her to the wall and kissing her senseless.

I shouldn't be here.

Not giving myself any time to second-guess or over-think, I release her neck, pull away, and step toward the door.

In one swift movement, I throw it open and disappear into the hallway.

Clenching my fists at my sides, I stride down the hall, much smoother than the trip to her room the first time, sobering up faster each second.

Fuck, I shouldn't have done that. I should NOT have done that.

What was I thinking?

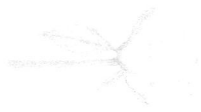

It's been two days since I drunkenly wandered into Alora's room. Two days since I had my hand on her waist, the other around her throat with her lips brushing against mine.

It's only been two days, and it's felt like for-fucking-ever. I've been distracting myself from the inevitable awkward encounter, skipping all my classes and staying glued to the ice. It's helped so far, although I know I can't do it forever. But another day or so won't hurt.

Besides, we have a big game tonight, and I need to be on top of it. We're playing the Titans, one of the best teams in collegiate hockey right now. They are ranked number one in scoring.

Not only will we need to get pucks deep in the net to counteract any of their goals, but we'll also need to be on our toes to stop them from scoring at all. The problem is, they don't have two or three players that do the majority of scoring that we can stay on top of; it comes from multiple players on each line.

I know we're the better team. That's not a question. But I don't want to win by one. I want to dominate them from beginning to end.

Before games, I usually mentally lock in by messing around with the guys—either by kicking around a soccer ball or a Hacky Sack to pass the time. Thankfully, that helps keep my mind distracted.

I just need to get out of my head and try to forget about what happened. But, fuck, I don't think I can.

Which doesn't do anything to help the hatred I feel any less confusing. How can I want someone so badly and loathe them at the same time? Make it make sense.

After warm-ups, the starters set up for puck drop at center ice.

It's a blood battle from the very beginning, every player out there working their bodies to the max. By the time the first period ends, no one has scored, but everyone is gassed. The exhaustion doesn't matter though; it fades quickly, replaced with the desire to win.

The second period starts off just as equally matched. Blow for blow. Shot for shot. Block for block. We need an edge, an advantage to push us over the wall.

This is where I come in occasionally. Not forced by any coach or teammate. A decision made all on my own. One I *love* making.

Number thirty-one has been picking on Asher all night. I already gave him a warning. But the next time I see it, I'm crushing him into the ice. I'm making a scene, making him regret ever touching Ash. As a bonus, it will rile the team up and hopefully push the momentum our way. I'll take the penalty happily, every day of the week.

Finny blocks one of their shots, and it rebounds

right near me. Taking it with my stick, I skate around the goal as their team makes a move to change a few of their players.

We take full advantage of the opportunity.

Elias taps his stick on the ice up ahead, and my body moves in sync with my thoughts as I pass the puck through the neutral zone. It glides effortlessly, landing right on the end of his stick, and he sinks into our offensive zone.

Asher flies into the zone on the other side, only one defender between the two Legends.

Elias passes it to Asher, who overexaggerates and pulls back the puck like he's going to shoot, but at the last second, he fires it back to Elias, who tips it midair past their goalie and into the net.

One of the Titans players is racing toward Elias, who has his arms in the air, celebrating.

"Don't you fucking dare," I shout, gaining speed and catching up to him.

He checks into Elias and sends him flying awkwardly into the boards. He collides with a deafening thud.

And all hell breaks loose.

Wrapping my arm around the soon-to-be dead guy's neck, I yank him backward, far away from Elias, who is still lying on the ice. His helmet comes undone and falls off.

"You're going to fucking pay for that," I promise him.

Releasing him, I let him gain his balance, but I'm not patient. Flicking my gloves to the ground and ripping my helmet off, I grab his collar and jerk him toward me.

Cocking my arm back, I release my fist, swinging my weight into it as it collides with his cheek. He grunts and throws his knuckles my way, but I dodge with ease.

The arena erupts as a full scrum breaks out around us. But the only thing I'm focused on is him and breaking his fucking jaw.

Rearing back, I land another blow and another. I knock him off-balance, and he drops to his knees, his arms flailing out beside him.

The refs begin skating over to us, surely to tear us apart, as he hit the ice—a typical cue for the fight to end.

But I'm not done yet.

Adjusting his collar in my grasp, I lift his head up, and his eyes fly open. But there's no mercy here. He shouldn't have hit Elias.

He knocked on this door; I'm simply answering.

Punching him on the side of the head, I watch the lights in his eyes shut off, and I drop him.

The arena goes berserk as he collapses to the ground, knocked out cold.

Adrenaline surges through me, and every single person in the building, aside from the Titans, cheer and shout.

The energy is electric as I skate away from him toward my bench.

I know I'll get heavily reprimanded for it, especially since I kept hitting him after he fell to the ice.

But I don't care. This rush is what I live for.

"Let's go!" I throw my hands up in the air.

The crowd somehow gets louder. My teammates smack their sticks against the boards as I step through the open board door.

"Fucking animal!" one of the guys yells at me with a huge smile on his face.

"Fuck yeah!" another howls, followed by a slew of compliments and shouts from the rest of the guys.

Striding down the tunnel toward the locker room, I can still feel the vibration through the floor from the pulsing energy behind me. It's palpable.

It's *everything*.

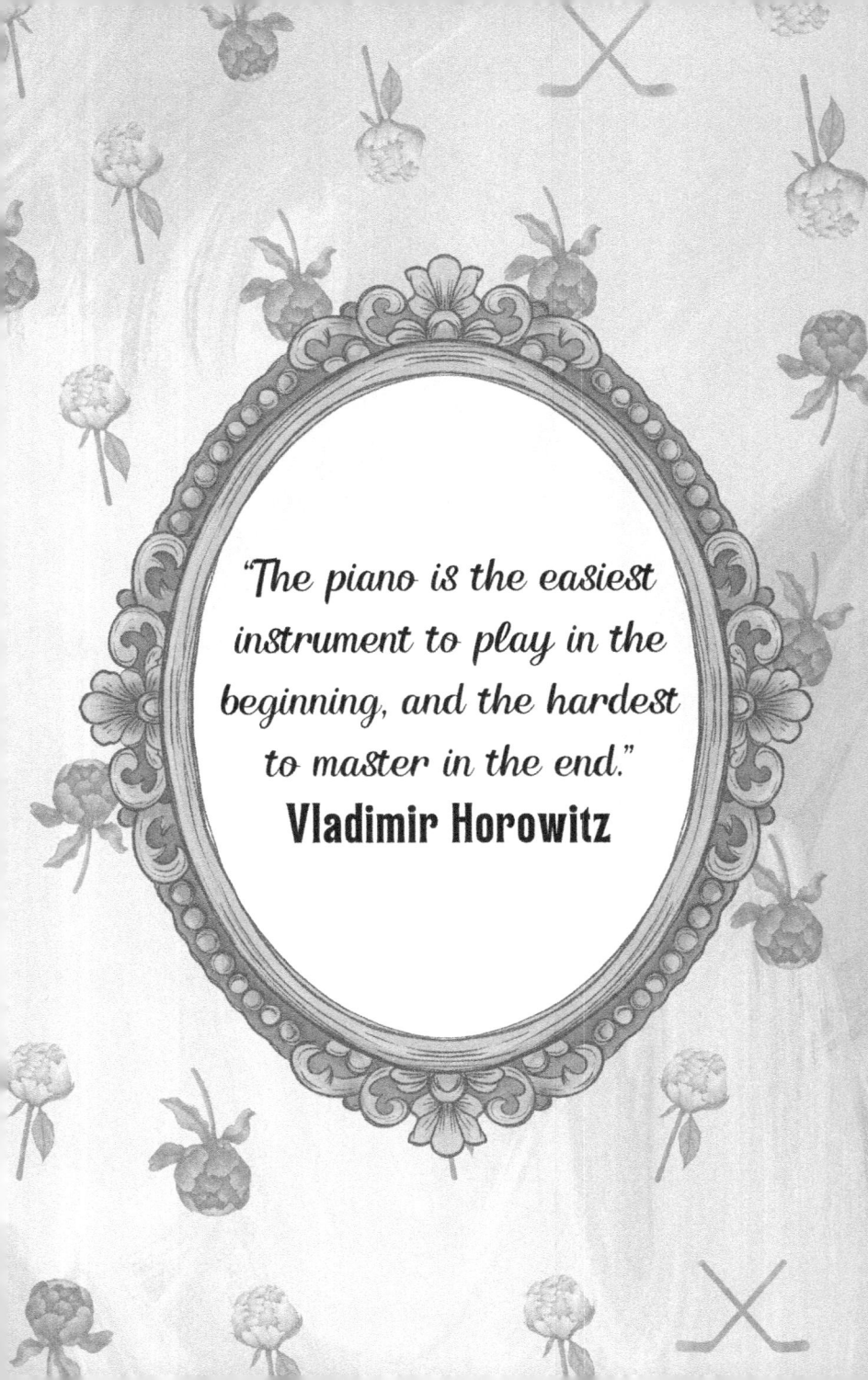

"The piano is the easiest instrument to play in the beginning, and the hardest to master in the end."

Vladimir Horowitz

chapter eleven
alora

A text is waiting for me when I wake up this morning. From someone I have no desire to see. But one I have no choice but to face. My dad.

It's been a long time since I saw him—almost two years now. Even that visit wasn't one from his own heart; it was a press tour for his most recent campaign. Back when he was just a mayor.

A political show is exactly what today will be, filled with smiles, handshakes, and waves as I'm paraded around like a doll—or worse, an accessory. My outfit was already personally picked out. Not by him, but by his team. It was dropped off to me at nine a.m., along with the itinerary.

His second assistant will be with me all today—in charge of keeping me in line, I'm sure. Not that I've ever given them a reason to doubt my performance. It's flawless every time.

The weight on my chest feels heavier than ever as I zip up the back of the modest pink dress. It might not be formfitting, but it's somehow still constricting, suffocating like hands around my throat.

Glancing in the mirror, I feel oddly proud of what I've pulled off in the last hour. Curled my hair, did my makeup, played piano for ten minutes, and even managed to have a cry session in there—before the makeup, of course.

I'd spent years perfecting the art of fighting back tears, especially the older I got. It seemed that as time went on and the memory of my mother faded from my dad's mind, the further he strayed from the man I'd once known.

This tweed dress, fitting for any politician or royal, fits me perfectly. Which is rather shocking, given the fact that I've put on some weight since I last saw him.

"Sunny, baby, June will be here in about an hour." I start filling her in on my plans for the day so she doesn't feel left out. "So, you'll only be alone until then."

She looks up at me with happiness in her eyes. I know she likes June, and June does a good job with her. I have no worries, especially with the deal I made with her.

I'm paying for all of her tuition for four years with some of my trust fund; in return, she's Sunny's sitter whenever I need. I'm flexible, of course, when I can be.

Sunny's a good girl and very independent, but I don't like leaving her alone for too long when I'm gone. It makes my heart hurt. Especially when I can pay for someone to be here and take her on nice, long walks and stimulate her.

I don't reach out to June every single time I leave my room, but if I'm going to be gone for more than a few hours, I like to have her there. If not just for Sunny, then for my peace of mind.

Sunny is my best friend and the most important part of my life right now. I would be so lost without her. No money will ever be too much to keep her happy and safe.

Grabbing my purse and the itinerary from my desk, I look it over once more before nicely folding it up and tucking it in my purse.

9:00 a.m.—Meet with Jess outside of Hans hall.

9:10 a.m.—Breakfast with the dean and the president of HEAU, and Congressman Briarwood.

10:00 a.m.—Photo shoot with the dean and the president of HEAU and Congressman Briarwood.

2-hour break—MUST REMAIN ON CAMPUS.

12:15 p.m.—Meeting with congressman.

That only sums up the start of my day in hell.

Unlocking my door, I catch one last look at myself in the small hanging mirror on the wall. Every hair is in perfect order. No smudged makeup.

Lifting my lips up into a smile that I don't feel, I force the energy to flourish into my eyes, making it as believable as possible. After letting my mouth fall and lift back up into a grin, I've achieved my goal—a flawless fake smile.

"Bye, Sunny. Love you, baby." I close the door behind me, and the automatic lock clicks into place.

It's like all the energy in my body shifts to my chest, welling up and expanding with every step I take down the hall toward the elevator. Pressing the button on the wall, I wait, hearing the mechanisms grind behind the double doors. The display screen above it changes, the light shifting from left to right as it gets closer to this floor.

It chimes softly, signaling its arrival, and I step forward toward the doors, patiently waiting.

The doors begin to slide open, and my heart jumps into my throat. My eyes fall directly onto his chest, the T-shirt drawn taut against his firm muscles.

Looking up, I lock eyes with Malik, sucking in a sharp breath.

I haven't seen him since that night, and I was not mentally prepared to see him this morning.

I'm such a different version of myself right now. So prim and proper. So controlled. A puppet of my father's.

His face is unreadable, his jaw tight. He looks at me with a blank stare.

Dean clears his throat, and I realize it's not just Malik getting off on the floor. The Kensington brothers are here, too, staring at us like we have a secret and they are desperate to hear it.

"Oh. Hey, Alora," Asher greets me with a smile.

Do they know that Malik came into my room that night? Did he tell them anything?

I don't know what I expect Malik to do. He's unpredictable on a good day. But after he came into my room and almost kissed me? I have no idea what he's going to do next. Or what I want him to do …

"Hi," I answer, glancing over at him as I step back and give the small group space to exit. But no one moves, aside from Dean blocking the doors from closing with his arm.

Awkward silence consumes all of us.

I want to move and get on the elevator, but I can't. Malik's stare pins me in place.

It hasn't left me. I can feel it caressing my face. Hot and heavy, as if his fingers were right there on my skin.

Dean looks at Malik, clearly noticing something is off about this interaction, more so than usual.

Malik's lips part as if he's going to say something. I wait, eagerly anticipating what's to come.

At the very least, I wish he'd address that I'm even here and acknowledge me. Or give me some clarity on what the hell happened that night. Like why, one second, he wanted to kiss me, and the next, he tells me he hates me. Then spends days avoiding me.

What is his deal? It was easier when he just despised me. It would be less confusing.

His mouth closes, and for a split second, it's almost like a veil dropped in front of his eyes and revealed a glimpse of vulnerability But I blink, and it's gone.

"Where are you headed, looking like a pretty, preppy princess?" Malik's lips tip up into a smirk, and I know he's teasing me.

But it feels more flirty than harmful.

"I'm heading to meet up with my dad." I glance away from them, my voice slightly shaky.

Dean nods. "Oh, that sounds—"

Malik cuts him off, striding forward and plowing through me, knocking my shoulder as he passes.

I stumble back a step but catch myself.

Asher's jaw is unhinged as he watches in awe as Malik storms down the hallway.

Malik's voice travels back to us as he calls out for the brothers, "Are you two going to hurry the fuck up or what?"

He doesn't look at me or acknowledge me at all before he disappears around the corner.

"We'll catch you later," Dean chimes in as they both politely brush past me and walk down the hallway toward their room.

I don't say anything, too dumbstruck to form a word as I step forward and press the level-one button, watching the doors close in front of me.

My phone vibrates repeatedly, and I pull it out of my purse, finding my dad calling me. *Shit.*

I glance at the time in the top corner as I answer the call. I'm late.

My father's voice is even harsher than I remember as he angrily whispers at me, the quietest of his words echoing in my ears, "Where the *hell* are you? Are you trying to make us look bad?"

"I-I'm in the elevator. I'm sorry. It took a while for it to get up to my floor." The apology rushes past my lips.

"Don't make excuses. Hurry up."

He forces a laugh at someone, his voice shifting to that fake tone he uses as he addresses them. "Hi, Kenneth. No, she'll be here in just a minute. Don't worry."

A moment of silence passes before he snaps into the phone, "You have three minutes to be at my assistant, Jess' side."

The call ends at the same time I reach the first floor. The doors open, thankfully without someone I know on the other side.

I can only go so fast. My heart rate needs to stay manageable, and I need to stay cooled off enough that I don't overheat. Maybe he should have thought of that before shoving me in this damn thick dress.

As quickly as I can, I head outside and begin the short trek to Hans Hall. Whether he likes it or not, it's going to take me longer than three minutes.

Which, of course, it does because it's a half a mile from my dorm. Which might take other people three minutes to complete, but not me.

Crossing the smooth cobblestone walkway, I stop at the bottom of the stairs of Hans Hall to catch my breath.

My heart rate's a bit higher than I'd like.

Giving myself a moment of peace, I take some deep breaths, even though right now, it barely feels like I'm getting anything in my lungs.

The door swings open, and a woman in a black pencil skirt and white blouse steps outside, her eyes dropping directly to me with recognition in them. "Alora, there you are. Come on. We gotta go."

Oh, I *know*. Everything's a rush—always. God forbid I take a second to gather myself.

But I don't say any of that.

Instead, I smile up at her and stride up the stairs, using the railing to help. Before I even reach the top one, her hand is hooked beneath my arm and pulling me inside of the door.

The dean, president, and the provost of HEAU, as well as my dad, are all waiting inside. All of their stares find me as we rush down the hall toward them.

The persona that exists inside of me for the times I'm the congressman's daughter more than myself surfaces, taking over. "I am so sorry that I am late! Please forgive me. I was feeling a bit under the weather when I woke up this morning."

They all brush it off, the president speaking for the group. "It is no concern at all. We're just glad you made it safely."

My dad is smiling at me, seemingly as happy as the rest of the men. But there's a sign—a tiny, almost-indiscernible darkness in his gaze—that tells me otherwise. He's fuming; he just won't show it in front of them.

"Shall we?" Jess asks, gesturing toward the door that's propped open.

The men nod and smile before allowing Jess and me to enter the room first.

"Thank you," I praise them, stroking their egos.

We file inside the Lockhart Room and make our way to the round table in the center of the circle rug beneath the tall crystal chandelier. Small name cards assign our seats, which we quietly take. I'm to the left of my father, then the dean, the president, the provost, and then Jess.

A server comes around the moment we're settled and removes the name cards before disappearing from the room.

A different server approaches us with an iced water pitcher in her hands. "Can I get anyone a glass of water?"

"Yes, please." My voice is almost unrecognizable, quiet and soft.

She starts with me, working her way around the table until the glasses are all full.

The president takes a drink before directing his attention my way. "Alora, tell us, are you enjoying your time here so far?"

I nod as a grin lifts my lips. "Most definitely. HEAU

has been a dream come true. It's an honor to be here, sir."

President Scott responds, "That's great to hear. We want nothing but success for you here. We're honored to be your school of choice."

The first server saves me from another political answer, walking over with the first two plates, setting them down in front of my dad and me.

Bacon, two small pancakes, scrambled eggs, fruit and a small slice of wheat toast. I see my dad failed to mention in the planning of this breakfast that I have to be careful with how much sugar I consume. The rest of the plates are brought out, and everyone thankfully spends the next few minutes eating while I pick around my plate and eat a few bites of the scrambled eggs and fruit.

After everyone clears their plate, aside from me, the guys talk shop for a while, which basically translates to kissing each other's ass for a half an hour. I'm here merely as a prop. I bet if I didn't say a word the rest of the day, no one would notice.

Once the breakfast table is cleared, we pose in front of an HEAU step-and-repeat backdrop for a few photos, which seems to take ages to complete.

I just need to get through the rest of this day, and I can relax again, without the hawk watching over me.

When the two-hour break approaches, I know just where I'm going—to practice piano until I feel more like myself again.

It goes by in a blur, and by the time the two-hour break comes to a close, I contemplate calling my dad and telling him that I'm too sick to come to our meeting.

But I know he would just come here instead, and neither of us wants that.

I'm meeting him in the dean's office, who turned it over to him for anything he needs for the day. Generous, as always when it comes to my family. I know I should be grateful, right? But all I feel is disgust.

"Come in," my father calls out after I knock on the hardwood door, his tone stern.

Twisting the doorknob, I push it open, finding him comfortably sitting in the dean's chair with his hands crossed on top of the oak desk. I shut the door behind me, knowing he'll want privacy.

"Have a seat," he orders, his gaze dropping to the two black leather chairs positioned across from him.

I do as told, quietly walking around the armchair and sitting on the edge of the seat. "Hi."

He clears his throat and lifts a piece of paper from the desk, handing it to me. I lean forward and take it.

Physically resisting my eyes from rolling, I read the headline. *Areas of Improvement.*

It's been a few years since I got one of these from him, although I was a teenager then, still in his care. Now I'm an adult, teetering on the edge of ending our relationship.

"As you can see, there is *a lot* to work on." He studies

his own copy. "But for starters, let's discuss today. First off, you were late. *Unacceptable.* You know how important appearances are in this world, and you failed to uphold them." His face reddens the longer he talks. "You barely spoke all afternoon, and I had to remind you to smile more than once. If you still lived under my roof, I would have taken everything from you as punishment. It's disgraceful, Alora. For both of us."

His face may be red with frustration, but my blood is boiling with rage.

Maybe it's from the small stint of being on my own that I've found this new sense of separation from my dad, more so than I did when I went to live with just my aunts. But I know that if he wanted to, he could have me revoked from this school with one phone call and upheave my entire life.

I don't care about the money. I know how to be happy without it. My aunts taught me that. But I won't say that I hate having the money I was born into. It's a blessing, one that I don't take for granted. But I don't need him to hold on to a majority of my money, thanks to my mom and the trust fund she had set up for me. The hundreds of millions set aside in the trust is the safety net allowing me to distance myself from my dad.

There's a tightrope between standing up for myself and pissing him off. I have to pick my battles, and I'm just not sure this is the one I want to choose.

"I apologize," I say as genuinely as I can muster.

He nods, dismissing it immediately. "Now, let's talk

about your time here on campus. You haven't been managing it wisely."

He checks the sheet again, and I follow, looking down at my own paper. I notice the second section, and my body goes cold.

"H-have you been having me followed?" My words are a ghost of a whisper.

He looks at me like I'm stupid. "Of course I have. You're an extension of my agency. What you do affects me."

My lungs empty, and a shiver skates across my shoulders. I know he values image above everything else and he has plans to run for senator and then president one day, but I never once questioned that he would completely invade my privacy.

Reaching into his bag, he pulls out a small picture. "I received word that you'd been spotted interacting with this individual."

He slides the photo across the desk, and my heart sinks.

It's a photo of Malik and me at the party, visibly angry with one another. Apparently, there's nowhere my father can't reach, including a college party with an invite-only attendance.

Did one of the brothers take a check from him to get whoever his spy is put on the list?

My mind starts racing as I try to remember if anyone stands out who I've maybe seen more than once that isn't a coincidence.

Then my eyes focus on Malik in the photo, and I recall the discussion at hand. "What about him?"

He shakes his head, disappointed I don't already know the answer. "You cannot be friends with this boy. Do you understand me? He doesn't have a great reputation. And certainly doesn't fit in the line of what we represent."

"It's a good thing we aren't friends. Merely old high-school acquaintances." My words are short and sharp.

I don't know why I feel so defensive of Malik. He's made my life hell. I know part of it is the daddy issues I have, wanting to defend anyone he dislikes. But I also understand the difference between the heat of anger I feel wanting to defy my dad, and the bubbling heat I feel beneath the surface when Malik's near me.

He remains quiet, and after I briefly scan the paper, I rise from my seat.

"If that's all …"

"That's all," he dismisses me.

Shit, I got up too fast.

When I lower myself to my seat, he watches me for a moment, and I swear I catch a glimpse of concern in his gaze. But it must be the black spots flashing in my eyes like glitter.

"It was good seeing you," he mutters softly.

The backs of my eyes burn, but I push it away, forcing the sensation back until it disappears. I won't cry for his love.

"Yeah," I whisper, pursing my lips and twisting them to the side.

"Have the room as long as you need." He gathers his belongings and walks to the door. "I love you."

I hesitate for just a second, wondering if I want to repeat the words to him. But at the end of the day, as crazy as he might have become, he's still my dad, and parts of me will always love him.

"I love you too," I murmur.

I hear the knob twist and then a brief hesitation. But a second later, he's gone, and I'm shut inside as my mind starts to race.

What just happened?

A few minutes pass by, and after drinking nearly half of my water bottle, I slowly stand up and walk to the door, feeling much better.

At least today is over, and I can just relax and hang out with Sunny for the rest of the day and maybe play some piano. Which is all I ever really want.

Strolling outside of the Administration building, I walk down the stairs and take a left to head back to my dorm. As I round the corner, I see my father and Malik face-to-face in what looks like a heated conversation. I freeze, stopping dead in my tracks as my veins run cold.

Tucking myself behind some overgrown vines that cascade down the building, I sink into the shadows. A perfect hideaway. They're too far away for me to hear anything, but I can tell from here that they're both fuming mad. Malik's fists are clenched at his sides, his face beet red.

What the actual hell is going on?

An entire minute passes, and they're still talking.

What could they possibly be discussing?

Malik steps forward, inching closer to my father's face. He says one more thing to him and then storms off in the opposite direction, his pace fast and aggressive.

My dad scans his surroundings out of habit, looking to see if anyone's watching with a smile on his face. His gaze passes right over me, but he doesn't seem to see me —thankfully.

He strolls away slowly and effortlessly, with his hands in his pockets, as if whatever just happened *didn't*.

Once he's out of sight, I untangle myself from the vines and continue walking home, the light breeze brushing my hair back and off my shoulders, the aroma of flowers floating in the wind.

My mind drifts away. I somehow feel even more confused than before, and I'm left with far more questions than answers.

It was odd enough to see the two of them talking in general. But that's not the part that leaves me unsettled. It's how they talked. There was a familiarity to it, like it wasn't the first time.

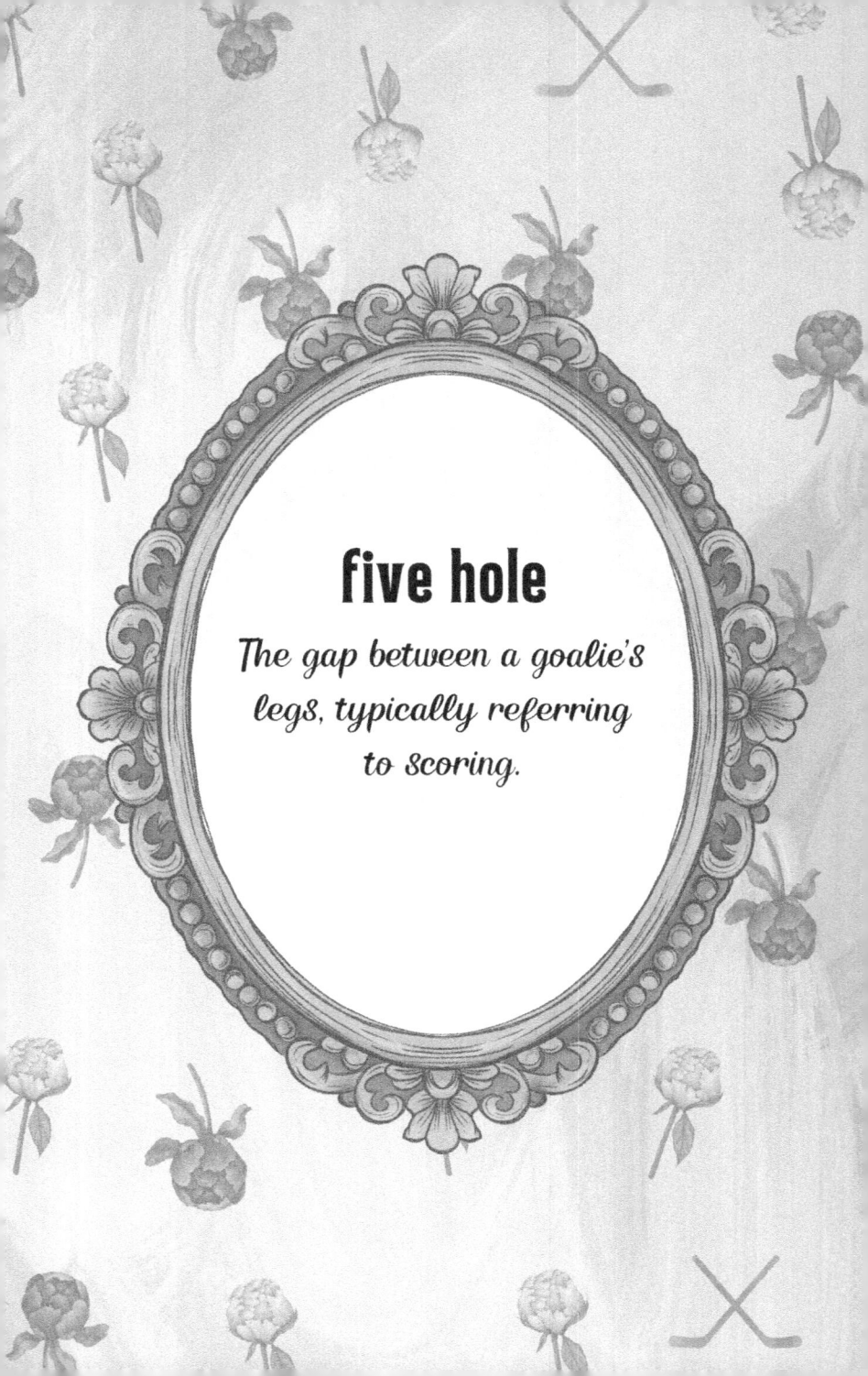

five hole

The gap between a goalie's
legs, typically referring
to scoring.

chapter twelve
malik

Music thumps in my headphones as I stroll through campus with my hood up, head down, and hands in my joggers pockets, heading toward World History. The class I have with some of my teammates, along with Lumi, Blair, and Alora.

This will be the first time I'll actually face her since that day in the elevator. I've been avoiding her like it's my job.

I'm confused enough with the emotions going through me without seeing her. But I can't do that forever, especially if I want to keep my grades up for my scholarship.

When I walk beneath a large willow tree, a few drops of this morning's rain trickle down onto my shoulders, the gloominess of the day matching how I feel inside.

A sense of dread always begins weighing me down this time of year. Nearing Micah's birthday and the anniversary of his death brings all the darkness to the surface. Like the demons inside of me know I'll be weak for a little while and take advantage—letting their anger out on anyone in our path.

Usually, during this time, I distance myself and isolate from everyone in my life. But last year, when I was ready to do the same, Griffin knew something was up and refused to let me be alone. The man slept on the floor of my dorm for three nights straight and woke me from my nightmares, and I from his. That stretch of a few days transformed our relationship completely, and we realized we were far more alike than we ever could have imagined.

He's my best friend, and I trust him with my past and pain—most of it anyway. Since last year, we've been inseparable. Except for when he's with Blair, I suppose.

I couldn't be happier for those two though. They're a perfect balance to each other. I've never seen Griffin smile as much as he does when he's with her.

They've got something really special.

Somehow, those two lovebirds allowed me to move in. The dorms had been killing me. I couldn't stand the noise and parties constantly going on. Which is ironic since I'm typically the first one to agree to attend them.

It wouldn't usually bother me, but my quiet, safe space became anything but. Sometimes, my mind is too loud, and I either need complete silence around me to help calm me or I need overstimulation to drown everything out. There's no real in-between, which can be rather frustrating when I don't even know which one I need.

It's been a lot better since they let me move in though. I have my tiny section of the mansion I stick to. I have everything I need. I don't think me living there is ever going to become a problem for them, but getting me to leave might. Because it's going to be damn hard to walk away from those amenities.

I've been lost in my mind all morning, running my brain ragged with nonstop thoughts—anything I can do to distract myself from the growing wound reopening in my heart.

I wish I could just black out and skip this part of the year and wake up after the fact. I feel like that would be less painful. Both for me and everyone around me.

My chest tightens as I stride into class. Alora's doe-eyed gaze locks on to me immediately. I stop in my tracks without meaning to. Her stare is blank and unreadable. But I can't miss it—the glimmer of hope in her eyes. My chest twists tighter.

She can't have hope that whatever happened in her dorm has changed something between us.

It hasn't, and it won't.

Right?

The class is nearly full already, but my seat between Asher and Griffin is waiting for me.

Needing to kill that hopefulness, I tear my gaze from her without so much as blinking and glance to the ground as I walk to the second row.

Slipping one side of my headphones off of my ear, I step past a few smiling girls, giving them a wave, and they giggle in response.

Walking past Dean and Asher, I drop into my seat, setting my backpack on the ground by my feet.

Griffin immediately greets me. "About time. Thought you weren't going to make it."

"Funny," I mutter, slipping my headphones off, folding them up and tucking them into my sweatshirt pocket. "The professor's not even here yet. We still have, like, three minutes."

His stare lingers for a second too long, and I can feel the concern in the weight of his gaze.

He leans over, turning his head to the side so only I can hear what he's about to say. "You all right, man?"

I shoo his concern away with a nonchalant shrug. "I'm fine."

"You know I'm here whenever you need. Even if you just need someone to listen. Don't bottle it up," he murmurs.

His kind words would probably soften anyone else, but all they do is lock down my heart even more, the thorns of my emotional barricade tightening and constricting more by the second. It's not his fault though; it's my own fucked-up brain's.

Nodding sharply once, I take my notebook out of my bag, along with a pen. Setting it on my notebook, I bend back down to get my water bottle and bump the desk. As if frozen, I watch in slow motion as it rolls off of the notebook and drops to the ground ... right beneath Alora's seat.

Fucking *great*.

It makes a loud sound as it hits the metal of her chair leg. She glances down and picks it up.

Just keep it. Just keep it and never turn around.

Sliding her arm across the top of the backrest, she twists in her chair and looks up at Griffin. "Did you drop this?"

He shakes his head, glancing at me. "It's Malik's."

Clenching and unclenching my jaw, I fight the urge to look straight down at her as her attention shifts to me. But when I see the redness around her eyes, I stare unabashedly.

She lifts it in the air toward me, and as I reach out, my eyes fall to the letters tattooed on my right hand's knuckles—*M* on my thumb, *I* on my pointer finger, *C* on my middle finger, and so on as Micah's name is spelled on my skin.

A surge of anger floods my system as I remember who she is. One of *them*. The ones who look down on everyone beneath them.

Someone who will never understand what my life is

like. Who could never understand why I am the way I am.

"Here," she murmurs softly.

Taking the pen, I snap, "Thanks."

Her eyebrows twitch. "You're welcome."

The next words flow from me without thought. I want her to feel as badly as I do. As badly as she *deserves* to feel. "What's wrong? Crying because Daddy cut down your allowance?"

She sucks in a sharp and pained breath.

Blair's head whips around. "Malik! What the hell?"

Alora doesn't turn back around or shrink. If anything, she sits up taller as a cold mask shifts over her face.

"Fuck you," she grumbles, her teeth grinding together.

Leaning down and over the small swinging desktop, I prop my head in my hand. "You'd like that, wouldn't you? Hmm? I bet you'd even beg me for it." I squint my eyes at her as I feel everyone around us shift to watch.

"Mal." Griffin utters my name like a warning, but I ignore it.

Asher and Dean sit up straighter to my right, and I can feel the agitation coming from Ash. I know he has a fondness for her, one I wish would die.

She stands from her desk and turns completely to face me. But I still have the high ground, being on the second level.

She leans up on her toes and over the divider. Grabbing the neck of my hoodie, she pulls me forward as she gets in my face. "I think it's *you* who wants that. You're just too embarrassed to admit it to yourself."

"Whoa, whoa, whoa." I hold my hands up, but she doesn't let go of my sweatshirt. I chuckle darkly. "Don't get mad at me just because Daddy won't buy you a new mansion or private island or whatever dumb shit you want to waste money on."

Her head cocks to the side as she swallows hard, yanking my head further forward. "You don't know anything about me, Malik. You *never* have. All you've done is spent years painting this image of who I am in your mind."

She tugs me toward her even more, the desktop digging into my abs as she continues, "Otherwise, you'd know that before yesterday, I hadn't seen him in almost two years, you asshole because he shipped me to Avandale to live with my aunts after I turned eighteen before senior year." Her eyes start welling with tears. "But, no, please keep going on about my dad's money. That seems to be all you've ever focused on anyway."

I'm speechless, unsure of what to even say back to that.

Could I actually have been wrong about her?

I scoff at the thought.

No. No way.

Her dog stands up and nudges her leg, drawing her attention away from me. She releases her grasp on my hoodie without looking my way again.

Blair's stare slices into me, more painful than I was expecting, and I sit back in my seat, averting my gaze.

She mumbles something to Alora before Alora gathers her things and stands up, walking out of the room with haste.

"Lumi, go with her. I'll be right there," Blair says, hooking her backpack on her shoulders, her posture rigid.

Scoffing at Blair, I cross my arms. "Not like you to miss a class—"

She cuts me off and juts a finger toward me. "Get your shit together, Malik. And stop being such an asshole to her."

"Blair, chill the hell out—"

"Malik," Griffin's deep voice grumbles next to me, "watch your fucking tone. I'm done giving you warnings."

Blair turns and strides out of the room after Alora, Lumi, and the golden retriever.

Tucking my hands in my hoodie pocket, I clench my fists, reminding myself to calm down. But it's not working.

My goddamn anxiety is spiking, and it's only pissing me off even more.

Griffin leans in closer to me, his voice soft yet firm. "Bro, I know this is a bad time for you, okay? And I get that. But you can't keep lashing out at Alora and especially not at Blair. There's only so much I'm going to let you get away with."

Everything inside of me is shutting down. Every emotion and sense of security. I'm a fortress, and even he isn't getting past my walls.

"Then maybe she should stay out of my and Alora's business," I snap, turning my head to fully face him.

He bares his teeth. "*Mal.*" He pauses and takes a quick breath. "Get your shit. You're coming with me."

"The hell I am." I scoff. "We have class."

"Shut up. Stop pretending like you actually care. You can get notes from Ash or D." He groans and runs his hand down his face. "For once in your goddamn life, just cooperate."

I consider his offer for a moment. I mean, I would rather be anywhere else but sitting in this boring-ass class right now, especially with the rage pulsing in my veins.

"Fine," I concede, grabbing my backpack and rising to my feet.

Storming out of the room, I rush outside into the gloomy, cold weather and scurry down the steps, stopping at the bottom as I wait for Griffin to catch up.

A moment later, he bursts through the door and joins me.

"What's your grand plan?"

"Stop being a smart-ass, Malik. I'm trying to help you." He grinds his words out as he passes. "Now hurry the fuck up."

"Where are we going?" I stride after him, less enthusiastically as him.

"To the rink. I figure there's no place I feel more at home. It's the same for you. And if you need to hit something to get some of that anger out, you can hit me. I can take it." He keeps walking forward toward the arena without looking back.

I follow behind him as we walk to Kensington Arena, the campus arena, paid for by Asher and Dean's family, where we quickly lace up and get on the empty ice in just our hoodies and joggers, no gear.

Twisting my stick in my hands, I smack it on the ice lightly, and he passes a puck to me. We skate around silently, passing the puck back and forth and shooting it into the net every now and then.

We understand each other here, like we're speaking a different language—hockey. Every hockey player feels at peace on the ice. We may feel a lot of other things during games or practice, but it feels right either way, like this is where we're meant to be.

Guilt strikes me like an arrow as the adrenaline in my veins begins to dissipate. I don't deserve a friend as good as him. Especially with how I just spoke to his girl.

Coming to a stop, I look up at him. "Griffin, I'm sorry, man. I'll apologize to Blair too; don't worry. But I'm sorry. I've been a real pain in the ass."

He chuckles. "That's an understatement. But we put up with your shit because we love you, man."

He waits, leaving a moment of silence for me to decide if I want to stay quiet or share more. I choose the latter.

"Look …" I bite down on my bottom lip, still hesitant to tell anyone the truth about Alora.

Gliding toward the bench, I lean down on the board, resting against my arms.

"Malik, whatever you need to say, say it. I, of all people, won't ever judge you. You know that. Just talk to me." He skates over and mimics me, leaning against the board.

"Fuck," I inaudibly whisper, rubbing my eyes with frustration that I can't even form one word about it. "It's complicated."

"I know I'm not the smartest guy ever, but do your best. I'll try to keep up."

He grins at me, and I chuckle hauntingly.

"Alora and I went to high school together." I spin around and lean backward against the divider. "She transferred during her senior year." I scoff. "You know, I actually kind of liked her at first." I swallow hard. "But then I learned who she really was, the daughter of Congressman Briarwood."

He pushes off against the board and leans back beside me as I continue, "I've never told anyone this, Griffin. You have to keep it between us."

He studies me for a moment, realizes I'm being dead serious, and nods. "Of course."

"The Briarwoods had something to do with Micah's death."

After talking to Griffin, I really do start to feel a lot better, which is an unexpected surprise. But I also feel like the reason the weight seems to be lighter is because I forced him to carry some of it. A burden that's not his to bear.

"See you in a few." Griffin walks across the parking lot to his pickup as I slide in my Corvette and close the door, bringing the engine to life.

The drive home is beautiful. The sun is already set, stars and the moon glowing up in the sky.

The air is nice and crisp, not too cold, but not too warm. It's perfect. Calm.

Exactly what I need right now. I'm tired. Emotionally, physically, I'm wiped. I just want to go home and crash after eating dinner.

By the time I pull into the driveway, I feel gravity harder than ever as the exhaustion from today starts to fully set in.

Finishing ascending the ridiculous set of stairs to the front door, I walk inside.

"Malik …" Blair widens her eyes as soon as she sees me, stopping dead in her tracks as she walks out of the kitchen with two glasses of water.

I actually need to apologize to her, so this works out. "Hey, can I talk to you quickly?"

Her mouth starts to form words, but nothing comes out. A beat of silence later, she murmurs, "I thought you guys were practicing later than this tonight."

Weird. "Nope. Why? What's going on?"

"Blair, is this okay to borrow? I'll bring them back to you once I can get home and change." Alora walks around the corner, smiling, but the moment she realizes I'm standing here, she freezes, her smile quickly withering away.

"Why are you here?" My question slices through the air, my words sharp and jagged as I step past Blair.

Blair purses her lips, answering for Alora. "We were studying and working on homework together. And then we were painting with Chip, and it ended in a little paint fight. Anyway, it's not just *your* house, Malik." She says my name like a warning.

Alora slowly walks closer to Blair, her cheeks reddening with embarrassment most likely. She whispers something to Blair.

"No, you don't have to go. Seriously, this is my house more than it is his. He can"—she raises her voice—"grow up!"

Alora's hair is up in a low, messy bun with loose, wavy strands pointing every which way. I have to stop the thought that I think it looks good like that.

The sweatshirt she's wearing instantly catches my

attention, the Legends hoodie looking oddly familiar. "So, why in the hell are you wearing my sweatshirt?"

Blair studies her for a moment. "It must have gotten mixed in with my laundry. I had to get her a change of clothes from the dryer after the painting incident with Chip."

Walking across the foyer, I'm once again reminded of our height difference as I stare down at her, a foot between us.

Fuck, she looks good in my hoodie.

But this isn't right. None of this is right.

Embers burn in her gaze as she looks up at me with firmly sealed lips. "I would *never* have chosen this had I known it was *yours*."

A smirk forms on my lips as I huff, a soft chuckle escaping. "Sure. Then give it back."

I challenge her, knowing she'll probably back down or say something snarky and insist on leaving with it— both sounding like a win in my book.

Her eyes ignite, and her spine straightens. "With *pleasure*."

Crossing my arms, I expect her to walk away. But instead, she surprises me.

Grabbing the bottom of the hoodie, she lifts it up and rips it off of her body with haste. Thrusting it into my chest, she makes sure to add some extra force behind it. "Here. Happy?"

Her cheeks redden even more, and I'm starting to

think it was never from embarrassment but rather frustration.

My eyes are traveling before I even realize it … down her taut neck to the lacy pink bra that is now on full display. They cup her big tits, and my fingers twitch, wanting to do the same.

Stop it.

Licking my bottom lip, I suck it between my teeth and force my gaze back up her chest to her eyes … her blown pupils and parted lips.

She knows what she's doing … teasing me. Taunting me. Asking me to make a move.

I hate it.

Fuck.

I *love* it.

"Much happier." I toss the sweatshirt over my shoulder.

She huffs out a quick breath and turns on her heel, giving me a show with her full hips as they sway with her strut to the laundry room.

Before she disappears around the corner, she lifts her hand in the air and flips me off with her back to me.

I chuckle, feeling an odd and unexpected burst of pride on her behalf.

Blair doesn't waste any time getting in my face, her voice an angry whisper. "Malik, I get that you don't like her. Fine. I'll be better about having her over when you're not here. But can you try to behave like a decent human being? I know that you have it in you."

"That might be the nicest thing you've ever said to me." I clutch my heart.

The front door swings open across the grand foyer, and Griffin walks through with no clue of what's happening. "I got pizza!" As he takes in Blair's annoyance, he pauses. "What's, uhh ... what's going on?"

"Alora's here," I grit out.

Griffin winces, understanding with his newfound knowledge of our situation. "Oh."

Speak of the devil ...

She walks back out, and my jaw fucking unhinges.

She's wearing a Legends T-shirt.

Yet again ... one of *mine*.

Only this time, it's missing the bottom half.

"Alora," I growl, "tell me you didn't just cut one of my favorite shirts in half."

Griffin bursts out laughing behind me, and I glare at him, my jaw clenching.

She winces playfully, teasing me with her sarcasm. "*Oops*. I thought it was one of Blair's."

I step toward her. "You're *such* a bad liar."

The only consolation is that at least my last name is on her back so everyone knows who she belongs to.

She winks at me and saunters closer. "Guess you'll have to find a new favorite. Although you might be able to pull off a crop top. If you ever get it back."

This girl is going to be the death of me.

When I glance at Blair, who is now having a full-blown giggle fit, she looks up at me with no remorse. "I'm sorry. But that's hilarious."

She looks back at Alora, and her face falls. "Alora? Are you okay?"

My head whips toward her.

She's suddenly gone pale, the rosiness from her cheeks out of sight. Blinking rapidly, she takes a few slow steps toward the sitting room behind me.

"What's happening right now?" Griffin asks, genuinely concerned.

Blair rushes to her side and hooks an arm around her waist, helping her walk. "Griffin, get me a glass of water right now, please."

My heart starts to race.

Blair stumbles forward, and in a split second, I realize what's happening.

Lunging forward, I reach out and catch Alora in my arms as she collapses toward the ground.

My heart jumps into my throat, and an aching-choking sensation wraps around my neck.

Scooping her legs up, I cradle her against my chest.

"What's happening? Blair?!" I shout at her, panic raking through my body like hot coals.

"Take her to the couch and lay her down," she instructs me with odd calmness. "She'll be okay. She'll wake up in a second."

Striding as long as my legs can manage, I gently

carry her into the living room and lay her down on the navy-blue sofa.

Blair throws a pillow at me from the other couch, followed by another. "Put them under her legs."

"Okay." I do as told, my palms sweating as I drop to my knees on the side of the sofa, my anxiety at an all-time high.

Brushing her hair from her face, I lift her head up slightly, not wanting her to choke on her spit when she comes to.

"Blair," I call out, "why are you acting like this is so normal?" I demand her answer, a beat of anger pulsing behind my words that she hid something like this from me.

She looks at me like I'm stupid. "You really don't know? You went to school with her," she says in disbelief. "You've seen Sunny, her dog How have you not put two and two together, you *idiot*?"

"Know what?" I whisper, racking through the memories in my mind for things that align with this. "She never passed out in school."

"She probably just did a really good job of hiding it. I don't think she had Sunny until after graduation."

Griffin walks in with a glass of water.

"She has POTS—postural orthostatic tachycardia syndrome."

"I've never heard of it," I mumble, an odd sensation of guilt sweeping over me. "What is it? What does it do?"

"It affects her heart." Her words rush past her lips. "Malik, *now* is not the best time for a study session, okay? Just take a breath."

Cupping her cheeks, I take a shuddering breath.

"Blair," I whisper, and her gaze softens. Something breaks in my chest, pain radiating outward. "Did ... did I do this?"

She hesitates, and her hesitation gives me enough of an answer to dig the knife deeper in my chest. "It's complicated. But stress can elevate her symptoms, yes."

"Fuck." I force the word out with my sharp exhale, my hands threading into the sides of my hair.

When I glance down at Alora, her eyelids flutter open slowly. She blinks, her stare blank.

Taking slow, deep breaths, she mumbles, "W-water."

Blair pushes me out of the way, and I back up without protest, letting her do whatever she needs to help.

"Right here." Blair hands her the glass.

"Sorry. I thought I was going to be able to make it," she apologizes, and I wince, standing to my feet.

Griffin looks over at me, his stare deep with emotion. He twitches his eyebrows, and I can practically hear him ask if I'm okay.

I nod and look away, feeling more vulnerable than I'd like.

What the fuck just happened?

"I'll be okay in a few minutes. And then I can call someone to come get me."

Who?

No.

Blair and Griffin are going to a movie tonight in the opposite direction of campus, so I know there's only one person here who can take her.

Fuck. I shouldn't do this.

"I'll give you a ride."

My offer shocks the room, all three heads turning my way.

"It's fine. I can have someone—"

"I wouldn't have offered it if I didn't mean it," I cut her off. "Let me know when you're ready to go."

Strolling out of the room with haste and without another word from anyone, I make the small trek to my room and lock myself inside, sinking down to the floor beside my bed, clutching my heart as my breaths heave in and out.

"Fuck!" I smack my hand on the ground.

Dropping my head into my hands, I close my eyes and take a few slow, steady breaths.

My heart is pounding out of control, and I have no idea why. But I need to get a grip.

Resting my cheek against the black comforter hanging off the side, and my stare lands on the row of framed butterflies on the fireplace mantel across from me, his photo centered between them all.

My jaw clenches.

Micah.

The image of him appears in my mind, as if he were standing before me. His black hair and purple eyes, so similar to mine. But he was so much younger and so much livelier. Innocent in the best ways.

God, I wish he were here to tell me what to do, to tell me how to act. All this time, I've been lost without him, and I don't think I'm ever going to be the same again.

Instead, I'll be broken and shattered like glass, trapped in a prison of rage and hatred that I'll never escape. The anger flares up inside of me, overpowering whatever else I was feeling before. It reminds me of why I hate Alora, of what she and her family have taken from me.

Who cares if she has problems of her own? So do I.

Someone knocks on my door. Probably Griffin to see how I'm doing.

Rising to my feet, I walk over to the door and pull it open. My nostrils flare as my gaze falls to *her*.

"Umm, I'm good to go when you are." She's nervous, her voice shaky. Her stare falls to my chest and then behind me. "Are those … butterflies?"

Something inside of me snaps, the villain within rising to the surface with vengeance.

Stepping in front of her, I block her view, and her eyes flick back up to mine.

"Get the *fuck* out of here."

Her face distorts in confusion. "You said you were going to give me a ride."

I shrug and laugh. "Yeah, well, I changed my mind. Call whoever you want. Don't let me catch you near my room again."

Her jaw unhinges, and she looks up at me with such pain … pain that *I* caused her. But I haven't cared for years, and that hasn't changed.

Right?

It can't. I won't let it. I refuse to become a pawn in Briarwood's game.

Slamming the door in her face, I turn around and go back to my spot on the floor, staring at the photos of Micah as every shred of respect I have for myself falls to the ground.

He would hate who I am now, who I've become.

It's probably a good thing he's not here to see me. He'd be so disappointed.

Walking on my knees to the fireplace, I grab his photo from the mantel and pull it against my chest as I go back to the bed and fall back on it.

A dam bursts behind my eyes, and a wail tears through my chest. Rocking back and forth does little to ease the agony. Tears drop from my lashes, chin, and nose.

I don't want to live in a world without him. I never have. I wish it had been me that night. If only I had been on that side of the sidewalk, I would have been the one to die. The way it should have been.

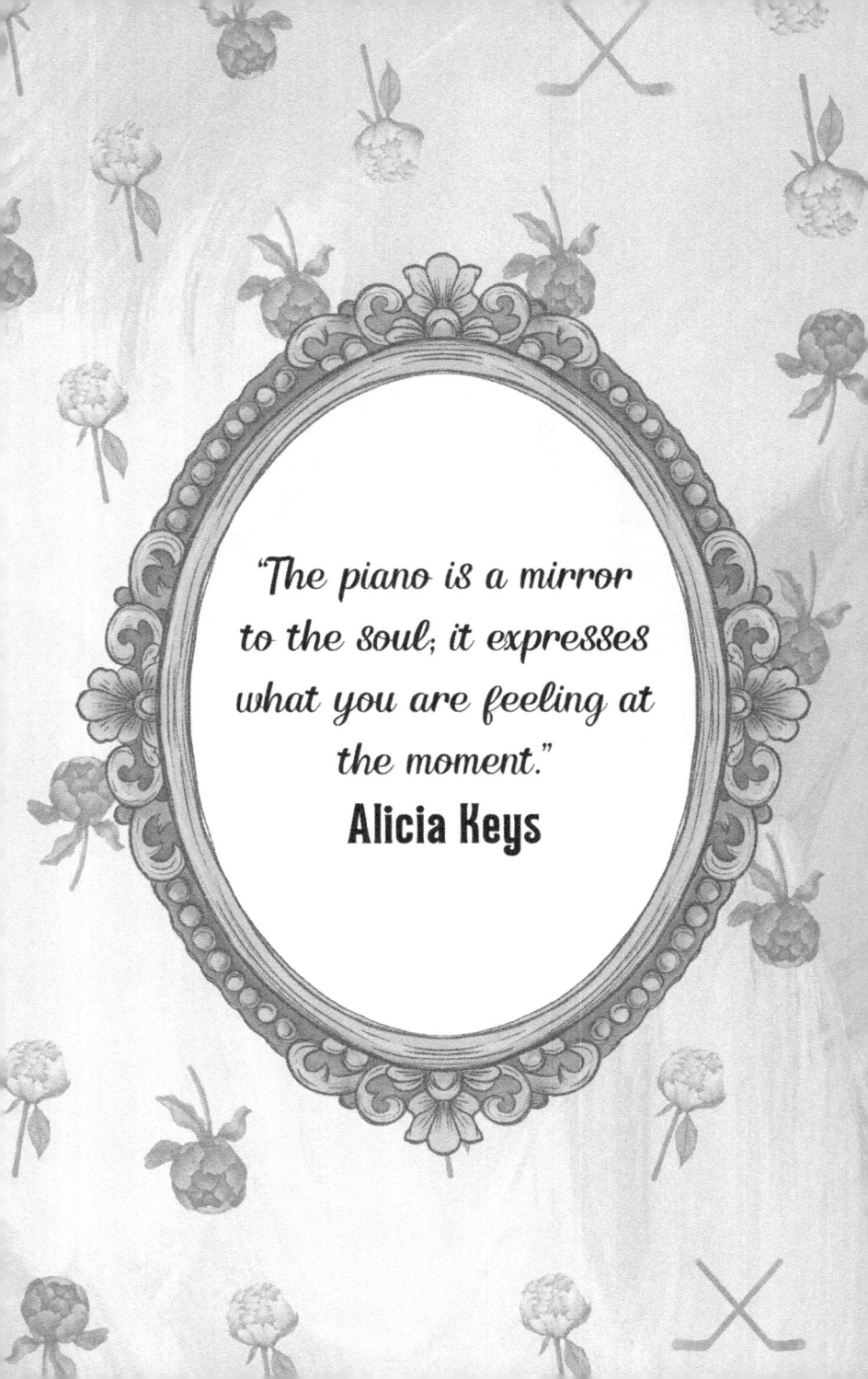

"The piano is a mirror to the soul; it expresses what you are feeling at the moment."

Alicia Keys

chapter thirteen
alora

My neck hurts from the whiplash Malik is giving me. I don't know whether to avoid him altogether or confront him. But I want answers one way or another because I have so many questions.

Why is he so hot and cold with me but steady with everyone else?

Why does he look at me with disgust and then attraction in the blink of an eye?

How does he know my dad?

Why does my dad want me to stay away from him?

Why the hell can't I stay away from him?

At this point, I think I need a full-blown interrogation to get the answers I need. But I'd be lucky if he answered one question.

After last night at their house, I feel somehow even

more conflicted. One second, I woke up, looking up at his wide and concerned eyes. The next, he slammed the door on me after basically telling me to fuck off.

People act the way they do because they have reasons to do so. I just want to know his. Maybe, in the end, he's just an asshole … or maybe there's more to the story.

I also need to get control of my life again because since I met with my dad, I feel like I'm under his thumb all over again. But I'll start with one thing at a time, something that I might be able to make sense of.

Maybe I'll get some advice from someone who knows Malik better than I do. At least whoever he is now.

When class is over, Blair and I hang back for a moment, both of us far too invested in our schoolwork to not finish taking notes from the board.

I finish before her. "Can I talk to you about something?"

She playfully side-eyes me as she writes. "Is it about a certain *someone*?"

I twiddle my thumbs. "Yeah."

"Of course. I'm always here for you." She sets her pen down and turns my way, giving me her undivided attention.

From hanging back after class before, we've learned there isn't another class in here for an hour after ours, so we don't need to rush out.

"I don't even know where to begin." I groan, sinking down in my chair.

"Can I ask you a question?" she asks hesitantly.

I nod.

"Do you like him? Romantically, I mean." She says it so casually, as if there aren't years to unpack before I can give her an answer.

"It's"—I sigh—"complicated."

"Of course it's complicated. It's Malik." She grins. "New question. If he kissed you, would you kiss him back?"

My cheeks heat by a thousand degrees as the image of him in my dorm room flashes in my mind. If he had kissed me that night, would I have reciprocated?

I fight the answer, knowing the one I want to say and the one that's true. As much as I want to deny it, I would have melted into his kiss.

If he hadn't been such an asshole in high school, I would have drooled over him. I've always hated this attraction I've had. Like my heart and mind are betraying me by liking him.

"That's a long pause." She smiles, reading me like a book. "Your secret is safe with me, as long as you want it to be."

"Yeah, I mean, I like him. But I also hate myself for it. It's jarring." I sit up in my seat, resting my chin against the palm of my hand on the desktop.

"He likes you, you know? And I think he's in the same boat you are … in denial and regret for the feelings he has. I don't know what happened between you guys in the past, but I know he cares about you. Even if he's an ass at showing it," she says matter-of-factly.

I watch her intently as she continues, "You should have seen him when you fainted. Alora, I've never seen that look on his face. He was scared out of his damn mind for you."

His concerned frown appears in my mind, tugging at my heart.

"Then why did he slam the door in my face?"

She looks away in thought. "I wish I had an answer for you. Malik is an enigma. He's got a lot of traumas in his past."

Remaining quiet, I hope she keeps sharing, desperate for any and all information.

"I actually hated Malik at first. I thought he was just this cocky asshole. Which he *is*—don't get me wrong." She chuckles. "But he's also loyal. To an absolute fault. He's passionate about the people he cares about." Her voice softens. "When my ex was threatening me last year, he and Griffin came home with bloody knuckles. That hadn't been his fight, but he had taken it on because the people he loved were hurting."

A girl walks into the classroom, grabs something from the second row that she must have forgotten, and turns around before leaving.

Blair reaches out and sets her hand over mine. "I don't have a handbook to help with Malik. But my advice? Go talk to him. He cares about you, even if it's in some fucked-up Malik way."

***

After debating for two hours on whether or not I was going to come here, I open the door and step inside of the arena. I still think this might be my worst idea yet.

Blair said their practice should end around seven p.m.

I check my phone. *Six fifty-seven.*

My heart is racing … a controlled amount but erratic because of where I am and what I'm doing. I left Sunny back at my dorm because I didn't want anything to distract me from going through with this. I need to do this on my own.

Waiting in the entryway of the rink, I stand off to the side, time slipping by in slow motion.

A door opens down the hall, and two players walk out—Asher and Dean.

They smile when they spot me, Asher greeting me first.

"Alora, if you wanted to see me, you could've just called."

Always a flirt.

"Hi, Asher." I smile at him and Dean.

"What are you doing here?" he asks as they approach me.

"Umm … I'm waiting for someone."

Why on earth did I not even run the possibility

through my mind that I would run into other players, like these two, who would certainly ask me questions?

He taps his chin like a cartoon character. "I wonder who that could be. Griffin? *Nope*. Elias? *Nope*. Finn? No, it wouldn't be him. Right, Dean?" he teases.

"Yeah, yeah, yeah." I roll my eyes.

The door swings open again, and Malik walks out, his aura immediately drawing my attention like a magnet. I'm frozen as he spots me, his searing stare keeping me in place.

No one should look that good after practice. He showered, and his hair is all wet and messy, falling over his forehead. He's too hot for his own good. I can still hate him and acknowledge that.

He slowly walks down the hallway toward us, his stare never wavering from mine. I'm not even sure he's blinked.

Asher lightly pats my shoulder. "Later, Alora. Bye, Malik."

Malik stays quiet as the brothers walk past me and out of the doors to the parking lot.

His voice is even and calm, but firm. "What are you doing here?"

Swallowing my fear and hesitation, I stick out my hand. "I want a truce. An understanding between us."

He studies me, his eyes scanning my face, as if I'm going to suddenly burst out laughing. Staying quiet, he looks at my hand and then back up.

Hearing laughter and chatter, he grabs my hand

and pulls me behind him as he walks down the hallway to my right.

"Where are you taking me?"

"Somewhere private," he bites out.

If this is an olive branch, I'll cooperate. If this is some sort of game, I'm going to kill him.

He twists the knob on a random door, and it opens.

He pulls me inside, and it swings shut behind us, sealing us in darkness.

He flips the switch, and light floods the room, which I can now tell is some sort of equipment room. Hockey sticks, gloves, skates, blades, tech I do not understand, and equipment I don't know decorate the room with a desk in the center, the only things on it being a couple of binders.

Keeping his distance from me, he leans against the door, and I take up a nice seat on the desk. Resting my butt against it, I ease myself up and over it, letting my legs dangle over the front of it.

Reaching over, he locks the door so we're not interrupted. Either that or he's about to murder me. Honestly, it could go either way.

"As you were saying …" He trails off, crossing his arms over his chest.

Sitting up tall, I clear my throat. "I want a truce between us."

He clicks his tongue against his teeth. "What exactly are you proposing?"

"Two options. You and I call whatever this is quits

—the banter and the fighting—and we become friends."

He pushes off of the door and takes a step toward me. "And the second option?"

Nervously swallowing, I wring my hands on the edge of the desk. He takes another step toward me.

"We forget about each other, and we stick to our sides of the world. We don't talk. We don't exist to one another."

"Hmm." He takes another step, leaving only a foot or so between us. "What if I have issues with both options?"

"What are they?" I counter, all the nerves in my body starting to come alive at his nearness.

He drifts forward, stopping between my knees, forcing me to look straight up. "I don't think forgetting each other is possible."

My mouth dries. "W-what do you mean?"

"I've tried to forget you." Reaching out, he lifts a strand of my hair and twirls it between his fingers. "Over and over, I have tried. Endlessly. And I've failed every *single* time."

My brain is empty, like he hit a reset button. I'm speechless.

Inching forward, he pushes my legs further apart as his voice changes, angrier and rough. "Do you know how aggravating it is to me that I can't get you out of my head?"

"I do." I sit further forward, our faces only inches apart. "*More* than you could ever know."

"You hate me, Bug?" He smirks. "Talk dirty to me again. I like it."

Rolling my eyes, I push at his chest, but he catches my wrists, pulling me forward and into him, my legs stretching as wide as they can go.

"Do you know how hard it is to hate the only person you want?" The words hiss through his teeth. "You torture me with every glance and every breath you take."

Tilting my head further back, I look straight into those haunted purple eyes. "Then why bother with this? Why come into my room and almost kiss me? Why do any of this at all?"

His stare drops to my lips and back up as a war brews behind his eyes, a myriad of emotions contorting his face. "You're my curse, Alora. I can't escape you if I try."

Searching his eyes, I wet my lips. "Your curse?"

Reaching up, he cups my cheek in his hand, brushing his thumb along my bottom lip. "My curse. My tragedy. They're all the same." He glances down to my now-parted lips. "The worst part is that no matter how much I hate you and how much I wish I could forget all about you, I *can't*. That's my destiny … to live in a never-ending loop of loathing you and wanting you."

My breaths are fast and ragged. The same as his next words.

"Do you know what it's like? Wondering how every inch of your body will writhe beneath my touch. How I picture you spread out, helpless and begging me for more?"

His lips brush against mine as his other hand drops to my waist, and I arch my back.

"I want to ruin you. Corrupt you. Make you suffer the same way I do. Make you hate me for the rest of your life. At least if you did, I would be free from the torment of choosing or losing you."

He steps back and walks away without another word. He unlocks the door and strides through, leaving me breathless and warm as my thoughts spiral out of control.

wave off

Referring to when a referee waves off a stoppage of play, such as icing or offsides.

chapter fourteen
malik

I'm so fucked.

Lying in bed, I hit play on one of the songs I recorded while outside of her practice room. From one of the times I followed her, waiting for her to get lost in her music before I emerged from the shadows.

She's *incredible*.

Once her song comes to an end, I open Instagram and search her name—something I've done a thousand times over the years. The most recent photo she uploaded is one of her and Sunny.

She looks so happy, so cheerful, posing with her girl. A pang of jealousy shoots through me that I've never made her smile like that. I mean, I've seen her happy like that before, but never by my own intention.

I shouldn't be surprised, given the fact that my goal

has always been to take that very thing away from her. But now, everything is getting muddled and confusing, and I don't know how to navigate the growing urge to make her smile rather than frown.

Scrolling through her page, I find one posted from this past summer. Location set in Italy. It's of her and some guy posing for the camera in front of a pool the size of my childhood home.

She's wearing a ruffled pink bikini set that I'm hoping she still has because it looks fucking incredible on her.

The blond guy's hand is wrapped around her hip as they smile for the photo.

My blood pressure spikes. *Who the hell is this guy?*

Mentally, I replace his image with my own and suck in a breath at the thought. We would look so good together, like yin and yang in so many ways.

My phone suddenly rings, tearing me from the delusional imagination that I need to run far away from.

As I read the name of the caller, my stomach drops to the floor.

No. I'm done with him. I've been done with him. He already got everything he wanted. What else could he possibly ask of me?

Answering the call from my uncle, I remain silent.

"Malik? Are you there?"

The sound of his voice forces me upright in bed, my fist clenching at my side.

"What do you want?" I spit.

"Just checking in. Seeing how things are going. Seeing if you're holding up your end of the deal." His last sentence is full of doubt and accusation.

As if I have any other choice. "Do you still have Micah?"

The only thing he could ever hold over my head to buy my silence...my brother. I've never seen the urn, never been able to hug or hold him. Instead, my uncle used it as a bargaining chip. As long as I never speak about the deal he made with Alora's dad, then I know his ashes are safe. If I talk, my uncle said he would flush them or discard of them one way or another. I know he's telling the truth.

In a weird way, I trust his word more than most people because he's never lied to me. He never tried to pretend to be the loving and kind guardian. He showed me exactly who he was and only hid it from anyone else.

I won't take a chance when it comes to Micah.

He scoffs, and I grind my teeth.

"Yes, of course I have him."

"Then I haven't said a word." I swing my feet over the side of the bed and drop my head into my free hand, propped onto my knee with my elbow, shrinking into myself.

"Good boy, Malik. I knew I could count on you." He pauses. "Have you gotten a deal to go pro yet?"

This was an inevitable question in this conversation. I haven't heard from him in nearly three years since I moved out of the house and started living in my car.

Which can only mean one thing … he needs money.

"Not yet. Besides, you're not getting a dime from me when I do."

His laugh straightens my spine and flares my nostrils. "We'll see about that."

"The only reason you are even allowed to breathe right now is because I don't want to lose Micah for good. He's not only your bargaining chip; he's your lifeline." I stand up as my words and anger bubble out of me. "The second you spread his ashes, I would be on your doorstep, and I would gladly become the last face you ever saw. Whether you know it or not, he's the only reason you're alive. Killing that connection only kills you too."

He exhales loudly. "You've always had a smart mouth on you, haven't you?" His Southern accent comes out strong in his next words. "I should have hit you harder. Maybe then you would have learned to show some respect."

Ending the call, I chuck my phone across the room, much harder than I intended, leaving a dent in the drywall after it falls to the floor.

My breathing is ragged, my chest spasming as I start pacing in my room, trying to calm myself down. But nothing's working.

Unbridled rage punches through my lungs as deep-rooted and buried pain fights to the surface. I should have killed him when I was younger. I should have done it the night my uncle and Alora's dad struck that deal. You'd think there was a finite amount of regret one person could feel, but you'd be wrong because I feel more every single day.

As if Griffin somehow senses my distress, he knocks on my open door, and I turn, finding him leaning against the doorframe.

"Everything okay?"

Biting my tongue, I tilt my head side to side. "It'll be fine."

He holds my stare for a moment as he searches my face, but I shut the fortress down, becoming a blank and unreadable canvas. But I can't slow down my erratic heartbeat and heaving breaths.

He steps into my room and shuts the door behind him. "What's going on?"

I chuckle, the sound shaky and fake. "What? I'm fine."

Slowly nodding, he walks over to me and sits down beside me on the bed as I sit up next to him. "All right."

Hooking his arm around my shoulders, he squeezes me against him, and something about it makes my resilience shudder. We sit in silence with his arm around me, and I feel every muscle in my body start to relax as the next few minutes tick by. Eventually, my heart calms and my quivering breathing stills.

Griffin senses my calm and continues with what he

came in here for. "Are you riding with us this morning? Wasn't sure if you were crashing in the Kensingtons' room tonight after Ollie's party."

Fuck, I forgot that was tonight. Ollie is a good friend of Dean and Asher's. Since last year, the rest of our little group have grown pretty fond of him.

"Yeah, is riding with you cool with you? I can be ready in just a couple of minutes." Moving across the room, I grab a pair of sweatpants and a T-shirt from the dresser and a sweatshirt from my closet.

Griffin stands up and walks back through my door.

"Yeah, no problem. Meet you outside. There are muffins in the kitchen if you want one," he shouts back into my room as he heads to the staircase.

Hunger is escaping me right now, but I know I need to eat something.

After changing, I slip on a pair of my tennis shoes and grab my backpack before heading to meet them, stealing a muffin and bottle of water on the way out.

The ride to campus seems faster than normal, but that may be because I'm merely existing in my mind today, zoning out without any effort.

We have World History class this morning, the one I have with Alora. My heart jumps at the idea of seeing her again, and I mentally smack myself for the thought.

She's not in her seat when we walk in, and a giddiness I didn't know I was feeling plummets. She's never late. As long as I've known her, she's been Miss Punctuality.

Quietly, I find my seat to the right of Griffin as Blair takes a seat in front of us, typing into her phone. I wonder if she's talked to Alora at all.

Is she feeling okay?

Last night, I fell hard and fast down a rabbit hole, uncovering and devouring as much information about POTS as humanly possible. I had made the mistake of looking it up at midnight and didn't go to bed until after three a.m. because I couldn't stop reading and watching videos about it.

I don't ask Blair. The thought of forming any words seems exhausting as I twirl my pen between my fingers.

Everything feels heavier today. Gravity, the weight of succeeding, the pressure of not letting Alicia and Darius down. I'm being crushed into smithereens.

I don't even notice when Asher and Dean walk into the room and find their seats to my right or when Lumi sits down next to Blair. I'm too distracted, zoning out and forcing my mind to stay empty of thoughts.

"Blair," Asher murmurs, "Alora sick or something?"

Part of me hates the affinity he has for her, and the other part of me is even more confused as to why I hate it at all.

Blair turns in her seat, her brown eyes finding mine before shifting over to Asher. "Yeah, she isn't feeling well. She's staying home today."

Asher groans, unaware of the invisible illness she faces every day. "Ugh, I wanted to see my girl so bad."

This earns a turn of my head, and I cock it to look at him as he fights back a laugh.

"*Sunny* is my princess." He chuckles with a knowing grin. "My *girl*." He looks at me fully. "Malik, what were you thinking? Did you think I meant Alora, you silly goose?" He pauses with a shit-eating grin. "You all right? You seem on edge today."

Biting the inside of my cheek, I nod my head and force a fake smile. "Screw you."

He chuckles as the professor walks in and steals our attention. As invigorating as this class is, my mind is nowhere near the lecture as he talks for the next hour straight.

When he dismisses us, I'm torn between going to the arena and practicing for an extra three hours today before tonight's actual practice. Or going to the Kensingtons' room and plopping on one of their beds for the biggest nap of my life.

Deciding on the latter, I head to their dorm hall, forcing myself to walk past Alora's room without knocking, even though everything inside of me tells me to stop.

When I get to Asher and Dean's room, I swipe the spare key fob they gave me, but the reader blinks red, denying me access.

What the hell?

I try it again. Once, twice, three times before giving up with a groan.

Did these fuckers change my access?

Glancing down the hall toward Alora's room in the corner, I contemplate wandering down and doing yet another thing I'll regret.

But thankfully, the brothers round the corner, stopping my thoughts dead in their tracks.

"Did you guys lock me out?" I call out to them, grumpy, irritable, annoyed, and now tired as hell.

They both squint at me in confusion nearly at the same time.

Dean shakes his head. "Nope. Sure didn't. Are you positive you aren't just stupid?"

Rolling my eyes, I take a step back and give them space to unlock it. I twirl my keys around my finger. A fob spins around the ring, and I realize my mistake. I tried to use the wrong one.

No wonder it didn't work. It's not programmed for this room.

I follow them inside and take over Dean's queen bed, sprawling out and getting comfortable.

"Make yourself at home." Dean laughs, taking a seat on the small futon across the room.

"I'm taking a nap." I announce, quickly setting an alarm on my phone before collapsing back into the pillows.

"Sweet dreams, babe," Asher says sickeningly sweet, and I can't help the chortle that slips past my lips.

After I work my body until it's as exhausted as my mind, I'm happy to be back at Dean and Asher's dorm, waiting for a few other people to show up for Ollie's birthday.

Ollie is a friend of ours, but we haven't seen him much lately since he got a new girlfriend. But we made sure to steal him away for a night to celebrate him turning twenty.

Some more guys from the Legends should be coming, along with a couple of his friends outside of our team.

"Are you going to mope around all night, or is Malik going to join in on the fun?" Asher asks, trying to get a rise out of me as he starts filling up a cup with Sprite and Crown Royal Regal Apple.

I'm not sure whether I should refrain from drinking tonight so I don't do anything I'll regret or get plastered so much that I forget about everything around me for just a little while.

But that's a dumb thought because I already know how this night is going to go.

Three hours, seven drinks, and who knows how many shots later, it's clear which choice won the battle.

The fogginess in my mind has only been clouding more and more, relaxing the tension in my body.

Lying back on Dean's bed, I close my eyes, the earth beneath me spinning, rocking me back and forth. Such an odd sensation, so *freeing*.

The one downfall of drinking so much is the never-ending bathroom breaks. When I slowly sit up, the room seems to shift with my steps, tilting on its axis as I wander toward the door.

"Malik, where are you going?" someone calls out behind me.

To take a leak, is what I mean to say, but it comes out in one connected breath, "T-take-a-leak."

Walking out of the door, I forcing myself to avoid heading to her, no matter how strong the tug may be.

Walking into the men's restroom, I take a piss and empty my bladder, feeling much better afterward as I head back to the hallway after washing my hands.

Falling through the door, I catch myself on a poor passerby.

With the next breath I take, I realize I know exactly who it is, the one person I was trying to avoid tonight.

But we can never seem to stay apart from one another as hard as we try.

We are the same in the end, two tragedies in the universe, forever tethered by our souls.

"Malik?" she murmurs, my name on her lips sounding like pure ecstasy.

"Yes, baby?" I trail my fingers down her hairline,

caressing her cheek as my other hand slides down her back, stopping above her waist.

Her tongue darts out and swipes her bottom lip. I pull her tighter against me.

Placing her hands on my chest, she pushes away, but I don't want to let her go. She stays in my grasp, looking away from me with upturned eyes.

She groans, her eyes pinching shut. "You're so goddamn confusing."

Running my hand down over her blonde hair, I memorize how soft it is, how far it flows down her back. How pretty it looks, tangled up with the tattoos on my hand as I lift it off her.

"I can't get you out of my head." I swallow hard, wanting that to be an internal thought, one that stays there. "You've taken up permanent residence, and I can't get rid of you."

Her gaze falls to my lips. "Do you think you're the only one who feels that way? The only one fighting their own feelings? I question my sanity every day when the first person I wake up thinking of is you."

My breath stills in my throat, and my mouth dries at her confession. She can't feel that way ... she just can't.

"This isn't good for me. You're not good for me. And I'm certainly not any good for you. There is no world where we would ever belong to one another." I crush her hope with my harsh words.

Her bottom lip trembles, and a dagger slices into my

chest, carving this image into my flesh so I'm forced to relive the anguish I cause her.

"Will you tell me one thing?" She bites down on the inside of her cheek.

I nod, hoping I can give her what she wants so she can walk away from me for good.

She leans forward and lifts her hand, sliding it up my jaw. My body fucking explodes at her touch. She is the sun, and I am Icarus, burning up, ready to fall for her.

"Why do you hate me, Malik?" She nervously bites down on her bottom lip. "What did I do to you?"

Her question oddly sobers me up, enough for me to realize that I've yet again gone too far. I can't tell her. I know her and her father might not be close anymore. But I can't risk her mentioning it and that somehow getting back to my uncle.

Her eyes start to water, and I feel the thorns around my heart constrict tighter But I didn't even notice the hold loosening.

She's dangerous, bringing my guard down without my knowledge.

She's my one weakness in this world.

Leaning forward and standing up taller, she closes some distance between us, and my emotional fortress locks back down.

Her gaze is intense, too passionate, too overwhelming. She's looking at me like she wants me to kiss her, to claim her right here and now with abandon.

"Don't look at me like—" My voice cracks, surprising me as I feel a burn sting the backs of my eyes. Forcing the choking warm sensation as deep as it will go, I look anywhere but at her.

"Like what?" Her voice is almost inaudible.

"Like you're starting to not hate me." Lifting my other hand to her face, I drift closer to her. My forehead slowly rolls against hers as a pain I've never felt shreds my chest apart. My eyes flutter shut. "I can't handle that. Cut me. Hurt me. Do anything you want to me. But don't fall for me, Alora."

A teardrop wets my thumb, and I clench my jaw.

"You wanted to ruin me, Malik?"

I stay silent, the ability to form a single word escaping me.

"You've succeeded." She pulls away from me and wipes the tears away from her eyes. "I'm tired, Malik. Tired of whatever this is." She gestures between us with her hand.

I'm frozen in place as she turns and walks down the hallway, away from me and toward her room.

My voice is a ghost of a whisper, contradicting what I *should* want. "I'm not tired. I need you."

"A piano is a living, breathing thing. It can be a friend and a companion."

Lenny Tristano

chapter fifteen
alora

My skin is buzzing with energy as I finish playing one of the hardest pieces I've ever attempted. To perfection, might I add, and in front of one of the most infamous pianists of the century.

Professor Von London claps his hands as I turn to him, desperate to hear his feedback.

"Brilliant, Alora. Just *brilliant*." His face is lit up with joy as he praises me. "You are a true talent."

My heart leaps out of my chest. "Thank you so much."

That compliment from anyone is special, but from him, it's everything.

Digging into his bag, he pulls out a few sheets of music and hands them to me. "Next week, I want to hear this piece from you. It's a bit different from the others we've worked on so far, but I think you'll have some fun with it."

Reading the music, I can practically envision how my fingers will move along the keys. It's a bouncy tune, upbeat and bright. A definite shift from the melodramatic, emotional songs we've been focusing on.

"I'm sure I will." I smile up at him.

He rises from his seat at the small table in the practice room and grabs his bag. "A pleasure, as always. I look forward to our next session together."

"Me too." I grin, gathering my music from the piano and slipping it back into its sleeve in my binder.

He walks out of the room, leaving Sunny and me, as I bathe in the compliments I'm replaying over and over in my mind.

I can't believe he believes in me. Pride blooms in my chest, warming every bone in my body. It's an honor to work with him.

If I'm lucky, he'll select me for the showcase at the end of the semester. From what I've heard, it's typically for seniors as a farewell showcase, but every now and then, undergrads are selected to perform as well.

My phone rings as Sunny and I walk out of the practice room to head back to our dorm room.

It's my aunt Flora.

"Hello?" I answer.

Her bubbly voice sounds through the speaker. "Hi, Alora! How are you doing? How's school going so far?"

Holding Sunny's leash, I lead her down the steps

outside as I respond, "It's been good. Yeah. Nothing too eventful. Aside from my dad showing up for a donation event—one made just for him, of course ... oh, and him letting me know that he has spies on campus to ensure that I'm behaving."

"No, he didn't ..." She trails off in disbelief and shock.

"Flora, you know I wish I were kidding." I sigh, feeling better, getting some of his bullshit off of my chest.

"Oh my goodness. I'm sorry, honey." She does her best to console me.

"It's okay. I didn't give him any more attention than what was required."

"Good. He doesn't deserve your love, Lore. You're too kindhearted for him." Someone says something in the background of the call, probably one of my other aunts. "I have to go before Fauna burns the entire house down. Call us soon, okay?"

"I will," I answer honestly. "I love you guys so much. Give everyone hugs from me."

"I will pass them along if they'll let me. You know how Fauna gets when she's hungry." She laughs. "We love you too, sweetie."

The call ends, and not a second later, a new one starts ringing on my phone. But this time, it's Phillip.

"Hello?" I answer his call.

"Hey, you. Guess what." His voice is loud yet seemingly far away, like he's yelling toward his phone that's across the room. "Too impatient. I'll be back in Evermore this afternoon. Took longer than planned but I couldn't help myself, I'm on vacay. Please tell me you don't have plans tonight. We have to do something."

Sunny and I walk into the dorm building and get on the elevator. "Not yet I don't. What do you have in mind?"

"Dinner," he answers almost immediately. "I'll pick you up. Does seven work?"

I nod, then realize he can't see me. "Yeah, sounds good! I'm excited you're actually going to be here at school with me. I'll have a friend of my own."

"No more putting up with the peasants." He chuckles.

"Oh, stop it," I lightly scold him. "Dress code?"

He blows a raspberry. "We're going to Mataquin, a fancy place, so wear something a bit dressy."

I've been there before. It's pretty extravagant. It's a good thing I have a few dresses and gowns that my dad insisted I keep with me for emergency events that required my attendance.

"Seven o'clock. Got it." I smile.

"See you then, hot stuff." He ends the call right as Sunny and I reach our room and slip inside.

I guess I'd better figure out what the hell I'm going to wear. Maybe something that would drive Malik insane if he saw me in it.

I wonder how he'd react, knowing I'm going out to dinner with a guy tonight.

Would he be jealous? Would he even care?

My worries and questions fade to the back of my mind as I spend the next two hours playing on my piano and practicing this new piece until I run out of procrastination time and I have to start getting ready.

Opting for a new gown that I haven't had a chance to wear, I pull it from my closet and hang it on the back of my door while I quickly pop some curls into my hair and apply some glowy, soft makeup on my face.

After finalizing my look with pink lip liner and gloss, I step into the gown and zip the zipper on the back.

The feat of getting ready alone has already fatigued me, one of the more understated symptoms of POTS.

It's the little things that really weigh me down. Aside from the episode at Blair and Griffin's, I haven't fainted in almost a year. But the shortness of breath and never-ending spurts of nausea, fatigue, and brain fog are the soldiers on the front lines, trying to bring me down.

Taking a moment to calm my breathing and heart rate, I lie in bed, resting my feet up on a pillow to keep the blood flow even and smooth. Sunny jumps up in bed next to me, lies down, and rests her head on my stomach.

I brush her soft hair back on her head, and the cute aggression threatens to take me over.

"You are just the prettiest girl, Sunny Bun."

Her big eyes look up at me, and my heart melts.

Knowing that we're only going to dinner, I'm not going to bother calling Sunny's sitter to come over.

She'll be okay for a couple of hours. Besides, she likes her alone time sometimes.

Drinking a few sips from my water bottle, I slowly sit up, taking my time and listening to my body as I rise to my feet. Feeling steady and okay, I grab my purse at the same time that my phone rings. It's Phillip.

"Hello?" I answer.

"Hey, I'm downstairs. I would greet you at your door, but the building apparently has security."

Grabbing my keys, I chuckle. "Yeah, no worries. I'm on my way down."

"All right. See you in a second." He ends the call.

Looking back at sweet Sunny, I blow her a kiss before stepping into the hallway.

My head swivels as I look for any familiar, cute boys. But the hallway's empty. Making my way into the elevator, I'm shocked as a hint of sadness slithers into my chest, making my heart ache from not seeing Malik.

But what did I expect? For him to just be waiting outside of my room twenty-four/seven?

No hockey players are spotted when I step off the elevator and head outside. The chilly air flutters my dress, and I hold it down as I spot Phillip and his Rolls-Royce waiting along the curb for me.

All done up in a suit and tie, he leans back against his car. If I were any other girl and we had any other relationship, I might swoon. But it's just Phillip, and I'm just Alora.

We already tried testing that dynamic out years ago,

and we quickly learned we are *definitely not* romantically compatible.

His face lights up when he sees me. "Well, look at *you*." His voice is musical, humming through the air with whimsy. "You look gorgeous, Lore."

My heels click on the pavement as a smile stretches across my face. "So do you. And you're *so* tan."

"Well, I did just spend the last like week in the Bahamas so …" He trails off as his gaze darts to my right.

I follow his stare, and my stomach flips.

Asher, Dean, Elias, and Malik are walking side by side. An intimidating image—four ripped, over six-feet-tall guys walking toward me. I swallow any lingering fear.

Asher, of course, is the first one to speak. "Alora, my God, you look hot!"

But I'm not looking at him. My eyes are glued to the dark-haired man staring at me so intensely that I think I might catch on fire.

He wets his lips as the group approaches, not deviating his gaze for a second.

My breathing shallows, and I force myself to look over at Asher. "Thank you."

"You are …" Asher asks Phillip, his tone indiscernible.

"Phillip Stephens." He sticks out his hand, polite, as always.

Asher shakes it. "And what might your intentions be with our Alora tonight?"

My gaze finds Malik again, but he's no longer looking at me. Those breathtaking purple orbs are stabbing into Phillip like daggers.

"Friends of yours?" Phillip glances over at me with a smirk on his lips, and I nod. "Alora and I go way back. We've known each other since we were kids. We're going to grab some food and catch up."

"I love food." Malik smiles, but there's no friendliness in his pearly, sharp grin. "What do you guys think? I, for one, could eat."

I can practically see the steam rolling off of him in waves. I wonder how far I can push this and get under his skin before he snaps. It's only fair after all …

Closing the distance between Phillip and me, I hook my arm in his. "We only have a reservation for two."

Malik's nostrils flare, and his jaw tics. "Is that so?"

I nod firmly. "Yes. Maybe you guys can join next time."

He steps toward me. "Next time, huh?" Licking his lips like a predator about to pounce, he takes another step toward me without blinking. "Next time, make sure to add another seat to your reservation. I'd love to come."

Phillip interjects, "Of course. The more, the merrier, right?"

Malik's gaze flashes his way in a tight squint, and a breathy chuckle chills the air. "*Right.*"

Asher and Dean step up to Malik's side.

"Well, we'd better let you guys get going before you're late," Asher says, lightly patting Malik's chest.

Malik works his jaw before his lips part. But he doesn't say anything.

Instead, he takes off, storming toward the dorm hall with the rest of the guys on his heels.

"Well, he seems … *intense*," Phillip mutters, opening the passenger door for me.

Sliding into the seat, I buckle myself in. "You have no idea."

The ride to the restaurant is anything but silent. Phillip starts hounding me with questions. But the moment I mention who the grumpy guy really is, he starts to understand. At least slightly.

"But you hate him," he says, his words hanging in the air as we pull up into the valet line.

I sigh. "Yes, and no …"

"Oh God," he groans. "You're going to have to start from the beginning, Lore. Fill me in."

Which is exactly what I do.

Phillip's always been a rock. Confident, strong, and sure. He knows exactly what life will look like for him, and so far, he hasn't been wrong.

Aside from his girlfriend cheating on him last month and moving in with her new boyfriend days later.

Cheating on Phillip is just gross.

I assure him that he'll have no problem finding someone new, but he wants to take a break from dating and just focus on his schoolwork for a while. If only I could do the same.

Instead of classes and studies, my mind lingers on Malik. I'm not even sure when that really began, but I know that everything has changed between us. We can't go back to just hating each other. We're forced to figure out where we go now. I think I know what I want, but it depends on him. I won't play his games anymore. I'm tired of them.

But if playing them gets me one step closer to breaking down his walls, I might be willing to play one or two. Even if it means I'm the dumbest, most naive girl in the world who's assisting in breaking her own heart.

After we devour delicious pasta, Phillip takes me back to my dorm and makes sure I get inside the building safely before pulling away.

I'm exhausted and so excited to kick my heels off, climb into bed, and cuddle with Sunny.

Unlocking the door, I step inside, flicking my heels to the ground and hanging my purse on the hook behind my door.

Sunny's paws hit the ground, and she trots over to me.

"Hi, baby. How was your night?"

When I bend down, she gives me a little kiss on my chin while I pet her head.

Standing up and rounding the corner, I slam to a halt, my stomach jumping into my throat.

"What the hell are you doing in here?" My heart starts doing flips in my chest while butterflies take flight in my stomach. "How did you even get in here?"

Malik smirks, lying in my bed with absolute ease, his ankles crossed and arm stretched out behind his head.

My body heats from the intensity in his stare, and I suddenly feel like a bug flying headfirst into a trap, confusing the tingly warmth of electricity with the sun.

His voice is raw and sharp. "How was your *date*?"

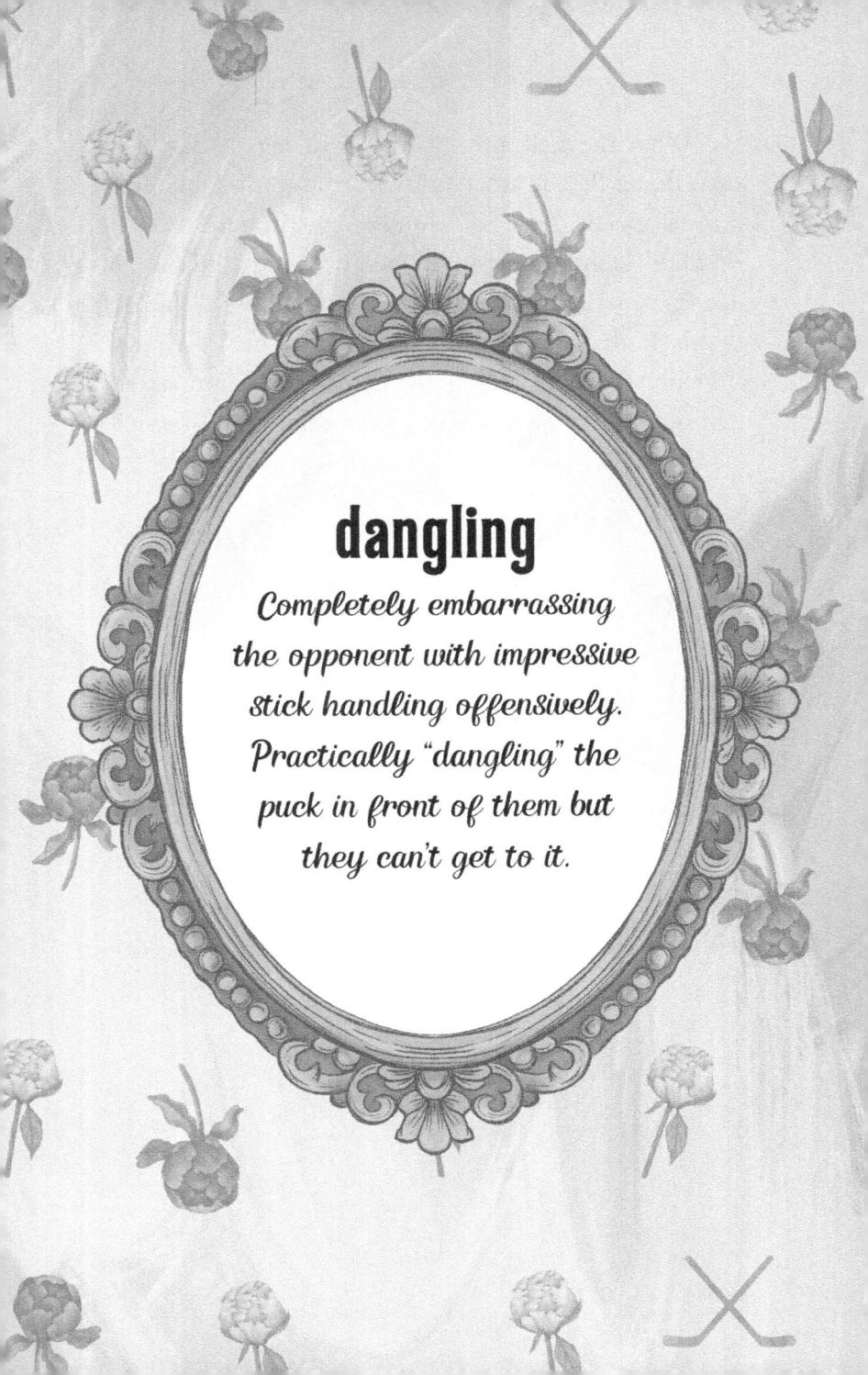

dangling

Completely embarrassing the opponent with impressive stick handling offensively. Practically "dangling" the puck in front of them but they can't get to it.

chapter sixteen
malik

I told myself not to come here, to leave her alone. Let her find happiness with that guy.

But I couldn't, not when she already belonged to me.

"My date?" Alora's lips show the slightest hint of amusement. "It wasn't a date."

Petting Sunny once more, who trotted back over to me after greeting Alora, I swing my legs off the edge of the bed and sit forward, resting my elbows on my knees as my eyes eat her alive, traveling from the bottom of the slit in her dress to the top of her thigh, up and over every inch of her until I land on her parted lips and her curious stare.

"*That* dress, and you want to say it wasn't a date."

She crosses her arms, only making it harder for me

to stay seated in her bed. "Why do you care? You don't want me anyway."

"Don't push it, Alora. You have no *idea* what I want." My words are quick and thick with emotion as my eyes slam shut.

"You're right. Because you don't know how to open your mouth and tell me," she snaps. "So, how the hell would I?"

I shouldn't find her feisty, fiery side so goddamn hot, but my throbbing dick says otherwise.

She takes a step toward me. "Now, are you going to tell me how the hell you got in my room?"

The corner of my lips tips up into a smile. "I have a key, silly."

Her lips part, and her eyes widen. "Are you serious?"

Nodding to the desk where I left the fob, I prove it. "Very."

Her face contorts with a thousand emotions as she tries to comprehend how I came to possess it.

I'll save her the effort of a question. "It was hanging on the back of your door the first night I ran in here."

Her head whips back to me. "You've had it since *then*?"

"Yeah, but don't worry. This is the first time I've used it. I mean, you had it hanging in plain sight. Anyone could have taken it."

"Nope, not really, Malik. Unless they broke into my room first, you psycho."

I've been called worse, especially by her.

Now that we got that out of the way, let's get to the important part.

"I answered your question. Now you have to answer mine. How was your not-date *date*?"

She rolls her eyes and points to the door. "Get out of my room."

When I stand up to my full height, she cranes her neck to look up at me, her confidence never wavering.

"Make me, Bug."

Her jaw clenches. "I hate you."

Striking fast and taking her by surprise, I wrap my hand around the side of her neck and push her back toward the wall, softening the landing with my other hand on the back of her head.

Her breathing quickens as her wide eyes find mine. "What are you doing?"

"Tell me how much you hate me when I bury my face between your legs." My gaze travels down her body. "You look so fucking good in this dress." My eyes fall to the length of her neck, adorned with my new favorite necklace … my hand. "Too good."

She swallows hard. "You're in my personal space."

"Oh, really?" I chuckle, dropping my head even closer to hers.

She arches her back to look up, pressing her tits closer to me, only weakening my resolve even more.

She nods hesitantly.

I thread my fingers into her hair and tug gently.

"Baby, you aren't allowed personal space when it comes to me. It's mine just as much as it is yours."

She sucks in a sharp breath, and her pupils dilate, the blues of her eyes darkening with desire. I know she wants this as much as I do. But my innocent little Bug isn't ready to admit that yet. I'll help her get there.

"Was your date everything you wanted?" I tease, trailing my hand that was wrapped around her throat down to the thin strap of the dress, inching it off of her shoulder. "Did he touch you? Hmm?" My voice deepens. "Did he kiss you?"

Ever so slightly she shakes her head, her body responding to my touch greedily.

I should leave. I *need* to leave. To stop whatever's happening right now and run to the opposite end of campus.

I was supposed to be the one to corrupt her, but she's already ruined me.

"Malik." She whispers my name, and something deep inside of me throws all caution to the wind.

I need her more than I care about any of the consequences. She's mine. She always has been.

"Fuck it," I whimper and crash my lips to hers, breathing in her essence like the freshest breath of air.

Stilling for a second, she doesn't kiss me back.

Pulling away, I wonder if perhaps I read her wrong. *I didn't.*

Her hands thrust into my hair, and she yanks my

head back to her, her pillowy lips claiming mine with their own ferocity.

We're wild, untamed, two storms colliding for the first time.

"You're fucking mine," I growl into her parted lips. "Your mouth is mine, Bug." I kiss her again, marking my claim.

Easing my tongue through the seam of her lips, I take more of her, as much as she's willing to give. She lets me in, and I devour her, tasting her with abandon.

Threading my fingers further into her hair, I pull her head back more, giving me the perfect angle to kiss her senseless.

My other hand works down the back of her dress, quickly finding the tiny zipper and tugging it down. She pulls back and looks up at me with wide eyes.

"I want to see you," I mutter, tugging at the zipper more. "Is this okay?" She nods, but I want to hear her pretty voice tell me. "Say it, baby."

"Take it off of me," she murmurs, her voice heavy and sultry.

Easing the dress further down her back, I hook my fingers under the strap still on her shoulder and slide it off.

The dress cascades down her full tits, leaving them bare and begging for my touch. The red silk slides down her curves, like water flowing down a waterfall, and I'm suddenly parched.

My mouth waters at the sight before me. She's

nearly naked, the only barrier between my eyes and her body are the black panties on her hips. I study every inch of her, committing it so intently to memory. Every freckle, line, valley, and curve of her perfect body. If this is the only time I get to touch her, I'm going to remember it for the rest of my life.

Her cheeks flush, and her gaze falls to the floor. Oh, that won't do. She's not doubting herself in front of me.

Lifting her chin, I force her to look at me. "Don't shy away from me now. You're perfect, Alora."

The softest smile lifts her lips, and I kiss her, our lips forming together as if they were made to do just this.

A shiver runs through her. "Malik, I thought you hated me."

Pulling away, I slide my fingertips up and down her sides. "And who says I don't?"

She giggles. "Well, you have a hell of a way of expressing it. Is this what you do to guys on the ice when they make an enemy of you? Tease them until they surrender?"

God, this woman.

"Are you going to surrender? Hmm? Or do I need to tease you a bit more?"

Her laughter stalls as she sucks in a quick breath.

Leaning down, I press my lips to her jaw, my tongue darting out and swiping the curve of it before continuing lower. I trail my kisses down her neck and along her collarbone.

Dropping down onto one knee, I hook my arm

around her waist, pulling her stomach against my chest. She melts into my grasp.

I take a mental screenshot as I look up at her, desperate to remember how angelic she looks, standing above me as I drag her down with my sin.

Lifting my free hand, I cup her breast and straighten my spine. "Fuck, these are so perfect."

I can't wait any longer.

I suck her nipple into my mouth, grunting as I dig my fingers into her back, needing her to be closer. Needing all of her.

Flicking my tongue back and forth across the hardened peak, I wrap my mouth around it and tug.

She gasps, "Oh my God."

Giving the other nipple the attention it deserves, I switch, devouring that one the very same. With every lick and caress, her hips start to roll into me, her body coming to life from my touch.

Fucking hell, I need to taste her sweet pussy on my tongue.

Trailing my kiss down her stomach, I work my way to her panties. Her back falls against the wall, and I wrap my hands around the tops of her thick thighs, pinning her in place.

Taking the black lace between my teeth, I look up at her lust-blown eyes and ease them down.

Her panties get caught on the roundness of her hips, and I help them along with my fingers, pulling them all the way down until they're pooled at her feet.

She's completely exposed, vulnerable, and raw, laid out for me like my new favorite snack.

Rubbing my hand back up her leg, I push her thighs apart, opening that pretty pussy for my eyes to devour.

"Umm ..." She trails off, and my gaze snaps up at her.

"What's wrong?" I freeze in place, waiting for her answer.

She looks away from me, her posture shrinking. "No one's ever ... done that before."

My brows pinch. "You've never let anyone's mouth between your legs before?"

She bites down on her bottom lip and shakes her head.

God, I'm going to make this her new favorite thing.

"Let me show just how good it can feel. How good *I* can make you feel." I inch closer to her center.

Grabbing her ankle, I lift it up and place it on my bent knee, opening her up to me. Leaning forward, I breathe her in, my cock throbbing in response.

Pressing my lips against the inside of her thigh, I nibble at her skin, eliciting quick breaths and soft whimpers from her.

We haven't even begun.

Glancing up at her once more, I hold her stare as I run my tongue up her center, her wetness coating my tongue.

Growling, I do it again. "So fucking sweet."

Her head tilts back as my tongue works her entrance, plunging inside with purpose.

I want to get lost in her, bury myself so deep inside of her that she forgets what it feels like without me.

"Malik …" She moans my name, and I grip her tighter, working her clit with fast sucks. "Holy *shit.*"

That's it, baby. Fall apart on my tongue.

She starts writhing in my grasp, her hips rolling back and forth as I push her closer to the edge. My dick is so hard that I think it might bust through my pants.

I need her like I've never needed someone, and that's fucking terrifying, chilling me to the bone.

Her mouth forms a perfect O as she moans on an inhale, seconds from coming for me for the first time.

Rubbing my mouth against her pussy, I quicken my assault, feeling the exact moment her body falls into ecstasy.

"Malik," she cries out, her body convulsing as she comes undone.

But I don't stop. I devour her through her orgasm, feasting on every drop, moan, and whimper she's willing to give me. I asked her to surrender to me, but I'm the one on my knees in front of her, begging for more.

As she starts to come down from her high, she leans forward, resting her hands on my shoulders. "I think I need to, umm … sit down."

Oh my God, I didn't even think about how this would affect her. *Shit.*

Acting instantly, I drop to the floor and open my

legs, lifting my arms to help ease her down. "I've got you. Come here."

She looks at me hesitantly and shyly, as if a moment ago I wasn't tongue deep inside of her. Gradually, she uses my arms to help herself down to the ground, positioning herself between my legs.

Slowly, I turn her around so her back is to me. I ease her into my chest, wrapping my arms lightly around her. She leans back into me willingly, settling into my embrace.

"How can I help?" I ask, wanting to make this easier for her.

From the research I've done so far, I know that sitting down, slowing the heart rate, and elevating the legs are the best things to ease the symptoms. And staying hydrated.

"Just give me a second. I'll be okay," she murmurs, taking slow, long breaths. "I'm sorry. It kind of killed the mood …" She trails off, and my heart fucking sinks.

Leaning around the side of her head, I tip her chin up to look at me with my left hand, her blue eyes wide and vulnerable. "Never *ever* apologize to me again. Especially when it comes to *this*."

She stares at me deeply, her eyes penetrating my goddamn soul.

"I'm serious, Alora. I never want to hear you say you're sorry for that. Do you understand?" I brush her hair away from her cheek.

She nods. "Yeah. I just didn't want to interrupt you."

"Why?" I wince, guilt following the sharp pang, knowing her mistrust comes from my actions in the past.

She purses her lips to the side, her cheeks reddening before answering, "I was scared you'd stop, and I *really* didn't want that."

With my right hand, I cup her breast, and my left hand tightens its grip on her jaw. My voice is clear and sharp. "These are mine." I shift my hand down her stomach, sliding my fingers between her legs and through her wetness. "This is *mine*."

Her legs part, resting against mine, and my fingers start to circle that sweet bundle of nerves. But I pause for a second, waiting for her permission to continue. I don't want to push her too fast if she's still feeling lightheaded.

She nods, wetting her lips.

My thumb hooks beneath her jaw as my fingers slide to her throat, pulling her tighter against me as my other fingers continue their torment on her pussy.

"No one touches you but me, Alora," I growl, leaning down and kissing her ferociously. "No dates. No other guys."

Her body starts tightening, her back arching hard.

"Tell me you won't let anyone else discover how delicious you taste, how dreamy you feel. Tell me, Bug. Tell me you belong to me."

Her head falls back, her cheek crashing to my chest. "Please don't stop."

I chuckle darkly. "So greedy for another one already?" Using my thumb, I open her parted lips further, lining her mouth up below mine before spitting down between her parted lips.

Her eyes widen, but her pupils darken, showing me just how much she loves being under my control.

"Surrender to me, baby. Tell me who owns you."

She licks her bottom lip, her whimpers and soft moans creating the most beautiful music in the room. "Y-you do, Malik."

Slowing my hand just slightly, I watch frustration take over her face.

"I—what?" Malik prompts me to say the full line.

I give her the pace she wants, and she gasps, her body convulsing from the shock waves.

"Say it, or I'll stop right now," I threaten.

She gives in. "You own me. You own me. You own me." Her confession and my tantalizing fingers make her come once more, and satisfaction blooms through my body. "Oh fuck! Malik, oh my fucking God!"

She writhes between my legs and I don't think she's ever looked more beautiful than she does right now— her hair messy, lips red, and skin flushed from what I did to her.

"What a good fucking girl, Alora." Lifting my fingers from her, I bring them to my lips as she watches. "Look at the pretty mess you made."

Sucking my fingers into my mouth, I clean them, savoring the taste of her on my tongue. I never want it to leave.

Sudden embarrassment widens her eyes. But there's no going back from this, so she'll have to get over it. Because I'm fucking addicted to her now.

"That was …" She trails off, biting down on her bottom lip. She spins in place, tucking her knees to her chest and facing me.

If there's any doubt in her mind—which I'm sure there is, given our past—I want to wipe it away. "I meant what I said. You're mine. You've always been mine, Alora. And I'm never letting you go."

"What does that mean?" Her eyes are clear as day, the walls that are usually there long gone.

"It means that I'm done trying to stay away from you. I *can't*." I pause, and she waits patiently. "It's not just confusing for you, *trust me*. But I'm done pretending like I don't want you. Because I do, more than I want to fucking live."

The air is electric, thick with the shift that just transpired, the permanent change between us.

Micah's name starts to form in my mind, and shock smacks me in the face at the idea that I even want to tell her about him.

There's still a part of me that's unsure about her and who she really is, given her family. Another part of me is terrified that she might already know the truth, and that … that would *destroy* me.

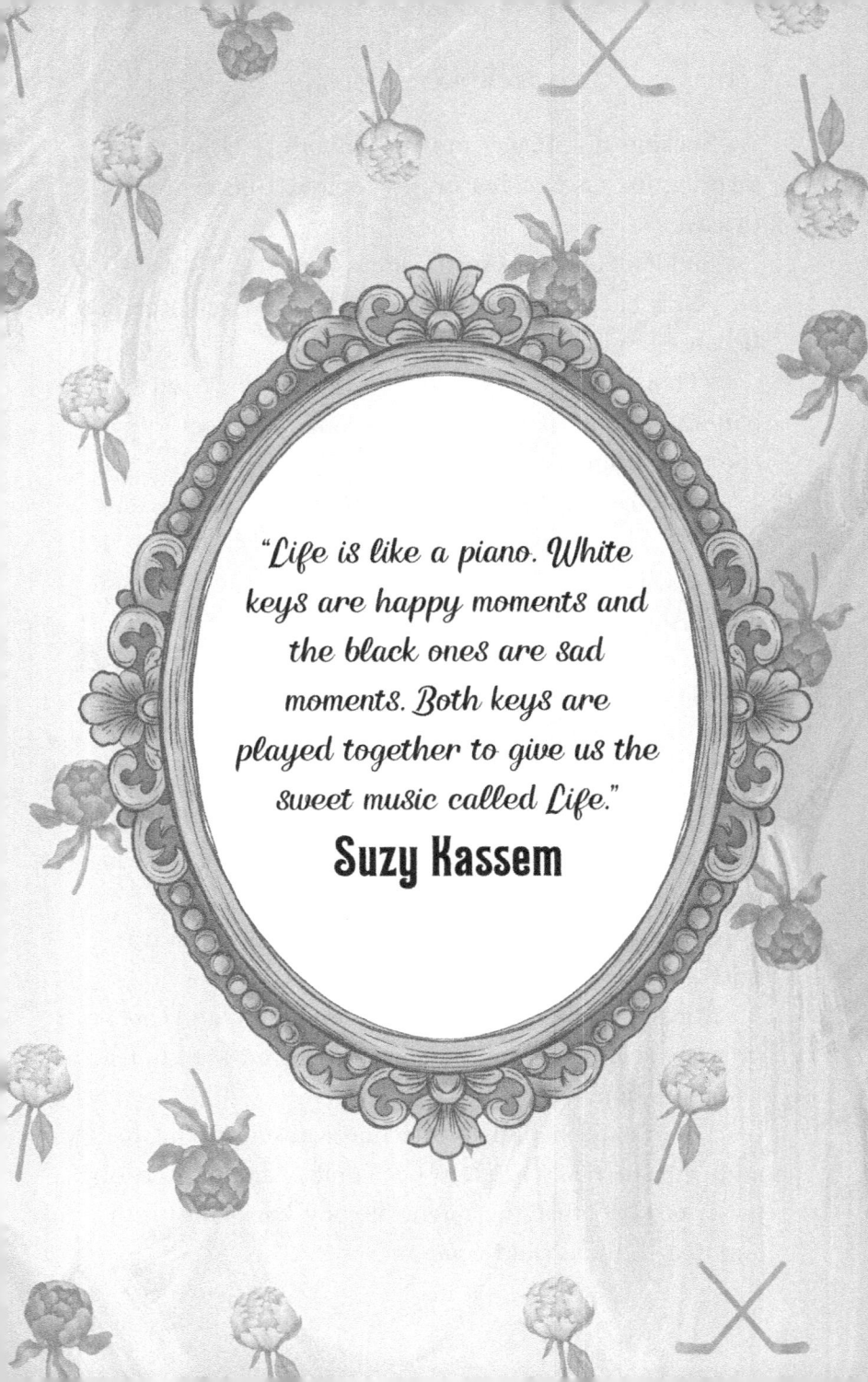

"Life is like a piano. White keys are happy moments and the black ones are sad moments. Both keys are played together to give us the sweet music called Life."

Suzy Kassem

chapter seventeen
alora

Phillip texted me this morning and let me know that he had the same World History class as me. Which will be very interesting, given that I also have it with Malik; after last night, I have a feeling that he will be very needy for my attention.

Who knows? Maybe this is all one really strange prank, and I'm just the butt of a joke. But the look in his eyes and the passion in his touch in my dorm room tell me that isn't the case. He wanted that as badly as I did.

As usual, I arrive at Ivy Hall early to get settled into my seat with Sunny before anyone else shows up. But as I turn into the room, I see that someone else beat me.

I hate the way my heart skips a beat when my eyes land on Malik, sitting in his seat with a smug smirk on his lips. His tongue darts out, wetting his bottom lip, and an image of him on his knees before me flashes in my mind. The same devilish gleam in his eyes right now as when he licked me like a lollipop in my room.

My body warms instantly as I enter the room and walk over to my desk, waiting to see if he says anything.

Immediately, he leans forward in his seat. "Good morning, Bug. Sleep okay?"

Sunny settles into her spot next to my desk.

"Hi. Umm ... yeah, I slept well. I was *exhausted*."

His eyebrows twitch, and he bites down on his lip. "Really? Well, I know how important sleep is to you. I was just trying to help."

I giggle. "So selfless of you."

He shrugs. "I know."

My phone buzzes in my pocket. I pull it out, finding a text from Phillip.

> Phillip: I know I'm the worst, okay? But I'm running so far behind this morning. Meet up after class? I'll bring some coffee.

I laugh, knowing I shouldn't be surprised by his tardiness. He's always run on his own clock. I type a quick response.

> I'll take notes for you.

> Phillip: You're a lifesaver. I owe you.

> Yeah, you owe me a coffee, LOL.

Sliding my phone back in my pocket, I look back up at Malik, finding his stare burning into me.

"I told you there's no going back after last night. My name might as well be tattooed on your skin and yours on mine."

My lips part, and butterflies take flight in my stomach. I know he's a man of his word, but I wasn't fully prepared for what being Malik's would entail.

Stepping toward my desk, I lean over the small railing dividing our rows. "Who said I wanted to go back?"

"That flirty smile on your lips when you were texting." He lifts his hand and cracks his knuckles.

This shouldn't turn me on … right? But there is something so incredibly hot about seeing him bent out of shape over a text.

"You know you're a little possessive, right?" I bite down on my bottom lip and grin, watching his lips twitch upward.

Reaching forward, he wraps his fingers around my throat and squeezes just the *right* amount. "Oh, baby, you have no idea."

"Jesus, Malik. I know you don't like her, but there's no need to choke her out in class." Asher bursts out laughing as he walks in the room.

"Careful, Ash. You'll be next." Malik laughs.

Malik releases me, although I could have stepped away anytime I wished. Embarrassment floods my cheeks, and I take my seat next to Sunny.

Sunny looks up at me, and I wonder what she thinks of Malik. Clearly, she likes him enough to have snuggled in my bed with him last night while I was at dinner.

Images keep playing in my mind, flashing clear as day as I remember what happened. I think he might be right though; no one else could make me feel the way he does. As alive, as on fire, as euphoric.

Part of me wonders if this is only about sex to him, but I find it hard to believe. Especially after the way he held me once I relaxed between his legs, wrapped in his embrace. I could feel it like a tangible being—the connection between us. The kind that doesn't just happen after one encounter, but one that has been building for years and years, manifesting and warping into the beast it is now.

"Alora?" Malik calls out my name.

Hearing it tears me from my thoughts, and I turn to find Malik, Asher, and now Dean all staring at me.

"You all right?"

I nod. "Yeah. Sorry. I think I zoned out. What's up?"

Malik's eyes and smirk tell me he knows exactly what I was thinking about.

Malik interrupts Asher as he opens his mouth. "Nothing. He's just being a little fuck."

Asher glares at him but remains silent.

Ooookay.

The rest of the class starts filling up, and the next

hour flies by as I take notes like my life depends on it. I know that my family's money and name could buy my degree. But I want to earn it the right way.

After I finish jotting down notes from the professor's last PowerPoint slide, I pack my things up.

Slipping my backpack over my shoulders, I lift Sunny's leash, and she stands up, stretching her legs. Blair walks out with Griffin and Lumi, giving me a little wave as they whisper to each other, clearly deep in conversation. I'll catch up with her later.

I'm the last one in the room to leave. We head outside into the sunny day to make our way to Moor Hall for piano practice.

The second I step off of the stairs, I feel his presence in front of me before I even look up. Like a part of ourselves exists in one another, an extension of our own bodies.

I'm scared of how much I'm drawn to him. It's like the moment I stopped fighting it, it somehow got ten times more intense.

"Where are you heading next?" Malik asks, and his friends look our way, shocked that we are politely speaking to one another instead of bickering.

Blair looks at me with a sassy smirk and a knowing gleam.

"Alora!"

I hear Phillip's voice and watch Malik's jaw tic.

Spinning around, I see Phillip walking toward me with two cups of coffee in his hands.

As Phillip closes in on me, Malik wraps his arms around my shoulders, tugging me snug against him.

God, he's ridiculous.

Phillip chuckles at Malik's poor attempt at marking his territory. I'm surprised he hasn't tried peeing on me yet to warn other men off.

"For you." Phillip smiles, stretching his hand out toward me.

As I start to take the cup from Phillip, Malik tugs at my arm, and I lose my grip. The cup slips through my fingers and falls to the ground, splashing and spilling everywhere.

I gasp and jump back as the coffee goes flying, barely able to move at all since there's a human wall behind me.

Spinning in his arms, I glare up at him. "*Malik.*"

He holds his stare on Phillip for a moment longer before dropping it to me, his eyes softening immediately. "Yes, baby?"

"You're a brat. You know that?" I cross my arms over my chest.

I can't tell if I'm more pissed off at him for spilling a good cup of coffee, disappointed that he can't behave for two seconds, or turned on that the thought of a man giving me coffee threatens him.

If he wants to fetch my coffee for me, he can, all day long. But now, I'm coffeeless and sad.

Asher and Dean laugh at him. I'm sure they'll give

him shit later, too, for suddenly being Mr. Protective instead of Mr. Bully.

Glancing up at Phillip, I find humor dancing in his eyes and a smirk on his lips. I mouth the words, *I'm sorry.*

He chuckles. "It's okay. Malik, I have no interest in Alora romantically. So, next time, try not to ruin her coffee just to make a point."

Malik stays quiet behind me.

The giant clock tower at the center of the quad chimes, and I look to see that I'm now also *late.*

Pulling away from him, I roll my eyes. "Be *nice.* I'm late for practice. I'll see you later."

When I turn away from him, he strikes, catching my jaw in his hand and pulling me back to him.

His lips are on mine in a heartbeat, his other hand threading into my hair as he kisses me like it's the last chance he'll ever get.

Everything around us fades away as I greedily take from him. If he wants to claim me in front of everyone, then he can do it.

I'm breathless and dazed when his lips part from mine. His eyes are darker than normal, his eyelids heavy, and his breathing is shallow.

"I'll find you later," he murmurs.

Asher and Dean walk over to us.

Dean takes a jab first. "Malik, we leave you alone for one night, and you go and get all soft on us?"

He scoffs. "You think I'm soft?" He turns to look at them. "Want to find out how wrong you are?"

They laugh and put their hands up playfully, waving the white flag.

"Phillip's walking me to my practice room."

Malik's head whips my way.

"And you are going to deal with it because he's one of my best friends. And that's not going to change."

His eyes dance between mine, a storm brewing inside. So much has changed since I've been here at HEAU, but drastically so in the last twenty-four hours.

"Okay." The word is painful for him to say, but he lets Phillip and me walk away without another word.

He might not be trying to make me cry right now, but that doesn't mean that everything is clear as day. My mind is still clouded and not just because of my POTS.

I can still feel it though—the heaviness between us, like there's a wall I still can't climb or see through.

Getting caught up in the moment is one thing, but there's still so many unanswered questions. They just escaped my mind when he had his tongue between my legs.

But I need answers, sooner than later.

Sunny prances alongside Phillip and me as we head toward Moor Hall and I wave behind me at the group.

I'm showing Phillip where his afternoon class will be on the way before I head to the practice room that I have reserved for two hours. I already looked up which building and room his class is in.

"So, uhh, how was last night? The last time I saw you with Malik it was very cordial and now he's practically trying to piss on you to claim you." Phillip chuckles, putting no effort in hiding the amusement in his voice.

I glare at him. "Malik and I talked … a little."

He chuckles. "Yeah, I bet you guys used your mouths a lot to communicate with one another."

"Shut up." I laugh, which morphs into a sigh as I remember that this isn't a dream. That Malik really just kissed me in front of everyone without shame. "Do you think I'm stupid? Or naive for trusting him?"

He takes a moment to think, and I don't blame him. I don't know how I would react to him if the roles were reversed.

Walking down the cobblestone path, he looks over at me. "I've known you almost my whole life, and I've admired you for a lot of reasons. One of them being your ability to read people clearly, no matter who they pretend to be. You have good instincts, and if they're telling you to take a chance with him, then I trust your judgment." He rubs the back of his neck. "I can't lie and say that I'm not a bit worried. I mean, he is still the same Malik who tormented you in high school. Those moments are just as real as these."

"I know," I murmur, biting down on my lip as I contemplate his words. "I mean, I'm obviously a bit hesitant. I would be dumb not to be. I wish you could have seen him last night though."

"No, thanks. I do not want to see those parts of him." He winces, and both of us laugh.

Shoving his shoulder, I continue, "Not like *that*. But the way he was treating me when my POTS started acting up. He helped me regulate and didn't make me feel bad in the slightest for interrupting the moment. He was so … *genuine*."

He can hear it in the silence, just like I can—the inevitable *but*.

"But I know that the other side of him is still there. What happens when he wakes up and realizes that his hatred outweighs whatever he's feeling now? Will it go back to the way it was? Because I can't handle that." I sigh. "I know he's keeping secrets from me. I just don't know what they are yet."

Phillip stops me. "Just take it day by day. Don't start making wedding plans or shopping for rings. Don't rush into anything too serious until you can fully trust him," he cautions me.

"You're right," I murmur.

But it's too late. I'm already falling, plummeting really, and I guess we'll find out eventually if he'll be there to catch me before I hit the ground.

"Go through here, and about halfway down the hallway, the door will be on your right," I instruct him, seeing the structural layout clear in my mind.

I already memorized campus like the back of my hand, including all the buildings. I like to know things to avoid ever getting lost. What can I say? I'm an over-preparer.

"Thanks, Lore. I'll catch you later, okay?" He winks at me as he backpedals toward the building, spinning around just in time to climb up the stairs.

My senses tune in to everything around me as I'm left alone.

The birds chirping, the sound of a water fountain flowing and splashing to my right, the smell of fresh flowers in beds.

This place really is incredible. I need to remind myself to slow down and smell the roses sometimes … literally.

I make the quick walk over to the music department, and I seal Sunny and me inside of the practice room, intent on not leaving until I've perfected the new assigned piece from Von London.

Time melts away as I play, and by my tenth time through the music, I can perform parts without the glancing at the sheet music, my fingers following the patterns of the notes while my eyes memorize the music.

"You're incredible."

Malik's voice startles me, and I jump at the sound, turning to find him standing in the doorway.

God, I was so locked into the music that I didn't even hear him open the door.

"What are you doing here?" I ask, calming myself back down. "Also, you really shouldn't try to scare me.

It's not exactly good for my heart," I tell him, slightly kidding, slightly serious.

His eyes widen and soften. "Shit, I'm sorry. Are you okay?"

I nod and pat the piano bench next to me. "I'm fine. I was mostly giving you shit."

He walks into the room, the door shutting behind him. Walking around the side of the piano, he sits down on the bench.

"Would you play something for me?" He glances over, looking down at me with a gleam of vulnerability.

Oh God, I don't know if I'm ready to open this part of my life to him. It's my most sacred piece.

"Please?" Reaching out, he outlines my cheek and jaw with his caress.

Nodding slowly, I set my fingers back on the keys.

Quickly racking my brain for what to play, I settle on a song that feels like a representation of our relationship, whatever that may be.

Striking the minor chords, I play from recollection, holding his stare as my fingers dance across the keys.

This was one of the first pieces I ever wrote. I used to love how haunted it started off, mixed with soft major notes. It's a war between light and dark.

I actually wrote it so the pianist selected the ending. It can either end with one side winning over the other or the two coming together in a perfect balance.

As the music fills the room, he watches me in complete awe and admiration. Our breathing begins to sync, his breaths quickening with mine as the music picks up.

It's getting to the point where I need to deviate and choose a path to end the song. Maybe just for today, I'll let the haunted notes win. Besides, darkness doesn't always mean bad. It could have simply gone without light for so long that it forgot what it felt like.

My eyes drift close as I play the last part of the piece. Striking the final note, I open my eyes. Malik's gaze has darkened, much like the music.

"You are fucking perfect, Alora." His voice is breathless as he cups my face and claims my lips with his.

He deepens it, parting my mouth with his tongue. A soft moan vibrates from me to him, and he groans in response.

A knock on the door tears us apart, and I once again find myself jumping in shock. Either I'm way too on edge or everyone else is being far too sneaky.

Rupert Von London smiles through the window and opens the door. "Alora, there you are."

Malik stiffens beside me. You'd think some fifty-year-old man wouldn't pose a threat in his mind, but I'm not too surprised. It is Malik.

Professor Von London looks over at Malik, and his gaze falls to his arms, decorated in countless black-and-white tattoos. He grimaces slightly, so insignificant that I'm not sure Malik even notices.

When he glances back at me, his smile resumes. "I

am proud to officially extend an invitation to HEAU's annual showcase." Striding over to the back of the piano, he hands me a wax-sealed envelope.

Jumping to my feet far too fast, I take a deep breath and accept the invite. "Thank you so much. I am so honored to have been chosen."

He beams at me. "I look forward to hearing your performance." He pauses, looking Malik's way with an indiscernible look in his eyes. "I'll leave you two to it."

Turning around, he strolls out of the room.

Looking down at Malik, I find him staring at the door with a snarl on his lips.

"I don't like that guy."

I roll my eyes. "You don't like any guy who talks to me."

That earns his attention, and he shifts back to me. His hands fly to my waist, and he pulls me down onto his lap.

Planting a kiss on my temple, he shrugs. "I don't like people thinking they can take you from me."

"Afraid I won't stop them myself?" I ask cautiously, wanting to gauge his trust.

He studies my face. "It's not that, Bug. I just protect what's mine. I won't survive losing another person close to me."

My heart aches. "And I'm one of those people?"

"The top of the fucking list."

michigan

A Michigan is a lacrosse style goal where the player picks the puck up on their stick, skates around the back of the net, and throws it into the net to score.

chapter eighteen
malik

Darius called me this morning, letting me know that he and Alicia will be visiting soon to watch a couple of my games. I know they're just being nice, but I can't help but feel happily overwhelmed by the gesture.

He could have forgotten about me the day I moved out, and I still would have been forever grateful for all they had done for me. I certainly wouldn't be here without them.

I don't know what it's like to have parents, let alone ones who care about me unconditionally. But they're the closest I've ever gotten to begin to understand.

Maybe Alora would like to meet them.

What the fuck? That thought came out of nowhere, taking me by complete surprise.

That's not happening, especially not yet. Not when

we just started … whatever the hell this is. But at the same time, in a way … she feels permanent.

I'm still confused about everything that's transpired recently. But I can't go back, and I don't want to. I meant every word I said to her, even if it scares the absolute hell out of me.

The more I get to know her and sneak beneath the masks she wears, I think the likelihood of her being anything like her father is slim to none.

Even that thought feels like a betrayal to Micah and to myself. Because if it's true, then the years of pain I caused her were only out of pure cruelty and not out of justified vengeance.

If she's truly innocent, then I really am the villain. Maybe I have been all along, but I was too blinded by grief and rage to ever see clearly.

The other side of the coin is that she is the epitome of who I thought she was and I am but a pawn to her. But to be honest, as long as I get to have her, I'll play whatever game she wants for the rest of my life.

Getting home from morning skate, I find Blair and Mrs. Potts in the kitchen. Griffin and I walk in together and join them.

"Hello, dears," Mrs. Potts greets us with a smile.

"Mmm, that smells delicious," Griffin praises, walking over to Blair and stealing a quick kiss.

Chip races into the room and runs straight to Griffin, squeezing him as tightly as he can. Their dog is right behind him.

"Hey, buddy!" Griffin hugs him back, bending down to embrace him.

Chip smiles up at him.

He has autism and is nonverbal, but you can always tell what he's thinking because he has the most expressive facial expressions, as if closed captions were written on his forehead.

He's Mrs. Potts's son, who—along with Mrs. Potts—has lived with Griffin for years, nearly Chip's entire life. I know Griffin looks at him like a little brother and would do anything for his found family.

I want that. *Desperately*. And I want it with Alora.

"Hey, Blair." I clear my throat.

She, along with Griffin, turns to look at me. "Yeah?"

I'm terrified, scared shitless. But maybe it's time I start following my heart instead of my head.

"Can you invite Alora to tonight's game?"

She fights back her smile. "And why can't you do it yourself?"

Rubbing the back of my neck, I sigh. "I don't want her thinking it's a prank."

"Why the hell would she think it's a prank?" She scoffs, and I watch the moment her gaze shifts from confusion to anger. "You asshole. Did you pull that kind of shit on her in high school?"

I remain quiet for a moment before owning up to it. "Yeah, all the time."

Her jaw unhinges. "Malik ..." She says my name with disappointment. "The fact that that girl is even talking to you, let alone kissing you, is nothing short of a miracle."

My lips tip into a grin. "Oh, trust me, *I know.* And I'm not about to fuck it up now."

She pulls out her phone. "Promise me you aren't going to pull any shit. I don't want to be your accomplice."

Crossing my heart with my finger, I answer her with the utmost sincerity, "I swear it."

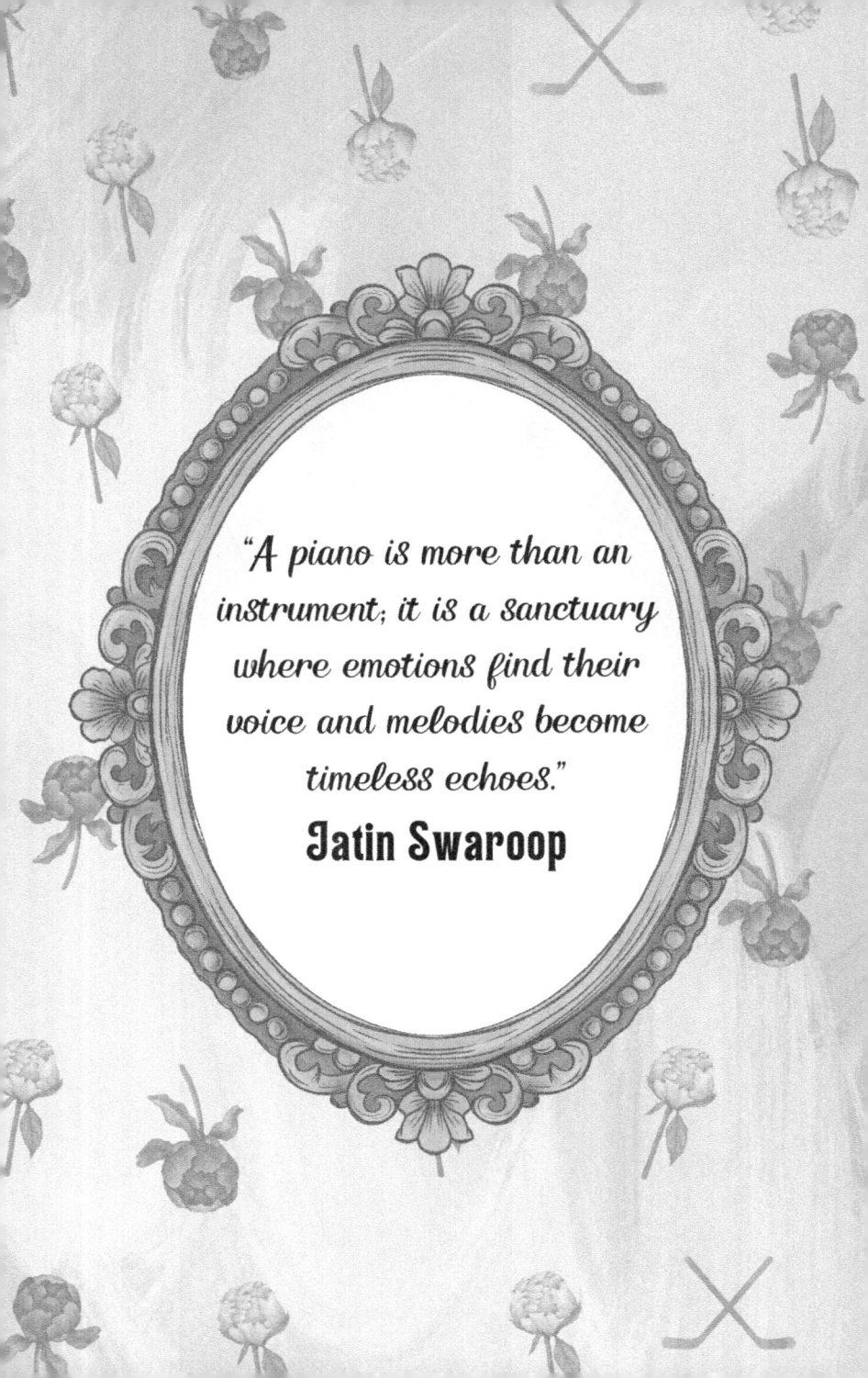

"A piano is more than an instrument; it is a sanctuary where emotions find their voice and melodies become timeless echoes."

Jatin Swaroop

chapter nineteen
alora

"**A**re you sure this is okay? Griffin won't be mad?" I glance down at the Legends jersey I'm wearing.

Blair insisted that I wear the jersey to the game tonight and I wasn't about to question her.

She chuckles. "No, not at all."

"Okay …" I drag out the word. "Thank you for letting me borrow it. I might look like I actually belong now."

She looks over at me as she starts her car. "And why wouldn't you?"

"I don't know …" My insecurities wrap around my throat. "I've only ever been to one hockey game before, and it wasn't exactly a great experience."

She reaches over the divider and grabs my hand.

"Malik told me, and I'm so sorry. But I made him promise that he has no bad intentions tonight."

I'm surprised he told her about the incident at all. I've noticed he likes to keep that version of himself reserved. Well, at least, he used to.

A shiver shakes my bones as the memory flashes in my mind—when Malik had the staff escort me out in front of the crowded arena for being his "stalker." God … the rumors that started after that were hard to bear. The jokes, the laughter … it still haunts me when I think about it.

But I also know that I'm not that girl anymore. I'm not in that school, and Malik isn't the same Malik I once knew.

"I wouldn't have come if I thought this was a setup." I glance out the window at the Hawthorne mansion. "Were Malik and Griffin friends when you two started dating?"

She nods, pulling onto the street and driving toward campus. "The best of friends."

"D-did he ever mention me?" I don't know why this question bubbled to the surface, but I can't help but be curious.

Shaking her head slightly, she winces. "No, but don't take that as a point against him. Honestly, I've never even heard him talk about his life prior to coming here."

"Really?" My ears perk up.

She nods. "Yeah, the only person I've ever heard

him mention is someone named Darius, and that was only in passing when I overheard Griffin and him talking."

My mind starts to shift back in time, wondering what I might have missed all those years ago. But I was usually so busy hating him that I left no room for empathy.

I want him to open up to me more, tell me all the secrets he keeps locked in his mind. But we just started crossing the line from enemies to lovers, and the last thing I want to do is chase him off and reverse the progress we've made.

We pull into the arena and find a decent parking spot. Blair said she wanted to get there before warm-ups so the choices were pretty open.

Grabbing my purse, I pull out my lip gloss and take one quick look in the pull-down mirror.

God, I'm nervous. I wish Sunny could be here just for moral support, but I know she'd be far more comfortable in our room with June than in a loud, cold rink.

My blonde hair cascades down my shoulders in loose, wavy curls. Brushing my light-pink-tinted gloss across my lips, I take a deep breath and check my monitor on my wrist, the one I only usually wear when I'm not with Sunny. Heart rate is under control.

"Ready?" Blair asks me, killing the engine and grabbing her own purse.

"As I'll ever be." I close the mirror and step outside

of the car, the cold breeze skirting through the jersey material.

When I walk into the arena with Blair, my heart is in my throat, and my stomach is rotating like a rotisserie chicken.

Blair holds her phone up for the ticket guy to scan. He scans the two tickets and lets us through. We must be some of the first people to arrive as the concession area is barren.

I've never been on this side of the arena. The only time I was here was when I came to confront Malik, and he pulled me into some equipment room on the opposite entrance.

"Our seats are this way. I always sit in the same one," she tells me, leading the way.

Turning left, I follow her into a short tunnel until we're at the top of some stairs.

"Wait." I stop. "How far down are we?"

She turns around and pinches her brows. "Row eight. Is everything okay?"

When I glance down the seemingly never-ending stairs, my palms start to sweat. I didn't even take this into account, and I totally should've.

"I should probably go to the restroom first. Going up and down a lot of stairs can really wear me out fast. Would you be able to point me in the right direction?"

"Of course. I'm sorry. I could have gotten seats higher up. I should have asked." She sighs angrily at herself. "Next time, we'll get seats closer to the top!"

Feeling like a sudden burden, I shoo her offer away with my hand. "Oh, no. It's okay. As long as I go to the bathroom first, I should only have to get up, like, one time. I should be okay—"

She cuts me off, "No, no. There's no reason you should subject yourself to that when I can see perfectly fine from a different seat."

Walking past me, she turns and points down the hallway that wraps around the rink. "They are just down there to your right."

I smile at her. "Thank you."

She nods. "I'm going to get a drink. Do you want anything?"

"A water, please," I say politely as I start to walk away, following her instructions.

"You got it."

Walking down the hallway, I stop when my eyes land on a poster hanging on the wall. It's a giant photo, stretched out ten feet wide with nearly life-size photos of some of the players. The main boys—Griffin, Asher, Dean, Elias, Finn, and Malik. But I'm only staring at one.

He's somehow more intimidating in this photo. If that's even possible. His face is rigid and threatening as he poses with his stick. With his helmet in his hand, his messy black hair is in full view, as are his stunning eyes, and I take a second just to study unabashedly.

After a few moments, I tear my gaze from his

intense stare and continue down the hallway to the restroom.

After using it, I wash my hands and run my fingers through my hair in the mirror before taking a few deep breaths. Giving myself an internal pep talk, I start heading back to Blair.

Turning the corner into the hallway, I slam to a halt, finding Malik leaning against the wall, waiting for me, his arms crossed over his wide chest.

Holy shit.

No one should look that good in hockey gear.

My God.

My eyes travel to his even broader shoulders, his jersey pulled over the pads beneath. I've never really found a lot of other hockey players attractive, but he … he is on another level. And standing in his skates and the little skate guards over the blades, he's even taller.

"Are you done ogling me?" He smirks and pushes off of the wall, walking toward me.

Craning my neck to look up at him, I shake my head. "Not yet."

His gaze falls to the jersey, and he cocks his head to the side. "Did you stop by the merch shop?"

I shake my head, looking down at it. "No, Blair let me borrow it."

He growls, his jaw tightening. "Turn around."

"W-what? Why?" I ask, and he lightly grabs my shoulders, spinning me around.

"No, she fucking didn't," he mutters under his

breath, his voice deep and angry. He twirls me back around. "Come on."

Taking my hand in his, he tugs me behind him. My body warms slightly, and my lungs tighten like a warning sign that I need to rest.

"Stop." The word falls out of my mouth effortlessly.

He turns back with a look of genuine concern. "What's wrong?"

"Will people get mad if I sit on the ground here?" I ask, waiting for his answer.

Brushing my hair back from my face, he assures me, "No, but I don't give a fuck if they do. Sit down if you need to, baby. No one will say a word with me here."

I slowly ease myself to the ground, and the coldness of the concrete floor seeps through my leggings, feeling nice.

Malik drops to the ground beside me and watches me with worry.

"I'll be okay."

Reaching over, he wraps his big hand around my thigh, brushing his thumbs back and forth.

"Do you need to lie down? Get your legs up? I can take you to a room that has a sitting area. I can have someone get a Waterboy packet from my bag and some water." He pauses, studying me while my chest blooms with emotion.

He noticed my Waterboy packets and stocked some in his bag? Maybe he just had some of his own. They are a pretty popular brand.

He holds my stare, and I can see a question in his gaze, but apparently, he doesn't want an actual answer.

Getting on his knees, he hooks an arm around my waist and beneath my legs. "Actually, I'm not going to ask you, I'm just going to do it. If I leave it up to you, you'll decline because you'll be worried you're being *too much*."

He lifts slightly and waits for my go-ahead to continue. I nod, and he gently raises me up as he stands to his feet, cradling me against his chest.

Vulnerability skates across my skin, making me feel exposed and raw. I didn't realize that he'd watched me so closely. Or that he knows more about POTS than what I've told him.

He's doing research of his own?

"Doing okay like this?" His voice softly caresses my ear.

"Yeah." I force myself to continue to take deep breaths even though I'm already feeling better.

I want it to keep going that way, even if Malik's close proximity is threatening my breathing to shallow out.

"Aren't you supposed to be somewhere right now?"

He lowers me slightly and twists a doorknob with his hand, pushing the door open with his foot. "I'm right where I need to be."

My heart skips in a beat—in a safe and loving way.

Carrying me through the threshold, he brings me

into some kind of lounge room, locking the door behind us.

Walking over to the couch, he turns and sits down on the far-left cushion, setting me in his lap with my feet resting up on the armrest.

"Better?" he asks, and a smirk lifts his lips.

"Much." I grin, feeling almost as good as new. "You didn't care about my well-being at all. You just wanted to get me alone, huh?"

He throws his head back on the couch and laughs. "Absolutely. You've figured me out."

His smile is big, his pearly whites on full display. I don't know if I've seen him smile like this. It's reaching all the way up to his eyes, twinkling at me as he gazes down.

"Do you need to lie like this for longer?" he asks.

"Oh, I'll be okay if you need to go. I'll be fine. I can find my way back—"

His hand cuts me off, sliding over my mouth.

"Stop." His spine straightens, and I feel his excitement shift beneath my ass, pressing into me. "I'm not leaving you, Bug. I'm just wondering how long you need before you can sit up."

My cheeks burn at what I'm about to do, and I haven't even done it yet. I sit up in his lap, moving my hips left and right as I hook my arm around his neck.

"Alora." My name leaves his lips in a mix of a growl and a groan, his hand snaking around my waist. "Careful. You aren't feeling the best right now, and I don't want to exhaust you even more. But if you keep that up, it's going to be very, *very* hard not to."

My core pulses from his words. "What are you going to do? You have a hockey game to get to." My lips tip up into a smirk.

His stare darkens as he runs his finger across my collarbone before wrapping his tattooed hand around my throat. "You think I won't stay up here with you and say fuck the rest of the world? Test me, Alora. I *dare* you."

He wouldn't actually though, right?

Like, he has to go back downstairs at some point. I'm sure he's supposed to be somewhere right now even.

But … he did tell me to dare him.

Tilting my head toward him, I press my lips against the base of his neck. Sticking the tip of my tongue out, I run it up the length, over the black ink running vertically on his skin.

"Alora." His chest vibrates as his deep, spine-tingling tone rattles through the room.

This is such a bad idea. But then why am I so excited?

"One more move, and I'm not letting you out of here until I get to taste you," he warns me, as if that's not what I'm trying to achieve.

I breathe against his ear, "I *dare* you."

All of a sudden, I'm on my back on the couch, and he's leaning over me, his hair falling forward and his chain dangling out of his jersey.

He eyes me like a starving animal. "Don't say I didn't warn you, baby." He attacks, his mouth assaulting my neck in torturous kisses and flicks of his tongue. "Mmm. You smell so good."

It's like his mouth knows where all of my buttons are and his tongue pushes every single one. I moan, and his hand clamps down over my mouth.

"You've got to be quiet for me if you don't want me to stop." He pulls away, and his lust-blown pupils find mine. "Are you going to be a good girl and keep that pretty mouth shut?"

Nodding, I pull him back to my neck as my breathing quickens. He scoots forward on his knees, forcing my legs further apart as his kisses trail lower.

"Lift your arms," he orders, and I obey, stretching them over my head.

Grabbing the bottom of my jersey, he scrunches it up and peels it off of my body, leaving me in my bra. He doesn't stop there.

Hooking his fingers in my leggings, he wiggles them down my hips to my ankles. "I'll never tire of seeing you like this. So fucking beautiful."

My heart hammers at his compliment. I want him to show me *exactly* how he feels.

Running his fingers down my stomach, he slides them between my bent legs and over the lace of my panties, rubbing my clit in small, tantalizing circles.

"Oh my God … yes," I whimper from the heat pooling in my core.

"You are so fucking pretty with my fingers on your pussy and your back arched like that." He slips his hand beneath my panties and finds the same rhythm as before.

Sliding two fingers through my center, he groans and licks his lips. "So wet for me already? I can't wait to feel you soak my hand."

Gently, he sinks a finger inside of me, easing it in and out. The sensation is foreign at first, but then it bursts with pleasure as his pace increases.

I watch him as intently as he's watching me when he inches another finger inside of me, pumping them in and out as his thumb circles my clit.

His eyebrows pinch together in curiosity. "You are *so* fucking tight."

Oh God, I didn't think he'd be able to tell that nobody has ever done this—or fucked me either. He's taking almost every one of my firsts.

The mountain of ecstasy builds with every thrust of his fingers and circle of his thumb, and I can feel that I'm not going to last much longer.

"Malik …" I exhale his name as he brings me closer to the edge. "*Please.*"

His purple gaze grows even darker. "Say it again. I like it when you beg."

"Please, please, please," I whimper, giving him exactly what he wants.

And he does the same, his pace quickening just enough for my orgasm to tear through me.

"Ahh!" I cry out, and his hand slaps down over my mouth, a stinging sensation spiking the pleasure.

"Shut those lips before I shove my cock down your throat and use it as a gag." His voice is menacing and almost cruel, and it makes my core pulse with desire.

I think I like this side of him too. I want all of it, every version. Nice Malik. Dirty Malik. Villain Malik. Give me every one.

I ride my orgasm out on his hand until it starts to fade, and I decide to tempt him just one more time. I stick my tongue out, and it hits his hand; he pulls it away, grinning.

Sliding his other hand out from my center, he sucks his fingers into his mouth and groans.

Pushing my tongue out of my mouth, I lean back against the headrest of the couch, my head falling back as I hold my mouth open and show him what I want.

It takes less than a second for him to realize what I'm offering. "Oh, *really?*"

Tilting my head back up, I nod. "I've only done it a handful of times, so I might not be very good at it … but I can try."

His jaw tics, and his eyes darken. "First off, *never* mention another man's dick in your mouth. Secondly, I'm going to need *all* of their names. Thirdly, anything you do with your mouth will make me come in seconds. You have no idea how long I've fantasized about how good your throat would feel."

He steps off the couch, takes his skates off and strips

his bottoms from him, leaving him in only his boxers. Doesn't he usually have to wear a cup with that? Never mind that.

My brain empties of every thought, except for … *Holy shit …*

When he cups himself, my jaw drops as the huge bulge throbs against his hand. His eyes twinkle as he walks to the edge of the couch behind my head, standing over me.

Hooking his thumbs in his boxers, he tugs them down his hips, freeing his rock-hard erection. It bounces from release, and I wet my lips.

Nerves start to flood me. I want to be good at this. I want to make him feel as good as he makes me.

"Should I stay like this?" I murmur.

"Is it easier for you to lie on your back?" His dick pulses above my face.

I nod, less than an inch between my mouth and his tip.

"Then open that filthy mouth, Alora," he demands.

Sticking my tongue out, I take his tip into my mouth as he inches forward, sucking and running my tongue along the soft skin.

"Oh, yeah, baby, you're going to do perfect," he moans. "Open wider. I want to feel my dick fill your goddamn throat."

Stretching my mouth as wide as I can, I take his thick cock as he thrusts forward, pushing it as far as it will go. I gag immediately.

"Fuck, that feels like heaven." He threads his fingers into my hair on each side of my head. "Try again. You can take more than that. I know it."

Nodding, I flick my tongue back and forth across the underside of his shaft, earning a soft moan.

Gripping my hair tighter, he thrusts hard into my mouth, and I fight the sensation to gag, focusing on taking him as deep as I can.

"Oh fuck, baby. Just like that." He pulls back, and then he jams it back down my throat, using my mouth as his own personal toy. "Such a good little slut for me, aren't you, Bug? Taking this dick so well."

My pussy pulses at his praise. I want more of it.

Resisting the urge to gag, I last as long as I can without inching away, but eventually, I rear my head back.

He reads my cue and slows down, sliding his dick out of my mouth until just the tip and an inch or so remain. Catching my breath for a second, I tip my head back, taking more of him between my lips.

"That's my girl. Greedy for this cock, aren't you? Let me give you every inch." He fucks my mouth with abandon, his face contorting with pleasure as he brings himself to the edge. "I want my cum dripping down your throat when you cheer my name at the game tonight."

His words are his own undoing, and he spills into my throat as a deep moan grumbles out of him. He whimpers, "Oh fuck, baby."

He pulls out to the tip. His dick pulses in my mouth for a moment until every drop drips onto my tongue, and I swallow. Flicking my tongue, I clean him, looking up with hooded eyes.

With a dirty smirk, he steps back, removing himself completely. Reaching over, he grabs Griffin's jersey from the back of the couch and wipes himself with it.

My jaw unhinges.

"Malik!" I scold him. "I still have to wear that!"

Ignoring me, he balls the jersey up, cocks his arm back, and launches it across the room, throwing it straight into the garbage can.

"Oh my God! Wait!" I reach for it, but it's far too late. "Now I'm going to smell like garbage and your cum. *Great*."

Bending down, he kisses me ferociously. "There is no way in hell I was ever letting you walk out of this room with anyone else's name on your back." Reaching behind his head, he grabs his jersey and lifts it off his gear, handing it to me. "My name only, Alora. Only mine. Always."

"Always," I murmur, taking it from him with hearts in my eyes. "You don't need it?" I ask, dumbfounded.

"I'll get a new one. Even if I had to play in someone else's jersey or sit the game out, I'd rather have it on you."

He slowly helps me sit up and watches me carefully as I slip his jersey over my head and thread my arms through the sleeves.

It's oversize on me, and it falls to the tops of my thighs as I rise to my feet and pull my panties and leggings up. "How does it look?"

He whistles and clicks his tongue. "Sexy as hell."

My cheeks burn.

Quickly, he gets dressed before we walk to the door. He puts his ear against it and listens for a second.

"I'd better get you to your seat before Blair accuses me of kidnapping you." He smirks, taking my hand in his as we step out into the hallway.

A few girls walking toward us glare at me with murder in their eyes when they see our hands interlocked before eye-fucking Malik right in front of me.

"Look the other fucking way," he snaps, and they gasp in shock but listen to his order anyway.

As we reach the top of the section Blair and I are sitting in, I spot Blair and her black hair bow. But she's definitely not in row eight anymore.

Only two rows down from the top, she must sense our stare, turning to us almost immediately. She waves kindly, and I wave back, knowing I'm doing a shit job at hiding the redness on my face.

Turning me to him, Malik grabs my jaw and pulls me up for a kiss, sinking his tongue into my mouth. A few people break into cheers and shouts in the crowd as they watch us.

Oh God.

Pulling away, I can feel my cheeks darken even more. "Good luck."

He winks at me. "Don't need it." He kisses me once more on the lips and then places one light one on my forehead. "Have fun."

"*Malik Ravenwell*." Griffin's voice is deep and scary as he calls out Malik's name a few feet away. "Get your ass in the locker room. You're late as shit."

Walking down two rows, I stride over to Blair and sit in the chair to her left. She's giggling as I approach, a knowing gleam in her eye.

"Find the bathroom okay?" she asks mockingly.

I cover my face. "I mean, yeah, I found it just fine. Ten out of ten experience."

She laughs. "I bet it was." Her gaze falls to my jersey. "New look?"

My face pales. "Oh God. Malik, he—"

She reaches out and gently touches my arm, calming my worries instantly. "I know. I figured as much when I gave it to you to wear."

My jaw unhinges.

"How do you think he knew you were in the restroom? He came to find you when you were gone."

Sitting back, I look at her in awe. "A little mastermind."

She flips her hair over her shoulder. "What can I say? I just love *love*, and I knew him seeing you in Griffin's jersey would drive him absolutely insane."

"It certainly did." I can't contain the smile on my lips. "I can buy you a new one."

She bats my offer away with the back of her hand.

"Please don't. I bought it just for this reason. It won't be missed."

"*Blair*," I scoff.

She shrugs. "I figured a little shove wouldn't hurt anyone. Besides, Malik can be dense sometimes, and I knew this would get under his skin. Something about these guys, their girls, and their jerseys. They foam at the mouth when we wear someone else's. It's not my fault they're all so predictable."

Laughing along with her, I reach down and pick up the bottle of water she got me as an announcer's voice roars through the speakers.

"Here are your HEAU Legends!"

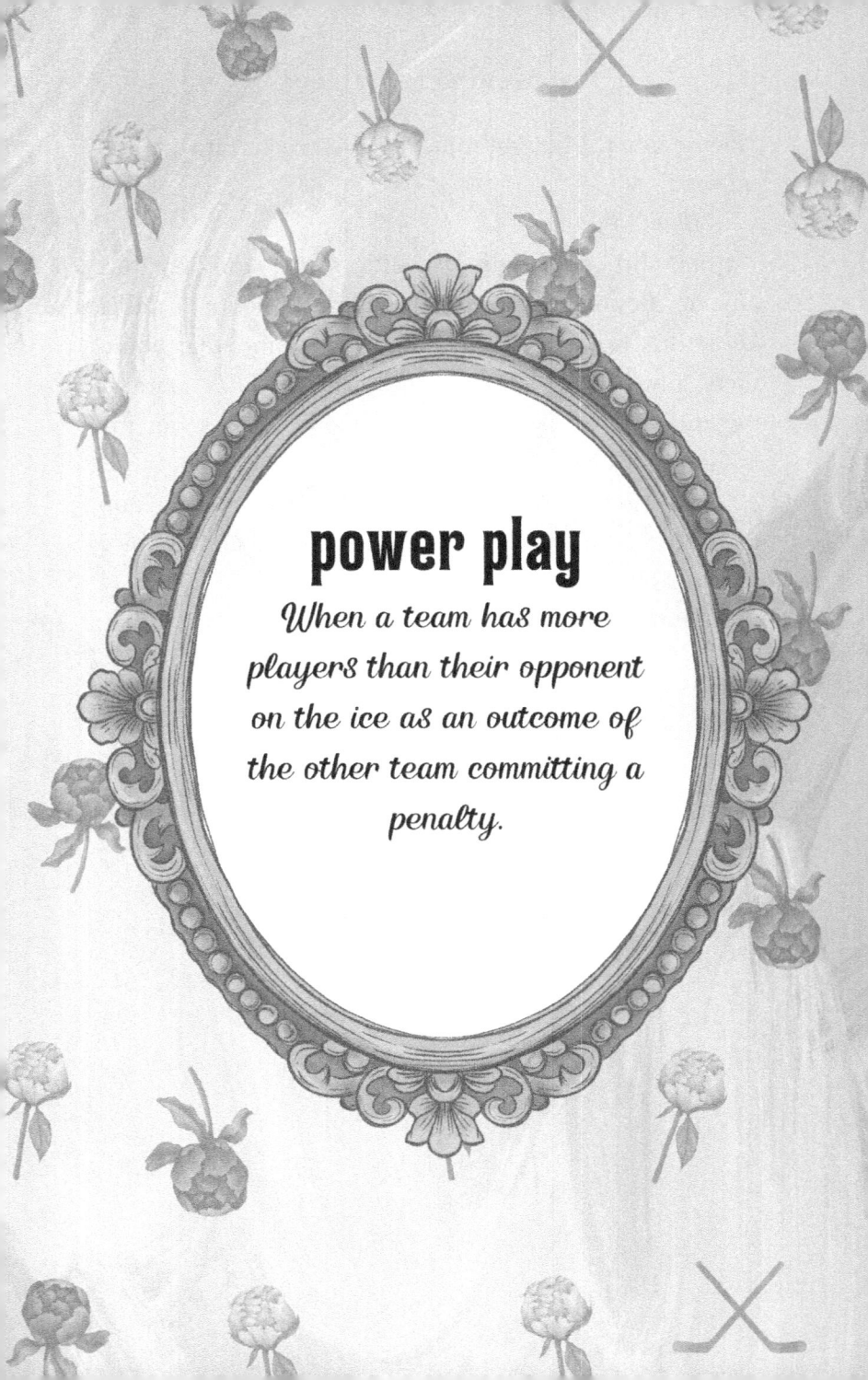

power play

When a team has more players than their opponent on the ice as an outcome of the other team committing a penalty.

chapter twenty
malik

Why did I have to wake up at all today? Why couldn't I have just slept through the entire thing?

There's a brief moment, a split second in time, when you wake up and your mind is empty. There's no pain, or grief, or sadness. It's not something you notice when you have nothing to fear. You simply wake up and move on with your day.

But when agony waits for you on the cusp of your first conscious breath, it's one of the worst phenomena. Because for that small moment, you just exist peacefully … and then suddenly, everything hits you at once, like a cannonball through the chest.

That's what this morning felt like, but worse … because when I first woke up, I thought of Alora.

The surge of self-hatred that came next was unlike

anything I'd ever experienced before. The first thought in my mind, especially today, should have been of Micah.

He would have been fifteen years old.

Birthdays in general were never really something we celebrated—at least not loudly. I would always find a way to hide a present for him or scrounge a few dollars here and there to get him a small cake or cupcake.

My uncle told us that we had to earn our birthdays, and to no one's surprise, we never did. We were naughty and big disappointments. He never let us forget it.

But no matter how many times he told Micah he was worthless, I would tell him how special he was twice as many. I refused to let Micah ever believe a word out of our uncle's mouth. I like to think that I succeeded in the end.

I wish I could visit him today in some way, shape, or form. Maybe that's what makes all of this so much harder. He's imprisoned somewhere, wherever my uncle is hiding him.

All I have are a few pictures of him that I managed to steal from the house before I ran, along with his butterflies. He would've wanted me to keep them safe, and I always will.

Below the tattooed word *Villain*, I rub over the black-and-white tattoo centered on my chest—a *Siproeta stelenes*, also known as a malachite butterfly, his favorite one. He used to say that he loved this one because of the green-and-black coloration and because the name reminded him of me.

The backs of my eyes burn as tears form.

"Fuck!" I shout.

My fists need to hit something, to punch this blood-boiling rage out of my system.

None of this would be happening if I hadn't made Micah join me for a walk that night. I just wanted him to get some fresh air and ice cream. I just wanted him to get out of that damn house and away from our uncle.

Tears roll down my lashes and fall, plummeting toward the ground.

How can I face Alora today? How can I look at her and not think of the person responsible?

I know it's not her; I know my hatred lies some-where else. But I also know she's connected to him whether I like it or not. I've treated her terribly over the years, and I don't want to do it again.

Sometimes, my mouth gets in the way, my words lashing out and whipping toward people who aren't deserving of the wrath. It's always been my downfall, but it's also been my shield.

If the rest of the world fears me, they won't dare get close to me. They won't get under my skin and sink their hooks in. They'll never make it past the fortress I've spent years building.

I think avoiding Alora today would be the best thing for both of us. Besides, I need to spend time with the butterflies today, brush up on the species he had and the new ones I've added to his collection.

A thorn stabs into my heart as I remember the horrible things I once said to Micah about his love for these tiny creatures. Things that I can never take back.

But I can learn—for him. I can keep his collection going for the rest of my life.

Honestly, the more I read or hear about butterflies, the more fascinated I become. Like the fact that they taste from their feet—which is insane—or that their wings are made up of microscopic scales. Butterflies are like the world's smallest dragons.

A knock sounds on my door. I'm sure it's Griff.

"Come in," I call out, wiping my eyes clean.

The door opens, and Griffin walks in, noticing my emotional state immediately. "Hey, man. How are you holding up?"

I could tell him I'm fine and that everything's great. But he would know it's a lie, just like I do. Besides, out of respect for him, I won't.

"You know ..." I trail off.

He nods solemnly. "Do you want to talk about him?"

I shake my head. "Not really."

"I get it, man." He pauses, a similar sadness skating across his features as his mind drifts away for a moment. "Are you staying here today then?"

"Yeah. Let me know if I need to do anything for class, please."

He nods. "Will do. Let me know if there's anything I can do to make today easier for you."

I force a smile his way, and he closes the door on his way out.

I don't know if today is supposed to be easy. If it's not painful, does that mean I love my brother less?

It sure feels that way.

I walk over to the fireplace, and my gaze travels over the black-framed bugs.

Alora flashes in my mind. *Bug.*

I remember when I gave her that nickname and the meaning I told her. One I created to inflict as much damage as possible. But I don't use it like that anymore. To be honest, I haven't for a long time.

When my life became complete chaos after Micah was killed, Alora became one of the only constants. A revolving focal point in my life. She was always there, whether she was aware I was watching or not.

For so long, I fought my feelings for her, but they've been there since day one. I just hid them so deep beneath the anger that I couldn't see them clearly.

I mean, what was I supposed to do? Fall for the daughter of the man responsible for my brother's death? I couldn't.

Because every day that she came into that school, showing up in her fancy car and wanting for nothing, I knew the blood that existed on every dollar of her wealth.

She was an oasis that I punished myself for wanting

to drink from. It would have been the utmost betrayal to Micah, even if he wouldn't see it that way.

There's still a part of me that feels guilty for letting her get close to me at all.

But the more I sink into her mind, the more I think she's in the dark about everything her father has done. She's not greedy or snotty like I gaslighted myself to believe.

However, it's not like her dad is completely out of the picture. Especially after he pulled me aside when he was here on campus. The audacity he had to say my name. To say Micah's. It took everything in me not to beat him into the ground until his blood stained the stones.

I know Alora might not be close with her father, but he's still her dad. I can't change that. I worry that when she discovers the truth, she'll take his side.

I feel like I'm walking on a tightrope, teetering back and forth between pulling her closer to me and shoving her away.

Turning on the TV that's mounted above the fireplace, I put on Micah's favorite Transformers movie. I wonder if he'd still love it as much now. Would he laugh at the same parts?

I lie back in bed, looking up and watching the movie. Today is about honoring him. I'm going to make his favorite sandwich later for lunch and pick up a small, personal-sized chocolate cake.

My stare locks on the screen as images flash from

the movie, but my eyes don't focus; they just stay in place as I cower inside of my mind.

After eating a hot ham and cheese, I grab my keys and wallet to head to the grocery store. I know Mrs. Potts would have been more than happy to get the cake for me when she did her grocery shopping for the house. But it would have felt wrong.

She's not part of my story; she's part of Blair and Griffin's. This is something I have to do for myself.

Walking out of the front door, I find Blair, Lumi, and Alora walking up the steps.

Shit.

This is *exactly* what I was trying to avoid today. But I haven't exactly told Griffin *all* the details regarding Alora's dad and his involvement. Just that he played a role in that night.

But I know he hasn't shared any of that with Blair out of respect for my privacy, so she would have no reason to not invite her over.

Stepping back through the threshold, I realize it's too late. They've already seen me. I can't run and hide, as much as my body is telling me to.

"Hey." Alora's face lights up when she spots me.

Mustering as much joy as I can into my voice, I flash a smile. "Hi."

"Where are you off to?" Blair asks, nosy as ever.

"I've got to run a couple of errands," I respond, hearing the coldness to my voice, even colder than the chilly air whipping around us.

Alora walks up to me and snakes her arms around my waist. I freeze, feeling like my consciousness is separating from my body.

She notices and looks up at me with worry. "What's wrong?"

God, I hate how attentive she is right now. I can't hide anything from her. "What? Nothing. I'm fine."

Blair eyes me angrily, and I wonder if my words came out crueler than I realize.

"Need some company?" Alora's doe eyes tempt me, but I need space right now, especially from her.

I'm not ready to tell her the truth. Frankly, I don't want to tell her at all. I don't want to hurt her with the secrets I keep.

"Not right now," I snap, stepping back from her embrace.

Pain strikes her eyes, and my heart constricts, the thorns digging into my flesh.

"Oh … okay."

Blair walks toward the door with Lumi. "Alora, we'll meet you inside."

She turns to me and scolds me with her glare—mentally threatening me, I'm sure.

The door closes behind them, leaving Alora and me all alone.

"What's wrong, Malik? I can tell something's up." She pushes her question again.

But I can't tell her. Especially today. This is his day, and I won't let a Briarwood, even her, take that from him.

She reaches and touches my hand. I jump back from the contact as it shocks me. I can't. I just can't. Not today.

Her eyes start to well with tears, and I bite the inside of my cheek so hard that blood bursts in my mouth.

"Alora, please."

"Please what?" she whimpers. "You haven't told me what you want me to do. You've barely said anything at all."

"Just go inside," I say, telling her what I want her to do.

"Why are you being so cold right now? I don't understand. Everything's been going so well." Confusion contorts her face as a mask in her eyes falls back in place.

This is *exactly* why I didn't want to see her today.

Reaching up, she cups my cheek, and my throat burns.

"Talk to me, please. Don't shut me out."

Lightly grabbing her wrist, I remove it from my face. There are a thousand words I want to say to her. A million things I want to share. But I can't even muster enough bravery to open my mouth.

"*Fucking pathetic. You're a fucking coward.*" My uncle's words echo in my mind, and for the first time, I agree with him.

I'm worthless. Weak. A pathetic excuse for a man.

Letting her in was one of the hardest things I've ever done—but above all, it was the most selfish.

I'm falling for her. I want to grab her, kiss her, and confess it all.

But today isn't the time for that conversation. She shouldn't hear those words from me until she knows the truth about our pasts and how intertwined they really are.

She wipes her eyes. "It was easier when all you did was torture me. At least then, I knew what your intentions were. Instead of getting comfortable with your compliments, constantly waiting for this shoe to drop."

Pushing past me, she bumps my arm, and I reach out for her wrist.

"*Alora.*"

I don't want to hurt her. *Fuck*, I don't want to be the reason she ever cries again.

She yanks her arm from my grasp and whips around. "Figure your shit out, Malik. Please." She pauses, her bottom lip quivering. "If this was all just another stunt, another taunt, then, yay, you got me good."

"It's not," I whisper, but it's far too late.

She's already gone inside.

I'm crazy about her, wild even, and I don't think that anything is going to stop that train. Maybe I could prove it to her in another way … how serious I am about her.

Ripping my phone out of my pocket, I shoot a quick text.

I need your next available appointment.

I've been itching to get another tattoo and this one will be perfect.

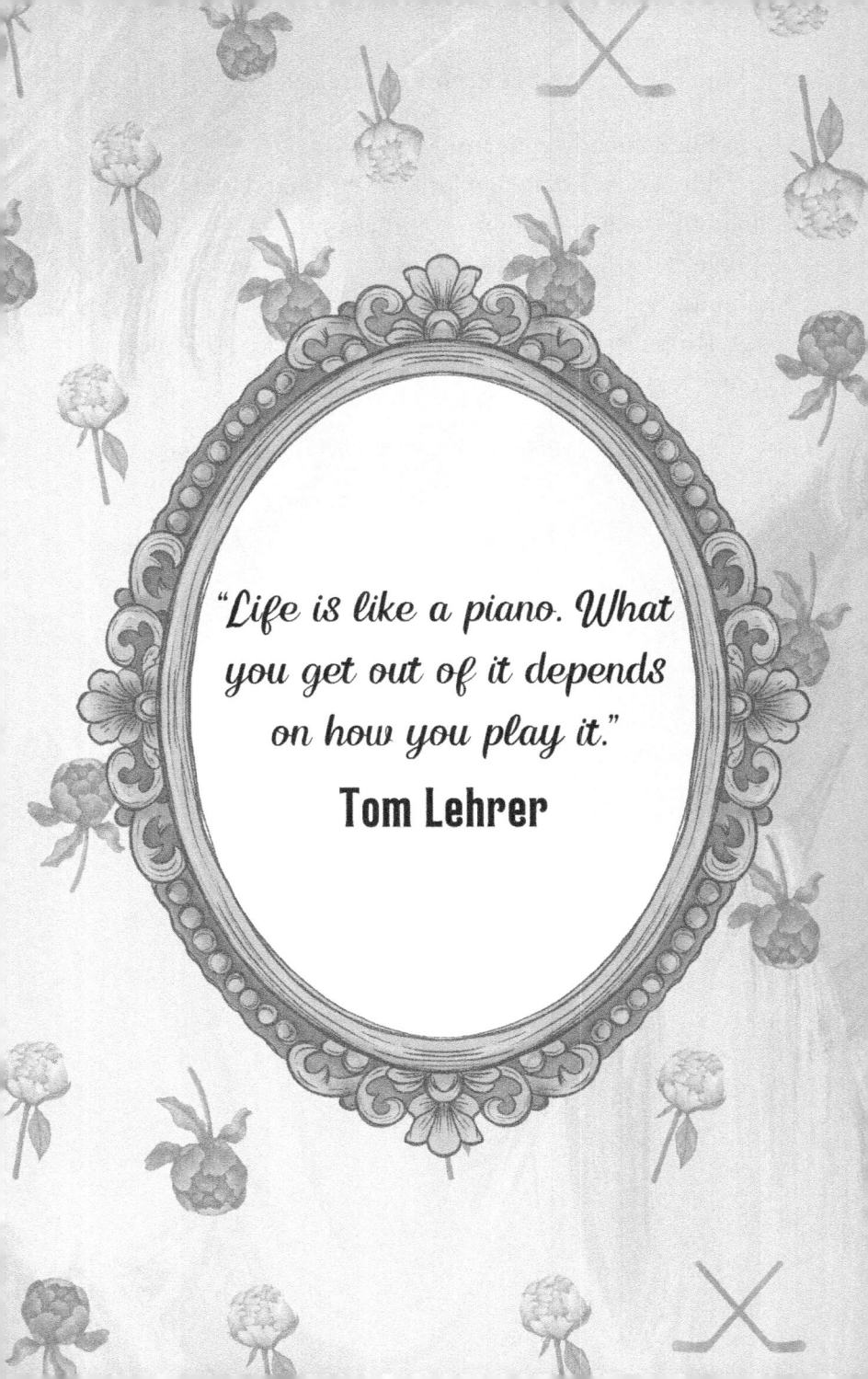

"Life is like a piano. What you get out of it depends on how you play it."

Tom Lehrer

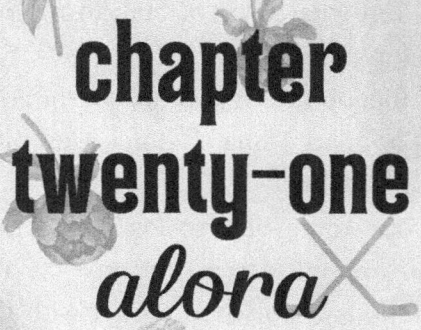

chapter twenty-one
alora

"Hello?" I answer my dad's call, and Sunny sets her head on my stomach like she somehow knows I need her support.

"Alora," he says angrily. Although I'm not surprised —that's the only tone I seem to hear from him. "Was our conversation not enough for you to understand?"

My mind flashes back to his visit on campus. "Are you talking about the secret spy you have?"

"Did you think I was kidding when I told you to stay away from Malik Ravenwell?" he snaps.

Why does he care so much about Malik?

"Not really, but I didn't think you'd mind that much. Why? Do you know each other?" I challenge him, wondering if he'll fess up to the conversation I caught them in.

"Not at all," he answers immediately, his tone unwavering. "But from what I've got here in my report, he's not a good fit for you."

Gripping the phone tighter in my hand, I exhale sharply. "It's a good thing I don't care about your approval of who I date."

"Watch your tone," he scolds. "You may be an adult, but you are still a representative of this family. You can't be a floozy, spotted at dinner with Phillip, and then be spotted, kissing Malik later. That is not the Briarwood way, Alora."

"Honestly, Dad, do you really think that Mom never went on dates with different guys?" I punch back, knowing that bringing her up will strike a nerve.

"Do. Not. Speak. Of. Your. *Mother*." The facade of a caring father is missing from his tone, the congressman himself showing up instead. "It doesn't matter what your mother did before we met, only what she did after. Don't disrespect her name by using her as a pawn in your argument."

"Why?" My anger spikes. "You've always used her in yours."

He sighs angrily. "The only thing I've ever cared about since losing her is protecting you. That's all I've ever tried to do—keep you safe."

"You have a hell of a way of showing it."

"Phillip Stephens." He says his name matter-of-factly. "Do you remember me telling you when you were younger that Phillip was the prince of your story? The one who would sweep you off to a happily ever after. Well, Malik is your villain, the one who curses you from ever rising up to your potential. He's the one that will destroy you in the end."

"Dad …" My eyes burn. "Have you ever considered that perhaps the villain all along is you?"

He's quiet, taking his time to respond. "If you view me as the bad guy, then I can live with that. I can't live with you falling under his spell."

"You speak a lot on his behalf for someone who claims to not know him at all."

"You speak a lot on a subject you don't truly understand for someone who relies on the kingdom that I've spent decades building." He takes a shaky breath. "Do you like school there? Do you like your accommodations? Because I could change it like *that*," he snaps.

He can do whatever he wants to me. I'll prevail.

"How about your aunts? Would they be supportive of your new relationship if I stopped funding their lives?"

My blood runs cold.

They have money of their own, but it's not enough to sustain them. When they left the umbrella of this life, they gave up the wealth, making a deal with my father to live off of a much smaller allowance. But I refuse to let him hurt them because of me.

"You wouldn't." I'm breathless.

"Push me, Alora, and you'll find out that some lessons are harder to learn than others. I've never coddled you, but I've always done what's best for you in the end. This is one of those times, Little Rose. One day, you'll thank me."

Hearing his childhood nickname for me tugs at my heartstrings, but it does little to ease the bone-chilling fear rattling me to the core.

Three beeps signal that he hung up, but I don't move the phone from my ear. I'm frozen in place, stunned by what just happened.

I can live with him taking money from me, but from my aunts? The three strongest women I know who gave up everything to raise me? I won't hurt them in the process.

When I drop the phone into my lap, the screen lights up, and I see the time. Crap, I need to get going. I have practice with Von London. I'm performing the hardest piece today for him.

Sliding off of the bed, I step into my white tennis shoes. They might look odd with the flowy pink corset top and jeans I'm wearing, but I care more about the blood flow in my body than I do the fashion sense.

Hooking Sunny's leash onto her new pink service dog harness that finally arrived, I grab my purse and water bottle and head to Moor Hall.

I haven't been able to stop thinking about the invitation to the showcase this spring. I'm going to prepare the most perfect piece for it.

Music is what makes my soul feel full, and I'm honored that my talent and passion are being recognized. Especially by someone as infamous as him.

Von London waits outside of our usual practice room, his face lighting up when he spots Sunny and me. More nervous than usual, I take a few steady breaths before I reach him.

"Good evening, Alora," he greets me with a light hug.

"Good evening, sir."

I awkwardly accept his hug, and he lingers for a moment too long, but I try not to think anything of it.

We have been spending a lot of time together in sessions. It's normal to grow a fondness for someone, I suppose.

Pulling away, I open the door, letting Sunny lead the way inside.

Taking a seat on the bench, I lift the piano lid and run my fingers over the keys out of habit. Von London walks in behind us, sitting in his usual seat at the table.

"I've been looking forward to hearing you play this one. It's my all-time favorite work." He gestures with his hand. "Whenever you're ready."

No pressure, just playing Rupert Von London's own piece to him, one he knows like the back of his hand.

Setting the music up on the stand, I close my eyes as my fingers find their starting place. I don't need the music; I've memorized it already, as I often do with any composition I play more than a handful of times.

Something about the music just clicks into my brain.

I inhale, and then I strike the first chords on the exhale, my breath flowing through the notes. And then I melt away into the song, my body simply a vessel to bring the melodic art to life.

I can see why this piece is special to him; there are two very distinct voices in it. Pushing and pulling back and forth until the song ends in an entirely different key, symbolizing the merging of the two and a birth of something new.

As I finish the song, I realize he's moved, standing a few feet right of the bench I'm sitting on.

He lightly claps and takes a seat on the bench beside me, his leg pressed firmly against mine.

"Beautiful as always, my dear." His voice is close, the warmth of his breath touching my ear.

Scooting away from him politely, I smile, turning my head just slightly his way. "Thank you."

He flips to the third page and points. "Can you play from here again?"

Nodding, I straighten my spine and align my fingers on the white keys. A second later, I'm once again lost in the song, my consciousness drifting to the back of my mind.

Bony fingers slide along my upper thigh, tearing me from my happy place and dragging me into a nightmare I never could've imagined.

My eyes fly open and land on Von London's hand on my leg. I should yell at him to stop; I should move away from his touch.

But it's like my brain is short-circuiting and I'm stuck in place as it reboots.

"W-what are you doing?" I gasp, coming back into control of my body.

He smiles at me as if this were a normal part of our sessions, as if we did this every time. Which we most certainly have not.

"You are incredible, Alora," he praises me, and a chill snakes down my spine chills.

I inch away from him, but he stretches his arm with me, keeping it secured on my thigh.

"Sir, this isn't appropriate."

He shakes his head with a smile. "I know there are guidelines against students fraternizing with teachers. But don't worry; I won't let anyone find out."

Scooting closer to the wall at my left, I realize I'm nearly trapped between the piano, the wall, and him, the only gap between the wide bench and wall a few inches. Shit.

This can't be real. This can't be happening. Is this some kind of sick test to see if I'm willing to cheat to get ahead?

"Mr. Von London, there is no us." My voice is shakier than I'd like.

Sliding closer to me, he moves his hand from my thigh to the back of my waist, wrapping it around my side and tugging me into him in one surprisingly strong move.

He presses his lips against my ear. "I understand your reservations. But it's okay, really. You know as much as I do how important music is. Imagine what we could create together."

My head shakes back and forth as I lean away from his hot breath. "No. No, I do not."

Surely, this is just a misunderstanding, and I've led him on somehow.

His brows furrow, and his eyes darken. But they don't give me the same giddy feeling Malik's darkened gaze does. Rupert makes my skin start to crawl.

I told him no. I showed him that I was uncomfortable. Any reasonable person would recognize these signs and back the hell off.

My stomach twists when the realization hits me … he is anything but a reasonable and respectable person.

The tips of his fingers sink into my side, pressing into the silky pink corset top. "Just relax, okay?"

He presses his lips against my cheek, and I slam my eyes shut at the contact.

"Please stop," I whimper, understanding that the person I've idolized for years is just a creep who doesn't deserve the pedestal he lives on.

He kisses my cheek again, this time closer to my mouth. "You were invited to the showcase." His tone unsettles me. "Do you want it to stay that way?"

My eyes fly open. "Are you blackmailing me to sleep with you?"

Shaking his head with a smile, he murmurs, "No, doll, I'm blackmailing you to get you on your knees. I'm not *that* much of a monster."

"It's hard to tell when you're assaulting me." My words gain stability as an eerie calmness settles into my skin.

Maybe this is the moment of freeze, fight, or flight. Maybe it's not a pick or choose, but an order of actions. I already froze, which means I'm onto step two.

For the first time in my life, I'm going to do something I've always hated my father for—wielding his name, title, and place in the world as a weapon.

Turning my head to face him, I snarl, "I assume you know my last name."

He nods thoughtlessly, his fingers still wrapped around my waist. "I do."

I chuckle darkly, and it sounds like a warning bubbling out of me. "Then you know it's the same one who just made a five-million-dollar donation to the music department. Do you think my name holds no weight at this school? Because you would be very, *very* wrong."

He stays quiet, studying me intently.

"You may think you're the one with the power in this dynamic, but you're sorely mistaken. I can have your job eliminated with a single call. I can ruin your tenure with HEAU and make sure you're not hired at any school in this country."

He begins to shrink as I sit up taller and taller, feeling a hint of power igniting in my blood.

His seemingly sweet demeanor falls, his lips twisting in a snarl. "You spoiled brat. You have a lot of confidence for someone who lives in her dad's shadow."

"Yeah? Are you willing to take your chances?" I challenge him.

"I sure am," he growls unexpectedly.

Shit.

He launches himself at me, and his lips crash against mine before I get a chance to even react.

Oh God, eww. Stop!

His other hand falls to the front of my corset, slipping inside of the top. He cups my bare breast, and my soul begins to leave my body as my chest tightens.

"Get off of me! Why the hell are you doing this?" I scream, and he rips the hand from my top and slaps it over my mouth.

An odd calmness finds him, as if he has no fear in the world of being caught or me overpowering him. A terrifying sight.

"Because everyone who finds success in this industry has to make sacrifices to get there. This is yours."

His words sear into my mind, and I know they'll be there forever.

I tried to *freeze*. I tried to *fight*. Only one option left.

He leans back in for a kiss, and I rear my arm back and punch him straight in the throat. A goose-like honk sounds from him as he gasps for air and clutches his neck.

Standing from the bench, I hop over his legs. But he

grabs the strappy back of my top, yanking me back toward him.

But I don't stop. I stride forward as hard as I can, hearing fabric tear as I pull away from him, feeling cold air hit my lower back.

"Stop!" I scream at him, hoping someone outside of the room will overhear, but I know it's unlikely. These rooms were built to be nearly soundproof.

But he doesn't stop as he rises to his feet. Sunny rushes over to me, starting to become well aware of the threat.

She positions herself between my legs, standing guard.

He looks down at her and laughs. "A little golden isn't going to hurt me. Alora, stop making this such a big deal. It was just a few kisses from someone who admires you. I had to pay my dues to get to this level. And eventually, you'll have to pay yours."

For a split second, I consider his gaslighting words, and I wonder if I'm really blowing this out of proportion. But as he steps toward me again, with my lip gloss smeared on his face and redness on his neck, I know that I'm not.

"Give me one more kiss and I'll forget all about this, including you threatening a teacher. We can keep all of this just between us. Right?" He steps toward me, and Sunny starts to growl.

This has already gone on for far too long. He

somehow senses my urge to flee and lunges forward, wrapping his hand around my wrist.

"Ahh!" I yelp as someone else screams.

Looking down, I see Sunny's teeth clamped down on his arm, blood oozing around the bite.

He kicks his leg at her but misses. But I won't.

Planting my hands on his shoulders, I drive my knee as hard as I can into his groin, feeling a gross, squishy, bursting sensation as my knee flattens against his pelvis.

Collapsing to the ground with Sunny still latched on to him, he screams out in pain, but I don't waste a second grabbing my purse and Sunny's leash.

"Drop it," I tell her, and she releases his arm like she would a chew toy.

"Good girl. Come on," I grab my purse and rush out of the room into a nearly empty hallway.

There was no one here who was going to save me if Sunny and I hadn't done it on our own. But not everyone has a Sunny, and the thought that he's tried this before makes me want to puke.

Walking as fast as I can manage, I exit Moor Hall, feeling the cold air peel his choking grip from my body. My eyes start to well up with tears as I swallow hard.

A wave of disgust and vulnerability washes over me.

Tears start to roll down my cheeks as I look left and right, my gaze bouncing between two paths.

One to my dorm. One to the rink, which is a lot closer to me than my room. It also has the one person in it who I need more than anything else right now.

My feet are moving before I realize it, rushing toward the arena. My breathing starts to rattle in my throat.

Keeping my arms tight to my sides to hold my shirt up, I race to Malik, needing to feel him wrap me up and shield me from the world.

My heart constricts. I didn't realize how fast he had become my safe space.

I don't care if things are a tad shaky with us. They are bound to be after everything we've been through. But all I know is that right now, the thought of anyone's else's touch makes me want to gag. I need him.

Throwing the arena door open, I rush inside, getting stopped by security.

"Excuse me, ma'am. What's your name?"

He looks at me more intently, recognizing my distress.

"A-Alora Briarwood."

"Are you okay?" He checks a list on a clipboard. "I've got you down here as approved visitors. But do you need any help?"

Shaking my head, I rush past him with Sunny, hearing the sound of pucks smacking against the boards getting louder and louder as I reach the double-door entrance to the rink.

The cold feels good against my skin—extra cold on my cheeks, where my tears are still flowing.

When I walk into view of the players, a few of them

spot me immediately. But I don't recognize any of them.

Someone shouts down to the ice, "Ravenwell!"

And then I see him.

On the opposite end, his head whips my way, and even through the cage, I can feel his stare find me instantly.

Without a second thought, he digs his skates into the ice and takes off toward me, followed by Griffin and Asher.

One of the guys near me ushers me over to the board, opening the door. But I don't tear my stare from Malik as his gaze becomes more and more worried, the closer he gets.

I start to shiver, my teeth chattering.

Malik jumps off the ice and rushes over to me, panic straining his eyes.

When I look up at him through blurry tears, my voice cracks. "I didn't know where else to go."

Pulling me forward, he encases me in his arms, shielding me from the world with his head on top of mine. "Always to me, Bug. Always to me."

The world starts to fade as he keeps me in his somehow-warm embrace. But as he pulls back and cups my cheeks with his hands, the tear factory starts back up.

"Alora, what happened?" His voice cracks with sorrow and pain.

But for some reason, I don't say anything at all.

His thumbs gently brush back and forth as his eyes

travel over every inch of me, looking for any answer he can find.

"Holy shit," Asher says in shock as he nears us.

"Asher, go get my sweatshirt from the locker room!" Malik orders him away, and he listens without hesitation.

My mind starts to feel foggy, like a few wires have come unplugged. His eyes are staring at me so deeply; I can feel his gaze reach inside of me like a hug, warming me from the inside out.

Sniffling, I shiver more and more as Asher runs back over, holding a black sweatshirt.

"Turn around," Malik snaps at everyone, and they listen instantly, turning their backs to us.

Pressing my corset against me, he holds it in place with one hand. "I'll hold this. You slip this on, okay?"

His words are soft, but his jaw is tight, like he's far angrier than he's letting on.

I take the sweatshirt from him, lifting my arms and sliding the hoodie over my head, down past my stomach. He pulls the broken top out from beneath the sweatshirt, tossing it to the ground beside us.

"Hey, look at me, baby." He grabs my cheeks again and bends over, lowering his eyes to my level. I didn't even realize I wasn't looking at him. "Who did this to you? Who hurt you?"

"R-Rupert." My voice sounds like a stranger, and as the adrenaline begins leaving my system, I become all too aware of what's coming next. "Malik, I don't feel good. I'm going to puke."

He rushes over, grabs the big trash can, and places it in front of me just in time.

Leaning into it, I heave, all contents of my stomach exploding into the trash bag. My hair is pulled back from my face as my stomach contracts again, upheaving anything it can.

He rubs my back as I expel all of my energy. Sunny licks my leg, showing her support. It also means that my heart rate is getting too high. It's already too high.

Once I feel the nausea fade, I straighten my spine and turn back toward him. I open my mouth to say something, but nothing comes out as a high-pitched sound rings in my ears, drowning everything else out.

And then my vision goes dark.

My eyes flutter open, and it takes me a moment to realize where I am and to remember what happened. The brain fog is thick and hard to think through.

My throat is dry as I look up at the man carrying me. "Malik?"

His gaze drops to me. "There you are, Bug. Open those pretty eyes for me."

"Where are we?" Glancing around, I have to stop

trying to take in my surroundings because everything's still a bit wavy.

"Heading back to your dorm room," he murmurs softly. "We're almost there."

Resting my head against Malik's chest, I bunch his jersey in my fist and squeeze my eyes tight. But the moment I do, I see Rupert's face inches from mine.

"You're safe," Malik whispers to me. "Don't worry about him. He'll never get near you again."

I want to ask how he's so certain, but right now, I don't care. I don't want to think about him. I want to focus on the one who has walked almost a mile with me in his arms.

My heart grows a new soft spot for this boy. "You've carried me the whole way?"

He grins down at me. "Sunny helped."

As the ringing in my ears fades away, I hear her pitter-patter on the concrete next to us. I chuckle. "Yeah, she seems to be carrying a lot of my weight. If you give me a second, I can walk."

"No," he states firmly. "I'm carrying you. You need to rest. I don't care if I had to carry you a hundred miles, I would do it."

And there he is—that warm, affectionate Malik that I've come to lov—

Whoa. That thought came out of nowhere.

"Are you okay?" He looks down worriedly.

My eyes are wide, but I quickly fix them. "Yeah."

We reach the front entrance of the dorm building.

"My keys are in my purse," I tell him, seeing the strap looped over his shoulder.

He smirks deviously. "Don't need them, remember? I have one of my own."

I hear his keys jingle beneath me in his hand.

"I forgot you were batshit crazy."

He winks at me. "Only for you."

Unlocking the front door, he carries me inside, Sunny right behind us, her leash hooked on Malik's wrist. When he brings Sunny and me into the elevator, I protest at his chivalry.

"I can walk, Malik. You can put me down."

"I know," he murmurs, tightening his hold on me. "But I can't."

Unlocking my door, he lets Sunny in first before carrying me through the threshold and setting me down on my bed.

Scooching up against my pillows, I see all of him and recognize that the shoes he's wearing aren't his—at least ones I've never seen. "Are those yours?" I point at the all-black tennis shoes that look too small for his feet.

He chuckles. "Nope. Borrowed them from our security guy." He kicks them off.

I don't want him to leave. I want him to stay here with me, but I also don't know if that's something he'd be comfortable with.

"Do you have to go back?" My voice is quiet.

His eyes lift, vulnerability twinkling in his gaze. "You want me to stay?"

Nodding, I scoot over in bed to make room for him.

A smile takes over his lips, revealing that perfect grin. "Are you sure?"

"Positive." I peel the blanket back. "I can change into pajamas if you want your sweatshirt back."

"I don't need it." He takes his jersey off and the rest of his chest gear and undershirt, until he's standing before me in only black socks and boxers. "I may need you to help keep me warm though."

Blushing, I chuckle softly. "I think I can do that."

He rubs the back of his neck and glances away from me. "Is that what I think it is?"

Following his line of sight to the folded-up Legends T-shirt on top of my desk, I laugh. "It sure is. You can wear it if you'd like … but it might be a little short on you."

Biting his tongue, he looks at me playfully and menacingly. "Thank you for your permission to wear *my* shirt."

Clicking my tongue, I grin. "Of course."

When he slips the half shirt over his head and broad shoulders, I giggle at the sight in front of me.

The shirt stops at the top of his absolutely shredded abs. The kind of physique that extends up his sides, every inch of his torso at peak strength.

Maybe I should cut all his shirts in half.

He walks over to the bed with a smile on his lips and slides in next to me, hooking his arm around my shoulders to pull me closer to him.

When I curl into his chest with my arms tucked between us, the air seems to weigh down on us, heavier than before, as if I can feel the questions loading in his mind.

Brushing my hair with his fingers, he softly asks, "What happened, baby?"

Swallowing hard, I know I want to tell him. But

forming those words on my lips feels like an impossible task.

He gives me silence, letting me mull through the thoughts racing through my mind. Leaning forward, he kisses my forehead and breathes me in.

Taking a shaky breath, I tell him what happened— from the very beginning when Professor Von London hugged me to when I ran from the room with Sunny. Every detail, every moment, every thought.

Listening intently, he stays quiet, not interrupting once. And when I finish, his eyes are watery, and as if his feelings for me are tangible, I can feel them wrap around my heart.

Holding me tightly, he consoles me, constantly reminding me that I'm safe and that he'll never let anything happen to me again. We embrace one another for what feels like forever, until I fall asleep in his arms.

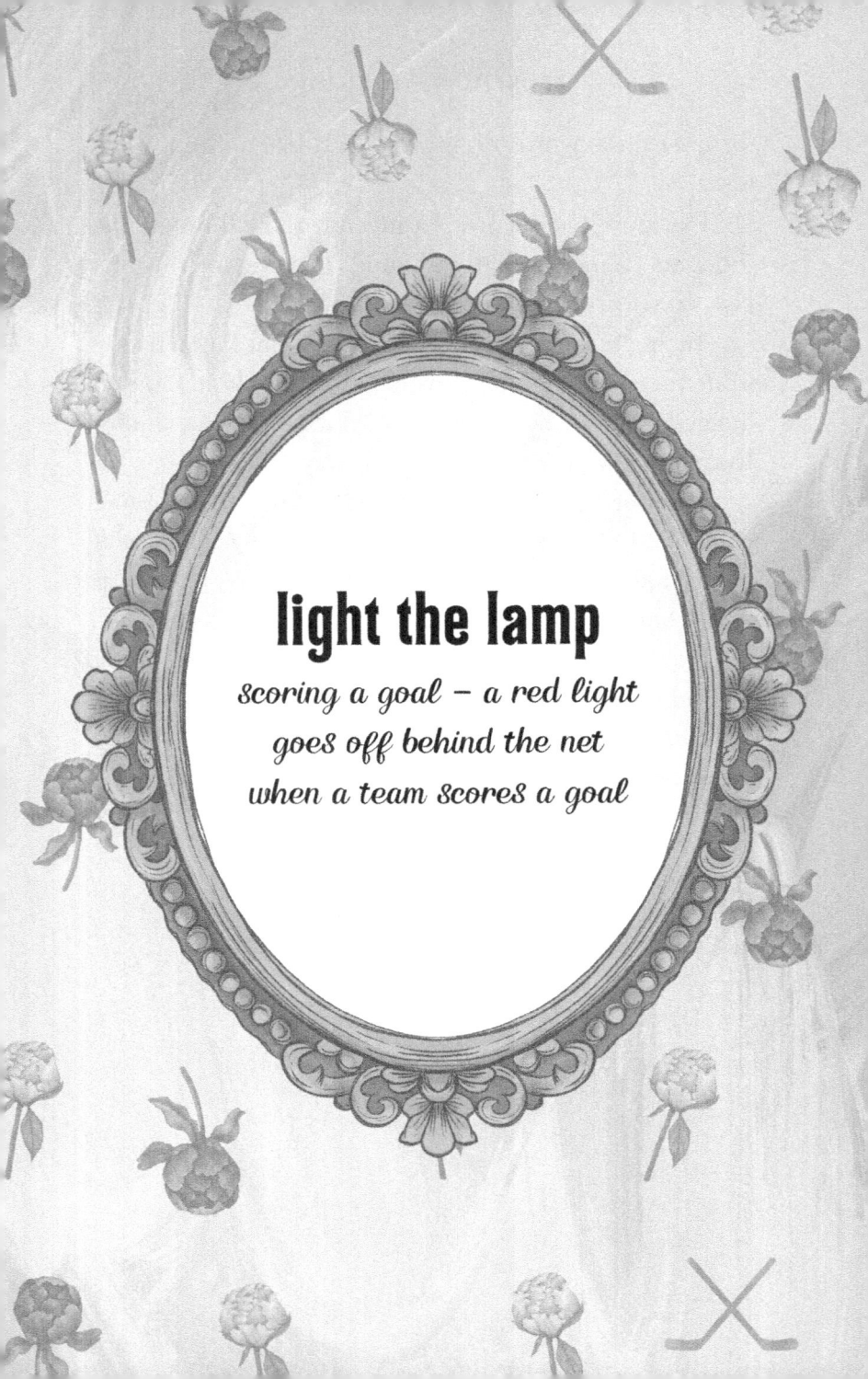

light the lamp

*scoring a goal — a red light
goes off behind the net
when a team scores a goal*

chapter
twenty-two
malik

Waking up this morning, I find a thousand texts in the boys' group chat, all checking in to see if she's okay. But the final one came from Griffin.

> Griffin: I've got his home address if we need it.

> Asher: And his phone number. I also hacked into his email and set it up to send me automatic notifications for his schedule. He seems to use it religiously.

God, I love these boys. I also have a special adoration for Asher's computer skills. I knew they'd come in handy at some point; I just never imagined it would be to help track down the creep who touched my girl.

I owe you guys. Thank you. At Alora's right now. I'll catch up with you guys soon.

Setting my phone down, I turn back to Alora, who is sleeping on her back with the hood of my sweatshirt up over her head. She looks so peaceful; I don't think I can bring myself to wake her.

So, I don't.

I watch her sleep for the next hour, bouncing between fawning over her and playing games on my phone.

Sunny stretches and yawns, stealing my attention. She prances over with a smile, and I pet her soft head. I wonder if she needs to go out.

Stealthily, I slide off of the bed without moving the mattress and disturbing Alora.

"Good morning, Sunny," I whisper and tiptoe over to the sliding glass door, unlocking it and inching it open.

She prances out, and I follow her, gently sliding the door closed behind us. She spots something in the grass and takes off toward it, trotting back with a ball in her mouth. When she drops it at my feet, I pick it up and throw it across the large yard.

Taking off, she bolts toward it and picks it up in her mouth, squeezing and squeaking it as she comes back to me. I throw it for her again, over and over until she tires, plops down next to me, and chews on it instead of giving it to me to toss.

"Ready to go inside?" I ask her, shivering in my boxers and crop top, walking to the door and sliding it open.

She hustles inside and drops the ball by the door before jumping onto her dog bed and curling up.

"Who's a good girl?" I whisper to her, rubbing under her jaw.

I've always wanted a dog since I was little, but I never dared bring one home or ask for one, not with my uncle living in the house. I didn't want to give him something to use against us, and that's exactly what he would've done.

When I glance over at Alora, she stirs beneath the cozy pink blanket with a grimace on her face.

What's she dreaming about?

Her head rolls to the side, and a scared groan slips past her lips. Should I wake her?

She grimaces again, and I can't bear to watch her face twist with fear a moment longer.

Rushing to her side, I kneel by the bed and gently rock her shoulder. "Hey, baby, wake up. It's just a bad dream."

Her eyes flutter behind her eyelids rapidly, and I nudge her again.

"I'm right here."

Her eyes fly open, strained and widened with fear,

and those bright blue irises land right on me. Her chest is rising and falling so fast, her breathing erratic.

Running my hand over her hair, I take loud, slow breaths. Following my lead, she forces her inhales to match mine, slowly calming down.

"Hi." Her voice is raw and frail, like she's been screaming for hours.

Grabbing her water bottle from the bed, I gently set it next to her. "Hi. How are you feeling?"

I read that POTS episodes can last days at times, and she may need to rest and relax for just as long, if not longer, to feel better.

She takes a few sips of water and clears her throat. "Umm … not great. My head is pounding, and I just feel … nauseous."

"Can I do anything to help?"

She shakes her head, and my chest pains because I know I can't take it all away for her.

Yesterday was a lot for Alora, not just the physical exertion, but the stress of dealing with that fucking creep. I'm going to kill him for touching her, rip and pry his soul from his body with my bare hands.

"Would you let Sunny out for me? She probably has to go potty," Alora asks, rubbing her temples.

Smiling down at her, I lean down and plant a soft kiss on her forehead. "Already did. We played fetch and everything. We're actually best friends now."

Alora giggles. "Oh, are you?" Her face softens, her stare deepening. "Thank you, Malik."

I brush her cheek with my thumb. "Do you want to talk about yesterday?" I whisper.

She holds my stare like an anchor, grounding her to the present as her mind drifts away. "The one thing I can't stop thinking about is that everything he ever told me was a lie. A ploy to get me to let my guard down around him." She slams her eyes closed. "God, it's like I can't shake the feeling of his hand on my chest … his lips on my mouth."

My blood runs cold at the admission that he kissed her. "I'm going to make him pay for what he did, I promise you."

She scoffs, doubting me. "No one's going to believe me over him. He's a legend."

"So am I, baby." I kiss her hairline. "And I guarantee you, he will regret what he did when I'm through with him."

"Malik." Her gaze flicks up to me. "I think it'd be better if I just forgot about it. I don't want to make a scene and make everything worse." She pauses, her mouth ajar, but she closes it without another word.

She might hate me for it, but I'm doing it anyway.

"He's not getting away with it. You deserve to get justice."

Her bottom lip quivers. "I just feel so stupid."

Jumping up, I slide into the bed next to her and pull her into my chest. "Don't say that. You aren't stupid, Alora. You're trusting and kind. You idolized him, looked up to him; there was no reason you would have thought differently about him."

She looks up at me. "But even you said you didn't like him."

I shrug. "I saw something in his eyes. But I like to see the worst in people and prepare for the harm they'll cause. You see the best, and I would give anything to see the world through your eyes."

Leaning down, I grab her chin with my thumb and forefinger and tip her head back, kissing her gently. Her lips meet mine with the same warmth and passion.

Part of me wants to tell her what I did in her practice room, but I'm scared it might run her off.

I can't simply like her and hold her hand, smiling. I need to protect her, consume her, obsess and devour her. Which is why I might have hidden a small camera in the room …

After the day I saw him look at her a little too closely, I had Asher help me install it in case he ever tried something.

It's not a matter of someone believing Alora's account. I have him on fucking camera, every moment documented. I swear, every single place he touched her, I'll break on him.

My phone dings. Once, twice, three times.

Checking it, I find more texts from the boys.

Griffin: ETA? Ready and waiting.

Asher: Schedule says he'll be at home
for the next two hours, so we might
want to hurry it up …

Dean: I've got Elias and Finn with me.

Heading to Griffin's in a minute. Meet
up there.

"Hey, would it be okay if I go run an errand quickly? I'll be back in just a little bit." I'm hesitant to leave her at all but this needs to be taken care of sooner than later.

Her warm gaze meets mine. "Of course. Sunny and I will snuggle and watch a movie or something until you get back." She stutters, "I-If you were coming right back I mean."

Leaning down, I kiss her forehead. "It's the only place I want to be."

The first thing I do when I get to Griffin's is change from my hockey gear and jersey that I switched back into before leaving Alora's. And then I pull up the footage of my hidden camera to see exactly what the fuck he did to my girl. I won't let anyone else watch it; that's Alora's business, and no one else needs to see it without her permission. But I almost can't even keep my eyes on it.

The way he cornered her, forced himself on her ... it makes me feel sick and feel an anger that I never knew was possible. One so deep that I'm scared what I will do when I see him.

I give the guys the gist of the information, and then we load into Griffin's truck and my Corvette, following the directions Asher gave us.

We haven't even made it to the professor's house yet, and my fists are already clenching so tightly that my fingers have gone numb.

Wringing my hands on the steering wheel, I force myself to take deep breaths—in through my nose, out through my mouth. But nothing will calm me down, no matter how hard I try.

"About a minute out," Asher mumbles, riding in the passenger seat next to me.

The rest of the guys are in Griffin's pickup behind us.

Taking the last right turn onto Spindle Street, we pull up to a ridiculously nice house. One that this fuck doesn't deserve.

I kill the engine, and Asher and I get out, followed by everyone in Griff's truck—Dean, Elias, Finn, and Griffin. I wonder if Rupert has noticed us yet.

I lead the way up the sidewalk toward his front porch, climbing the few stairs and ringing the doorbell.

I heard him in that video, telling Alora that no one was going to believe him. Well, he's wrong. Because I sure as fuck do, and so do the guys behind me.

Sound rustles inside, growing louder and louder until the door is opened and Rupert steps into view.

He looks us over. "How can I help you boys?" His voice is shaky. His gaze lands on me, and his face falls. "Look, I don't want any trouble now."

Stepping through the threshold of his front door, I spin my baseball cap around backward, wanting an unobstructed view of the man I'm about to destroy for touching my girl.

Lifting his hands up in surrender, he cowers and stutter-steps backward.

I chuckle and grab his hand, digging my fingers between the tendons. "Too late for that."

"Please. It was all a misunderstanding." His arrogance fills the room, fueling my rage even more. "Whatever she said, she was lying."

Laughing maniacally, I snap one of his fingers back, hearing the crunch echo in my ears. He cries out in pain and tries to pull free from my grasp. But he won't escape it.

"What do you want from me? Money?"

I break another finger, and he screams.

"Do you really think you can buy us off? Not everyone is as greedy and corrupt as you," I growl in his face. Wincing at his crooked fingers, I bare my teeth. "I bet it's going to be awfully hard to play piano with these."

"What's your plan? Attack me? Beat me up? The police won't let you get away with this." He scowls, clearly having no idea of who he's talking to.

"I'm sure, as a teacher at this school, you've heard of the name Kensington or Hawthorne?"

He swallows hard and nods.

"Then I'm sure you're well aware of the power they hold, not only just on campus, but in Evermore. They fund this town, and if you think threatening them is a good idea, I can't wait for you to find out the consequences."

"All for a lying girl?" He scoffs, flabbergasted, as if he can't even fathom what I would do for her.

My right fist is flying before I can blink, crashing into the side of his face. "Don't even talk about her! You don't deserve to speak her name."

The guys step forward, lining up at my sides as my fists bunch into his shirt, lifting him up.

"You're going to quit your job. Today. While we're here," I inform him very clearly.

His eyebrows lift. "I'm not *resigning*!"

"Asher," I grumble, "show him."

He takes my phone and pulls up the security camera, showing him the live feed of someone playing violin. "Do you see that? That's live right now. Isn't that interesting?"

Rupert's face pales, his body sagging into my grasp. "Y-you recorded it? Without my consent?"

"Oh, now you care about consent?" The taped-up knuckles of my left hand bury into his abdomen. "I'm sorry. I should have asked. Are you okay with me recording you assaulting one of your students?"

"I-it's not what it l-looks like ..." He trails off, and I shake my head in disappointment.

Dropping him back to the ground, I shove him. "Get your phone out. You're quitting right now. No notice. No letter. Over the phone. Right. Now."

He chuckles nervously. "You can't be serious."

"Do you want to find out if I'm bluffing?" I smirk, looking at him through my lashes, my head tilted to the floor.

He starts pacing back and forth. "And if I don't?"

I shrug, letting him answer his own question with his best guess.

"You have sixty seconds before I forward the footage to the president."

His eyes bulge out of his head, and he rushes over to me with his hands lifted in prayer. "Wait, wait, wait! I need more time, please!"

Cocking my head to the side, I click my tongue against the roof of my mouth. "Ticktock."

"Fuck!" he cries out and grabs his phone, unlocking the screen. His finger hovers over an app, but he doesn't press it. "And if I don't call?"

"Your gamble. Your consequences." I cross my arms over my chest.

As I look over him as he contemplates what to do, my stomach twists sharply. How could he do that to her? A gross man abusing his power. I'm well aware of men like that; they are my least favorite kind.

"Ten seconds," I warn him, ballparking the time in my head.

As he spends the next ten seconds sighing and crying, I unwrap the dressing on my left knuckles. They're wrapped up from my most recent tattoo appointment. I haven't been ready to show Alora yet, so I've kept them hidden, making it look like an injury from hitting someone on the ice.

"Time's up," my deep voice calmly tells him as I toss the bandage to the ground. "Go ahead and read this for me." Lifting my knuckles in the air, I make a fist.

His gaze drops to my hand, and he sounds the tattooed letters out in his mind. Then his terrified brown eyes fly up to mine.

"Say it. Say her name," I snarl, stepping toward him.

He quivers. "A-A-l-lora." The coward of a man before me can barely speak, his voice frail.

Nodding, I smile at him—not in a friendly manner, but in a warning of what's about to happen. "That's right. And this one's from her."

My fist drives upward, colliding into the bottom of his jaw, clanking his teeth together. He wobbles back, trying to catch his balance, but it doesn't matter because I'm not done yet.

My right fist slams into his stomach, his kidney, his face, and then my left does the same, his cries filling the house as I pummel into him.

He touched her, he made her feel helpless and weak, and he stole pieces of her that were not for the taking. Images of her walking up to the boards at the rink flash in my mind.

Her tangled blonde hair, her torn top, splotchy red skin, smeared lip gloss. But the most vivid of all is the mascara streaks running down her cheeks and neck, telling me everything I needed to know—she didn't want that, and I was going to obliterate him.

Falling to the ground, I collapse on top of him, ramming my fists as hard as I can against his bloody and swelling face.

"Malik."

My name echoes in my ears, but I push the sound away, focusing on the whimpers and dry-heaving of Alora last night. Of when the thought of him made her throw up either from disgust or fatigue. *He* did that.

I'm tired of powerful men thinking they can get away with hurting anyone in their path. He is just another one in the long line of demons who have no compassion for those around them.

I'm tired of feeling like I'm constantly fighting a losing battle. Like I'm not in control of my own life. Of feeling like everything I do will end up amounting to nothing in the end.

Then there's her, the glowing light that calls me home. We're simply opposite sides of the same coin ... both falling victim to the manipulation of arrogant, greedy men.

The shiny fucking star in my life, and he thinks he can just touch her and get away with it?!

Pounding my fists into him over and over, I feel his blood splash back in my face, mixing with the sweat beading on my forehead.

Sound starts to fill my ears, gargled and muffled, but I piece together the end of Griffin's sentence.

"... enough. You've done enough!"

Hands and arms wrap around me, yanking me up and off of the bloody mess on the floor. Tuning my surroundings back in, I realize that I might have hit him a few more times than I thought.

Out of breath, I stand to my full height and spit down at him. "Your job is already gone. I just wanted to see if you'd do the right thing. Clearly not."

I drive my foot into his ribs, and he grunts. He opens his mouth to speak, but nothing comes out.

When I step away from him, he grabs my ankle. "What do you mean?" His voice is raw.

"That video was already given to the president— before we even got here." I yank my leg from his grasp.

Asher chimes in, "I put word out to my parents about a professional pianist harassing and assaulting students. You're part of the Hartford Association, right? The elite and private organization for the best pianists in the world?"

Lifting himself up, he slumps against the wall, blood spilling out of his mouth as he nods.

Asher winces. "I'm honored to tell you that you're not anymore."

He coughs. "P-please."

Crouching down next to him, I grab his jaw in my hand, and he screams in pain. "Oh, what a shame. It looks like your pleas don't mean anything to us. Just like hers meant nothing to you."

Two policemen walk in the door, and Dean greets them.

I would be nervous about cops walking into this situation, except that we were the ones who called them.

"Whoa, did he get into a car accident?" the older one asks, eyeing Rupert's injuries.

"Sure did," I answer him, dropping Rupert's jaw. Turning back to Mr. Von London, I hold his weakened stare and whisper, "Don't bother crying wolf. It's not like they're going to believe you anyway."

"Stand up for us." The cops walk over to him, and I back out of the way.

Rupert struggles to his feet, and the younger cop twists his arms behind his back.

"You are under arrest for sexual assault and false imprisonment. You have the right to remain silent ..."

I tune him out as the cop escorts him outside.

The older one stays behind for a moment. "Thank you, boys, for bringing this to our attention. We'll make sure he is well taken care of."

Reaching out my hand, I offer to shake it, but when he looks down, he freezes. I follow his gaze, finding my knuckles and hand bloodied.

His lips part as if he wants to say something, but he remains silent.

I mutter, "Thank you."

He nods and walks out of the house, catching up to the younger cop.

"Hey, Malik?" Asher pats the back of my shoulder as we walk outside. "I promise to never piss you off."

Chuckling at him, I shake my head. "Too late."

"You didn't even need us anyway." Griffin chuckles.

Looking over at him, I correct him, "That's where you're wrong. I didn't ask you to come so you could help me fight him. I asked you to come so you could pull me off in case I almost killed him."

"Touché," Dean mutters.

We get in our cars and head back to Griffin's, where everyone else's vehicles are. When we arrive, the Kensingtons get on their bikes and ride away, followed by Finn and Elias in their own vehicles.

"Oh my God, that's a lot of blood." Blair gasps when we walk in the front door, her eyes landing on my soaked shirt and splattered skin.

"Don't worry." Griffin laughs. "None of it is ours."

"Does that make it better?" she asks, waving to me to follow her into the kitchen.

Griffin teases her, "So, you'd rather us be hurt than hurt someone else?"

She glares at him. "Oh, shut it."

Walking over to the sink, I wash my hands well, scrubbing the dried blood with soap and hot water until there's not a trace left of what I did. Well, aside from a couple of splits in my skin that the soap makes damn sure to find.

"I'm going over to Alora's tonight," I tell them, drying my hands off with a rag.

"Finally, we get the house to ourselves again." Griffin sighs.

"Fuck off." I laugh, throwing the towel at him and walking toward my room. "I'm leaving in a few."

Heading to the bathroom, I rewrap my left hand, hiding the tattoo I got for Alora. It might seem crazy and soon, but I don't fucking care. She's it for me; I'm done. It's her or no one.

Quickly throwing a bag together with some clothes and the essentials, I hop in my car and head to Alora's. But first, I make a pit stop and pick up a few things at Toads Grocery.

When I get to her dorm, I knock on the door, and she calls out, "Come in!"

Using the key fob I still have, I let myself in, my arms full of bags. "How'd you know it was me?"

She sits up in bed as Sunny rushes over to me, greeting me with a wagging tail and kisses.

"You're the only one who would show up at my door without calling first." She smirks.

When I set the bags down on her desk, she eyes them. "Whatcha got there?"

"A few things I thought you might like." I start emptying them, revealing a box of the Waterboy hydration packs she always has with her, her favorite bottled water, a veggie tray, and her favorite guilty-pleasure treat—strawberries and whipped cream. Thank you, Alora, for posting about it on your socials.

"Malik," she murmurs adoringly, "thank you."

"And of course"—I pull the last thing out of the bag, a toy for Sunny—"something for the best girl."

Sunny lights up and immediately sits down, waiting for me to give it to her. I toss it into the air, and she catches it, rushing over to her bed and squeaking it with vigor.

"Such a sweet gesture, Ravenwell. Are you buttering me up to kill me?" She slowly rises from her bed and walks over to me, wearing a cute two-piece light-blue lounge set.

"Maybe." I pull her closer to me. sliding my left hand into her hair and lowering my lips to hers, I kiss her desperately.

Her phone starts ringing loudly, cutting through our moment.

She walks over to her bed and sighs. "It's my dad.

I'll just call him back later. God, he hasn't wanted to talk to me this much since I was a kid."

My blood chills at the reminder of Congressman Briarwood. I feel like my happily ever after is in my grasp, but we're not safe yet. It can still be ripped away from me, from us, shattered into smithereens.

But I won't let him take anything else from me for as long as I live. Even if he tries to slay me like a dragon, I'll burn his fairy tale and lies to the ground.

I just hope that when I show her who he really is, she won't hate me for it in the end.

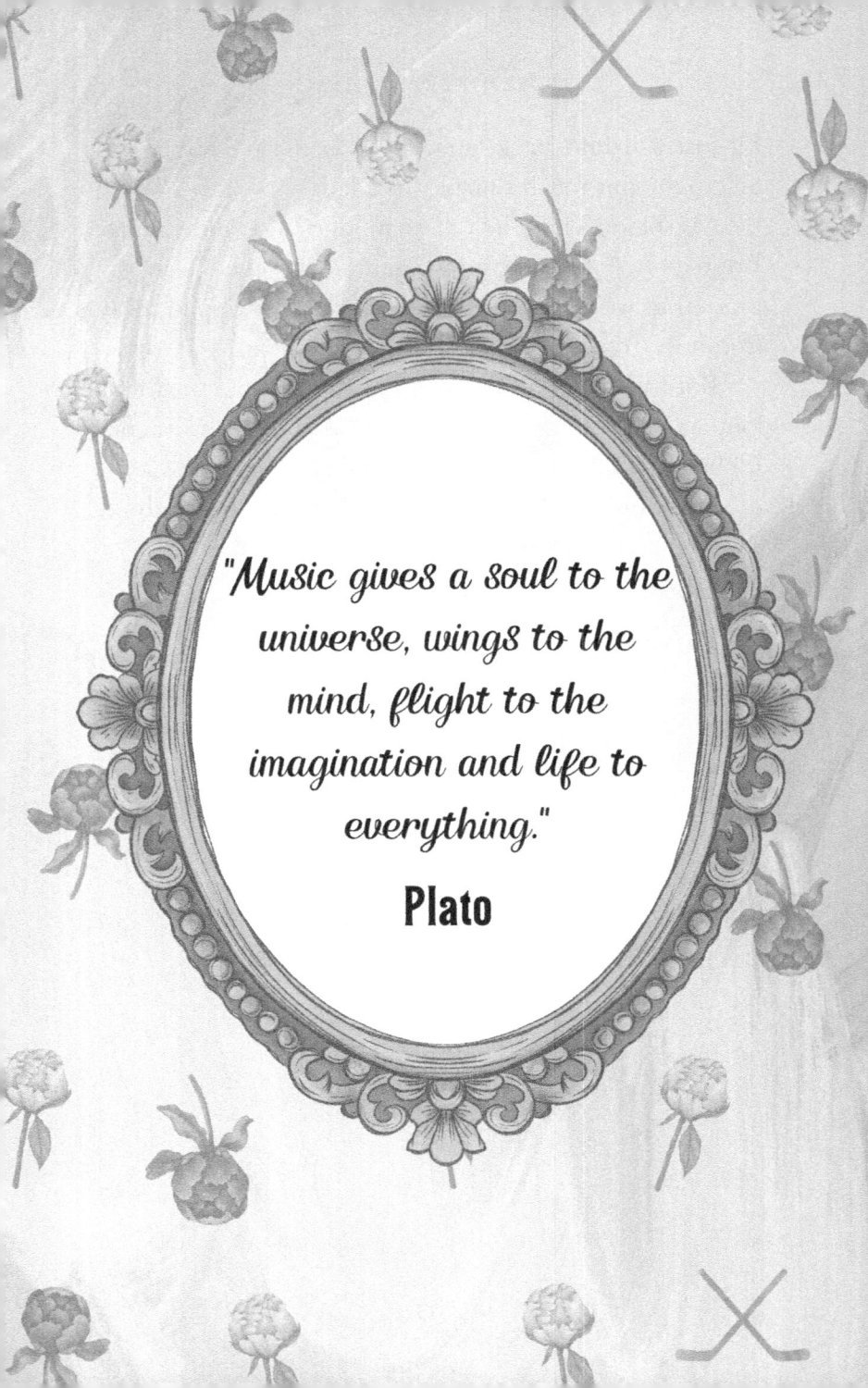

"Music gives a soul to the universe, wings to the mind, flight to the imagination and life to everything."

Plato

chapter twenty-three
alora

The last few days have been brutal with one of the worst flare-ups I've had in a long time. It took almost three days for me to start to feel back to my normal self.

Thankfully, I had great company to keep me entertained. Malik barely left my side the entire time, and I can't even begin to express how … comforting that was.

I don't know when everything truly shifted between us. Part of me is still scared he'll suddenly change his mind. But frankly, I don't care. I want him for as long as I can have him.

There's something in the way he stares at me, like he sees through every shield I've ever hidden behind. Like he can see me unabashedly and chooses me anyway.

Whether taking a chance with him is the smartest or

dumbest decision I've ever made, all I know is that I'm falling for him.

There's no use in fighting it; it's too late to stop it. I'm simply a snowball racing down a snowy hill, my feelings growing bigger and bigger every day.

But I have to remind myself that this very well could end in absolute turmoil. Especially with secrets lurking in the dark. I know there are things going on that I'm not privy to. I intend to find out. Maybe I'll ask him tonight, when he gets back to the house after practice.

Blair, Lumi, Phillip, Sunny, and I spent the afternoon around the pool in Blair's backyard, some of us enjoying it more than others. Now, we're lying in Blair and Griffin's living room, watching a movie.

Sunny and Rex, their dog, have really become the best of friends. It's adorable to watch her bond with him. They're snuggled up together next to me, Sunny's big head on his small body, using him like a little pillow.

"Holy shit. Alora." Phillip's head pops up behind his phone. "You need to see this."

He tosses his phone over to me, and I catch it and stare at the screen, my jaw unhinging and crashing to the floor.

My shock is barely audible. "Jesus."

An article was just published to *Evermore Daily News* —"HEAU Professor Assaults Student, Facing Multiple Charges."

My heart drops, and I skim the article, looking for any indication that I was the student. But the more I read, the more my shoulders relax, as no details are mentioned. When I scroll to the bottom of the article, my breath catches in my throat. Rupert Von London's mug shot is centered on the page. But that's not what took me by surprise.

It's the fact that more of his face is black and blue than not. Parts of his face are split open, clearly repaired with stitches and bandages. The article notes that in a provoked attack, multiple fingers were broken, and he had an occipital fracture and a fractured jaw.

Holy crap.

"I wonder what happened," I mutter, zooming in on the image, seeing every scratch and bump on him.

Blair looks over at me with a knowing gleam in her eye. "Wait, what do you mean?"

Confusion thrums through me. "What do you mean, *what do I mean?*"

Her mouth forms into an O as she inhales, her eyes widening. She sets the remote down on the coffee table in front of us. "Umm, maybe I'm not supposed to say anything."

Sitting up taller, I turn to her completely, Phillip following suit. "Do you know what happened?"

She swallows hard, contemplating whether or not to tell me. "Yeah …" She pauses. "I assumed that you knew. I didn't know that Malik hadn't told you."

I wait for her to continue, the hair on the back of my neck rising with anticipation.

"The guys paid him a visit the day he was arrested.

They were the ones who called the cops. And that"—she glances down at the phone, pointing at the mug shot—"was Malik."

"All of that?" I gasp, shocked that he could cause so much damage.

She shrugs nervously. "He can be an overachiever when it comes to the things he loves."

Her choice of words sends a jolt through me. I can't imagine a world where Malik Ravenwell would ever love me.

Maybe it's because I've spent most of our time together hearing him tell me how much he hated me. But love? I don't know.

My phone rings, and I jump from the full volume. Grabbing my phone from beside me, I see my dad calling.

That can't be a coincidence.

"Excuse me. I have to take this." I stand.

Phillip looks my way, and I can tell he's asking if it's my dad. I nod and stroll out of the room into the quiet foyer.

"Hello?" I answer, chewing on my bottom lip.

My dad's sigh is the first thing I hear.

Well, this conversation is going to be delightful.

"How many times do I need to tell you to behave before I have no choice but to enforce your consequences?"

My spine straightens, and my shoulders drop, a chill skating across the nape of my neck.

"Dad, I've been on my best behavior lately." I pause, knowing that it doesn't matter what I say; I know his mind is already made up.

He laughs with no humor. "Is that why I received a photo of Malik Ravenwell carrying you across campus? I mean, what on earth goes through your mind when you call that behaving? I warned you, Alora. Please don't make me *make you* follow my rules."

"Then stop making them, Dad. I'm an adult. Besides, it's not like you've been in my life for a long time anyway," I snap, wondering if this will soften his anger or fuel it more.

He takes a deep breath. "I know you can't understand. I don't blame you. But sending you away to your aunts was for your own protection, Little Rose. It was to keep you safe from the dangers of my job. Which is only getting more dangerous since I'll be running for senator."

I always knew he would shoot for the stars in his career. I know he wants to run for president one day. But why does his success have anything to do with the way I act? More specifically...the way he wants me to act.

Tears well in my eyes. He might have meant well at the time, but that doesn't take away any of the pain he's caused. He can't take that back.

"Please, just stay away from the Ravenwell boy," he pleads.

"Why are you so insistent about it? What is your problem with him?" I beg him.

He sighs and clicks his tongue. "He was involved with a lot of bad people in high school. He's dangerous. I'm trying to keep you safe."

Malik was a lot of things back then, but he was far too busy ruining my life to get involved in shady shit.

As much as he watched me, I watched him back. I needed to know where he was, so I didn't step on a mine and blow myself to smithereens.

And I know my dad's lying. He clicked his tongue before he started talking—the tell he's had for as long as I can remember. I just can't figure out why they're connected.

"Okay," I lie right back to him. "Is that the only reason you called? To yell at me?"

I can practically see him rubbing his temples in frustration.

"No. I called because I saw the article that was just published in *Evermore Daily News*. A piano professor. Did you meet him?"

"Yes." My voice is quiet.

He exhales heavily. "Christ, Alora. Do you know who was involved? Please tell me it wasn't you."

Should I lie to him? I feel like if I say the truth, he'll just find yet another reason to keep a closer eye on me.

"No, it wasn't me." The words feel like poison on my lips.

I hate lying. I hate liars. But this is for the best.

"Thank goodness. That would have been a media disaster."

My face pales at his utterance.

He clears his throat and quickly says, "And I'm sure it was very traumatic for whoever the victim was."

Yeah, it sure was.

"Good thing you don't have to worry about a new scandal or bad press," I snap, my voice cruel and harsh.

"Listen, I have compassion for the situation, but with the upcoming election, we don't need a distraction."

"Dad," I whisper in shock and disappointment.

"Never mind that. If you hear anything or any reporters approach you, stay quiet and keep your mouth shut. Please, honey, for the both of us."

"Yeah, Dad, anything you want." My voice is saddened and strained as I fight back the urge to cry. I've cried enough for this man over the years.

For the first time in a long time, his voice sounds kind and sincere as he says his goodbye. "I love you, Little Rose."

"I love you too," I mutter, wondering if that's the truth or just another lie.

Ending the call and shoving my phone in my jeans pocket, I spin around to head back to the living room and slam to a halt, finding Malik standing five feet from me, looking pissed as hell, his jaw locked shut and eyebrows low.

"Hey, what's wrong?" I ask him, walking up to him and reaching up to wrap my arms around his neck.

But he backs away and closes his eyes the moment I touch him. He breathes through his nose, taking a few breaths before opening his eyes.

"I'm sorry. Did I do something?" I ask, suddenly feeling incredibly lonely after the conversation I just had with my dad and now this.

He bites down on the inside of his cheek. "Sorry, I'm just … I'm just tired. I need to go lie down. Excuse me."

My heart cracks, the tiniest microscopic fracture. "Just talk to me, Malik. Maybe I can help."

His voice is cold and cruel, bringing me back to my childhood as he mutters, "You couldn't possibly understand."

When he brushes past me, I feel him take part of me with him as he rushes downstairs to his room, and I'm left standing in the foyer with the heaviest weight on my chest.

Feeling incredibly small and invisible, I fight back the tears welling in my eyes.

He's not good with communication—I know that. But he can't keep shutting me out and hope that we'll just continue on as is. We both need more than that. And I need him to let me in, to show me that this means as much to him as it does to me.

If I want this to work, I'm willing to put in the

effort, but he needs to meet me halfway. Maybe I'll just give him a little boost.

My feet are moving, crossing the grand foyer with no sign of stopping. I descend the stairs to the lower east wing toward Malik's room.

Don't stop now. Stand tall. Be strong.

Approaching his door, I grab the handle and throw it open, finding Malik sitting on his bed with his head in his hands.

My heart completely breaks at the image of him shattering, wetness gathering in his gaze as he lifts it to mine.

For a split second, I see the broken boy inside, the one so terrified of the world that he stays hidden behind the sharp and thorny shell he's worked so hard to build.

I take a step toward him.

"Don't," Malik warns me with one word. "You can't be in here."

I feel like I'm facing a lion in the wild, completely unsure of when or if the beast will strike.

My voice is steady and calm. "But you're in my room all the time. Why can't I be in yours?"

He bites his bottom lip in frustration, rising to his feet, his mouth drawn taut. "Because I said so, Alora."

"Just like that?" I lose my composure, snapping at him. "I mean, why can't you give me an *actual* reason?"

I take another step toward him, and the shell surrounding him stiffens even more.

"Tell me a *real* reason, something genuine, and I'll leave," I murmur. "Just open up to me, Malik."

His eyes blur over, as if a scene is playing out in his mind. "I …"

"Is it about my dad? You know, I saw you two talking the day he was here."

His gaze clears up, and the fury that ignites inside is unmatched to anything I've seen before. "You don't know what you saw. He—he was just asking for directions."

I scoff. "Oh, yeah, because when I give someone instructions, I yell at them and clench my fists."

"Well, he was pissing me off with his holier-than-thou tone. What can I say? I despise authority." He crosses his arms over his chest.

Running my hands through my hair, I sigh, realizing we're getting nowhere. "Malik …" His name is a plea on my tongue. "Is it about Rupert? I saw what you did to him. What, do you regret it or something?"

His brows furrow. "What? No. *Fuck no*, I don't regret that. If anything, I wish I had done more to him."

Something inside of me warms just slightly.

Closing my eyes, I sigh. "Then can we please stop playing this guessing game and you just tell me the truth?"

A war plays out behind his eyes as his stare bounces back and forth between mine. His lips part to say something, but he doesn't.

"I can tell you're going through something right now. And I'm here for you just as much as you are for me. But you can't just lock me out of your mind, your heart, your room." I flex my hands. "I need more of you, all of you."

Silence consumes him as he listens to every word I say, leaning forward as if he was hanging on to my words for dear life.

Patting my jeans, I exhale. "I'll give you your space, okay? Good night."

Spinning on my heel, I walk back toward his door to leave, but before I reach it, he steps past me and shuts it with his hand while his other hand finds my waist, pinning me to the closed door.

"Wait. Please, just wait."

Looking up at him, I do just that. I'd sit here for an eternity if he needed me to.

His eyes slam closed, and agony flashes across his face. "I'm scared to tell you anything, Alora. Fucking terrified."

He looks at me, and I see it—the broken version he usually hides from the world.

"Because no one has ever been as close to my heart as you, and you could absolutely destroy it in a second if you wanted to. I'm scared that the more I give, the more you'll find a reason to leave."

Reaching up, I grab his jaw with my hand. "You think opening up to me will make me want to leave?"

Slowly, he nods.

Sliding my other hand up, I cup his face. "That will never happen."

Disbelief flashes in his gaze before he glances away. "There's a lot about me you don't know, Alora. Stuff that will change your view on the world."

Brushing my thumbs back and forth, I stand onto my toes and gently press my lips on his. "I want it all, Malik. All of you. Always. Because …" My heart launches into my throat. "Because I'm falling in love with you."

His hand tightens on my waist. "You know you deserve better than what I can offer you."

"Well, I don't want anything else. I want *you*." I inch closer to him, sliding my hand down his chest and fisting his shirt, tugging him toward me.

"What if it's not enough?" he whispers.

"Malik, *you're* enough." I kiss him, breathing him in. "You're everything."

Something inside of him snaps, and he grabs my face, kissing me ferociously. Words aren't his forte, so perhaps he wants to show me how he feels instead of telling me.

Parting my lips with his tongue, he slips it into my mouth. His touch overwhelms me—in the best of ways. He devours me, showing me just how much I mean to him.

He pulls away and looks down at me with hooded eyes. "I know you deserve more than a coward who can't speak. But I'm way too selfish to ever let you go.

So, please, just for tonight, let me get lost in you. Please, baby, I need you."

The pain and anguish in his reddened stare dissolve any reservations I had left. Slowly, I nod, agreeing.

"Thank you," he whimpers before crashing his lips to mine, his fervor unmatched.

Pushing his body against mine, he parts my legs with his knee, grinding and rolling against me as our mouths dance together.

His hands slide down and around my hips. I gasp as he lifts me up and wraps me around his waist, our lips never parting.

Bringing us over to the edge of his bed, he gently lowers my back to the comforter, stepping between my legs. "I need you, Alora. Fuck, more than anything else in the world."

Trusting Malik with my heart may be the most dangerous game I've ever played. But as I open my eyes and find the look in his, I've never been surer of what to do.

He may be broken and flawed. But so am I.

Grabbing his shirt, I pull him back on top of me, our lips colliding and melting together with the fire in our kiss.

His hands make quick work of my top and bra, tossing them to the side. Wandering down my body, his greedy fingers undo the buttons of my jeans, slipping them down my legs effortlessly. His lips follow the path of his hands, trailing down my neck to my breasts.

He sucks my nipple into his mouth, flicking his tongue back and forth, making my back arch off of the bed. When he palms my other boob, it spills through his fingers, and he kneads it roughly, sending a hot bolt down my spine.

Dropping to his knees on the floor in front of me, he hooks his fingers into my silky pink panties and shimmies them over my hips. As he tosses them into the pile beside him, he inches forward, sliding his arms beneath my knees and pulling me toward him.

"Fucking hell, Alora," he groans, pushing my legs further and further apart.

The warmth of his breath caresses my center, and I gasp.

"You have no idea how many hours I've spent fantasizing about the filthy things I want to do to you."

He runs his tongue up my core, and I moan.

"The ways I've imagined burying myself so deep inside of you that you forget you ever hated me. You've haunted me for years, for far longer than you'll ever know."

His words electrify my body, and his name leaves my tongue in a whimper. "*Malik*."

Circling my entrance with his finger, he slides it inside. "Tell me you've thought the same, Bug. How you've pictured all the dirty things I'm going to do to you."

As he slowly pumps his finger in and out, his tongue laps at my clit.

"Yes, yes, *yes*, I have."

A second finger fills me. "Let me show you just how fucking good I can make you feel. Let me mold your pretty pussy to every vein on my cock."

Moaning, he picks up his pace, thrusting into me faster and faster as I race closer to my first orgasm.

"Malik, *please*."

He flicks his tongue. "Then come on my fingers like my good little slut, and I'll give you every goddamn inch."

When he sucks on my clit, waves of pleasure start to pulse through my body.

"Oh fuck," I cry out as ecstasy fills me.

Relentlessly, he continues his worship of me until my breathing starts to slow.

Easing his fingers out of me, he sucks them clean and stands up. "How are you feeling?"

My heart warms at the simple yet thoughtful question. He knows he's getting my heart to race, but lying on my back with my legs in the air certainly helps.

"I'm doing good."

A smile tips his lips up as he slides his joggers down his legs, exposing even more of his tattoos, scattered across his thighs and V-line. His boxers are tight, struggling to contain the pulsing and throbbing erection.

"It's ridiculous that you can be *that* hot," I murmur, greedily eyeing him up.

"Oh, yeah? You think I'm hot?" He winks at me.

"You know you're hot." I roll my eyes.

Lightly, he slaps the inside of my thigh, and my pussy pulses from the sensation.

"That's not what I asked, Bug."

"Malik, I'm obsessed with you—for reasons far more than your looks. But, yeah …" I trail off, letting my eyes wander up and down him. "You're a fucking god, carved from marble."

He huffs proudly. "Damn straight, baby."

The air thickens between us as he pushes his boxers to the ground and tosses his shirt to the side, not a shred of fabric left on either of us.

Wrapping his hand around his shaft, he pumps himself once, twice as he stares at my center and wets his lips.

"Malik," I whisper, pulling his gaze to mine. "I, uhh … I haven't had sex before …"

Something washes over him, and I can't quite decipher it.

But as he parts his lips, his voice is raw with emotion. "You've always been mine, Alora. Since the fucking beginning. This just proves what I've known all along." He leans over me, grabs my throat, and claims my lips with his. "Don't worry, baby. I'll go slow until you beg me for more."

Nerves start to pulse through me, but the best kind. The ones that only come from special moments like this. I want it to be him. Maybe I always knew it would be him, and the realization didn't surface until recently.

His fingers graze my inner thigh as his tongue splits the seam of my lips, grinding against mine.

"Spread those juicy thighs for me," he orders, and I happily obey, pushing them further apart.

When he slides two fingers back into me, I start to get anxious that it's going to hurt. I mean, *fuck*, he's huge.

As if he can sense my worry, his thumb finds my clit as he murmurs into my mouth, "Your body was made to take mine, Alora."

Slipping a third finger in with his sensual thrusts, I gasp, feeling him play my body like an instrument. He works me with precision, bringing me to finish two more times before he stands up to his full height, fisting his cock with his big hand. Stepping closer to me, he swipes the tip through my wetness and slaps it against my inner thigh. Once, twice, three times.

Spitting down on himself, he coats his length and lines himself up with my entrance. "Look at me, Alora."

I find his stare, darkened and intense. I do as he asked and lock my gaze on to his.

Leaning down over me, he plants a soft kiss on each cheek before claiming my lips with his once more in a passionate declaration. Pulling back to look into my eyes, he pushes inside of me, and I gasp at the pressure.

He threads his fingers into the back of my hair and pulls my head back enough to expose my throat. Running his tongue up it, he nips and sucks, easing the pressure in my core with each touch.

"This pussy is mine, Alora." He looks at me, waiting for my confirmation before continuing, and I nod, wanting him to fill me completely.

Thrusting forward, he plunges further into me, and I sharply inhale.

"Fuck, you're so tight. I never want to leave. Let me stay buried inside of you forever, baby, *please*."

Ever so slightly, his dick slides out of me to the tip. Gently, he eases back into me, igniting a pleasure I never knew could exist.

"Holy shit," I moan, every cell in my body jolting to life.

He chuckles arrogantly as he does it again, pulling back and thrusting into me, but this time, he sinks deeper. "You're doing so fucking good."

The pleasure starts to completely outweigh the pain, and I want more—faster and faster.

Wiggling my hips, I bite down on my lip as his dick twitches inside of me. "Ahh!"

"My greedy little Bug. What, you want more?" A devilish smirk lifts his lips.

"Yes," I beg. "Please, I want *all* of you."

He pulls out to the tip, then thrusts forward, and I cry out as he fills me to the brim.

"Malik!"

"Mmm. I like hearing you scream my name." He bites my neck and runs his tongue over the stinging sensation.

His restraint is gradually snapping with each thrust

into me. This is affecting him just as much as it is me, and there is something so satisfying about that.

Staying quiet, I can't fight the smirk on my lips as he slowly eases in and out of me, using all of my energy not to make a sound.

His eyebrow cocks up. "Oh, yeah? You want to play that game? Be a little brat? Let me show you just how fast I can have you moaning my name."

Wrapping his hand around my throat, he squeezes at the sides, and a burst of euphoria erupts in my core. My back arches off of the bed as his other hand wraps around my ankle. Lifting my leg up in the air, he leans it against his chest, hooking it over his shoulder. The position change somehow opens my body up more for him.

Fighting the absolute need to moan, I bite my cheek as he sinks deeper inside of me.

"Oh, baby, you are going to drive me fucking *insane*."

His chain hangs in the air between us, like his dark hair, as his pace picks up, pounding into me over and over as my resolve begins to disintegrate.

Those long fingers of his hold my thigh in place, and the image alone has me nearly exploding.

Wait, what is that?

"Malik," I whimper as he slams into me, clouding every rational thought in my head, "is my name tattooed on your knuckles?"

Growling, he digs his fingers into my thigh, and it nearly sends me over the edge.

"I'm obsessed with you. You consume every thought in my goddamn head." He thrusts harder. "Isn't it clear, baby? I'm yours just as much as you're mine."

His confession tears through my body, and I cry out, moaning and whimpering through each shuddering breath. "Malik, Malik, oh my Godddd!"

My eyes slam shut.

He squeezes my throat and commands me, "Open them. I need to see the look in your eyes as you come on my cock."

Somehow, every nerve in my body electrifies, and wave after wave of pleasure pulses through me.

"There you go, my good fucking girl. Come on me. Drench it, baby." He fucks me passionately, his thrusts long and sensual as I float above the bed.

Standing to his height, he grabs my hips and pulls me toward him as he slams back into me, each thrust from tip to hilt.

In four long and fevered thrusts, he groans and pulls out of me. Pumping himself vigorously, he moans.

"Oh fuuuck," he growls, coming hard, his cum shooting onto my stomach.

For moments or hours—who the hell knows?—our breathing fills the room like a harmony I want to play over and over again.

Stepping away from me, he walks into the bathroom and grabs a towel.

With the biggest smile on his face, he cleans me up and then himself before tossing the towel in the hamper.

Walking back to me, he slides into bed beside me and kisses my forehead.

"How are you feeling? Need water?"

His attentiveness warms me to the core.

"Maybe some clothes?" I laugh, propping myself up onto my elbows.

He taps his chin. "Hmm … no can do. I prefer you like this."

Rolling my eyes, I shove his chest lightly and lean away from him, but he catches my jaw and pulls me back, aligning his mouth with mine.

"What am I going to do with you?" he murmurs.

"Keep me?" I whisper, pressing my lips into his before pulling back.

He closes the distance between us, his mouth on mine in a heartbeat. "Letting you go has never been an option."

shorthanded goal

A goal scored while the team is on a penalty kill

chapter
twenty-four
malik

G lass shards decorate the pavement as I push myself to my feet, my entire body numb. A roar of heat pulses to my right, and I turn my head to it, blinking rapidly to clear my vision.

As I squint my eyes, the orange blur shifts into hungry flames, lapping at the oxygen around the burning car.

What happened?

His purple eyes appear in my mind, and my heart drops.

Micah.

A roar tears through me, his name a prayer, slicing through the air around me. *"Micah!"*

"Malik!"

Hands are on my shoulders, and without thought, I

swing at the blurry face above me, my fist colliding with a strong jaw.

He's not going to get away with this.

"Malik!"

The familiar voice suddenly registers. It's not my uncle yelling my name, but Griffin.

Rubbing my eyes, I wince. "I'm sorry, bro. Fuck, my bad."

He steps away from me and leans against the fireplace. "It's been a while since you had one of those."

I sigh as agonizing pain strikes my heart. "It's about right. It's almost the twenty-first."

He knows what happened on that date … Micah was killed.

"I know, man. I'm sorry," he says genuinely, knowing some of the pain I'm facing.

"I'm sorry if I woke you or something …" I trail off, covering my eyes with the back of my hand, blocking out the blinding light that he must have turned on when he came in.

"You're good. You're not the only one who's woken up, screaming, in this house before," he admits, and I remember when he told me Blair had to come and shake him awake a time or two.

"And that's why you're my best friend." I grin.

He chuckles. "Because I also have terrible recurring nightmares?"

Lifting my hand, I glare at him. "No, smart-ass. Because of our *trauma*."

"Oh, right." He clicks his tongue.

A moment of silence passes between us, as neither of us quite knows what to say.

"Do you want to talk about it? Was it Micah?"

Nodding, I sit up, back myself against the headboard, and wipe the beading sweat from my forehead. "Yeah …" *But there's more to it than that.*

"The accident?" he asks, and I nod.

"Fuck," I grumble, tossing my head into my hands, fighting the real story trying to come out, something I'm starting to get really exhausted by. "So many times, I wish it had been me that night. I mean, shit, every time I think about it, I feel that way."

Griffin walks over and sits on the opposite end of the bed, bending one leg on top of the comforter with his other foot planted on the floor. "Malik, you, more than anyone, know I understand that guilt, that weight. It's something you've got to stop running through your mind. I know that's easier said than done. But eventually, you'll forgive yourself for surviving when the one you loved didn't."

A sob heaves out of my chest as tears flood my eyes. I punch the bed beside me. "Fuck!"

As if my heart were skinned alive, it burns and writhes inside of me. My cheeks dampen as the anger, frustration, and sadness roll down my cheeks.

Griffin sits across from me, silently, but not absently. He's letting me feel this moment, live through it, while being here for support.

My heavy gasps for air begin to settle, and I wipe my eyes clean. "It was Alora's dad, Griffin. He killed my brother."

His voice is horrified and quiet. "What?"

Even that simple terrifying sentence feels good to speak out loud, as painful as it is.

"Congressman Daniel Briarwood. Trustworthy. Kind. And true. A man for the people. A man who got so intoxicated that he had to be carried out to his car. A man who got behind the wheel. A man who plowed Micah over like a pebble in the road."

The hyperventilating cries rip through me. "The man who paid my uncle for his silence. The same uncle who is hiding Micah's ashes from me so I don't say a goddamn word. The same uncle who brokered the deal with the fucking devil."

Speaking the truth into existence for the first time suddenly makes everything so clear—that I'm a piece of shit and Alora deserves better.

Griffin lets me get it all out.

"Alora attended our high school our senior year before I realized exactly who she was. I even liked her, but the second I heard her last name, I knew I could never be with her. Hell, there's a part of me that still thinks it might end up that way. But not because of us, but because of him.

"I put her through *hell*. At a high school hockey game, I had the entire school laugh at her until she ran out, crying. Had people harass her every day if it wasn't me personally doing it. But even though I couldn't have her, I couldn't bear seeing anyone else with her. God, there were so many guys I beat into lockers, the ground, the ice, all because they wanted her. But I couldn't stand it, and I made sure they never succeeded."

Tears and snot pool together as years of built-up emotion pour out of me. "She graduated early just to get away from me. And the moment she was gone, it was like I was on my own all over again. I hated her. I hated her family. That she got this life of luxury and no worries while I lived out of my car until my coach found out and opened his home to me."

"Then ..." I sniffle, unable to stop. "Then I ran into a random dorm room to get away from Dean and Ash because I pranked them and they were chasing me, only for it to be *her* room. I mean, what are the odds? Of us attending the same high school? Of me getting a scholarship here? Of her transferring to HEAU? Just for us to come together after I wrote *the end* on our story."

I ripped the lid off of my mouth, and it's like I can't quit. Every thought, worry, and fear fall from my lips as much as I want it to stop. "Now ... now everything's changed, yet somehow, so much hasn't. Her dad is still threatening me; he made a little appearance on campus a while back and told me to stay away from Alora.

"I tried. But I can't. I stopped fighting my feelings for her, and I'm not going back to the way it was. But I don't know where to go from here. I mean, am I the monster if I choose her? If I tell her the truth and ruin her reality forever, will it all end anyway?"

Utter exhaustion from crying so hard starts to sink into my body, and when I force my eyes back to Griffin's, I find tears of his own.

"Christ, Malik." He pauses, looking at me carefully. "Why the fuck did you keep all of that locked in?"

Glaring at him, I point out the obvious—that he did a very similar thing with his pain; he just hid it in the west wing of his house and forced it out of his mind.

"Touché." He smiles heavily.

Silence, comforting and free, lightens the room. It's like a thousand pounds has lifted from my chest, and I can fucking breathe again.

"I don't know what to do."

Looking at me with confidence and pride, he mutters, "Yeah, you do. Because you love her—that's plain as day—and you'd be an idiot to fuck it up just because you're scared."

Resisting the confirmation in my mind, I sigh, but it's no use. Because he's right—I fucking love her.

"Music was my refuge. I could crawl into the space between the notes and curl my back to loneliness."

Maya Angelou

chapter
twenty-five
alora

"I'm sorry, what did you just say?" I'm pulled from my dissociative stupor.

The two girls in front of me in class look back at me with shocked expressions.

"Oh shit. I'm sorry."

I wave her apology away with my hand. "Forget that. What did you just say? A photo?"

She lifts her phone up for me to see. My vision focuses, and my bottom lip starts to quiver as I realize what I'm looking at—or rather who.

The headline reads, *A Congressman's Daughter Assaulted on School Grounds by a Faculty Member.*

Pictured beneath the ridiculously long title is a photo of me … being cornered in the practice room by Rupert. Eerie shivers straighten my back and twist my stomach.

How? There aren't even cameras in those rooms. Where did the photo even come from?

"I'm sorry. I didn't realize you … that it was you."

The girl starts to pull her phone away, but I grab it and quickly scroll, skimming the article as shock rolls through me.

My dad knew about it, told me to stay quiet, and then spoke about it in an exclusive interview? How could he use my fucking trauma for his own benefit? And without even telling me?

Are you kidding me?

My mother's kind face flashes in my mind. She would be so disappointed in who he ended up becoming. I might not have known her for a lot of my life, but I knew her enough to know that she would hate who he is now.

My dad spills in his interview about how hard this has been for me and how I wanted to keep everything private. But apparently, I changed my mind and wanted to use this to advocate for campus security.

Laughing angrily, I hand her phone back to her and grab my stuff. "Thank you." Without another word, I grab Sunny's leash, who looks up at me concerningly.

Dogs are perceptive, but especially my Sunny girl. I swear she's the biggest empath I've ever met.

"Come on, baby."

We walk out of class, which was seconds from ending anyway, and stride out of Hubert Hall to head back to our room.

Taking my phone out, I call Phillip, someone who

understands politically manipulative parents. But I find that he's already calling me.

"Hello?" I answer, realizing my voice was sharp and quick.

He sighs. "I imagine you've seen it?"

My blood boils. "Oh, yeah. Definitely saw it! What the hell, Phillip?! I mean, I feel like I'm dreaming, and this is a crazy-vivid one that feels so real. But then I'm going to wake up because there's no way in hell that my dad is using my assault to win over voters."

Sunny and I turn the corner, passing Happily Ever After Floral, then Cogsworth Coffee, and then the biggest quad on campus. Of course, I had to find this out when I was in one of the farthest lecture halls from my dorm.

"I'm sorry, Lore. It's a dirty fucking move. Did he even tell you about it?"

"No!" I shout, realizing it was more like a scream as students' heads whip my way. "He didn't even know it was me."

"He found out somehow," he mutters.

"What the hell?" My voice is quiet as I squint at the buzzing group three hundred feet in front of me. But by the time I recognize the threat, it's too late; they're already striking.

"Alora! Alora Briarwood! Tell us …"

"Alora! How do you feel, being on campus after the attack?"

"Miss Briarwood! How does it feel, having such a caring father?"

"Alora, with your father running for senator, are you hoping for change to be implemented on campus for student safety?"

Phillip's voice cuts through the overbearing questions. "Where are you?"

"Main quad!" I nearly shout into the phone because I'm stuck in a circle of human vultures, moving slowly as I take small steps forward, Sunny tucked tightly against my side.

"Please, move!" I shout, the polite response to the media flowing from me with muscle memory. And then I remember that I don't give a fuck anymore when it comes to appeasing my dad. "Get the hell out of my way!"

"Has the attack made you bitter?" a guy asks, shoving his phone in my face.

Grabbing it, I turn around and launch it as far as I can without thinking twice. "What do you think?"

Sunny yelps as they close in tighter on me, someone probably stepping on her, and I feel like I'm going to explode like a bomb.

I have to protect her first. I know she's just confused and scared.

Crouching down, I wrap my arms around her and take a deep breath before hauling her up. "Move!" I yell, my voice cracking with frustration.

I kick my leg out, and one of them grunts and shifts out of the way, opening a tiny gap in the wall of flashes. Bursting through it, I run, carrying Sunny's fifty-pound body in my arms, each step feeling heavier than the last.

The group follows me at an uncomfortably close distance. When I set Sunny down, she immediately starts to jog with me, and we round the corner to the path toward the dorm.

"Thank God," I exhale, seeing my heroes running right toward me.

I couldn't be happier to see Malik and Phillip as they lead the group of hockey players, closing the distance between us.

Malik instantly tucks me behind him, spinning to me as the rest of the guys rush past us, chasing the reporters away.

"Hey, I'm right here," Malik murmurs, assessing me for injuries, but he won't see any on the outside.

My heart rate is rising, not only from the physical exertion of picking Sunny up and running, but also the stress of whatever the fuck *that* was. God, it's been years since I had to deal with the press. But it's even worse with my dad's announcement of his run for US senator.

Walking out of the way of everyone else, I drop my backpack to the ground.

Crouching down, Malik stops me, but only for a second as he drops to the paved walkway, pulling me down into his lap, my side against his chest.

"I've got you. Deep breaths, baby." Malik kisses my temple repeatedly, lightly wrapping his arms around me.

Sunny lies down, resting her head over my thighs, and I pet her, trying to distract my mind while I force the breaths in and out.

Sometimes, my panic will only worsen my symptoms. I need to calm myself, calm my heart rate. Freaking out only worsens it.

Malik rubs my back, whispering softly in my ear, "There you go. That's it."

After about five minutes, I'm feeling good enough to get moving. I just want to get home and lock myself inside. A few of the guys trickle back over to us after scaring the media away.

"Thank you." I look up at them as they come to a stop in front of us.

"No problem." Asher smiles. "It was fun actually. Besides, you're practically a legend, like the rest of us." His gaze falls from me to Malik.

Phillip crouches down in front of me. "Hey, how are you doing?"

Shrugging, I sigh. "Feeling better. But you know ... how loving our dads can be."

He clicks his tongue. "Sure do."

"Come on, baby. Let's get to your room," Malik murmurs into my ear, sliding his arm beneath my knees and his other around my back.

I inch forward to slide off of him, but he grabs me firmly.

"Uh-uh. You're not walking."

I'm surprised he didn't freak out over Phillip being here.

Phillip sticks his arm out, bends down, and grabs Sunny's leash. "Why don't I take this pretty girl for a walk while you get her settled in?"

Malik smirks. "Sounds good to me. Bug?"

Nodding, I agree, "She would love that. Besides, you're probably far more at her pace than I am. Would you grab my backpack, please?"

He nods and picks it up from the ground, handing it to me.

Phillip calls Sunny to follow him. "Come on, Sunny Bun."

"Go." I release her verbally, knowing she wants to stay at my side.

Lifting me up into the air, Malik stands to his feet. I bite down on my bottom lip and watch him intensely. I could get used to this princess treatment.

Griffin clears his throat. "You guys all right? Want us to walk you back?"

Malik shakes his head. "No, I've got her from here. Thanks though."

They nod before splitting off in the opposite direction. I have no idea how he got so many of them to drop everything at a moment's notice to come to my rescue. Or how Phillip even found Malik in, like, a minute. But regardless, it was a happy coincidence.

"How are you actually doing?" Malik's voice caresses my cheek as he lifts me higher in his grasp.

Looking over at his stunning purple eyes, I answer truthfully, "Like I need a good *distraction*."

His eyebrows lift, and he chuckles. "Oh, really?"

I giggle. "Yeah. But you'll have to do most of the work because—"

He interrupts me, "Don't worry, baby; I'll keep your legs in the air—for the blood flow, of course, not any other reason."

I cackle. "Oh sure, okay."

"You think you can handle it?" he murmurs, his voice sweet and kind, but I can't help to take it as some challenge.

"I think I can handle you just fine." My tongue swipes my bottom lip, and I smirk.

"That's cute, Bug. But you have no idea the restraint I used when I fucked you for the first time. The sheer willpower not to pound into you all night long, *over* and *over*."

He approaches the entrance to the dorm hall, and I use my key fob to unlock the door.

When he carries me inside, a few onlookers ogle the tattooed and jacked hockey player as if I wasn't even in his arms. Something about it lights a fire in me, the smallest flame of possession igniting.

They can look all they want, and I don't blame them so long as they don't try to touch.

He's mine.

Malik uses my foot to press the Up button outside of the elevator, and I giggle as we stride inside, the doors closing behind us before ascending.

When we step off of the elevator and turn down my hallway, there's a gentleman waiting outside of my door, with a garment bag in his arms.

Malik slowly sets me down, striding ahead of me with me tucked behind him.

"Miss Briarwood?" the man in a suit asks.

I nod.

He juts the bag toward Malik and me. "A delivery from Mr. Briarwood."

"Thank you." I smile kindly at the messenger, taking the bag. There's no reason in taking my anger out on him; he's just doing his job.

He immediately leaves, and I feel bad, not knowing how long he had to wait for me, but the tag hanging on the hanger steals my attention away from any guilt.

Next Friday, seven p.m. Gala at Triton Harbor Event Center. Wear this.

"He's lost his mind," I whisper in shock that this is all very real and not just a bad dream.

Malik unlocks my door, and we slip inside. I hang the bag on the back of the door.

Malik leans against the wall, waiting for me to make the next move.

"It's from my dad. He wants me to attend a gala with him next Friday." I rub the bridge of my nose. "It's sad. I don't even recognize that man anymore—and I don't mean the progressive balding. It's like he's not even my dad. Not in the ways that matter."

Slowly walking over to me, he cups my cheeks, brushing his thumbs back and forth. "I'm sorry, Alora. You deserve a much better father than *him*."

Looking up into Malik's eyes, I take a slow and steady breath, reflecting for just a moment on how far we've come.

When I was in trouble, being swarmed by the media, he dropped everything and came to me. He carried me back to my dorm ... *again.*

Time and time again, he's shown me how he feels. I know expressing his emotions verbally is harder for him. Maybe right now, I can speak his language.

"Distract me," I whisper sensually, sliding my hands across his shirt, feeling the mounds of muscle beneath.

He smirks. "Distract you? Hmm? How do you propose I do that?" The sassiness disappears for a moment as something dark washes across his features. "Are you sure you don't want to talk about it?"

Shaking my head, I trail my hands lower, slipping my right hand beneath his joggers and boxers, wrapping my hand around his already-hardening cock. "I'm sure. Now, are you going to fuck me or not?"

He snaps, fisting the hair at the nape of my neck and tipping my head back at the same time his tongue plunges into my mouth. His hands make fast work of my clothes, stripping my sweater, bra, leggings, and panties to the floor, and his stare hungrily devours me.

"Goddamn, Alora, you're perfect," he groans, his hands palming my breasts with need. "Now get on your bed and spread those legs for me."

Doing as told, I walk over to my bed and lie down on my back, propping myself onto my elbows as I watch him tear his clothes from his body.

Ripping his shirt over his head, he throws it to the floor before quickly stepping out of his boxers and joggers. "Wider, baby. I want to see how wet and ready you are for me."

Opening my hips more, I feel so bare waiting for him as he prowls closer, his gaze exploring my body.

He pumps himself from base to tip with his left hand, the same one with my name tattooed on his knuckles.

I still can't believe he did that, but there is something so goddamn hot about my name being permanently engraved in his skin. There's no question in his mind that we belong together, or he wouldn't have done it. So, I won't let there be any doubt in mine.

I want to feel exposed with him, down to the core. He's the only person in this world I want to experience this level of vulnerability with.

Running his thumb over the bead of pre-cum on his hard erection, he softly groans, his eyes traveling back up my body to mine. "We don't have a lot of time."

I nod, opening myself up even more. "Then you'd better be fast."

He scoffs, his eyes darkening. "Careful, baby. You might bring out a side of me you aren't ready for."

Sitting up taller, I reach forward and wrap my hand around his velvety shaft, pumping him over and over. "Try me."

A sexy, deep groan vibrates through him. "You're not going to be able to walk tomorrow when I'm done with you."

I bite down on my lip as my cheeks erupt in redness. "Good thing I have you to carry me."

"I don't want to warm you up with my fingers this time, baby. I want to feel your sweet pussy stretch for my cock." His finger hooks under my chin and tips my head up, and he stops at the very end of the bed, between my legs. "It'll be intense, but, fuck, so good."

I know he won't push me more than I can handle. If I tell him it's too much, he'll stop. I want all of him, in any way I can get, in *every* way.

Leaning back, I palm my breasts and jiggle them gently, watching his dick throb.

His resolve breaks, and he bends over, running his tongue up my center. I gasp as his tongue works vigorously, bringing every nerve in my body to the surface.

Standing to his full height, he grabs his dick and brushes the fat head up and down through my soaked center. His thumb circles my clit as he lines himself up.

"Malik," I moan, instantly covering my mouth.

He grabs my arm and pulls it down. "Don't you dare stay quiet. I own your every moan, whimper, and cry. Give them all to me."

When I nod, he pushes into me, and I audibly gasp at the pressure.

"So fucking tight, baby," he whimpers as he works himself deeper inside of me.

It's so much less painful than the first time we did this, but still overwhelmingly intense.

I moan softly as he fills me up with every inch. "More. *Please*."

A sharp sting slaps against my thigh from his palm as he slams into me at the same time, and I cry out, "Holy fuck!"

His tattooed fingers reach toward my throat and circle it as he rears back and rocks into me. "You want more, baby?"

Nodding, I realize he might have been right. I don't know if I can handle unbridled Malik. But I want to, and I'm not going to stop.

Slipping his thumb into my mouth, he growls, "Such a greedy little slut for this dick, aren't you?"

SLAP! SLAP! SLAP!

His fingers whip against my inner thigh as he pounds into me, the mix of pain and pleasure like nothing I've ever felt before, bursts of euphoria erupting with each slap and thrust. His thumb leaves my mouth, and his hand wraps back around my throat, squeezing tightly. I'm not going to last another five seconds at this rate.

"Malik! Oh fuuuck! It feels *so* good!" I whine.

"Yeah, baby?" He pulls his hips back and rails into me, fucking me rough and steady. The sounds of our bodies colliding echo through the room. "Don't you hear how good it sounds when I fill your juicy pussy up? Like fucking music."

My body starts to levitate as the volcano inside of me prepares to erupt. "Please, fuck, yes!" I cry out, my back arching as my orgasm tears through my body.

As I fist my hands in the comforter, he continues to pound into me, making every pulsing wave even more intense.

He slaps my breast, and I whimper at the sting on my nipple.

"I'm not letting you go until I feel you come one more time, Alora."

I wiggle my hips. The sensations are mind-blowing. "Malik …"

He hears my plea, his thumb finding my clit again. "Come on, baby. Be my good fucking girl and come on my cock again."

As he rolls his hips into me, his breathing picks up, the same as mine. My second orgasm is seconds away from tearing through me.

"Yes. Just like that. Oh fuck, your tight pussy is heaven," he moans, and I'm gone, plummeting off the edge of the earth and floating through space as my body convulses with pleasure.

He circles my clit harder, riding me through it. But as I shift my hips, he whimpers, "Fuck, baby."

Pulling out, he comes on my center, the warmth running down my folds.

His heavy breathing mixes with mine. Then he fetches a towel from my hamper, cleaning us both up with a shit-eating grin on his face.

Inching myself off of the bed, I walk over to my dresser and grab new clothes, slipping on comfy lounge shorts and an oversize T-shirt before climbing in bed. Malik puts his boxers on before joining me.

Sliding his arm beneath my waist, he pulls me against his side and kisses the top of my head. "I don't know what I'd do without you."

My heart warms, and I look up at him, finding his stare soft and gentle and so, *so* passionate. The urge to tell him I love him is overwhelming.

But I don't know if he's there yet, and I want to wait for the right moment. I'm going to tell him very soon, but I want it to be perfect.

"Good thing you'll never have to find out again." I kiss his firm pec.

He leans his head back and stares up at the ceiling. "Are you going to any of your other classes today? I can walk you so you don't get bombarded again."

"Probably not today." I shake my head, glancing at the clock, and I suddenly realize he shouldn't be here.

"Oh my God, Malik. You're going to be late for the bus!"

His smile tips up with a secret, sparkles in his eyes. "No, I won't. I'm not going."

I repeat his words to him in a stupor. "You're not going? To your away game?"

He looks me deep in my eyes, and his voice is loving and serious when he says, "There will always be another game, Bug. I want to be here with you in case you need me."

My eyes well up with tears, and the biggest smile stretches across my face. "*Malik.*"

His cheeks redden, and he melts into my bed. "How about we watch a movie?"

I nod, snuggling deeper in his embrace as he grabs the remote from my nightstand, turning my TV on.

KNOCK! KNOCK! KNOCK!

Malik looks at me smugly. "I'll get it."

Striding over to the door in only his boxers, he throws it open and leans against the wall.

"Jesus Christ," Phillip scoffs. "Glad you could at least get those on before opening the door."

Sunny rushes past him and beelines it to the bed, jumping up and pouncing on me.

"Hi, baby! Did you have a good walk?"

Excitement widens her big brown eyes as she pants heavily.

"Oh my goodness, what a happy girl you are!"

Calling out to Phillip, I shout my gratitude. "Thank you for taking her!"

He pops his head around the corner. "Anytime!" He winks at me and smiles before heading back out.

Malik shuts the door behind him and walks back over to us, sliding back in bed. I pull the covers over Malik and me, and Sunny snuggles up between our legs.

The cutest family.

The thought equally terrifies and excites me. But that's what we're slowly becoming—each other's family.

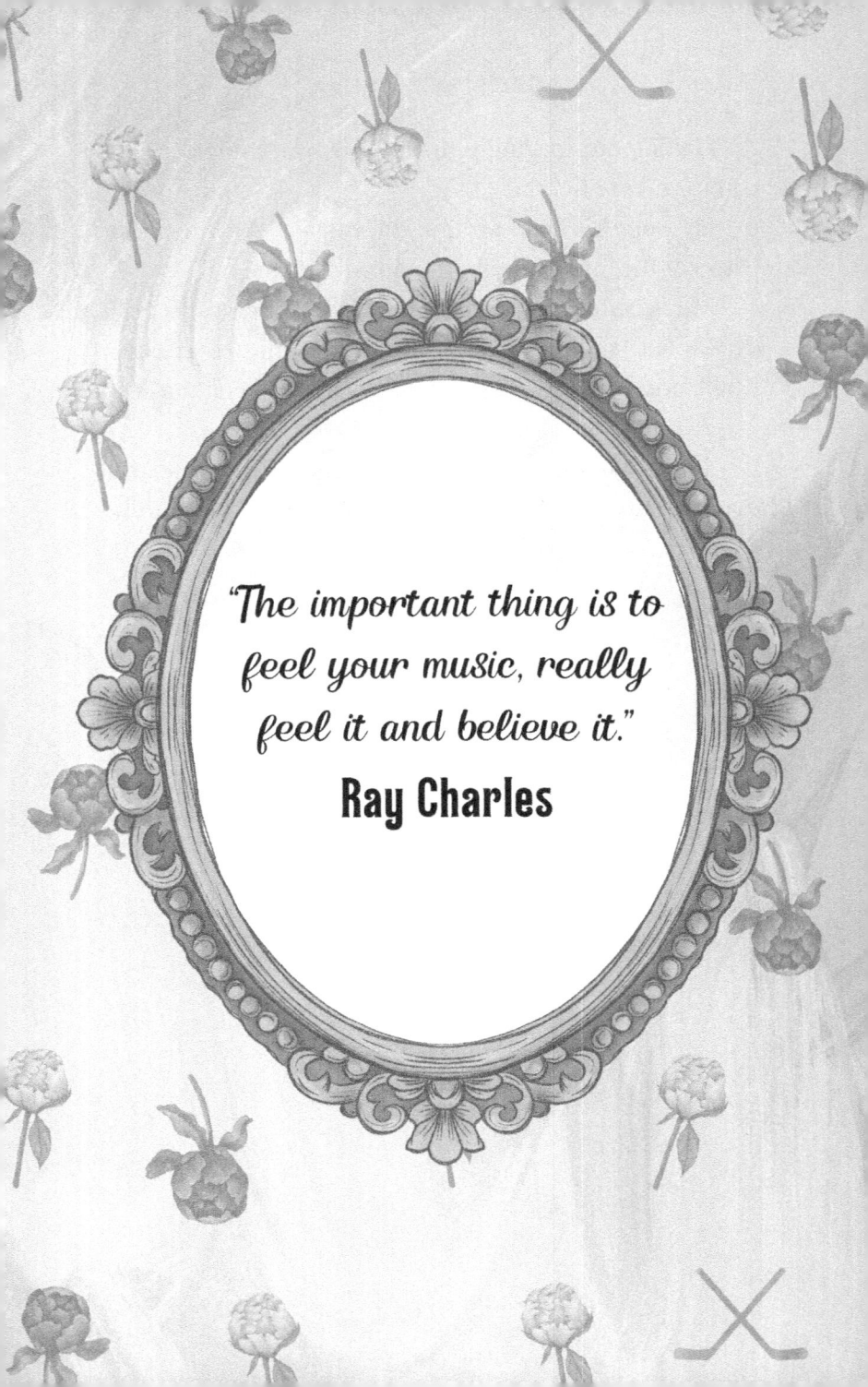

"The important thing is to feel your music, really feel it and believe it."

Ray Charles

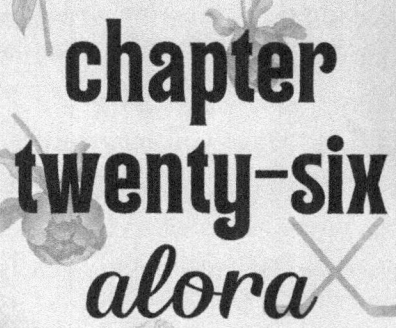

chapter
twenty-six
alora

Ten minutes into class, and Malik still isn't here.

Grabbing my phone from my backpack, I check for any texts or calls from him, but there's nothing.

I open our messages and shoot him a quick text.

Me: Hey, are you feeling okay?

Setting my phone down on my desk, I do my best to pay attention to the professor, failing miserably every second that passes. My mind is stuck on him. I hope everything's okay.

The rest of the hour is no different. I don't hear a word coming out of the professor's mouth, and all I can think about is Malik. He hasn't answered my text either.

When we're dismissed, I grab my things and stand, turning to Griffin. "Hey, can I talk to you?"

He nods, walking down his row and stepping to the ground level, striding over to Blair, Sunny, and me. "What's up?"

Nervously, I ask, "Have you heard from Malik? He wasn't here, and I haven't heard back from him."

Griffin looks away instantly, clearly knowing the reason for his absence. He rubs the back of his neck.

"What is it?"

Biting his lip nervously, he murmurs, "Today is really hard for him. This date holds a lot of bad memories. Just … give him some space today. He'll reach out when he's ready."

My chest aches. I wish I had known. I could have done something to help distract him.

Nodding, I flash a smile. "Thanks for letting me know."

He and Blair walk out. Sunny and I follow them out of Ivy Hall.

My phone rings, and I pull it out, hoping it's Malik. But it's not; it's Flora.

"Hello?"

"Hi, dear! We are so excited to see you this week!" she cheers in my ear, and my heart sinks.

"You're coming for the gala?" I ask, clearly left out of the conversation between my family members.

"Well, we certainly can't leave you to deal with your father alone. Especially after the last stunt he pulled."

My throat burns.

"And we need our Sunny fix. It's quiet without her prancing around."

"Wait, when are you getting in?" I ask eagerly, an idea popping into my mind.

"Thursday! Why? What's up, sweetie?" Her bubbly energy sounds through her words.

"I … I might have someone I want you guys to meet." I fidget with Sunny's leash as we walk back home.

She gasps audibly, the shock lasting seconds. "Oh my goodness. Who is it?"

"A boy." I smile as his face appears in my mind.

"Fauna is going to lose her mind. She went to a tarot reading the other day; the lady said that her Prince Charming would come in an unexpected form and that love would be entering her life in one way or another. Maybe she was talking about yours."

I'll never tire of the uniqueness of my aunts. They are wholly themselves, and no one will tell them differently.

Chatting with Flora for the next fifteen minutes about any little thing, I distract myself on the dreary walk home before saying goodbye.

I'm going to do my best to give Malik the space he needs today even if the only thing I want to do is show up at his door and throw my arms around him.

But instead, I'm going to spend the next few hours playing piano in my room. It's been too long since I had a lengthy practice session, and on a rainy day, it just feels right.

Time drifts away as I force myself to stay occupied so as not to bother Malik. Before I know it, it's nearly ten o'clock, and I still haven't heard back from him.

Rain splatters on the sliding glass door, creating the best pitter-patters, which I could listen to for hours.

I know Griffin told me to give Malik space, and I am, but knowing Malik needs it doesn't make it any easier to stay away.

I wish I knew what this day meant for him, the weight it holds. I just want to know more about him— the good, the bad, and the twisted.

Hopefully, he'll trust me with his secrets one day. I'd be honored to keep them.

Maybe if he's feeling up to it, he'll want to come to the gala with me on Friday. At the very least, it may be a nice distraction from whatever's on his mind.

I pull my focus back to the present and line my fingers up on the keys. I begin to play "La Campanella" by Franz Liszt, the volume on my piano turned way down.

The head of the music department told me that they would be reviewing every student who had been invited to participate at the showcase, given Rupert Von London's *incident*.

It would be horrible to know that the only reason I qualified was because he liked me. I want my music to be cherished and loved solely because of the music, not because of who I am.

So, until I hear that I won't be performing, I'll keep practicing as if I am.

I get lost in the sound, transporting myself to a different world as I perform the piece in my room, the only audience member being Sunny. But she listens intently nonetheless.

KNOCK! KNOCK! KNOCK!

My hands freeze, and I inhale sharply as I'm yanked back to the present.

Who the hell would be knocking on my door this late?

Standing from my piano bench, I walk to the door and peek through the hole. The air thickens, and my hand fumbles for the doorknob.

Soaked head to toe, Malik stands there, his face pulled down and his eyes red and puffy.

When I throw the door open, he looks up at me, and I watch everything inside of him crumble to pieces.

Backing up, I make room for him, and he bounds through the threshold, wrapping his arms around my waist and pulling me tightly into his chest.

The water soaks through my clothes, but I don't care. All I care about right now is him.

Brushing his hair back from his face, I look up at him as my eyes burn. I've never seen him like this … not even close.

But whatever he's going through, he came to me,

and I'll do everything in my power to eliminate whatever or whoever is making him feel this way.

"Malik, talk to me. Please," I whisper, wiping the tears and rain from beneath his eyes. "I'm right here."

He cups my face and crashes his lips to mine, passionate and raw. He places his heart and soul in the palm of my hand. "I love you. No matter what comes next, I love you. Not the world, not your father— nothing will ever change that. If I can't be by your side, then I don't want to be here at all."

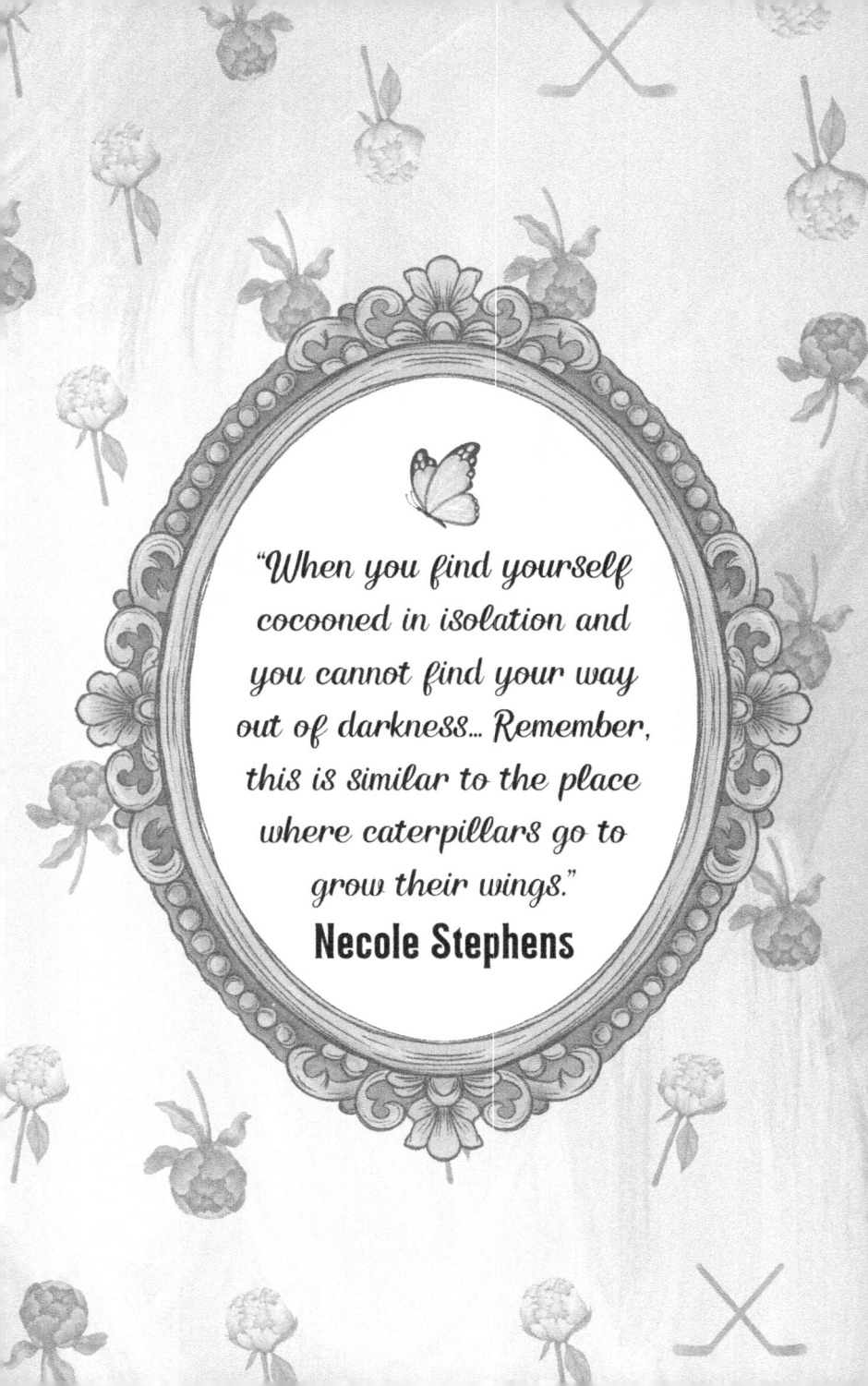

"When you find yourself cocooned in isolation and you cannot find your way out of darkness... Remember, this is similar to the place where caterpillars go to grow their wings."

Necole Stephens

chapter twenty-seven
malik
three years ago

Every breath is painful and sharp, thanks to my uncle's fists from earlier tonight. But I don't care how many times he hits me as long as he never touches Micah again.

"How about some ice cream, huh? I snuck a few bucks from my teacher's purse."

I pinch Micah's cheek, and he gasps in shock at the confession of my crime.

"That's not nice, Malik! It's not yours," my little brother says, looking up at me with big purple eyes.

"I'm just teasing. I found the bills lying on the side-walk. It was an unlucky day for someone, but really lucky for us," I lie, knowing he won't enjoy the ice cream as much if he thinks I stole the money to pay for it.

"Can we go to SB Ice cream?" he asks, as if that's

not the one I take him to every time I have enough money to bring him.

I nod. "Nothing less than the best for you." I rub his black hair, messing it up.

"Double chocolate swirl?" He beams.

"With chocolate sprinkles, of course," I say, finishing his order for him as we tiptoe down the stairs toward the front door.

Our uncle passed out from his bottles an hour ago, giving us the only free time we ever have. And I'm capitalizing on it tenfold. I have to; it's the only time I get to see Micah really smile.

Stepping over the piles of trash and bottles, I take his hand and lead us out of the front door.

"Malik, guess what," he whispers excitedly.

"What?" I ask, looking down at him.

"I'm so excited," he cheers as the front door closes behind us.

Messing up his hair with my hand, I chuckle as we turn down the sidewalk to head to SB's.

It's beautiful out tonight, just warm enough, but not too hot. It's just perfect.

Skipping, hopping, and racing, we finally reach the ice cream parlor, and Micah orders his usual.

"And for you?" the guy asks.

"Just his. Thanks." I slide the dollar bills across the counter.

Sometimes, I wish Micah weren't as perceptive as he is. His gaze whips up to me, and he frowns.

"We can share mine!" he offers, and my chest warms.

Shaking my head and smiling, I assure him that it's quite all right. "I don't want any right now. Thanks though."

"Okaaay." He drags the word out.

The worker walks back with my change and his ice cream cone.

Micah takes it happily, and I leave the few pennies I have left in the tip jar.

"It's so good. Here, take a bite." He thrusts it up at me as we head back outside.

I laugh. "You eat it yourself, chocolate monster."

"If you insist." He grins evilly. "Mmm, it's soooo good," he mockingly groans.

I shove his shoulder lightly, and he takes the opportunity to stroll along the edge of the sidewalk, walking on his tiptoes like he's on a tightrope.

"You little shit."

"Do we have to go back home tonight?" His voice is soft as he looks up at me with a sorrowful gaze.

My heart constricts as pain slices into me. "I'm sorry, buddy. Soon enough, I'll have my own place, and you can come live with me, okay? We'll leave that house for good."

"Promise?" he asks, lifting his pinkie in the air.

I hook it with mine. "I promise."

Staring into his purple eyes, I believe my words. I owe it to him. I have to get us out of this shithole our mom dropped us into before walking away.

I was six years old, and Micah was one year old when our mom said we were going to visit our uncle. But then she never came back, and we never heard from her again. She was found in a hotel days later. She had overdosed on heroin.

I don't remember much of her at all, the memories fuzzy more and more each day.

My uncle always says that Micah and I were her curse, that we were demons and that's why our eyes are purple. But I know he's wrong.

"I love you, buddy." I smile down at him, and his eyes light up.

"I love you too—" His finger slips from mine.

And time slows to a halt as I fall to my knees.

My ears ring from metal scraping, and his scream echoes in the air. The wind picks up around me as if the earth were yelling with us.

For a brief second, I'm stuck in time, frozen as I teeter on the edge of reality.

If I can stay here—right here—then I don't have to face what's really happening.

But my heart starts to race, thumping so loudly in my chest and ears that it sounds like gunshots. My adrenaline spikes, and my eyes burn with agony.

No. No. No. No. No. No.

NO! NO! NO!

This can't be real; this can't be happening.

But the longer I stand still and deny it, the longer I'm away from him when he needs me most.

Everything around us shifts into chaos, and my world goes up in flames.

A scream tears through the sound barrier, and it takes me a moment to realize that it's coming from me. But the moment it clicks, reality snaps back into place.

Glass shards decorate the pavement as I push myself to my feet, my entire body numb. A roar of heat pulses to my right, and I turn my head to it, blinking rapidly to clear my vision.

When I squint my eyes, the orange blur shifts into hungry flames, lapping at the oxygen around the burning car.

What happened?

His purple eyes appear in my mind, and my heart drops. Micah.

A wail tears through me, his name a prayer howling through the air around me. "Micah!"

I'm running before I realize it, my legs carrying me to where Micah lies twenty feet away, face down on the pavement. My ragged voice and cries fill the street as I throw myself to the ground beside him.

"Micah! Micah! Micah! Hey, buddy, it's okay!" I reassure him, gently grabbing his shoulders and rolling him over.

He winces, moaning in pain. "Malik …"

Tears blur my vision as I scoop his head into my lap,

and his eyelashes flutter as he looks up at me with wide eyes.

"I'm right here. I'm right here, Micah. Just stay with me."

I can't tear my gaze from his. I can't call out for help. I'm useless. Weak. All I can do is hold him.

Sobs bubble out of me as he lifts his hand and cups my cheek. I mirror his movement, lifting my hand from his chest and resting it on his small jaw.

What is that? Ice cream?

A dribble of something dark falls from the corner of his mouth, and I wipe it with my thumb. It smears across his soft skin, and I gasp as tears stream down my face.

It's blood.

"Malik?" Micah's soft voice is somehow even quieter.

"Yeah, buddy?" I ask, sniffling and hyperventilating.

"I'm cold …" His voice shakes as his bottom lip quivers.

Wrapping him up in my arms, I pull him against me, resting his face on my chest, hugging him tightly. "Is this better?"

He nods against me, and I cradle the back of his head with my hand, feeling wetness squish between my fingers.

Rocking back and forth, I soothe him like I used to when he was a baby. "It's okay. It's okay. Everything's going to be okay." My voice is raw and jagged.

Tilting my head back, I look up at the sky, my face wretched and twisted. "Please, if there's a god or someone out there …" I heave. "Please don't take him from me. Please." Rocking back and forth, I cradle him tighter. "He's all I have. Please don't take him. I can't surive without him."

Cupping his face, I lean down and press my forehead against his, and my tears fall to his face.

Slamming my eyes closed, I sob. "I love you, Micah. I love you so much. I'm so sorry … I'm so sorry!"

Something's changed—something I can't describe— and as I open my eyes, I realize it's because I can't feel him breathing anymore. His eyes are open, but he's not blinking.

My voice is a ghost of a whisper. "Micah?" I rock him gently. "Micah?"

He doesn't move.

"Micah?" I shake him harder.

Sirens ring in my ears.

"Micah! Wake up! Wake up, buddy!" I sob. "Please …"

His body is limp in my arms, and his eyes … his eyes are empty. The recognition of that mere thought makes me want to die.

A high-pitched cry slashes through my lungs. Pulling him back against me, I cling to him like my life depends on it.

Someone touches my shoulder, but I don't react. I just want to stay here with him. I don't want anyone to touch him or look at him. He's mine. He's my little brother.

"Micah …" My voice cracks into a thousand pieces. "Please don't do this."

An EMT grabs my face and forces me to look at him. "Let me take a look at him, okay? I need to help."

No. He's fine. He's just fine. He's just resting right now. That's all.

"Can you step away, just for a moment, sir?" someone else asks me, but I can't even respond. "We're going to move you, okay? We need to evaluate him."

A thousand hands are on me, pulling me off of Micah as I scream and thrash.

"Stop! Stop! No!"

They pull me further away.

"Stop! He's fine! He's okay!"

"They have to check him out," one of the people holding me back says, but I don't care.

I need to get to him.

The EMT glances over at me—no, to someone else, but it doesn't matter. I can read the look in their eyes because I already know the truth. I just don't want to admit it yet.

"No, no, no, no, no, no, no …" I whimper. "No!" I scream at the guy. "You're wrong! He's just fine!"

"Take a deep breath for me, son, okay?"

He's fine. He's fine.

A gurney suddenly appears, and they load his limp body onto it. I suddenly can't hide from the truth any longer. They wheel it away as I'm held in place by at least three or—I don't know—four people.

"P-please," I sob. "Please."

Someone's voice cracks as my back is rubbed. "I'm sorry."

I lose sight of him as he disappears around the corner of the ambulance. I don't know where to look, how to breathe. I don't know how to exist in a world that he's not in.

A man in a suit stumbles out of an SUV, and it's like my mind starts replaying the accident from the beginning.

He's the one who was driving. He's the one who hit Micah.

Shaking out of their hold on me, I take off running straight toward him.

"Hey! Stop!" they call out for me, but I'm already cocking my arm back and plunging it as hard into his face as I possibly can.

I deliver blow after blow, and his face becomes covered in blood. I can't even form a word; all I can do is swing at him, hitting him with as much force as I can muster.

But just like before, I'm pulled away, ripped upward by those damn strong hands.

Staring down at the man, I commit everything about him to memory. I will make him pay for what he did to my brother if it's the last thing I ever do.

But I didn't need to memorize his face or his license

plate because the next day, he shows up at my front door and talks to my uncle.

The day after that, two brand-new cars arrived on our doorstep. I don't want to take the car, but I know it's my only way to get away from my uncle, from the haunted house he's raised me in.

I pack everything I've ever cared about into two plastic bags—most of which are Micah's butterflies and a few odds and ends.

A week later, that house is empty. My uncle moves to a much nicer place, a place he doesn't belong, a place that was paid for with my brother's blood.

A month later, no service has been held, no memorial. It's as if Micah never existed in this town.

I threaten to tell the truth about that night, but my uncle says the moment I open my mouth, the police will put a bullet in my head. It isn't just the EMTs who are on Congressman Briarwood's payroll and helped cover it up; it's the cops too. The corruption runs deeper than I can probably imagine.

I wish I could fight for justice for Micah, but my uncle has one last thing to use against me. The only part I have left of my brother—his ashes.

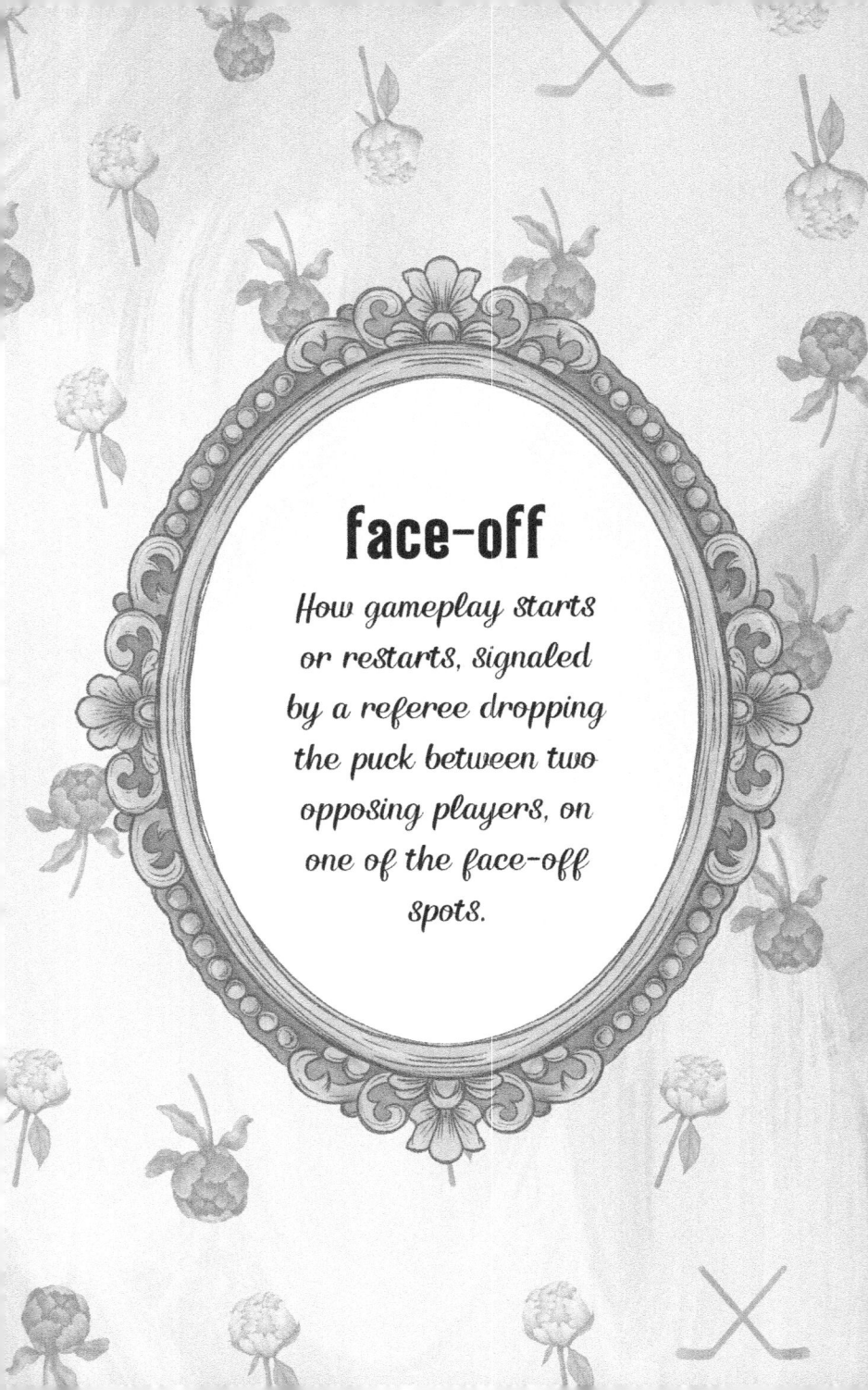

face-off

How gameplay starts
or restarts, signaled
by a referee dropping
the puck between two
opposing players, on
one of the face-off
spots.

chapter twenty-eight
malik
present

"Y-you love me?" Her voice is wary and thick with emotion.

Nodding, I grab her face, and her breath is warm on my rain-soaked lips. "Yes, Alora, I love you. I love you so fucking much. And I can't lose you. I can't pretend that you aren't it for me. You're the only person in this world I can't live without."

Her eyes well with tears, and her lips tip up into a quivering smile. "I love you too."

Every wall and reservation wash away from her as she melts in my grasp, like my declaration brought her the utmost peace. Little does she realize, it's done just that for me too.

Caressing the back of her head, I crush my lips to hers, kissing her like I never have before. It's different this time. It's more—*so* much more.

She fists her hands in my wet shirt, her body melting into mine, a hunger behind her every movement. As much as I want to continue down that path, we can't. Not yet.

"Wait."

She blinks rapidly, and I stroke her cheeks with my thumbs.

"I have to tell you something … a lot of things actually."

She stiffens slightly, and recognition dawns in her eyes, like she's been waiting for this moment. "My dad. You said you won't let my dad stop us."

I nod. "There's more to it than that." I wince, still hating that I have to be the one to ruin the image of him in her mind. "You might think I'm a dick for not telling you sooner. You might even hate me. I really fucking hope you don't, but I couldn't blame you if you did."

"Y-you're kind of scaring me now," she murmurs, walking over and sitting down on the edge of her bed, next to where Sunny is curled up in a ball. "But first, please change so you're not in freezing cold clothes."

I didn't even realize I had been shivering this badly. "Don't peek." I crack a joke, even in this insanely serious moment.

She rolls her eyes and playfully covers them with her hands before spreading her fingers apart and gawking at me fully.

Stripping out of my wet T-shirt, sweats, boxers, and

socks, I thank my past self for stashing clothes here. I change into a clean Legends hoodie, sweatpants, and socks.

She inches back on the bed to make room for me, but I can't help but be hesitant as I walk over to it, feeling that I might deserve to sit on the floor rather at the same level as her.

"First, I need to—" she starts to say at the same time I mutter, "I'm sorry to tell you about this.

"You go," I urge her, trying to gain confidence in the extra second it'll give me.

"The day that my father was on campus …" She pauses, holding my stare.

My shoulders fall because I know what she's about to say. *She already knows.*

"I saw you two talking. Not like new acquaintances. Like old enemies. You were *so angry*. And he was so … I don't even know how to explain it. I've never seen him quite like that."

My heart drops when she doesn't add anything about the conversation.

"You didn't hear what he said, did you?"

She shakes her head, and I sigh. Part of me was hoping that she had. At least then I wouldn't have to be the one to expose her father to her. But he would find a way to make me the bad guy.

"Alora …" I clench my jaw and swallow hard.

She reaches out and grabs my hand to console me,

and selfishly, I let her keep it, her delicate fingers stroking mine.

"Please tell me," she whispers, like she's scared if she says it any louder, I'll stop.

But there's no going back now. There hasn't been for a long time.

"I had a little brother."

Her eyebrows pinch in confusion, which, unfortunately, will fade as I continue.

"He was killed when he was ten and I was fifteen. I had taken him out for ice cream—an escape from our abusive uncle's care." My chest tightens, my throat and eyes burning as I force myself to speak the next words aloud. "On our walk home, he was hit by a drunk driver. He, uhh …" I feel a sob trying to break loose, so I clear my throat. "He died in my arms."

I look down at our interlocked hands, unable to hold her stare any longer. It's too intense, too *all-seeing*.

She lets me continue without interrupting, and I'm thankful because if given a chance to stop, I will take it.

"The driver was a man, in town for some … event."

She gasps, putting it together in her own mind.

A beat of silence consumes us as our breaths halt in our lungs. I don't even want to say it out loud, but I need to, for both of us.

"Your dad killed my brother that night. And it wasn't an accident." I pause. "Because afterward, he didn't take accountability. He paid his problems away."

When I flick my teary eyes up to look at her, her blue gaze is clouded with sadness of her own.

"What did he do?" Her voice is soft yet broken.

My heart constricts in an entirely new way.

Not a drop of doubt is in her tone or her body. She believes me. She really believes me.

That means more than she'll ever know.

Clawing at my throat, I sigh. "He paid *everyone*. Threw money at anyone who would take it. The EMTs, the cops, my uncle. He bought their silence, and they swept Micah under the rug like he was *nothing*."

Her eyes slam shut, and tears stream down her cheeks, rolling off her chin and falling to the pink sweater, darkening the fabric in a similar way I feel I'm darkening her. Taking away her naive image of her dad.

"I'm sorry," I murmur, and her eyes fly open in anger.

She inches closer to me, holding my hand tighter. "Don't you dare say you're sorry. If anyone in this room should be, it's me."

"It wasn't you who did it, Alora, even if it took me a long time to understand that. *Too long*." Lifting her hand to my lips, I kiss the back of her hand tenderly. "I hated you, Alora. I thought I did at least.

"Every time I saw you, I saw *him*. The man who had murdered my brother and then covered it up with money and bribes. As if he had hit a Stop sign and not the most important person in my life."

She cocks her head to the side. "Why didn't you ever say anything?"

Rubbing the back of my neck with my free hand, I spill the can of beans more. "Micah's ashes … my uncle … he has them. He and your dad have kept them from me to keep me quiet. As long as I know his ashes are safe, I'll never say a word to anyone I think will tell."

A blanket of silence falls on the room, and Sunny shifts beside us, wiggling over to me and resting her head on my knee, as if she can sense my distress.

Looking up at Alora, I suck in a sharp breath. There's something different in her stare right now—a seriousness.

Her sad tears boil into frustration. "I won't let him get away with it, Malik."

As much as I love her support, I can't help but wonder if she's second-guessing me at all. I mean, I wouldn't blame her if she did. He's her dad.

"You haven't defended him …" I trail off nervously.

Leaning forward, she presses her lips softly against mine, and I reciprocate the gentleness.

"Believe it or not, you're about the only person in this world I do trust. Of course I'm not going to defend him. I'll always defend *you*."

I swear I can feel a vine of thorns unwrap from my heart at her words. The dam bursts behind my eyes.

"Thank you." My whisper is a tendril of hope.

For the first time since that night, my shoulders

relax ever so slightly. Not completely ... but enough to matter.

"I'm not letting you get involved in this though. I don't want you to get hurt." I slide my hand over her crisscrossed legs in front of me. I just need to touch her, any and every part of her.

She shakes her head immediately. "You aren't alone anymore, and you won't be fighting that way either."

"We don't know what he's really capable of," I caution her.

"There's something he doesn't know, Malik." Her shoulders roll back as an aura of power washes over her. "He has no idea what *I'm* capable of."

She continues, "He raised me in his world—until the day I turned eighteen at least. Maybe it's time I use my last name and the reputation he's built for some good instead of hiding from it."

"You scare me, Alora," I murmur, and she smiles softly.

"Oh, yeah? I scare the big bad Malik?" she teases.

I nod. "Petrified."

Staring at her, I do my best to memorize this moment, committing every detail to my mind. "Especially right now, with that vengeful gleam in your eye. You're a force of nature."

"We are when we're together. I promise you that he will not get away with it."

"How?" I ask such a simple yet heavy question.

"We'll figure it out. But I promise we'll be careful,

and I'll make sure Micah is safe and sound before we pull the trigger on whatever plan we come up with," she says before waving her hands in the air dismissively. "I don't want to talk about my dad anymore."

I wait for her to continue.

"Will you tell me about him?" she whispers.

Nodding, I figure there's one good place to start. Grabbing the back of my hoodie T-shirt, I pull it over my head, setting it beside us.

Her eyes start to wander over my chest and arms. "Tell me about them. Why'd you get each one?"

"Of course, there's this." I hold my hand up, and she traces the five letters with her finger.

She starts to trace the word *villain* arched across my chest. "You know you're not a villain right?"

I shrug. "Aren't we all a villain in someone else's story?"

Her weighted stare warms me as I practically read her mind, that I'm no longer the bad guy in hers.

Silently, her hands slides on top of mine, flattened over the tattoo just below *villain*.

"And then …" I choke up, but I force it back down. "This."

I uncover the butterfly tattoo with my hand. She does the same thing again, gently tracing the outline, sending shivers through me.

"Butterflies were his favorite thing in the world." I smile as the image of him sitting and staring at one of his framed ones pops into my mind. "He was fascinated

… but I wasn't the most supportive when it came to it. Something I greatly regret."

Her eyes soften. "*Mal.*"

That's the first time she's ever called me that. Warmth spreads through me.

"I know what I said, the jokes I made. I hate myself for it. But instead of just dwelling on it, I've continued his collection, expanding it tenfold, even adding one to my skin."

A light bulb flashes in her eyes. "Your room …" She winces, lightly smacking her forehead. "That's why you freaked out on me that day." She pauses in thought. "The little things are making so much more sense now."

"I'm sorry I didn't tell you sooner. I just didn't know …"

"If you could trust me? I get it, Malik, seriously. I can't imagine what that was like. I'm surprised we've gotten to this point at all. It's a miracle." She looks at me with admiration.

Moving back to the Micah-inspired tattoo tour, I turn and show her my back. The two giant wings that cover my shoulders with three numbers between them. Six. Two. Three.

"His birthday. June 23."

She murmurs kindly, "It's beautiful, the ways you've honored him."

She runs her finger down the side of my neck unexpectedly. "What does this one mean?"

It takes me a split second to remember what I have there. Two words in Latin. *Somnium meum.*

"What does it mean?" She brushes the black ink back and forth.

"It was one of the first ones I ever got. For some reason, I was feeling rather hopeful that day and wanted something to remind me of what I was fighting for every day. It translates to *my dream.*"

Her lips part, and her eyes widen. "Are you serious?"

Nodding, I wait for her to elaborate on her shock.

"I had to do a paper in school; maybe you did, too, if you took Mrs. Humphries English class. We had to write an essay about the origin of our name. And in one of the rabbit holes I stumbled down, I found out that Alora means *my dream.*"

Chills run down my back and spine as I repeat the words. "My dream."

Something about that coincidence seems so … *right.*

Our paths have always been intertwined in ways we never could have imagined. I've never been one to believe in fate; it's hard to after everything I've been through. But maybe, once upon a dream, she's mine, a part of my story that was always inevitable.

"Can I just hold you right now?" I ask, wanting to feel closer to her.

She nods, and I move instantly, wrapping my body around her as I pull her back into my chest with our heads on the pillows.

With her ear near my lips, I apologize for things I did long ago. "I took a lot of the anger about my brother's death out on you, and I'm sorry. That wasn't fair to you, and if I could take it back, I would."

She nestles into me tighter, warming my heart. "Don't apologize for who you became in order to survive, Malik. You had to shield yourself from the world at such a young age. I forgive you for who you were back then. You just have to do the same for yourself."

Tears flow from my eyes again, and I sniffle. She turns around immediately, wiping them away with her thumbs.

"If you want, I'd love to hear some stories about him. If you're comfortable, of course." Her bloodshot eyes look into mine with such vulnerability and love.

I don't know how in the hell it's taken me this long to realize how far from her father she really is, but I'll never let myself forget it.

It's going to be hard to talk about him. Just the thought of it has my throat burning.

But I want to. He deserves to be remembered by anyone willing to get to know him.

With her wrapped in my arms, I start to open up about my baby brother.

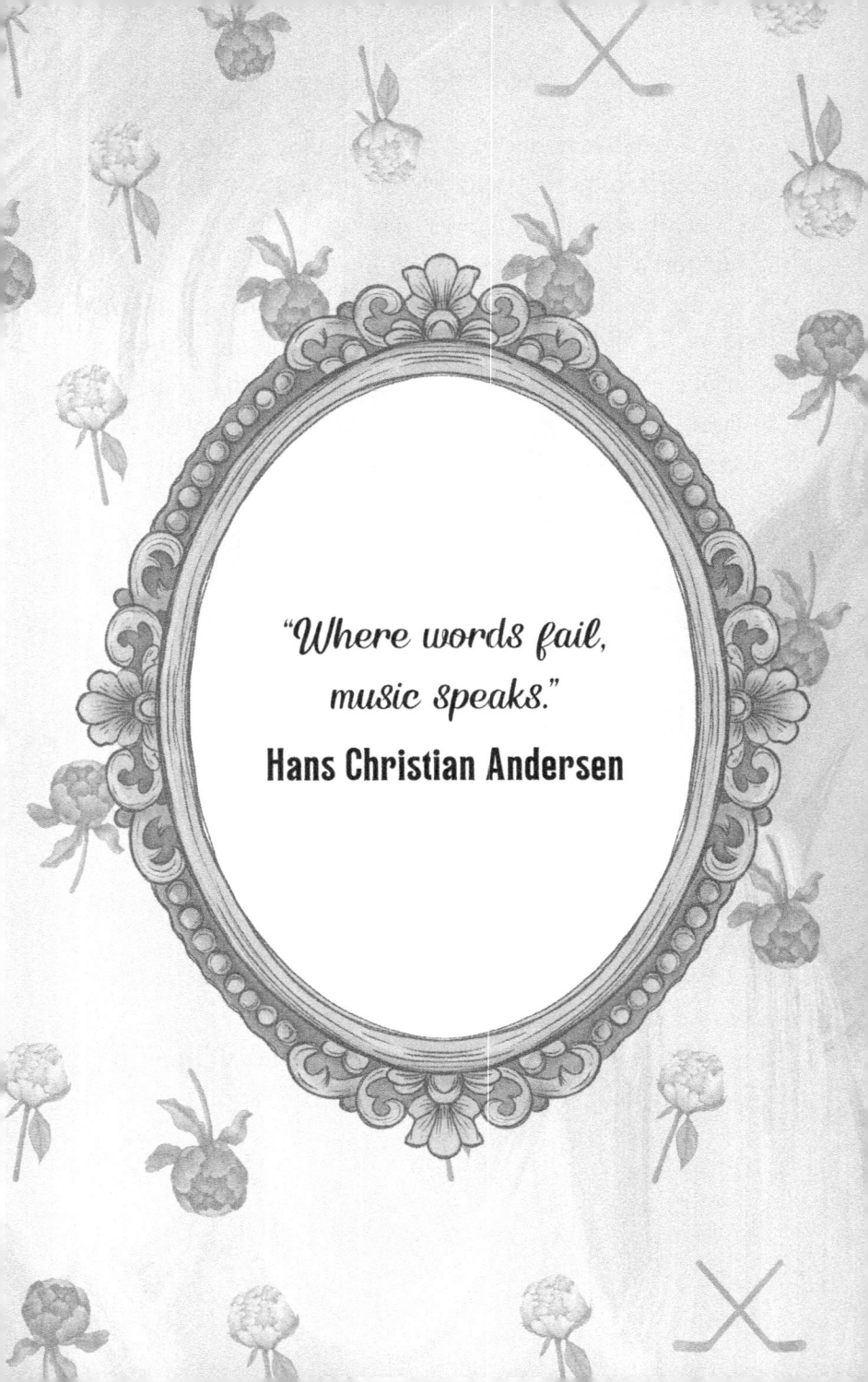

"Where words fail,
music speaks."

Hans Christian Andersen

chapter twenty-nine
alora

Today, the world feels heavier yet clearer than it's ever been. Like I've finally been handed the missing puzzle pieces that I was searching for, for what felt like forever.

But now that I have them, it's like everything has clicked into place.

Malik's hatred for me all those years wasn't for nothing. Was it directed at the wrong person? Sure. But at least there was a reason I can finally understand.

A part of me—the smallest sliver of my being—wants to think that my father's innocent. The little girl he used to tuck into bed and tell made-up stories to ... she wants to believe in him like she used to.

But I can't hide from the feeling in my gut—that he's not the man who once raised me.

He lost himself somewhere along the way, became consumed by the world around him and the chaos of his own creation. It's sad because, deep down, I miss him, the version of him I used to know.

I never realized you could mourn someone who was still alive. But I think I started doing that a long time ago. It's hard to move on completely when every now and then, you get glimpses of the person you once knew in their eyes, one that you desperately want to cling to.

He's who I think about while I perform this piano piece, *Liebestraum No. 3* by Liszt. His face is the one haunting me with each note and chord that echo through the small room.

The music board joined our Individual Study in Music Performance class this morning, putting each of us on the spot to perform. They want to confirm that those invited to the showcase deserve their place. They aren't just going to let anyone on the stage, and with Rupert's scandal, I'm sure they want to make sure that we were chosen for our talents alone.

As the final note fades out, applause breaks through the silence around me, goose bumps chilling my arms.

Rising from my seat, I bow my head and look up at the three board members, awaiting their feedback.

The woman in the middle, Martha Schumann—a legend—speaks first. "It's a shame we hadn't had the pleasure of hearing you perform until now. You are truly exceptional." She pauses, whispering to the other staff members. Then she continues, with a big smile on her face, "Please see me in my office after class today."

"Okay," I murmur, taking my seat at my assigned desk with Sunny.

The next performer takes their seat on the piano bench.

Nerves rattle my bones a bit as we wait for each minute to pass by. Everyone else gets immediate feedback and a yes or no to the showcase. Most of which are noes, but that's not surprising, given this is an entry-level class.

When we're finally dismissed, I follow the three board members down the hall toward Martha's office, I presume. Once we pass through the ornate wooden door, they close it behind me and offer me to sit. I sit down in one of the velvet Victorian chairs, and Sunny sits between my legs, as if she's also eagerly waiting for what they're going to say.

The male professor, Sergei Horowitz, speaks first. "Alora, where have you played before this? Did you study anywhere else?"

Slowly, I shake my head. "No, sir. Only in the privacy of my home."

Martha leans forward over her desk. "Firstly, we are going to need to drastically change your course load. There's no need for you to be in most of your classes. You're far beyond their levels."

She digs something out of her desk and slides an

envelope over to me. "Secondly, we would be honored to have you perform in our showcase."

Relief washes over me at her offer, and excitement builds within me at the idea of switching into harder classes.

I couldn't help but think that perhaps the only reason I had originally been invited was because of that creep's desire for me. But this one is all because of me, and he can't take that away.

I take the envelope and gently hold it in my lap. "Thank you so much."

She nods sharply and smiles.

Sergei clears his throat. "We would also like to apologize on behalf of the department. If there's anything we can do to make you more comfortable, please don't hesitate to reach out."

I nod, my mind racing. I'm wholeheartedly overwhelmed in the best of ways at everything that just transpired. "Thank you."

I'm not sure what else to say. It's not like it was their fault, and I'm sure they're just as angry as I am.

Carol Backhaus, the third member who's been waiting in silence, adjusts in her seat. "Alora, you have the makings of being someone truly extraordinary in any path you wish to take. This may be too personal to share"—she swallows hard with a smile on her lips and sadness in her eyes—"but I knew your mom a very long time ago."

My heart twists. "You did?"

She nods, pressing her lips together. "We attended the same university. I know she graduated with a business degree, but she hadn't started out in that major. She was originally a music major—for singing." Her eyes gloss over as she drifts back in time. "Gosh, she was *such* a gifted vocalist."

Memories start firing off in my mind of her singing me to sleep, singing in the car, singing all the time. She really was incredible. I just never knew it was something she had pursued.

"Do you know why she changed her major?" I murmur. I don't know why she'd ever give that up.

She shakes her head. "I don't. But I think that she would be so proud of you for being right where you are."

My eyes burn and well up with tears. "Thank you."

She leaves me with one more statement. "Don't confuse your success with your legacy. You earned the spot in the showcase on your own merit."

After leaving Martha's office, Sunny and I spend the afternoon lounging around in our dorm room and watching some of our favorite movies.

Malik is with his team most of today. They have a

game tonight and have been watching tape and doing … whatever the hell it is they do before games.

June will be hanging out with Sunny while I go to the game. Blair and Lumi will be going, too, and it'll be nice to have some company.

My phone rings, and I answer a call from Fauna. "Hello?"

"There's my angel. How are you doing?" she asks, and my chest warms when I hear her voice.

"Doing well," I answer, knowing I have a lot to fill my aunts in on, but I also know that this second probably isn't the right time.

"Glad to hear it! Well, we'll be flying into town Thursday for the gala this weekend. When can we steal you away for dinner?"

"Thursday will be good." Butterflies dance in my stomach. "Can I still bring someone with me?"

She gasps in playful shock. "Is this that same boy?"

"Yeah," I murmur.

"Then of course. And what is their name?" she asks, and I bite my bottom lip.

I can't exactly say Malik because they're wellllll aware of what happened between us in high school.

"It'll be a surprise," are the only words I can manage to form.

She hums. "So secretive." But then she agrees instantly. "Fine, you and your secret special someone meet us tomorrow at six. I'll send you the name of the restaurant."

"Okay." I smile.

"I'm excited to squeeze you, my little peanut," she coos.

My aunts are everything to me, and they deserve the same goodness that they put out into the world.

"I love you."

"I love you too, Lore." She blows a kiss into the phone before ending the call.

Well, dinner is going to be interesting. We have a lot to catch up on. And a lot to plan.

Wearing Malik's name on my back has me feeling giddy in an entirely new way as I walk into the arena with Blair and Lumi. Because right now, I'm not wearing it with uncertainty; I'm wearing it, knowing I'm his.

We get settled into our seats, and warm-ups are underway. I find him on the ice instantly, recognizing the movements of his body as he skates. I could blindly find him in a room full of people.

"Excuse me," a woman mutters, wanting to walk down our aisle.

We stand up, and a man and woman slide past us, sitting directly to my left.

The woman next to me murmurs to the guy, "Do you see him?"

"There he is." The man points. "Number fifty-five."

Fifty-five? I look at my arm and remember I'm wearing that same number on my jersey. *Who are they?*

"He's going to be so surprised when he sees us." She giggles.

Are they ... the ones who took him in?

Is it weird if I ask?

Malik shoots a puck into the net and turns toward me, looking up in the stands and waving. Lifting my hand, I wave back as my stomach flutters.

But I'm not the only one who waves.

The couple raises their hands in the air, and as if we're a reflection of one another, we turn to each other with a look of confusion.

And then we look back at Malik, whose hand is in the air with surprise. Pointing at all of us, he flicks his hands toward each other, and I read what he's trying to say, turning to face the couple.

"Hi. You must be Darius and Alicia?" I ask politely as they watch me with curiosity.

They nod, and Alicia smiles, reminding me of how my aunt Flora lights up when she grins. "Yes, we are. And what's your name?"

Sticking my hand out, I shake the man's hand, then hers. "I'm Alora."

"Alora ..." Darius mumbles my name with recognition, his face flat.

Alicia rolls her eyes at him. "Ignore my husband. He's clearly not putting this together as fast as I am."

Her eyes fall to the jersey I'm wearing. "It seems you guys aren't enemies anymore."

I chuckle, realizing they know exactly who I am—or at least have heard of me through Malik. "No, not quite."

Lumi butts in. "They're dating."

"He gave you his jersey." Darius's voice is filled with emotion. "You must be someone incredibly special to him."

That piques my interest. "What do you mean?"

Alicia sucks in a breath as Darius continues, "He's never given his jersey out before."

"Not to anyone?" I ask, goose bumps skating along my arms.

He shakes his head. "Never. Not once his entire high school career. The only person who ever wore his jersey was Micah. But once he lost him, he never did it again."

My eyes burn, and I blink back tears from forming in my eyes. "Thank you for telling me that."

Their stares are full of respect and adoration.

Darius smiles at me with wetness in his eyes. "Thank you for getting him to open up again. Until this moment, I almost thought that would never happen."

A tear rolls down my cheek. "It was a team effort from both Malik and I."

Darius laughs, a sob breaking free from his throat. "I know Malik. I'm sure it was one hell of a job. But we're grateful nonetheless."

I laugh as the brightness dims in the arena. The light show begins on the ice as the build-up song plays loudly through the speakers, cutting off our conversation. The announcer begins shouting into the mic, announcing each starter as they skate out onto the ice and take their place on the blue line.

Alicia reaches over and squeezes my hand with hers. Looking up to her eyes, I find them brimmed with tears. I can see the love they have for him, like he's their son.

She mouths, *Thank you.*

I nod and squeeze her hand back, enjoying the moment.

After the anthem is performed, they set up for the start of the game. The Legends versus the Kraken. Blair, my resident hockey expert, fills me in on all the stats of the team and the likely outcome. Honestly, it's so impressive that she can keep everything straight in her mind.

Apparently, the Kraken have two of the top scorers in all of college hockey on their team. Which doesn't sound super beneficial to us. But she assures me that Griffin and Dean are the best defensive duo, and the Kraken will have one hell of a time trying to score on them.

She's right.

By the end of the second period, the score is one to zero, with us in the lead.

After a quick bathroom break and concession stop, I head back to my seat.

Someone grabs my wrist, and I'm suddenly pulled inside of a room, the door shutting behind me.

"Ahh!"

But the moment his scent fills my nose, I relax.

"Hey, Bug."

"What are you doing here?" I gasp, playfully slapping his chest.

"I needed this." He grabs my jaw and tilts my head back at the same time his lips crash down onto mine.

He breathes me in with his kiss, devouring me as his tongue starts dancing with mine.

I moan into his mouth, and he groans, his fingers grabbing my waist. After getting his fill, he pulls back like it's the hardest thing he's ever had to do.

"Wait for me in the lobby with Blair and Lumi after the game. *Please*."

He kisses me again, and I melt into a puddle.

Pulling away, I bite down on my tingling lip. "What's in it for me?"

He squints at me. "Oh, really? Just seeing me isn't enough?"

Cocking my head to the side, I playfully wince. "I don't know."

Suddenly, I'm airborne, my legs wrapping around his waist as if it were their most natural position.

Pressing my back against the wall, he claims my lips with his. "How about I promise to love you forever?"

"That easy?" I challenge him between kisses.

He nods, his lips pressed into mine. "The easiest thing I'll ever do is love you forever, Alora."

My chest bursts with joy, and I kiss him ferociously as the world around us seems to fade away.

I've lived my life safely, following orders from my father, being the perfect student and the adoring daughter. I did those things for my dad, my teachers, and my peers to earn their love. But I don't have to earn Malik's; he loves me for free.

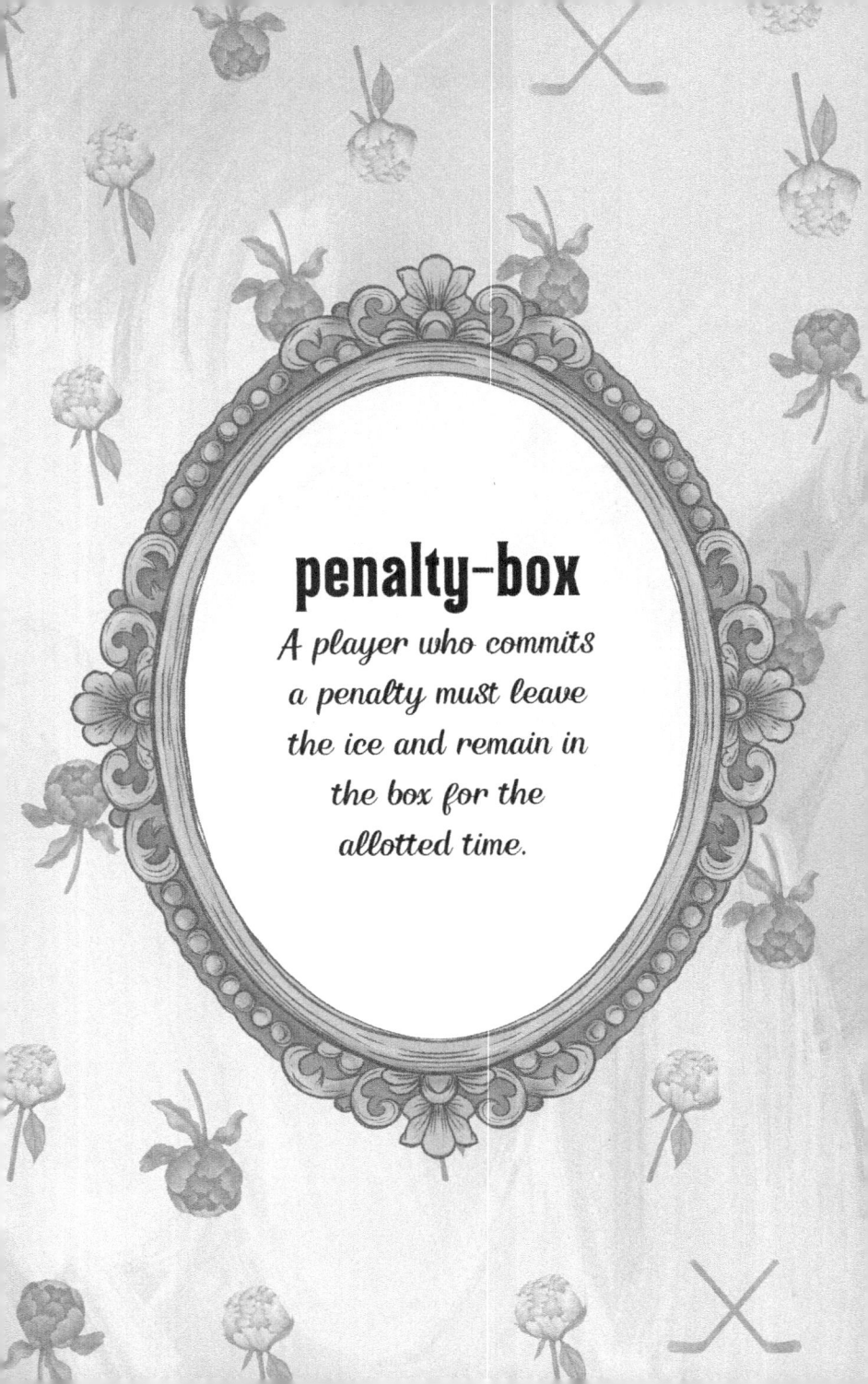

penalty-box

*A player who commits
a penalty must leave
the ice and remain in
the box for the
allotted time.*

chapter thirty
malik

I'm more nervous walking into dinner with Alora's aunts in a suit than I've ever been while walking into an arena. But with Alora's hand in mine, I feel damn near unstoppable.

As if she can sense my erratic heart, Sunny brushes against my leg and looks up at me.

"I'm okay, girl," I assure her.

When she gently tugs at my hand, I look down at Alora's sparkling blue eyes, framed by her long blonde waves.

"Don't be nervous. I know they'll be shocked at first, but once we explain everything, they'll love you. Seriously. They are nothing like my father, the furthest from him."

Rubbing the back of my neck, I lift our interconnected hands to my lips. "I trust you."

We walk through the double-door entrance, and three women's heads turn to us instantly.

Sunny's tail starts going crazy, and for the first time ever, I see her pull on her leash to try to get to them.

"Alora!" one of them calls out and races over, wrapping her arms around her while the other two greet Sunny with pets and kisses.

The one with pixie-cut hair looks up at me, and the glimmer in her eyes instantly fades. She steps back without tearing her stare from me.

"Why is Malik Ravenwell here?" Her voice is sharp.

The other two look up at me and rise to their full height, all of five foot one, scowls twisting their mouths.

Alora steps in front of me, her back brushing my torso, and I release her hand, resting it gently on her waist.

"Before you freak out, you need to hear us out. There's a lot you don't know yet."

"Briarwood. Table for five!" a hostess calls out.

The five of us look over at her and pause, the heaviness still in the air.

"Right here," one of her aunts answers, stepping toward the host stand.

"This way, please." She smiles.

Her aunts lead the way, followed by Sunny, Alora, and me. My heart is in my fucking throat as we are seated at a round table in an enclosed atrium.

A waiter comes over immediately and takes our

drink order before disappearing behind a stained-glass door.

Thrust back into the awkward disdain of the conversation, I swallow hard, sitting still with my hands in my lap.

Never more in my life have I ever wanted to impress three people as much as I do them. But I know I'm starting with a thousand negative points and have a hell of a long way to go.

They sit tall and proud, all three staring directly at me.

Alora drags their attention to her. "Hate him later. But I promise you will hate him less once I'm done telling you about my dad."

That ignites their gazes, and Alora tells them *everything*.

By the time she's done catching them up on the absolute chaos that has become our lives, their eyes soften when they look at me, and an understanding passes between us all.

Flora, Fauna, and Freya disclose that they have a few secrets of their own, ones they've kept for years, waiting for the right moment. Waiting for *this*.

Fauna slips away to make a quick phone call before coming back and telling us that she has an idea, a plan to bring some of his darkness to light without putting on a grand spectacle.

But if a show is what he needs to own up to the things he's done, then so be it.

The charity gala is tomorrow night, and I still haven't technically agreed to go with Alora, although she and I both know that I wouldn't be anywhere other than by her side.

As we wrap up and head to the front of the restaurant, I murmur to Alora, "I'll go tomorrow on one condition."

She glances up at me with excitement in her eyes. "What is it?"

"You wear a dress *you* want and not the one your father sent. Wear one that makes you happy."

Her demeanor softens, and she smiles. "I think that can be arranged."

"Ooh." Fauna butts into our conversation. "Wear blue. You look so stunning in blue."

Flora pushes her out of the way as we walk outside into the chilly day. "Pink! Pink is your color!"

Fauna scoffs. "Blue!"

"Pink!" Flora slaps her shoulder. "It has to be pink!"

Fauna steps in front of us and walks backward. "Blue. Like the color of the sky on a warm, sunny day."

"Pink! A soft, delicate shade. Something flowy!" Flora joins Fauna in her backward walk, and I chuckle.

Freya grabs the tops of their heads and spins them around. "I'm sure she is more than capable of picking out her own dress color."

They bicker quietly with each other but find solidarity at last as we approach my Corvette.

"Tomorrow, let's meet up two hours before the gala

at your dorm room to reconvene and make sure we are set and ready to go before the big event. My secret weapon will meet us there," Fauna instructs us, and we nod. "Alora, are you sure you want to do this, honey? One of us can take your place in all of this."

She shakes her head. "He won't talk with you guys the way he will with me. I can do it."

Flora rubs her hand up and down Alora's arm, and I squeeze her hand.

"We love you." Fauna smiles at her and then up at me, and my heart warms.

"Tomorrow." Alora mutters the word with finality.

"Tomorrow," I repeat, lifting her hand up to my lips and kissing her fingers tenderly.

Alora, Sunny, and I get in my car to head back to her place.

When we reach the dorm, we head upstairs. My phone chimes when we slip inside of her room, and I check it out as Sunny and Alora plop down on her bed.

I pull my phone out and read the text from my uncle.

The Devil: He's threatening me now because you can't keep your dick in your pants. Get your shit together, or so help me God, I will make you.

Shoving it back into my pocket, I grind my teeth and glance up at Alora, who's watching me with a worried gaze.

"Who is it?"

"My uncle," I murmur. "Nothing important."

"I'm sorry. It will all be over soon, I promise." She opens her arms, her legs draping over the side of the bed, and I don't waste a second to go to her.

She wraps her arms around my waist and rests her chin against my chest as she stares up at me. Fuck, she's so beautiful. It's intimidating sometimes how perfect she is. She fucking glows.

"I love you," she whispers as I push her hair back from her face with my fingers.

"Not possibly more than I love you," I murmur, brushing my thumb across her bottom lip.

"Will you help me with something?" she asks, and I'm already nodding in agreement before I know what it is. "Help me decide between a few dresses for tomorrow?"

"Watch you dress up in fancy gowns and ogle you unabashedly? It's a yes every time."

Her eyes pinch shut from the joy in her giggles. "When have you ever not stared at me unabashedly?"

I chuckle. "Touché."

She walks over to her closet and pulls out three garment bags taller than her and hangs them on the back of her door. "Turn around," she orders me, blushing.

Shaking my head, I smirk. "And miss the show? No, thank you."

Hooking her finger in the strap of her purple sundress—one I will certainly be desperate to see again

—she pushes it off of her shoulder before repeating it with the other one.

Oh, she's giving me a *show*.

Running her fingers down her sides, she tugs at the thin fabric, and it cascades down her body, leaving her in lilac-purple panties.

"Mmm." I run my tongue across my bottom lip. "Fucking hell, Alora. That ass of yours will be my goddamn ruin."

She sucks in a mocking breath and cups her big tits with her back to me, looking over her shoulder. "And what about these?" Turning on her heel, she palms herself, jiggling them up and down.

My cock twitches aggressively in my slacks. Fisting the comforter with my hands, I do my best to be good and stay seated. But, fuck, she's making it hard ... making everything hard.

When she drops her hands, my mouth waters at the sight before me. My burning gaze travels from the top of her blonde hair down to those devilish eyes, plump lips, over those big perfect breasts. A path that I desperately want to make with my tongue.

Goddamn, she's so hot—*too hot*. I'm going to combust.

Her wide hips are begging to be gripped as I plunge deep inside of her. My fingers and dick twitch at the thought.

Glancing back up at her stare, I'm almost burned

from the inferno scorching behind her eyes. "Careful, looking at me like that, Alora."

She takes a slow step toward me. "Or what?"

My dick throbs in my pants, begging to come out and play. Hooking my finger between us, I gesture her toward me. "Come find out."

Holding her hands behind her back, she sashays closer, but still out of my reach. "What are you going to do to me?"

Leaning forward, I adjust myself in these tight pants. "What do you want me to do to you?"

Her answer dances on the tip of her tongue as she continues to close the distance between us.

Killing any doubts she may have, I assure her, "There is absolutely nothing you could ask of me that I wouldn't agree to."

"I'm just nervous …" she murmurs and bites down on the side of her bottom lip. "I want you"—she holds my stare—"to take control."

I keep my hands to myself as she steps between my legs with her lips parted, like she has more to add.

Sliding her hands around my shoulders, she shimmies her tits in my face, and I growl as I fight harder than ever to restrain myself.

"Bend me. Shape me. Mold me. Do whatever you want." Her voice is sultry, and I roll my eyes as the air draws taut between us. "I'm yours, Malik. Take me."

I snap, my hand wrapping around her throat in the blink of an eye. She melts instantly into my grasp, her pupils dilating as I switch positions with her, pushing her to the bed as I tower over her.

Running my nose up the length of her neck, I breathe her scent in; that strawberry-vanilla blend is my own slice of heaven.

"You sure you want this?" I groan, running my free hand from the tip of her chin down her neck and between her tits. "Because I'll fuck you with abandon, Bug." My fingers trail lower, stopping just above her clit. "I'll pound into this sweet pussy until you can't fucking take it anymore."

Lost for words, she wets her lips and nods, wriggling her hips, desperate for any friction.

She whimpers, "*Malik.*"

I sink my fingers into her wetness beneath her panties, and then I bring them to my lips and suck them clean. Standing up, I undo the belt of my pants and step back.

"You want to be my good little slut, huh? Want me to do every dirty thing to you?"

I slip my thumb into her mouth, and she nods.

"Get on your knees," I demand. "And open your mouth."

She slides off of the bed and kneels on the pink rug as her hands find the waistline of my pants, tugging them down as she parts her pretty lips. She frees my erection from my boxers, and it springs in the air between us, hard as a fucking rock as I think about sliding it down her throat.

When she wraps her soft hand around my shaft, I stop her, pushing her hand away.

I step toward her. "Uh-uh, baby. No hands. Now stick your tongue out for me."

Her wet tongue protrudes from her lips, and I groan at the image of her on the ground in front of me. So fucking hot—that alone could do me in.

Fisting her hair in my hand, I tip her head back and grab my cock with my free hand, pumping it back and forth as I circle it around her open mouth. I slap it on her tongue, and the sensation pulses through me to the core.

"Put your hand on my thigh. Rest it right on my number, baby." She drops her hand to my leg, palming the number fifty-five tattooed on my thigh. I slide my tip along her tongue and into her mouth. "If it's too much, tap me once, and I'll slow down. If you need me to stop, tap me twice. Got it?"

She nods with my dick in her mouth.

"Good fucking girl," I growl before thrusting forward, slamming my dick down her throat. I moan loudly.

She gags immediately, and I ease out to the tip while she gathers herself. She doesn't tap me once or twice, so I keep going, rolling my hips and filling her back up.

While I fuck her mouth, I feel my dick grow, cutting her airway off as it hardens more and more. Her eyes start watering, and the sight nearly makes me come as I watch her struggle to take it, but I push on anyway.

But if I keep going, I'm going to come long before I want to be done.

When I back up, my soaking wet dick throbs in the space between us as it falls from her lips. She breathes heavily, panting and looking up at me with parted lips, eagerly waiting for her next instruction.

"Get on your knees on your bed, ass in the air toward me."

Offering her my hand, I help her slowly stand, and I claim her lips with mine, kissing her slowly and passionately as she takes a second to stabilize.

Turning around, she crawls onto the bed on all fours.

My eyes roll backward, and I whisper, "Fuck."

Fisting my cock, I pump it as I step toward her.

With no warning, I smack my hand across her ass, watching it jiggle and redden almost instantly.

She gasps in shock, her back arching for more as she peeks over her shoulder.

SMACK! SMACK! SMACK!

Her ass turns bright red as I leave my marks all over her backside.

"You like it when I spank you, don't you? You like how good it stings?"

She nods, looking at me with hooded eyes and swollen lips.

Palming both cheeks with my hands, I spread them and bounce them together, over and over. I'm hypnotized by how fucking delicious she looks.

Crouching down, I run my tongue from her clit and over both holes, desperate to taste every inch of her. "Mmm. So fucking good."

She whimpers, her hips bucking for more.

Kissing her cheek, I open my mouth and bite down firmly on her round ass, leaving indentations in her flesh. She gasps at the unexpected move but then wiggles her ass slightly, showing me she's good with it.

Standing back up to my full height, I push my hips forward, rubbing my tip against her center. "Beg me for it, Bug."

Her chest flattens on the bed, and my dick throbs.

"Please."

My chuckle comes out more like a growl. "Say it again. I love it when you beg."

She pushes her ass back and whines, "Please, Malik. Please fuck me."

Pushing my tip into her tight pussy, I rail into her, feeling her body struggle to fit me with every inch I thrust inside.

"Ahh!" she cries out in a mix of pain and pleasure. "Holy shit, Malik. You're so—"

I cut her off with my fingers as I wrap my arm around her hip and massage her clit.

"B—big."

Rolling my hips into her over and over, I circle that bundle of nerves with my fingertips, feeling her body starting to pulse around me in mere seconds.

"Oh fuck, baby. Already ready for your first one?" I

continue to fill her to the brim with each thrust forward, working her closer and closer to the edge.

Her words are muffled as she cries out into the blanket. "Yes, fuck, please!"

As she nears her orgasm, I quicken my fingers just enough to push her into oblivion. "Clench around my cock when you come, baby. I want to feel every pulsing wave."

"Ahh! Malik!" she cries out, and I sit up, grabbing her hips and pounding into her as her moans intensify.

SMACK! SMACK! SMACK!

"Maaaalik," she whimpers as I fuck her through her orgasm, not letting up once.

I want to see her face. I *need* to see her as she falls apart next. Every twist of her expression and bounce of her tits—I need to commit it all to memory.

Slowing my thrusts, I ease out of her and grab her hips, twisting her around until her ass lands on the bed and she faces me.

"Put your legs on my shoulders," I order her, watching relief wash over her features.

She was struggling to stay like that. But I never want her to push herself to the point of a flare-up.

"And next time, tell me you need to switch positions."

She holds my stare for a moment before nodding with a shy smile on her lips. "Yes, sir."

"Mmm. That's my good fucking girl," I murmur as she lifts her legs, hooking her ankles over my shoulders.

"You're giving me three more before I let myself come. And you're going to count them out for me after each one—got it?"

Her wide eyes and parted lips make me smirk as she nods. Grabbing my pulsing cock, I slide back inside of her, her core gripping me tightly as I plunge every inch deep into her pussy.

With my thumb on her clit and her eyes on mine, it takes me only a minute to make her fall apart all over again. And only three minutes more until we reach number three for the day.

Giving her a minute to recover, I grab her water from her nightstand and make her take a few drinks before we keep going. I don't want her passing out on me here. I want to push her limits, but never too far.

I don't want her coming this last time until I'm doing it with her, and this time, I'm not pulling out. I need to feel our bodies explode together.

As I pound into her, our moans, groans, and whimpers fill the room as our breathing quickens in sync.

"I'm coming in you this time, Alora, filling you up completely," I growl, leaning down and pressing her legs against her chest as my thrust adjusts, using gravity to slam into her.

She nods, a complete puddle beneath me. "Come wherever the fuck you want. I don't care. Please just … oh fuck. Malik, please."

Her body starts to writhe beneath me.

"Give it to me, baby. Be my good little slut and make a mess on me."

Her back arches, and she cries out, triggering my own orgasm.

Fisting her hair with my hand, I crash my lips to hers, kissing her between moans and gasps for air. Spilling into her, I fill her with every drop of my desire.

"Fuck, baby, you feel so good, filled up like this," I growl against her parted lips. "Mmm. I love you."

She's panting and out of breath as the biggest smile breaks across her lips. "I love *you*."

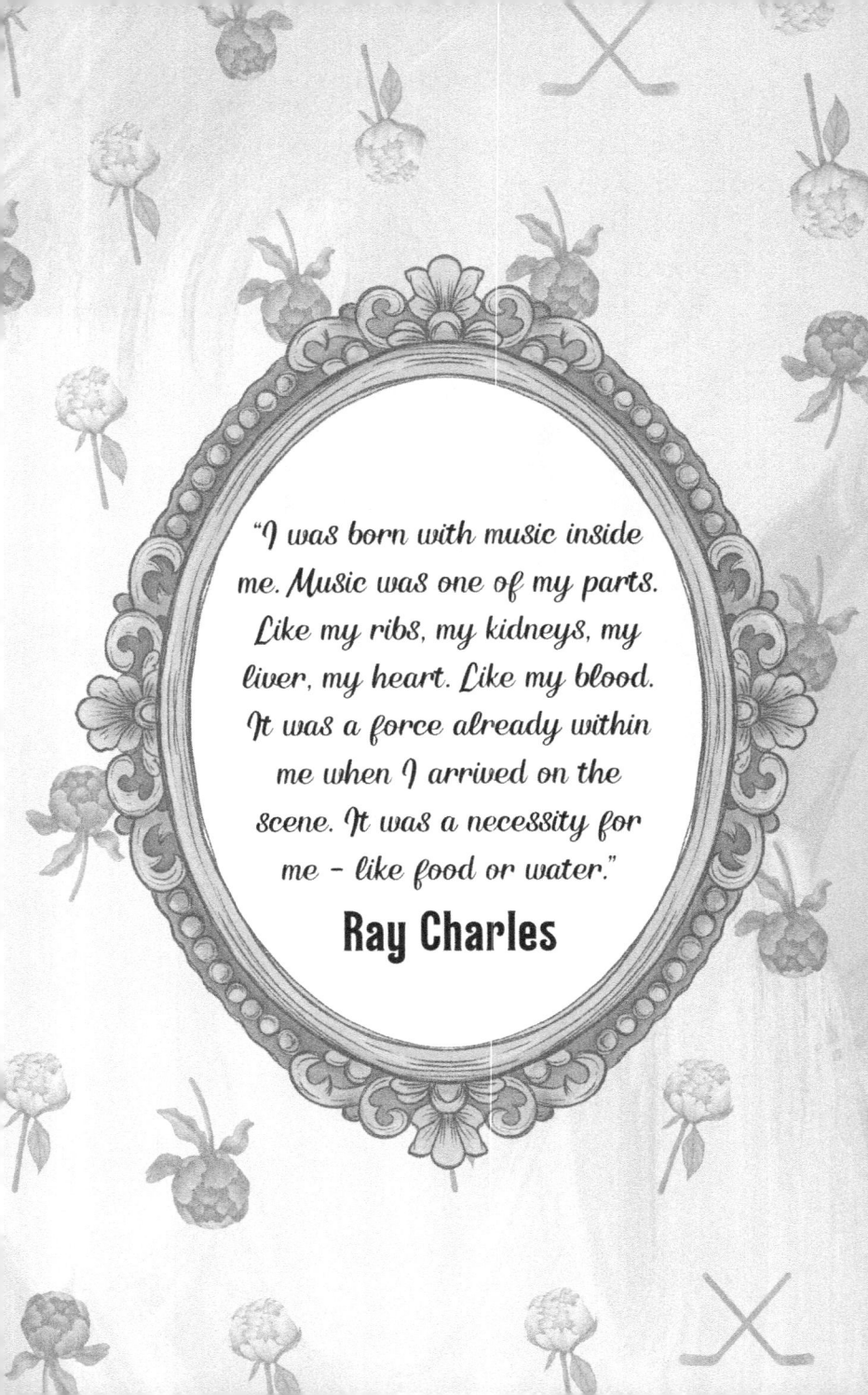

"I was born with music inside me. Music was one of my parts. Like my ribs, my kidneys, my liver, my heart. Like my blood. It was a force already within me when I arrived on the scene. It was a necessity for me – like food or water."

Ray Charles

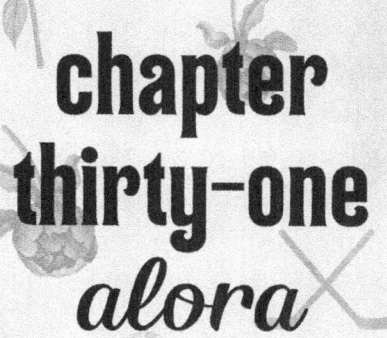

chapter thirty-one
alora

As Agent Hopkins, the Federal agent that my aunts contacted to help, secures the wire beneath the back of my dress as my heart hammers in my chest.

Everything is happening so fast, and even though I know the plan from front to back like the back of my hand, I'm still shaking with nerves.

What if Malik's wrong? What if he thinks my dad killed Micah, but he was just confused? What if the only reason two federal agents are in my dorm room now is because I put them there? What if we're wrong?

Agent Hopkins zips up the back of my shimmering pink satin dress, and I turn around as she starts to say, "You are all set to go. Just talk to him, see what you can get. We need his verbal confirmation about killing Micah before we move in."

My aunts are all three sitting on my bed with Sunny watching us intently.

"I understand."

When we filled them in on Micah and what had happened, they shared that they had been approached a few times over the years regarding suspicion around some of my father's business affairs, but they never had anything concrete to bring him in for. And when you're going to arrest a congressman, you'd better be sure before you slap accusations like that on them.

It looks like I'm going to be the nail in his coffin, as long as I can get him talking.

"We will be waiting outside of the venue," she states before throwing the Legends hood up on her sweatshirt. "Good luck."

"Thanks," I mutter and chuckle humorously.

"How are you feeling?" Flora asks as my door clicks shut.

Turning to look in the mirror, I relax my widened eyes and drop my shoulders. "I'll be fine."

The pink gown is held up by two thin straps. The bodice is boned and corseted tight to my waist, making my boobs look somehow even fuller than usual, as they're pressed against my chest.

My blonde hair cascades down my back, the front sections pulled back and secured with diamond barrettes.

Fauna walks over and delicately rests her hands on my bare shoulders. "You look beautiful, Lore."

My heart swells. "Thanks, Fauna."

She smiles, her eyes lighting up. I got awfully lucky to be raised by these three women. I couldn't have asked for anyone better. They might not be my mom—no one ever will be—but they are my closest family.

A knock sounds on the door, and the nerves somehow spike tenfold. I know Malik's attracted to me, and I often want to impress him, but this is by far the most effort I've ever put into getting dressed up, and I want him to like it.

Flora walks over and pulls the door open.

I can feel his stare on my profile, caressing my skin like a physical touch, burning down my body. Turning my head, I lock on to his intense stare, and my lips part.

God, he looks so goddamn good in a suit and tie. His hair is perfectly tousled atop his head.

"You look breathtaking, Alora," he murmurs softly as he approaches my side, his eyes glued to mine.

Even though I'm wearing five-inch heels, he towers over me, but it's a lot easier for me to do this. Grabbing the back of his neck, I stretch up and press my lips against his.

Pulling away, I rest my forehead against his chest and take a few deep breaths.

"Are you ready to go?" he asks, kissing the top of my head.

Sunny jumps off of my bed and waddles over to him happily. Malik bends down and gives her his undivided attention, and somehow, my heart warms even more.

Glancing up at my aunts, I see such a deep fondness and adoration on their faces while they watch Sunny and Malik together. Clearly, he has grown on them. I know they're still cautious, and I don't blame them. I'm just glad they're giving him a chance.

Grabbing my phone, I realize we only have fifteen minutes before I need to be at the Triton Harbor Event Center.

Hooking my purse over my shoulder, I tuck a water bottle inside, followed by my phone. "We should probably get going."

Tearing himself away from Sunny, he stands to his full height and walks back over to me, offering me his hand, which I happily take.

"We'll be there shortly," Fauna says warmly, pulling me in for a quick hug, followed by Flora and Freya doing the same.

"I love you guys," I swoon, struggling to keep the overwhelming nerves at bay.

"We love you too, darling," Freya says, heading to the door with Sunny's leash in her hand.

They are going to keep Sunny with them tonight at the event. I love her and would rather have her with me, but in case anything goes south, I want her safe with them.

Malik and I head downstairs, hand in hand.

Walking into the chilly evening air, I suck in a sharp breath.

Phillip honks the horn of his Rolls Royce, and we head his way. Malik slides into the back seat, and I sit up front with Phillip.

"You guys sure do look great together," Phillip coos with a smile on his lips.

"I know," Malik mumbles possessively, and I roll my eyes.

Turning, I find a smirk on his lips and chuckle at his ridiculousness.

Phillip drives us across town to the event center where the charity gala is being held.

Tonight's charity doesn't deserve to be tarnished by anything my father might have done. Which is why I plan on pulling him away when I get there to talk to him one-on-one.

My mind drifts away during the drive, replaying old memories of my dad and me. The version of him that I knew when I was little and when my mom was still around. When he was charismatic, funny, carefree, genuine, and ethical. He was the best dad when my mom was alive. So loving and attentive.

Her death changed him. It might not have happened drastically but more gradually over the years. As if he locked himself in a tower, and his obsession with building his empire drove him mad.

We pull around the giant marble fountain with a mermaid-shaped spout and come to a stop outside of the center. Three valet workers approach and open our doors for us, helping us out of the car.

Phillip tips them generously, handing his keys over to the one seemingly in charge, who slips into his car and pulls away, quickly replaced by the next car that rounds the fountain.

Malik slides his hand into mine and squeezes firmly, letting me know that even if it feels like it, I'm not here alone.

With Malik on my right and Phillip on my left, I stroll toward the door, my heels clicking on the pavement with each step.

The doors open for us, and we are immediately greeted by security. I present my ID, and Malik and I are allowed entry, quickly followed by Phillip once he checks in. Malik, of course, isn't on the list, but it doesn't matter because he's my plus-one.

Sauntering down the wide hallway, we turn into the grand ballroom, and my eyes widen. They sure went *all* out. Chandeliers hang from the ceiling, drapery hanging throughout the entire room. The round tables are decorated with gorgeous flower arrangements and candles.

I know this gala is for a good cause, but I bet if they'd donated half of the money they spent on decor, they still would have been able to put on a wonderful event.

The room is bustling with conversations, women in

flowing gowns and men in crisp suits filling the large space.

Teetering on the edge of entering the room and turning and running, I take a few shaky, deep breaths. Everything that comes next will be unpredictable. I have no idea how my father is going to react when he sees that the plus-one I brought is Malik.

I have no idea when our confrontation will occur, but I will need to get him alone at some point to talk to him.

He's the wolf in a room full of sheep. I just need to lure him away from the herd.

A shiver runs down the back of my spine, and I look to my right, locking eyes with the man of the evening.

My dad's smiling at something an older man in his group is mumbling, but there's no joy or humor in his eyes. Only anger and confusion when he sees Malik with me.

Comforting me, Malik rubs his hand up and down the small of my back.

A few of the guys next to my dad follow his stare, and I recognize them vaguely. My dad lifts his hand in the air and waves us over.

Oh shit.

Malik guides me forward, and I force myself to get out of my own head and start playing the part that I once perfected.

My spine straightens, and my shoulders shift back as I lead us across the floor with a smile on my face. As we reach the group, I nod politely, a slight bow to my head to show my respect.

Lifting my arm, I greet my dad with a side hug. "Hi, Dad."

"Alora." He grins, squeezing my shoulder tightly. "You look … lovely." The words are hard for him to spit out.

I know he's fuming inside … for a multitude of reasons. I'm not wearing the dress he sent. I brought a date other than Phillip. And I was late.

"I'm glad you could make it," he hums, getting a little dig in at my punctuality.

"I wouldn't have missed it for the world." My gaze skates across the three gentlemen to his left, all staring at me a little too intensely.

"A word," my father mumbles, trying to steer me away from the group, but I keep my feet planted.

It's not the right time. I was told to attend the evening as planned, follow the itinerary, and then get him alone when everyone was bidding at the silent auction.

Malik secures me at his side, and the look in my father's eyes is one of malice.

A waitress walks by with a tray of champagne, and I grab one, taking a sip.

"We can't leave yet; the event is about to begin."

As if on cue, the speakers in the room pulse as someone taps the microphone. "Good evening, everyone. Please make your way to your seats in the next minute or so, and we'll get started."

"Malik, should we find our table?" I look up at him, sliding my hand across his chest, feeling the hair on the back of my neck rise from the glare in my father's eyes.

"You are with us, Alora. Your … date can join. Phillip as well." My dad glances over at him. "Good to see you, Phillip," he adds politely, offering his hand for Phillip to shake.

He shakes it and nods. "Good to see you too, sir."

We follow my father to a table near the stage. He pulls my chair out for me as we approach. Taking a deep breath, I kindly sit, letting him push it in for me.

His hands slide over the tops of my shoulders, and he leans down, his warm breath hitting my ear. "What do you think you're doing? Embarrassing me like this. Alora Briarwood, you know better. Get rid of him in the next five minutes."

Tipping my head to the side, with a smile planted on my face, I whisper, "Or what?"

He goes silent, clenching his jaw as he pushes away from me before taking a seat at the chair to my right.

Malik sits to my left, and Phillip is to the left of him as the air in the room becomes heavier, making it harder to breathe as we sit and wait.

The announcer takes the stage again a moment later and commences the gala, welcoming everyone in attendance. Apparently, it's their biggest gala yet with high expectations.

Time seems to fly by as every item in my mental checklist is marked.

Introductions.

Opening speech.

Video dedication.

Silent auction.

After two hours of quietly sitting and waiting, it's nearly time for me to get up and lure my dad out. We didn't want to disrupt the event as much as possible. Tonight isn't about my dad.

I've run the conversation through my head a thousand times over, but I'm still not completely sure what I'm going to say when the time comes.

He's been fuming at my side this entire night— waiting for a moment to reprimand me, I'm sure. And now's his chance.

Leaning over to Malik, I murmur, "I'm going. I love you."

He kisses my temple and whispers in my ear, "I love you, baby."

I don't know if I could do this without him here tonight to support me. It certainly would have been ten times harder.

Turning to my father, I lean toward him and excuse myself. "I'll be right back. Going to use the restroom."

When he whips his head my way, the rage in his eyes is still as hot as ever. Although maybe it's been there all along, and I just haven't fully noticed until now.

He doesn't say a word, and I push my chair back, heading out of the back of the room toward the hallway.

Pushing through the door, I stroll down the well-lit hall toward the restrooms, away from the gala. Farther than needed, but out of the way so as not to be inconvenient to anyone else when my dad inevitably follows me and raises his voice.

My father is predictable as always when it comes to his anger. His familiar gait sounds behind me on the marble, the heels of his dress shoes clacking against the ground.

His voice is sharp, stopping me dead in my tracks. "Alora."

Spinning on my heel, I watch him speed-walk over to me, no mask hiding the disappointment on his face.

"What the fuck do you think you're doing?"

Scoffing, I cross my arms. "God forbid I wear a dress that I like."

He points his finger at me, lowering his voice as a few people turn into the hallway we're in. "You and I both know that your slutty dress is not what I'm talking about." With his hands on his hips, he squints at me. "Why are you so intent on defying me at every turn since you've been at HEAU?"

Something in my mind disconnects, and I stare at him as if he's a stranger—because who he is now is someone I don't recognize.

"What happened to you, Dad?" My voice cracks.

Taken aback, he scoffs. "What are you talking about?"

Standing up taller, I open my mouth and speak freely. "I mean, what happened to the man who used to tell me stories and tuck me into bed? Who taught me how to first play piano and ride my bike. What happened to the man who was empathetic and warm?" I pause, my gaze bouncing between his eyes. "Mom wouldn't like who you've become."

His face melts for a split second, revealing the dad I once knew, but then he's gone, the shell hardening back up.

My cheek stings like a hot iron scraped across it, and I gasp as realization dawns on me.

"D-did you just slap me?"

His mouth is open, shock stretching his features. "I'm sorry, Alora. That was out of hand."

He reaches forward, but I step back, and he winces at my withdrawal before standing taller.

My breathing quickens, and my eyes burn. "What do you have against Malik? I really like him."

"Alora, you can't believe a word that he says. He's a manipulator and a liar."

Running my hand down my face, I exhale. "It's funny, really, because that's the exact thing I would say about you."

Pain lances his expression, and he looks up at me with confusion. "You don't know what you're talking about."

I bite my lip as tears well in my eyes. "But, Dad, I do. I know firsthand how good of a liar you are. I've watched you do it my whole life."

Shaking his head, he sighs. "He's not good for you."

"Is it that?" I pause, readying to face the monster inside of him head-on. "Or is it because you're scared I'll find out the truth about what you did?"

He glances around us, but I'm not sure what he's looking for. Wrapping his hand around my wrist, he tugs me hard, leading me through a door into an empty banquet hall.

"Watch your mouth. You don't know what you're talking about," he snaps.

Smirking up at him, I push him closer to his tipping point. "Do you want to bet?"

He snarls, "You're acting like a brat—you know that? Spoiled and ungrateful for the things I've done for you."

"Ungrateful? For you shipping me off because you didn't want to parent me anymore once I got diagnosed? Ungrateful that you forced me to keep my piano playing a secret, only practicing in an empty room? That kind of ungrateful?" My blood begins to boil. "Or when you didn't even show up for my high school graduation? How about when you had someone follow me on campus and then suddenly pretended to be the caring father? It's far too late for that, *Congressman*."

A war brews behind his eyes as he studies me like an

enemy, looking for any weakness. But thankfully, he taught me how to hide all my cards well.

"What exactly should I be grateful for?" I snap.

His eyes well up with tears, frustration brimming at the surface. "For pushing you as far away from me as I could manage. For keeping you safe from the world I built."

"W-what?" I murmur, taken aback.

His eyes fall to the floor. "Do you really want to know the truth? Do you think you can live with the weight? Because there are days that I doubt it for myself."

My throat tightens, and goose bumps break across my arms. *Is there more than just what happened to Micah?*

"The things I've done to protect the life that you have would haunt you for the rest of it," he says casually as he brushes my hair off of my shoulder, his jaw twitching. "I've sold all of my humanity to the devil to ensure you can keep yours."

Silence consumes me, my voice nonexistent as shock waves course through me. An ache deep to my soul throbs in my chest at his confession.

In my mind, he was always cut and dry, no room for sympathy, not after what I learned about Micah. But unfortunately, villains aren't always one-sided. To some characters, they're not villains at all.

Tears well in my eyes as I look at my dad, the one who used to put me first. His foundation is cracking, the vulnerable man beneath peeking through.

"I'm sorry," he murmurs, and I can tell he means it.

A sob shakes free from inside of me, tears rolling down my cheeks. I want to run away, but I also want to freeze time and just stand still.

I want to pretend that none of this is real, that all of this has been a story that he's telling me as I drift off to sleep in my little princess bed.

Why can't I just hate him? Why can't I just write him off and leave him in the dust?

Why did he have to ruin us?

As tears continue to flow down my cheeks, my shoulders rise and fall with the quickness of my breaths.

But I can't walk away from this. I can't pretend that he didn't do horrible and terrible things. It's not fair to me, to Malik, or to Micah.

So, instead of wrapping my arms around him and accepting his apology, I mutter four words that bring his kingdom to ruin. "I know about Micah."

The room around us seems to spin as he holds my stare, layer after layer peeling away in his gaze.

Nodding ever so slightly, he takes a shaky inhale. "I assumed as much."

"Why, Dad? Why would you do that? He was just a kid!" My voice breaks, and he winces, his eyes slamming closed.

"So were you," he whimpers, tears falling from his lashes.

My throat burns as he opens up, his voice passionate and raw. "*You* were a kid. Your mom was gone. It was just us. I couldn't let that night change everything I had worked so hard to create for you." He drags his hand down his tear-soaked face. "I came from nothing, Little Rose—nothing. And I couldn't leave you with the same. You deserved better, and I made damn sure that was exactly what you got."

Shaking my head in disbelief, I sniffle as he continues, his heart breaking open in front of me as he pours himself out.

"I didn't send you away because you had gotten diagnosed. I sent you away because I hadn't wanted you living with a murderer … and that was what I had become. And that was only the beginning of the path I stumbled down." He quivers. "I couldn't bear to look at you for a while. To see the innocence in your eyes, the same look that little boy had that night." His eyes slam shut. "It's burned into my brain, and no matter how hard I try to scrub it out, it won't leave."

Reaching out, he grabs my shoulders and pulls me against him, wrapping me up in his arms and rubbing my back. And for some crazy reason … I let him. Because even though he's done horrible things, I just want a hug from my dad.

He speaks softly in my ear, emptying the can of worms. "I didn't want to be away from you ever, Little Rose. I wanted to be by your side for everything. But after that night, the plan changed." He pauses and sobs, cradling the back of my head with his hand. "I got caught up in it, in the people I surrounded myself with.

There are so … *so* many things I wish I could undo." He kisses my hair, his voice thick with emotion. "But it's too late."

Something inside of me breaks when I hear the truth of my past. Answers to all the questions I piled up over the years, always wondering what I did to make him not want me anymore.

"Alora …" He sobs. "I'm sorry. I love you so much, baby girl. I only held you at arm's length to keep you away from the things I did."

When he squeezes me tighter than ever, I hug him back, clinging to the last honest moment we may ever share. Tears stain his suit, mixing with my makeup, as I fall apart in his arms and him in mine.

"*Dad.*"

Rubbing my back, he nods his head in the crook of my neck. "It's okay, baby. It's okay. I already *know.*"

I melt into him, feeling the world start to crumble around me. Brick by brick, the castle walls he surrounded us with start to fall, crashing and disintegrating at our feet.

"It's okay, Alora. I understand why you did it," he consoles me as I shout and cry harder than ever into his shoulder.

The door opens behind us, but I can't move. I can't step away from him.

How did he know? How did he know? How?

"Daniel Briarwood," is called out by one of the agents.

"No, no, no, not yet," I whimper, holding him tighter. "No, please."

My dad pulls away from me, cupping my cheeks. His face is reddened and streaked with sorrow. He nods slowly, and I shake my head.

"Please don't go." My voice is barely audible as it squeaks past my lips. "*Please*."

I know he has to. I know he deserves to. But what about me? What do I deserve? To lose him forever? How is it fair?

How is any of this fair?

"It's okay," he whispers, resting his forehead against mine. "It's okay, Alora. You'll be okay."

I shake my head as arms encircle my waist from behind, and I recognize the feeling of his chest against my back as he tries to ease me away from my dad.

But I stand strong.

My dad looks up behind me and sobs. "I'm sorry for what I did. Truly." Looking back down at me, he exhales, his breath choppy, his face wet with snot and tears. "I love you."

Pushing away from me, he steps back, putting his hands behind him as the agents step forward and cuff him.

Charging forward, Malik holds me in place, no matter how hard I fight.

"Stop, please."

"I've got you," he whispers, his voice raw in my ear. "I'm sorry."

Spinning around, I hit him in the chest. "I don't want to do this. I don't want to be here. I don't want to—"

He pulls me into him, encasing me in his arms, and he starts to cry with me, clinging to me as tightly as I am to him. "I know, Bug. I know. But I'm right here. I've got you. Just take a deep breath with me, okay?"

Footsteps distract me, pulling my attention, but as I try to look, Malik holds my head in place, kissing my hairline.

The footsteps leave the room, and seconds or minutes pass by as our breathing starts to sync and slow.

"Alora?" Malik whispers my name with hesitation as exhaustion starts to weigh on me.

Inching away from him and looking up, I wipe my eyes, feeling the makeup beneath smear.

As he brushes my cheeks with his thumbs, his eyes show nothing but love. "I'm sorry you had to do that."

"I'm not." My voice surprises me, firm and confident. "That was the most honest conversation we've ever had."

Leaning down, he kisses my forehead. "Let's go home, baby."

Nodding, I slide my hand into his, our fingers interlocking.

We head out of the empty banquet and find my three aunts waiting in the hall.

My aunts look up at us instantly, their faces wet with tears and worry. All three of them walk over to us, but they don't stop until they wrap their arms around Malik and me.

"You were so brave, Alora. So strong," Flora murmurs.

Fauna and Freya tell me they love me before releasing me from their tight hugs.

"Where's Sunny?" I ask, my voice almost unrecognizable to my ears.

"She's with Phillip, waiting in the car for you guys," Fauna assures me.

I'm completely drained and mentally foggy. All I want to do is go home and crawl into bed, wrapped in Malik's arms.

I rest my head on his arm. They look up at him, and have some sort of silent conversation.

"We're going to be in town for a while, it seems. Call one of us tomorrow, okay?" Fauna asks me, squeezing my hand.

I nod, lifting my lips into a weak smile. "I will."

Malik bends down and scoops my legs out from under me, cradling me against his chest.

"I can walk," I whisper, looking up into his bloodshot purple eyes.

He sniffles, then smirks. "I know, but I can also carry you."

Walking down the hall, he carries me toward the entrance of the event center, and I close my eyes, suddenly so exhausted from everything that just happened.

This was the biggest stressor I might have ever had, and I know I'm probably going to spend the next few days lying in bed. But it won't be so bad with Malik and Sunny at my side.

My stomach twists with nausea, and I take a few deep breaths.

Malik somehow knew that it was my adrenaline saying that I was fine to walk. I'm drained.

Mentally, physically, I have nothing left to give.

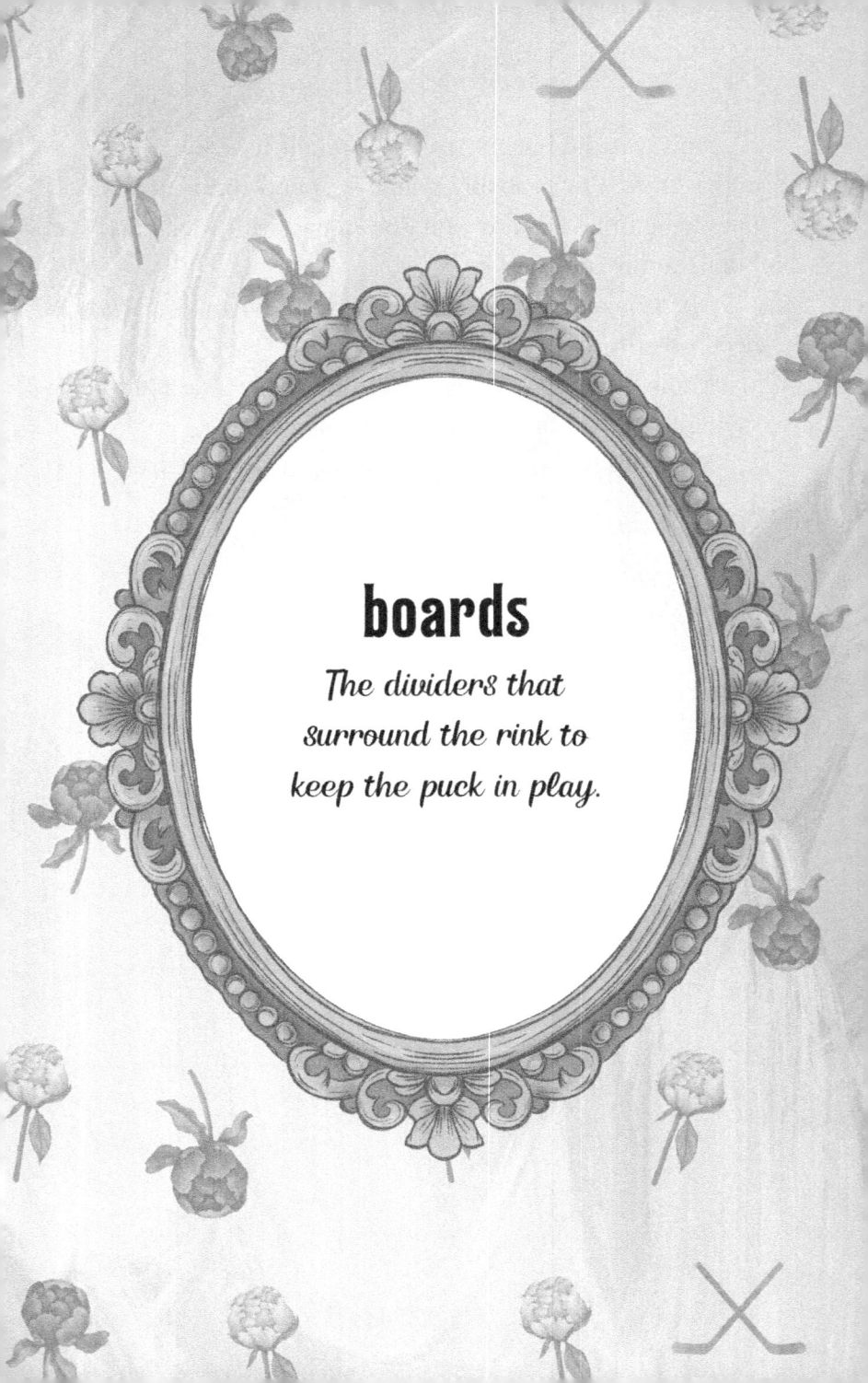

boards

The dividers that surround the rink to keep the puck in play.

chapter thirty-two
malik

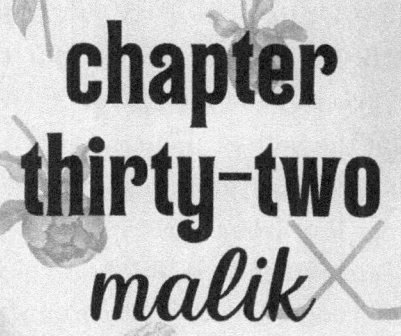

The aftermath of the last few days has been ... *intense*, to say the least. For everyone involved. But especially for Alora.

The image of her completely broken down in my arms when her dad was being taken away is burned so deep in my mind. That anguish was torture to watch because I couldn't take it away. Not then and not now.

Her POTS has flared up, the episode lasting over the last few days. I've done everything I can to make it easier for her, but it still doesn't feel like enough.

She lost her dad—and trust me, I know that he deserves exactly what he got. But that doesn't take away the ache in my heart when I see her in pain.

It's such a confusing feeling—holding her as she mourns her dad while I feel peace, watching my brother finally get justice.

There's still a lot to be worked out. Like my uncle and everything he did. But the agents assured us that he would be held accountable for his role. Now it's just a waiting game for the both of them.

It's complicated and murky. Although I wouldn't expect anything less from this situation. Everything about us has been complicated. But I don't care.

She's my life now, the most important part of my existence. Nothing will change that. She's who I look for in the stands of my games, the home that my heart has found solace in.

Thankfully, Alora's been feeling better today, and I don't have to play this game without her in the stands, next to Blair.

Glancing into the crowd, my eyes land on her immediately as we take the ice and skate around for a brief second before setting up for the start of the third period.

Lifting her hand, she blows me a kiss, and my heart fucking jumps out of my chest to catch it.

"Are you done eye-fucking your girlfriend yet?" Asher skates up beside me and smacks the back of my helmet with his hand, laughing.

Jabbing the top of my stick into his side, I scoff. "Why don't you try to make me stop?"

He rolls his eyes. "Okay, tough guy. Do you want to win tonight?"

Smirking, I skate around Asher. "Oh, baby, we're going to win. Don't doubt that."

"Awfully confident for someone leading by one," number eighty on the Gargoyles chimes into our conversation as our starting line sets up at center ice.

"Awfully confident for someone I knocked out last season," I mutter, locking eyes with him as we stare one another down, bracing for the face-off.

I win the battle, dishing the puck back to Asher. He flicks it forward, sniping the pass to the end of Elias's stick. Elias bursts into the zone, only one defender between him and the goalie.

Flying up on his left side, he drop-passes the puck to me. Winding up, I slap the puck with my stick, and it soars through the air.

It knocks the goalie's water bottle out of place as I add another goal to the board. The Legends raise their sticks in the air, and everyone races toward me in celebration.

"Fuck yeah!" I shout as they swarm me, my back hitting the board.

Breaking away from the group, I skate toward our bench, making sure that I gain enough speed to catch up to number eighty, who's heading to his own.

"Two now, huh?" I chirp.

Smirking, he challenges back, "Two goals is the worst lead in hockey."

"Don't worry, bud; we'll make sure to up that number to make you feel more at peace with your loss."

Turning away from him, I bump gloves with my

teammates, hollering into the arena as adrenaline courses through my veins.

The next eight minutes go by without another goal or even a penalty. Somehow, they've managed to hold us off. But we've done the same. The score is still two to zero.

But I can feel it in the air—that the tension is building up and something is bound to snap it.

The final guy of the last shift switches with Asher at the perfect time, completing our line. Dean steals the puck from number eighty, checking him into the boards as he does it.

Asher shouts to him, slapping his stick on the ice as he races into the neutral zone, "D!"

Dean passes the puck, whipping it down half the rink, right onto Asher's stick. Flying down the left side of the ice, one of their guys lines him up to smear him into the glass, and I dig my skates into the ice even harder.

He explodes into Asher, throwing him two feet into the wall, and his head collides with the boards. He's going to fucking pay for that.

Dropping my stick, I burst into the zone. He knows what's coming, but I'm faster than he expects.

When he turns around, his eyes bulge as he tries to brace for impact. But it's too late.

I drop my shoulder and ram into him, sending him into the boards, similar to Asher, but much harder.

Rage consumes me as I catch a glimpse of Asher

still lying on the ice as Dean and Elias stand in front of him to block anything from accidentally touching him.

Number eighty stands to his feet, a snarl on his face. "You want to go? Huh? You want to go?"

More than anything right now, but Coach told me to try to be on better behavior, as I've been too easily instigated to fight lately.

He scoffs cockily. "What a fucking pussy."

Ignore it. Ignore it. Skate away.

When I turn around toward Griffin, he nods at me with pride. I hate not breaking this kid's fucking face for his dirty hit on Asher. But I don't want to let my team down either. We got even.

He shoves my back, and I glide closer to Griffin, who stiffens, inching toward me.

The linesmen and ref get between us, pulling number eighty back like a kid in trouble. Cheers break out in the rink as we're escorted to the penalty box.

Elias, our captain, skates right behind us. He'll wait to hear the official call from the ref.

Number eighty is still roaring at me, trying to rev me up, and I'd be lying if I said it wasn't working just a little bit.

Before we reach the boxes, he gets one more dig. "Saw you in the news. Was your brother as much of a pussy?"

I snap my head toward him as my fists twitch. He doesn't deserve a response. He's not going to get one … not from my mouth at least.

Ditching the linesman holding my arm, I storm over to him, half into the penalty box. Grabbing him by the jersey, I shove him into the box, his head bouncing off of the board inside, the helmet falling to the floor.

Red is all I see—all I want to see. I want his blood to stain the ice when they drag him out of here.

Twisting him around, I pop his jaw with my fist as he tries to cover his face. Relentlessly, I land blow after blow as the white of his skin turns red.

My ears are silent, no voice or music getting through. Only this. Only him.

"I'm going to fucking kill you," I sneer, spitting down on him.

Someone pulls me backward, strong enough to move my entire body, and when I turn to see Griffin and Elias holding me, I realize that I might have gone too far.

My hearing starts to open back up, absolute chaos ringing out around me.

My knuckles ache, and I shake my hand, blood spraying to the ice. Although I'm not sure whose blood it is.

"You're a fucking killer. Leave some aggression for the rest of us." Griffin smiles at me proudly, chuckling softly.

When I look over at Elias, he shrugs. "He deserved that."

"Yeah"—I nod, smiling—"he did."

Pumping my arms in the air, I skate away from

them, directing my attention to the crowd that somehow grows even louder.

Hopping the board door, I'm pat on the back as I disappear into the tunnel. I won't be playing any more tonight—that's for sure—not after what I just did.

Medical is beside me the moment I enter the locker room, grabbing my knuckles and assessing the damage. But I'll be fine. I just split the skin on a couple of my knuckles. But it was worth it.

The Legends beat the Gargoyles, four to zero, making me feel even better, knowing that fuckhead is going home with black eyes and a big fat L.

When we get out to the lobby after the game, Alora and Blair are waiting for Griffin and me.

Alora's face lights up instantly, and my heart fucking melts. Every win feels better with her—hell, life feels better with her.

Dropping my bag to the ground, I charge over to her, cupping her face and crashing my lips to hers. She quickly finds my rhythm, kissing me back with the same intensity.

She moans softly into my mouth, only loud enough for me to hear in the bustling lobby. But it makes my dick twitch in my pants. God, I'm never going to get enough of her. It's impossible.

When we pull apart, her eyes are on fire. She's just as turned on as I am. Her lips tip into a devilish smirk, and an idea pops into my mind. A bad one … one we definitely shouldn't do.

Throwing my bag over my shoulder, I take her hand in mine. "See you back at the house, Griff."

"You too," he murmurs with confusion, but doesn't bother to ask any questions. It's better that way anyway.

"Malik," Alora squeals as I lead her down a quieter hallway, one she's been down before.

I twist the knob of the overstock equipment room, and when it opens, I smile, pulling her inside behind me and flipping the light switch on.

Maybe she won't feel comfortable with this, or maybe she will want to go back home first.

But as I turn to face her, I realize that my little Bug likes some adventure. Her hands are on my jaw, and her lips are on mine instantly, her tongue delving into my mouth with greed.

Leaning back against the door, I lock it before circling my hands around her waist.

"I need you so fucking bad," I groan into her parted lips.

She nods with her kiss as her dainty fingers find the bottom of my sweatshirt. The moment her hands slip beneath it and explore my abs, my cock twitches.

She loves my body and has no problem showing her adoration, making me fucking feral as she runs her hands up my pecs and then over my shoulders, tugging me closer to her.

Sucking her bottom lip between my teeth, I nibble at it, and a moan vibrates through her and into me.

She whimpers. "I want you."

I push my joggers and boxers down, and my erection springs free, bouncing between us. "Get on your knees and beg me for it."

Her eyes darken as she flicks her gaze down at my pulsing cock and back to my heated stare. She wets her lips as she wraps her hand around my shaft, dropping to her knees before me.

With her eyes big and sultry, she takes my tip into her mouth, circling her tongue repeatedly.

I flip her hair to one side. I think the hottest thing she's ever worn is my last name and number. "You look so fucking good like that, baby."

She takes more of me into her mouth, and I slide down her throat, filling her up until her lips press against the base of my shaft. She flicks her tongue out of her mouth, lapping at my balls, and the sensation nearly sends me spiraling over the edge.

"Holy fuuuck," I groan, my eyes rolling into the back of my head.

The warmth of her mouth leaves me, and I open my eyes, looking down at her. Her lips are pursed, and her eyes are hooded.

"How about *you* beg *me*?"

Her words take me by surprise, but my cock fucking twitches, bouncing off her chin.

"You want me to beg you?"

She bites down on her bottom lip and nods, standing to her feet and taking my shaft in her hand, pumping me slowly. "Beg me to let you fuck me."

Her hand feels so good on me, and for the first time ever, I'll beg. But in my own way.

Wrapping my hand around her throat, I lower my mouth an inch above hers. Using my other hand, I slide my thumb along her tongue, opening her mouth.

I spit down into her mouth, and my dick hardens as she sticks her tongue out further, greedily taking it. She swallows hard and licks her lips.

Guiding her by the throat, I spin us around, pressing her back into the door.

Leaning down, I run my tongue from the base of her neck to her ear, humming at how good she tastes and smells.

She pumps me faster as her heart rate picks up. I make sure to keep an eye on the pulse beneath my thumb, not wanting to push her too far.

"Please, baby," I groan, my breath caressing her ear. "Let me bury myself inside of your tight pussy. Let me fuck what's mine."

Her breathing is erratic as she pulls my head back and claims my lips with hers. Ferocious and feral, she kisses me with a hunger I've never seen.

Sliding my hands down her body and over my jersey, I hook my fingers in her leggings and panties, pushing them down to her knees.

My fingers find her core instantly. "Drenched for me. Just how I like it."

She nods, her back arched and eyelids heavy.

Her hands fumble for her leggings—to take them

off, I'm sure—but I stop her after she pushes them halfway down her legs. I know exactly how I'm going to take her, and she won't need them completely off.

"Wrap your arms around my neck," I instruct her, hooking my arm beneath both her knees with my right arm.

She does as told, and I lift her into the air, guiding her back against the door. Keeping her legs over my right arm, I stand up to full height, flattening my hand on the door at her side.

Grabbing my cock with my left hand, I stroke it through her wetness, and she inhales at the contact.

"Are you going to be my good little slut and take it like this?"

She nods, wiggling her hips. "Yes. Ugh, please."

"I knew you'd be the one begging me in the end." I smirk, line myself up with her, and plunge into her tight pussy in one fell swoop, the angle from her twisted legs nearly brings me to my knees.

"Ahh!" she cries out, moaning at the intense sensation.

With her legs pressed together and hooked over my arm, my dick stretches her pussy out in a whole new way, and it's fucking magical.

As I thrust every final inch into her, our breathing matches up as we cling to one another.

Rolling my hips back, I ease back into her, torturously slow for the both of us. But with how perfect she feels and how intense I feel for her, I'm not going to last long at all.

Palming her ass with my left hand, I lift her slightly, holding her in place as I pull back and rail into her.

She moans and gasps with every thrust.

Her pleasure fills the room, and I don't give a fuck if anyone hears us. I'm sure as shit not telling her to be quiet. Someone else can try if they dare.

"Oh fuck, Malik," she whimpers breathlessly. "Faster, please. I'm almost there."

Snapping, I give her every inch hard and fast, burying myself in her as our orgasms build to the surface together, racing toward the finish line.

I groan against her lips, "Give it to me, baby. I'm not going to last much longer. Your pussy feels too fucking good, clenching around me like this."

The praise sends her spiraling. "Oh shit. Fuck. Fuck. Fuck. Oh! God!"

The waves of her ecstasy push me over the edge.

My balls tighten, and I spill inside of her, moaning as unimaginable pleasure courses through me.

I need this. I need *her*. Forever.

When I ease out of her, our mixed cum trickles down her legs, dripping onto the floor. I lower her feet back to the ground, and she wobbles on her feet for a second, giggling.

Her cheeks burn darker as she grabs a tissue from the counter along the wall and wipes the floor up. It's funny that she's embarrassed by that, but she has no problem begging me for my dick.

She wiggles her panties and leggings up and walks back over to the door. "I should probably use the restroom."

Shaking my head, I slap her ass hard, palming it firmly. "Uh-uh, baby. I want my cum dripping down your legs when we walk out of the arena."

Arousal pulses in her stare, and she wets her lips. "Your place or mine?"

An image flashes in my mind, one I've never really seen, only imagined.

A place of our own.

I would say that it's crazy and too soon, but for fuck's sake, I'm clearly not sane when it comes to her.

Brushing my thumb along her bottom lip, I lean down and kiss her tenderly. "Wherever you want to go, Bug, I'll follow."

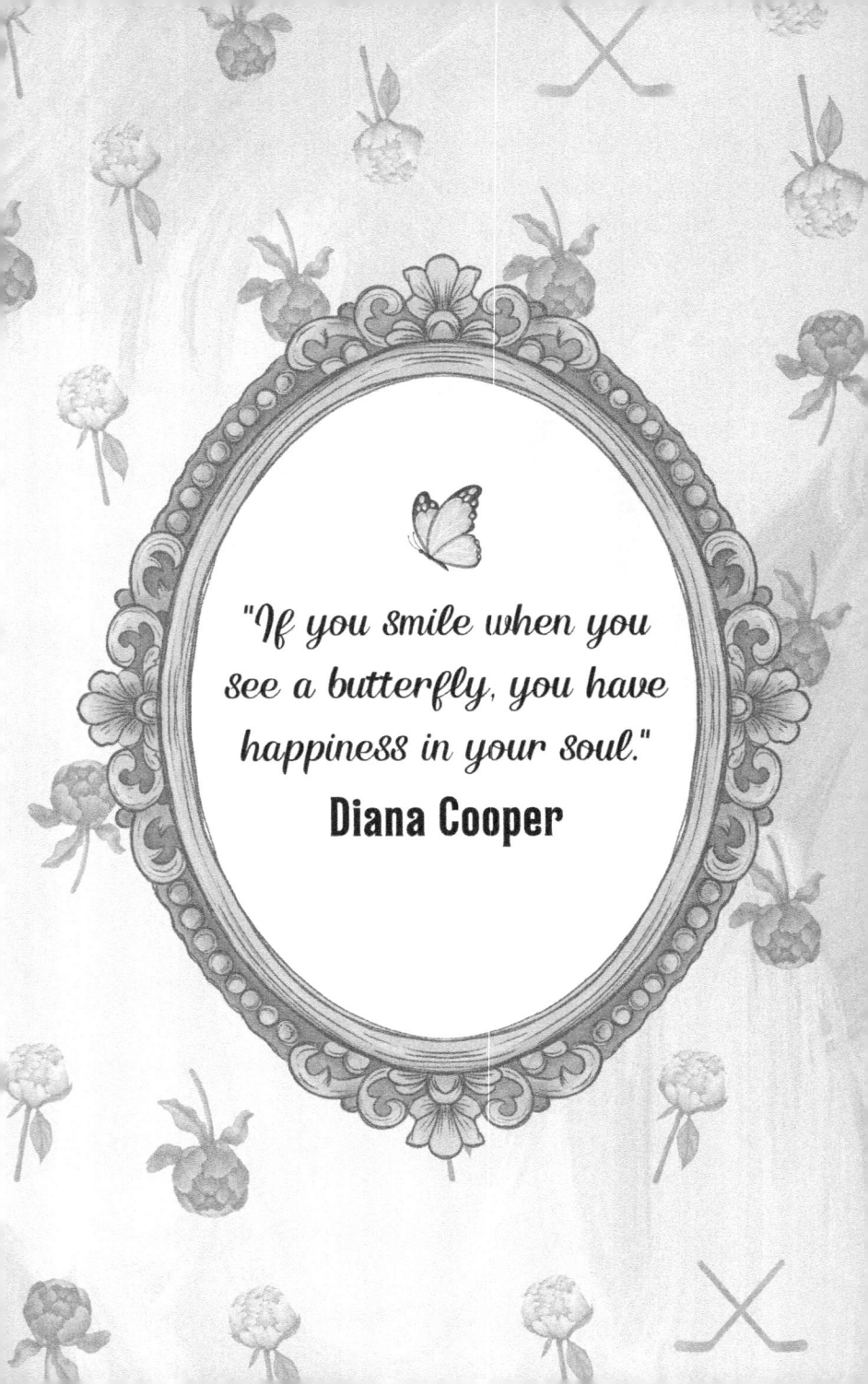

"If you smile when you see a butterfly, you have happiness in your soul."

Diana Cooper

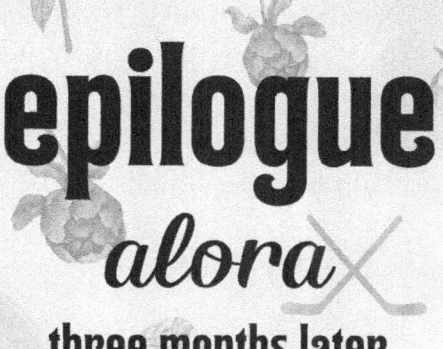

epilogue
alora
three months later

The lights on the stage burn into me as my fingers dance across the keys and my body rocks along with the song I composed for my showcase piece, titled "The Dream."

It's haunting and dark, but gradually, lighter and more melodic notes trickle into the score. The dynamic starts to shift and change as the brighter music begins to take over, pushing the darkness into the shadows. The audience listens intently, completely silent as I pour myself into my performance.

This is the first time I've ever played in front of a crowd, free to show my talent and love for the piano, and it's so incredibly freeing.

As I get lost in the dance of the keys, my mind drifts away.

So much has changed in the last couple of months.

Malik's uncle was arrested for accepting a bribe, conspiracy to cover up a murder, among a rap sheet that was pages long.

I've seen the peace settle into Malik's soul recently —that fight or flight he was constantly in before finally fading away.

He doesn't have to live on edge anymore or fear any manipulation from his uncle and my dad. He can just be himself however he chooses.

There's still one thing holding us back from closing that chapter for good. His uncle still won't reveal where Micah's urn is, but I refuse to let him hold that over him. I might have made a few calls and hired a couple of people to track them down. And today, I'll finally get to cash in on the results.

In the aftermath of my dad's arrest, my family was plastered all over the news, torn to shreds for his corruption. But my aunts stayed strong through all of it, not blinking an eye at the swarm of reporters that somehow always found us.

My dad won't ever see the light of day again, not after he's found guilty for all of his crimes. Micah was the tip of the iceberg of his secrets.

Bribery, embezzlement, fraud, and murder are just the beginning of what he's facing. I haven't visited him, and I'm not sure that I ever will. It's complicated … obviously.

Even with the ruins he left us in, he also left behind hundreds of properties, businesses, and investments. My aunts had chosen to leave that world when they took me in, but they didn't hesitate to step right in to take everything over. They divided the assets, splitting the responsibility between the three of them. Anyone on the outside would assume they were always proud and strong businesswomen.

My aunts are still living in Avandale, in the same home they've always had. They're still the same people they were before the money started flowing into their accounts instead of my dad's. If anything, they've doubled down on their kindness and humbleness.

Generous doesn't begin to cover it. They are going above and beyond in any capacity they can fill.

Without asking—because they know he'd say no—my aunts paid for Malik's tuition in full. They also set up an account in Malik's name for whenever he needs it.

He swears he'll never touch it, but I think I'll wear him down eventually. I know he doesn't want it because it's coming from a Briarwood and he doesn't exactly have a great history with our money ... but it's different now. It's clean.

Sometimes, it's okay to take a gift, especially when there's no negativity or guilt tied to it.

My aunts also gave Darius and Alicia a nice chunk of money for their support of their future son-in-law.

We're not engaged ... yet. But I swear I'm going to marry that man the second he asks. I would ask him, but knowing his possessive ass, I'm sure he'd say no just so he could do it himself.

Besides, I'm not in a huge rush. I know we'll be together in the end. I just want to have his last name on my license and not just his jersey.

But I guess having my name on his knuckles for the time being will do.

My music grows louder and louder as it builds toward its resolve. The final battle, the final tug-of-war between light and dark. Right when you feel the song start to crescendo and balance, a new harmony between the two emerges, humming softly through the air until silence is all that remains.

Applause breaks out in the concert hall. Slowly turning toward the audience, I rise to my feet, step out from the bench, and bow. The lights are blinding from here, blocking most of the faces and much of the enormous room. But I can feel his stare, and I find him in the front row. Malik stands up, applauding, and the entire crowd follows suit.

When I can make out the audience's faces, my smile becomes uncontained, and pure joy blooms in my chest as I see not only that Malik, my aunts, and Sunny are in attendance, but also the rest of his friends—my friends—Griffin, Asher, Dean, Elias, Finn, Blair, Lumi … and Lumi's new boyfriend, Matt.

Bowing once more, I spin and walk upstage, slipping behind the curtain. The host of the showcase, our university's president, thanks everyone for coming, bringing the night to a close.

I still can't believe that I was the closing performer.

After everything that happened with Rupert Von London, I wasn't sure I would be here at all, but to be selected to end the entire show is really special.

"There you are," Malik murmurs, spinning me around and kissing me softly. "You were … incredible, Bug. It was beautiful."

God, I'll never get over how good he looks in a suit. It's a good thing I'll get to see him wear one a lot when he goes pro. He might not be signed yet, but he did mention that a representative for the local professional team had reached out to him and Griffin recently to discuss an entry-level contract, which is a huge first step.

We walk out hand in hand, and our group is waiting for us in the lobby of the auditorium.

Praise and cheers overwhelm me as we approach them.

Taking the leash from Flora, I crouch down and kiss Sunny's forehead. "Hi, baby."

She looks up at me with those big brown eyes, and I have to fight the cute aggression from taking over.

After a slew of hugs, Malik, Sunny, and I head home.

My phone vibrates in my purse when we get into his new car—a Corvette still, but a brand-new one that doesn't hold any bad memories.

He wanted to get rid of the one my dad had given

him to cleanse that part of his life. My card was slapped onto the countertop the second we walked into a dealership so he could just "look." And of course, I refused to leave unless it was in a new vehicle … because I'm a spoiled and bratty princess … *right?*

I quickly check the text, and it's just the one I wanted to see.

> Investigator Lawrence: Waiting outside, ma'am.

> Perfect. Be there in a few.

Evermore has become my home, and I'm not sure I ever want to leave. But until that road comes where we might have to move for his future, I got us a place that we'll be comfortable in. One that's just for us three.

Sunny loves the gigantic backyard and the thousand blankets she buries herself in on the couches and beds. Malik loves it for basically the same reason, but I think his favorite might be the movie room, where we spend way too much of our free time.

We turn into our driveway, one nearly as long as Griffin and Blair's. The path is surrounded by huge, old trees, connecting at the top in a beautiful arch.

"Who is that?" Malik asks the second our home comes into view behind the sky-high hedges and thorny rose bushes.

"A surprise," I murmur, nearly bursting at the seams

as he pulls to a stop in front of the curb, not bothering to go around the corner into the garage complex.

The man in a suit waits at the top of our stairs, framed by the large wooden arch doors, a large box in his hands.

"Come on," I coo, grabbing my purse and stepping out of the car.

Malik appears at my side, his eyes glued on the strange man, but there's something else in his eyes, a sense of hope, and I can't wait for that seed to blossom.

"Good evening," he greets us, and I smile.

"Thank you so much for this. Seriously, we cannot express our gratitude enough," I say, carefully taking the box from his hands, surprised by how heavy it is.

With a sharp nod, he descends the stairs and leaves without another word.

Unlocking our door, Malik leads the way inside, walking backward as I follow him in, confusion etched in his features.

Sunny trots in behind us, her leash dragging on the floor. Malik quickly unhooks her, and she books it for her favorite spot—the window cutout that overlooks the waves of Evermore Bay—and curls up in one of her blankets.

Malik watches me cautiously as I carry the box over to our coffee table, setting it gently down on the glass.

"What is it?" he whispers, his voice already thick with emotion.

When I glance up at him, my vision starts to cloud as my throat burns.

Gesturing toward the box, I step backward, giving him space to do this himself.

He drops to his knees on the hardwood floor, and wetness brimming in his eyes as he tears off the top piece of tape and lifts the flaps of the box.

A white chunk of Styrofoam blocks any view of what's hidden inside. But he knows—I know it.

When he lifts the block, a sob cracks through the room, and he rocks backward onto his butt, lifting his hands to his face as a shudder rolls through him.

His cries shred my heart into pieces as he slowly gains his strength and reaches inside the box, wrapping his hands around Micah's urn.

"*You found him*," he whimpers, wrapping Micah up in his arms for the first time in years. "Hi, buddy. It's damn good to see you." His voice cracks.

Stroking the ceramic of the urn, he rocks back and forth as tears stream down his face. "You can rest now, buddy. I've got you."

The dam behind my eyes bursts, and I cover my mouth with quivering fingers.

My sob pulls Malik's attention up to me, and his eyes are so clear, so vivid, no walls or thorns barricading him from the world.

"I love you." His voice is almost inaudible.

Nodding and sniffling, I wipe the tears from my eyes. "I love you too."

Minutes pass by as he cradles Micah, taking all the time he needs. And I stay by his side through it all.

Eventually, he rises to his feet and carries Micah over to our fireplace, wiping the surface before carefully setting him down on the mantel, positioned perfectly between the frames of his butterflies.

Walking over to him, I slide my hand on Malik's back, rubbing up and down soothingly. "A perfect place."

He nods and wipes his eyes. "For a perfect kid."

Hooking his arm around my shoulders, he pulls me into him, encasing me in his arms, and he plants endless kisses to the top of my head.

My gaze drifts to the mantel, slowly shifting from butterfly to butterfly, and I can't help but wonder how our life would look now if one single moment had or hadn't happened.

The butterfly effect has never felt more personal. It's crazy to think that in some way, fate played a part in our story. If one rock, one pebble had been out of place, we could have never met. But I think we were always meant to be.

Because of every little moment leading up to this, I stand in the arms of the redeemed villain, in a castle free of curses and thorns, in a love story that is no one else's but our own.

Thank you for reading Redeeming the Villain! If you enjoyed it, please leave a review on Amazon and Goodreads!

Book three is coming soon! Title TBA!

Want to read more from Pru Schuyler while waiting for book three in the HEAU Hockey Legends Series? Check out her backlist below!

Nighthawks Series (new adult pro hockey romance)
Find Me in the Rain
Find Me on the Ice
Find Me Under the Stars
Not My Coach
Find Me in the Fire

Mrs. Claus Standalone Duet (adult holiday romance)
Stealing Mrs. Claus
Becoming Mrs. Claus

Wicked Series (young adult mystery/suspense romance)
The Wicked Truth
The Wicked Love
The Wicked Ending

Saint Eldritch Series (new adult paranormal romance)
Shut Up and Bite Me

Made in the USA
Coppell, TX
12 June 2025

50615228R10329